NOT *by* SIGHT

NOT *by* SIGHT

a novel of the patriarchs

Elizabeth Jacobson

WordCrafts

Not by Sight is a work of fiction, based on events detailed in the Biblical book of Genesis. The author has endeavored to be respectful of the Holy Scriptures with regard to all persons, places, and events presented in this novel, and attempted to be as historically accurate as possible. Still, this is a novel, and all references to persons, places and events are fictitious or used fictitiously.

Published by WordCrafts Press
Cody, Wyoming 82414
www.wordcrafts.net

To Mom, Dad, and James,
because iron sharpens iron.

For we walk by faith, not by sight.
2 Corinthians 5:7

Part One
Sight

1

The shriek rent the still air.

Joseph jolted awake. The palest light of morning seeped through the woven cloth of the tent, the braziers inside only giving off the tiniest glow. Everyone would be awake soon, but for now, Joseph looked around and only saw the snoring forms of his brothers. Well, four of them. There were seven others, sleeping in tents spread out across the camp. They were twelve in all.

Twelve. Nine months ago they had been eleven, and nine months ago his mother had been alive.

Pressing his hands to his forehead, he strained his ears, listening.

All was silent. He must have been dreaming.

He turned onto his side, and then the sound came again—this time quieter, almost a sob.

Sitting bolt upright, he looked again at his brothers. Still they snored. He grimaced, and then quietly raised himself from his bed and slipped out the opening of the tent. Now he knew where to go.

He stole across the sleeping camp, past the tent where the sons of Leah slept, past the cooking tent. As he hurried past the animal pens, a few of the donkeys lifted their heads curiously. Nothing else moved.

Would no one help her?

"Dinah?" he whispered as he arrived at the edge of one of the women's tents. There was no response. He shifted on his feet; he could not enter unannounced. The cry came again, this time almost a whimper. She must be dreaming.

"Dinah," he whispered a second time, a little more loudly. He shook the cloth of the tent near the place where her head would be and heard a gasp from inside.

"Dinah?"

There was a rustle and another quiet sob. After a moment, his sister appeared at the entrance to the tent, face pale and tear-streaked. She locked eyes with Joseph, and her face crumpled.

He went to her and held her close. "Would none of the women wake you?" he murmured.

She sobbed again against his shoulder. "I think they choose not to hear me."

Joseph grimaced and pulled her closer.

"I must stop this," she whispered. "It is the lot of many women, it was not so strange a thing—"

Drawing back in surprise, he clasped her shoulders and looked her directly in the eyes. They were large and despairing in the pale light. "It is not a thing that should *ever* be done," he said vehemently. "It was a vile thing, and against God."

"So is what our brothers did in my name."

He opened his mouth, but he had no response.

"It is clear why the Canaanite women do not care to wake me. They are here, with us and with nowhere else to go, because their families are dead. And their families are dead because of me."

"*Not* because of you. Because of Simeon and Levi and the prince of Shechem," he spat out the last name.

"It is all the same to them."

"It is not—" he stopped short. There was movement on the other side of the camp.

Joseph squinted in the dim light, straining to see across the camp. Dinah tensed next to him, clutching his arm. And they stood watching in horror as the figure of their eldest brother hurried away from a tent that he should never have been in.

"God help us," Dinah whispered, breaking their stunned silence. They watched his retreating form. "Why was Reuben in Bilhah's tent?"

4

Joseph tried to force down the sick feeling growing in his stomach and took a deep, steadying breath. "Perhaps—"

As if on cue, Reuben stopped midstride and looked their way.

All three stood, rooted to the ground, but it was too dark and too far to see Reuben's face clearly. Dinah was shaking next to Joseph. Finally, their brother turned and hurried away, rounding the corner of a tent.

"*He and Bilhah are*—" Dinah trailed off.

Shaking his head slowly, Joseph searched for an explanation. Something, anything. The sick feeling in his stomach tightened into a knot.

His sister made a sound like a caged animal. "First I am ruined, then our brothers murder in my name, then your poor mother. And now this? These are the years of Sheol."

He could only nod. The knot settled in the pit of his stomach like a rock. "Maybe they are."

The sun glared down on them through the colorfully woven canopy, and the day promised to be hot. Joseph thought the morning meal unusually silent, but he could not be sure if that were only his imagination—*for who else could know?*—or if something were truly amiss.

He watched Reuben, the honored eldest brother, from his seat with Dinah and her mother Leah at the far end of the long table. At fourteen, Joseph was no longer the youngest, but until Benjamin was old enough to join, this would be his place.

Reuben, seated next to their father, seemed as carefree as always. The concubine Bilhah, as she brought the tray of freshly-baked bread, also appeared content, nothing on her face like the haunted look that followed Dinah.

If it is so, then they are both complicit.

His stomach knotted again at the thoughts running through his mind.

5

It could not be so. It must not be so.

Look at them. He and Dinah must have misunderstood. No such betrayal could have so little effect on the participants.

He glanced at his father's concubine over and over as he ate. No sign showed on her face. Finally, he looked again towards Reuben.

His brother was watching him.

A chill shot through Joseph. Quickly looking down at his bread and milk, he could still see Dinah from the corner of his eye. As soon as their brother looked away, he saw her glance flick upward to focus on Reuben, keenly.

The morning passed peacefully in the camp, though Joseph's mind was distraught. He could not tell his father with such flimsy proof as a quick glimpse in early morning light and a strange look at mealtime.

A hot wind was blowing, and he chewed absently on his bottom lip as he made his way to the small tent where a woman from Shechem was caring for Benjamin. Joseph was to head into the fields shortly with Dan and Naphtali, Bilhah's sons, but he wanted to see Benjamin first.

He considered Bilhah as he walked. As his mother Rachel's former handmaid and his father's concubine, he supposed she was the closest thing he and Benjamin had to a mother now. Leah, his father's first wife and his mother's sister, was related to them by blood, but she had always despised him—she likely would Benjamin as well.

Frowning, he sighed and thought of Bilhah again. Before Benjamin had been born, Joseph had always thought he ought to have felt the strongest connection with her sons, though that had never been the case. But she was kind; she always had been.

If she and Reuben were truly doing this—

He shook his head distractedly as he stood outside the tent's entrance. "Mehetabel?"

There was a squeal from Benjamin, and he heard Mehetabel laugh. "Come in, Joseph."

His brother shrieked with laughter as he entered, and he saw one of the woman's young sons tickling the boy's stomach. Joseph laughed in turn, and Benjamin, now seeing him, held out his arms. His eyes, the color of the sky, as their mother's had been, beamed up at Joseph.

He picked up the little boy. "Oof!" he said. "I think he is heavier than yesterday."

"Very possibly." Methetabel smiled. Joseph liked her; she did not blame Dinah or their father Jacob for the actions of Simeon and Levi. But there was sorrow in her face, just as there was in all the Canaanite women's faces.

"I will take him out for a bit."

Mehetabel nodded.

As always, Benjamin received countless coos of admiration from the servant women while Joseph took him around the camp. And Benjamin, as always, smiled charmingly. "Oof," Joseph said again after a while, shifting Benjamin's weight on his hip. "It will be better when you can walk, little brother." Benjamin burbled a laugh in answer, almost as if he understood.

He was nearing Mehetabel's tent to return Benjamin when he heard shouts coming from the opposite side of the camp. Reuben's voice was alarmingly clear amidst the yelling. Joseph's stomach sank. Apprehension growing, he left Benjamin with a harried kiss and darted off to the other side of the camp.

A crowd was gathering outside his father's tent, all manner of servants and Canaanite women crowding around. Dan and Naphtali, Bilhah's sons, were screaming at Reuben. Joseph pushed through the crowd, his mouth going slack.

"You *wretch*," Dan howled. He shoved Reuben backward, but the tall man barely staggered before roaring and sending a fist flying into his attacker's face. Naphtali leapt forward and pummeled their oldest brother from behind.

"Enough!"

Joseph jumped. His heart was pounding. The three brothers froze, and the crowd fell silent.

Jacob stood at the entrance to his tent, eyes blazing as he surveyed his sons. "Reuben. Enter."

Everyone turned to look at the eldest son, who roughly shook off Dan and Naphtali's hands before making his way into the long tent, head held high. Jacob followed him in, and murmuring rippled through the onlookers. Dan and Naphtali stalked away like two roiling thunderclouds. Gad and Asher, the sons of the concubine Zilpah, emerged from the crowd and hurried after them.

The crowd began to disperse, and Joseph saw Dinah, leaving with some servant girls, glance back towards their father's tent. There was a grim look in her eyes.

Joseph's breath caught in understanding. She must have told.

If Reuben found out—

No, he told himself. None of that would matter now. Their father was dealing with the situation.

He let out a long breath before taking a few steps backward. Whispers hissed back and forth between the Canaanite women he passed, and one male servant leaned towards another and nodded towards Jacob's tent. Joseph winced inwardly. Talk would spread through the camp like wildfire.

Forcing himself to turn from the scene, he stood in thought, torn, before coming to a decision.

Yes, he was now meant to be heading into the fields. But Dan and Naphtali would certainly not go right away, not after this. And they would be volatile right now—most of his brothers had a temper, especially towards him, the eldest son of the favored wife. He had learned to bide his time and wait until they calmed before showing himself.

He very slowly returned to the tent he shared with the sons of Bilhah and Zilpah, casting a few backward glances toward his father's tent as he went. He listened at the entrance before stepping inside. All was silent. Relief settled in his bones. They had, as expected, gone somewhere else.

The tent was hot under the midday sun, but it was welcomingly quiet. He moved to his bed and pulled out the wooden box of clay tablets stored under it, determined to distract himself until enough time had passed. He sat down and shuffled the tablets, taking a final calming breath, until he found one of his favorites, a tale from his great-grandfather's homeland that his father had translated and dictated to him one day. It was the story of a launderer, driven to distraction by his wealthy client's absurd demands.

He glanced down at the cuneiform lines.

What you are talking is nonsense (said the poor cleaner).
The person who could come up with these ideas,
And accomplish them, doesn't exist!
These orders you are giving me and telling me to repeat back,
To recite over and over, I haven't the power to accomplish.
Come with me upstream of the city, on the city's edge,
And I'll show you a washery.
This big job you want accomplished—do it yourself!

He didn't know how long he was lost in reading the tablets. Only that out of nowhere Reuben burst into the tent and hauled him up by his tunic. Joseph gasped.

"Did you tell him?" Reuben roared.

Joseph could only shake his head mutely.

The tall man dragged him out of the tent and threw him to the rocky ground. The wind knocked from him, Joseph struggled to force himself upright. "I saw you this morning, you son of a jade."

Air rushed back into Joseph's lungs, and he screamed at the slight against his mother. "I said *nothing!*" He kicked his feet into Reuben's stomach.

His brother grunted and stumbled back a pace before advancing again.

Scrambling backwards, Joseph clambered to his feet, breath coming heavy and heart pounding in his ears. Every sordid bit of his suspicions must have been true, and it did not appear that speaking with their father had cowed Reuben in the slightest. *"Nothing!"* he shouted again, still retreating as Reuben stalked forward.

"Who then?"

"I don't know!"

He hoped with everything he had that Reuben was not being false in his seeming ignorance of Dinah's involvement. He would not harm her physically, but he was very capable of making her life even more miserable than it already was. Perhaps he had not seen her in the dim light.

Reuben snarled and made another rush at him. Stumbling, Joseph looked around wildly, bracing himself for a beating.

The instant before Reuben could reach him, Judah appeared from the blue and roughly dragged their oldest brother back.

Joseph let out a gasp of relief.

"Reuben," Judah shouted. "Get a hold of yourself!"

Reuben struggled against Judah for a moment before he stilled, glaring at Joseph.

"I did not tell him, Reuben. I swear it," Joseph said thickly.

The man grunted and threw off Judah's arms before stalking away.

It was only then that Joseph realized they had drawn another crowd. The faces of servants and Canaanite women swam before his eyes. He took a shaken breath, and Judah looked at him solemnly. "Thank you, Judah," Joseph whispered.

His brother walked over and put a comforting hand on his head before leading him away. "Come, lad. You're wanted in the fields." The crowd parted to let them pass.

Joseph nodded.

"Did you tell our father?" Judah asked quietly, once they were away from the crowd.

Joseph jerked away from his brother. "Judah! No! Do you not hear me?"

"I am only asking."

He couldn't help the little snort that escaped him. He often found Judah to be the calmest and kindest of his brothers, but he gave in too easily to the surrounding chaos. "I saw him," he said flatly. "But I said nothing. I did not think it would be wise or fair if I had no proof, only a guess."

Judah nodded. "Very well."

They walked on, and Joseph guessed his intention was to see him all the way to the fields. The stiff brown grasses and scrub brush of summer rattled around them as they walked, and the buzzing of insects permeated the air. "What will happen to Reuben and Bilhah?" he asked quietly.

"That is Father's decision."

Joseph bit his bottom lip, and they walked on in silence. Approaching the field where a portion of the sheep were kept, he saw Dan and Naphtali seated on a boulder. They both looked up, and Joseph nearly stopped in his tracks.

For the first time, it dawned on him that he might have made an error. Had Dan and Naphtali gone directly to the fields as planned, despite what had occurred? If so, he was late. Very late.

Judah did not seem to notice his concern, and they walked onward. Their two brothers stood as they approached. "I'm sorry," Joseph fumbled immediately. "I thought you would not go so soon."

"Go easily with the little one," said Judah. "Reuben's already been at him."

Keeping his head down, Joseph quickly went to check the water jars. It was always his first job. One was full enough, but the other had a wet ladle near it and was almost empty. "I'll fill this," he said and glanced up at Dan and Naphtali. They were scowling, and Judah was already on his way back to camp.

"See to it," Dan barked.

Joseph skirted away to the nearby well.

Joseph caught Dinah that evening as he was coming back from the fields with the sons of Bilhah. The two brothers had walked on in the evening light, not noticing when the small figure behind them darted away. Joseph snatched Dinah's arm and pulled her behind a tent.

"Did you tell Father?" Joseph hissed.

She eyed him. "No. But I told Dan and Naphtali."

He shook his head. "With no proof?"

"I only told them what I saw," she said firmly. "And our fears were not unjustified, apparently."

"Dinah," Joseph said, "if Reuben finds out it was you—"

"Dan and Naphtali promised they would not tell. And I know you will not."

They looked up at the sound of the loud clanging of metal pans. It was the signal for the evening meal. Slowly they walked together out from behind the tent and towards the canopy. "I only want you to be careful," Joseph murmured. "What you did was rash."

"Maybe, little brother," she said quietly. Joseph thought he saw in her face a bit of her old self-assurance.

The braziers were flaming high in the center of camp, and the space under the canopy was brightly lit. They all gathered to sit down, brothers and sister, and Jacob and Leah. Reuben's face was brazen, but he would meet no one's eyes. Joseph carefully ignored him as he went to the water jars to wash his hot face and hands, then moved back towards the table, slipping between a loudly talking Simeon and Levi. But before anyone could sit, Jacob called: "Joseph, my son, come to me."

All chatter died down. Everyone, family and waiting servants, turned to look at Joseph. Slowly, spine prickling with apprehension and confusion, Joseph walked from his place at the foot of the table up to the head. When he reached his father, Jacob looked coldly at Reuben. "Move down."

Gasps rippled through the canopy. Leah's face went ashen, and Reuben's became white. His mouth clenched, and his eyes met Joseph's.

Joseph would have turned away, had not Jacob's firm hand held him in place.

The next moment stretched for an eternity. Then Reuben stormed away, leaving an open place at their father's right hand. Wordlessly, Jacob guided Joseph to the empty seat and sat him there.

From far away came the sound of sheep, and wind rippled through the canopy. Among the family, there was only silence.

2

Benjamin threw the almonds at Joseph's face and then immediately broke down into hysterical laughter. "You … are … funny!" he managed between gasps.

Sputtering, Joseph laughed in turn before sweeping up the three-year-old and turning him upside down. "Well, I think *you* are!"

Benjamin continued his wild laugher, and Joseph began marching him through camp. He started to sing snatches of the lullaby their mother had sometimes sung to him, changing the cadence to a strong beat:

"In the garden, it is the lettuces *I have watered!"*

He near-shouted *lettuces* and Benjamin shrieked in amusement.

"Among the lettuces I have chopped the gakkul lettuce.

Let the lord eat this lettuce!"

He swung Benjamin outward, and the boy shrieked again. After one or two more swings, Joseph carefully righted his brother and set him down.

Benjamin immediately grabbed him. "Again! Again!"

"No, not again," Joseph said breathlessly, mopping sweat from his eyes. This weather was stifling. "You're getting too big!"

Benjamin continued laughing. "Yes, again!"

"Tomorrow," Joseph promised.

"Well, I see the two of you are having fun."

Joseph turned to see Dinah smiling at them. Balancing a tall jar of water on her head, one hand gently touched the rim for a moment.

"Di!" Benjamin ran to her, and Dinah swiftly put down the jar to catch his hurtling body in her arms. Joseph walked over and snatched it up, promptly pouring half the water out on his head.

Dinah looked at him dryly. "You'll be refilling that."

"Fine," Joseph said. He grinned and poured the rest on his head. Dinah rolled her eyes.

Benjamin was tugging at her skirts. "Is there bread?" he asked.

"You just threw almonds in my face, and now you want bread?" Joseph asked, looking at him through the beads of water that were running down his hair. Benjamin turned to look at him, covered his mouth, and laughed.

"Demanding, isn't he?" Dinah chuckled. She took Benjamin's hand and walked him to the nearby cooking tent. Joseph followed, carrying the empty water jar and shaking out his hair. It was almost winter, but autumn had come like a second summer, and no end was in sight.

They reached the tent, and a few of the female servants looked up as they entered its overhang. The air was thick with the smells of roasting meat and fresh bread. Dinah nodded to the women and pulled a loaf from a nearby basket. She knelt down and held it in front of Benjamin's face. "Now, this is for eating, not throwing."

Benjamin nodded solemnly. Joseph wasn't certain he trusted him, but Dinah unconcernedly handed him a piece of the loaf. She tore the second part in two and handed a piece to Joseph before taking the rest for herself.

Once back in the sun, she shooed Joseph off. "I need that water; go refill it. I'll see to Benjamin." Benjamin, surprisingly, was calmly eating the loaf.

Joseph ambled away, out of camp, and down the hill toward the nearest well. The landscape ought to have been beginning to green a bit by now, watered by the autumn rain. Instead, there was only brown, endless summer. But many of the wells, though low, were holding, and there were still gullies where the sheep could find food. Those were the most important things. He reached the well and let down the jar.

15

It splashed on the far bottom, and he let it fill. As he began the more rigorous process of pulling it up, he looked out at the hills. They were near Hebron, though they would have to move north soon. He would have liked to have gone farther south in preparation for the winter, but as he and his father had discussed, there would be even less water there. So north it would be.

The jar reached the top of the well, and he carefully hoisted it onto his shoulder before beginning the walk back to camp. He looked out over the landscape again and could just mark the figures of Issachar and Zebulun returning from the fields. He didn't bother to wave to his brothers. They would not wave back.

Reentering the camp, he found Dinah returning from taking Benjamin back to Mehetabel. She nodded towards the cooking tent as he approached, and he fell in step behind her. "You are seventeen tomorrow," she said.

Joseph nodded teasingly. "And then you will only be one year older than me."

Dinah laughed and looked back at him. "For two months." But then her face became strained.

He quickened his pace until he was even with her. "What is wrong?"

His sister sighed and looked away before answering. "Father wishes me to marry. I am late to it as it is."

All the unspoken meaning washed over him. He let out a deep breath.

"I am sorry," he murmured, not knowing what else to say. "To whom?"

"No one, yet. Thanks be to God." They reached the tent and Dinah took the jar from him. "It is nothing," she said in her way that meant the conversation was over. "I will see you at the evening meal." She gave him a thin smile and disappeared into the tent.

Watching her go with concern before turning away, he knew full well there was nothing he could do and wished there was something he could. He scuffed the dusty ground with his sandal before

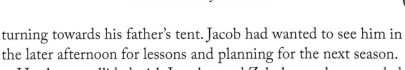
turning towards his father's tent. Jacob had wanted to see him in the later afternoon for lessons and planning for the next season.

He almost collided with Issachar and Zebulun as they rounded the corner of the tent. Hot and sweaty from the sun, they were in a foul mood. "Oh! Where are you off to in such a hurry?" Issachar's hands dug into his shoulders. "Finally going to exert yourself?"

Joseph jerked himself from his brother's grasp. He was as tall as any of them now, save for Reuben and Asher, and he didn't mean to let them think they could bully him around any longer. "Father wanted me in camp today," he said. "I'm to go out into the fields tomorrow."

Zebulun only snorted in answer, and they strode away. Joseph watched them go with a glare and righted his now-rumpled tunic. They were impossible. Nearly all his brothers were these days.

As Rachel's son, their father had always favored him. Everyone had known that and dealt with it. But after Jacob had given him Reuben's seat, everything had changed. Now most of his brothers were fully bent on making him miserable.

He reached Jacob's tent and entered.

His father looked up with smile. "My son, come in!"

Joseph watched his family as they ate together at the evening meal. Loud chatter filled the air, and if he alone was silent it was not unusual. He took a mouthful of lentils and watched his father thoughtfully. Glancing around the table and back towards Jacob, he could not help the thought that crossed his mind, though it immediately pricked him with guilt afterwards.

Was Jacob in the wrong?

He forced himself to consider it further, despite the guilt.

Had it been unjust of their father to set him up as the favorite all these years?

Even after Reuben had been so terribly in the wrong himself, was it truly right for Jacob to unseat him in favor of his eleventh son? Was it right, for that matter, to only do that and no more? For nothing else had been done.

Joseph shook his head to himself. He must stop this. He could not question his father.

And yet, the idea dogged his mind—until, as if in response, words he had heard spoken by his father years prior filtered into his thoughts.

"There are three things God requires of those who follow Him—to act justly, to love mercy, and to walk humbly in the path God has given them."

He frowned.

Did his father do as he had said? Did he act justly? Did he please his God?

Shaking his head, he made a final push against the thoughts. It wasn't his place to consider his father in such a way or interpret the commands of his father's God. He quickly attempted to join the conversation, pretending to smile at something Judah had said that made everyone laugh.

His brothers could not continue like this forever. They would calm one day, and then all would be well.

The next day dawned with the first signs of winter. Joseph and the sons of Bilhah and Zilpah were up and gone from camp as the sun rose, taking only some leftover bread and figs from the previous night with them. The air was chill for the first time in months, and their breath puffed in little clouds in front of them. *A welcome gift on this day,* Joseph thought, considering his now seventeen years.

"The weather is an agreeable change," Joseph said.

"It is." Dan's reply was terse.

The group once again fell into silence. Joseph grimaced to himself and took to watching the patterns his brothers' sandals left in the dewy brown grass as they walked. He pulled his sheepskin cloak a little more tightly around himself. They continued on over the next rise and Joseph looked down on the dull brown land. Sheep were scattered sorrowfully amongst the little gullies.

Three male servants who had kept night watch over the sheep lifted their hands in greeting and rose from their spots atop various hillocks. His brothers started down the hill, and Joseph followed. The two groups passed each other with a polite exchange before the brothers reached the bottom of the hill.

Dan motioned at the scattered flocks, some invisible behind the rises, and back at Joseph. "Bring them in."

Joseph's mouth opened a little. "Bring them *in?*" He motioned around them. "There's not enough food for all of them; they're scattered for a reason."

"We're not going to be bothered to keep track of hundreds of wayward sheep. We let the servants do that. They'll not starve."

Joseph shook his head in disbelief. "That's irresponsible, Dan."

Gad snorted. "That's rich, coming from you."

Bristling, Joseph snapped: "*I'll* watch the farther flocks. Then we won't have to be in each other's company all morning." He couldn't help the second part.

He walked off, anger smoldering. How long had this been going on? He counted the days since he'd been in the fields—seven? Eight? His brothers were difficult, but he hadn't expected *this* of them. This was how they handled their responsibility to their father? To their family?

Forcing himself to calm, he took a deep breath as he walked. It couldn't be all of them. Judah would never agree to it, nor Reuben, for that matter. He reached the top of a far hillock, making sure he could see all the scattered sheep, before sitting down in a huff next to a scraggly bit of scrub. A quick glance back showed the sons of Bilhah and Zilpah settling down in a similar manner.

The rest of the long morning saw him alone with his indignance. The sun rose fully, washing away all trace of the wintery morning in a blaze of heat. Near midday, he once again glanced at his brothers and caught them taking swigs of date wine. He scowled, and taking a draught of his own waterskin, turned his back again and faced the other direction.

When Reuben, Simeon, and Levi came after the noon hour to relieve them, he snatched up his bag and wordlessly marched back to camp without waiting for the others. If they could see him and knew where he was going, so be it.

He strode through camp, past the cooking tent, though his stomach growled, and on to his father's tent.

His father looked up in surprise when Joseph burst in. "Father, your sons are cheating you."

Jacob frowned at him. "Of what are you speaking, my son?"

Joseph pointed out the opening of the tent. "Dan and Naphtali, Gad and Asher. They have been mistreating the flocks. They do not let the sheep graze freely, to make the day easier on themselves. They are drinking wine while your flocks starve."

"Is this so?" His father's frown grew.

"It is."

Wordlessly, Jacob left the tent. Joseph sat down and wiped his brow, and felt a sense of grim satisfaction.

It did not last. Just before the evening meal, Simeon and Levi found him as he was pouring grain for the donkeys. Levi came up behind and bullied him away from the trough, pushing him into Simeon. The bag of grain pitched in Joseph's arms, trickling its contents haphazardly on the ground. Simeon grabbed him by the shoulders and whirled Joseph to face him.

"Let go of me!" Joseph spat, trying to pull away but still struggling with the sack of grain.

"You little rat," Levi returned with a snarl. "Going straight to Father. Can't keep your mouth shut."

Joseph gaped. "Reuben and Judah would have done the same!"

"We're not talking about Reuben and Judah, we're talking about *you*," Simeon said.

He roughly broke free as the sound of clanging metal pans rang in the air. Leaving the donkey pen wordlessly, he set the bag of grain outside a nearby storage tent before turning and walking away. If Simeon and Levi wanted to continue harassing him, they'd have to do so in front of everyone.

They trailed behind him, all the way up to the canopy and the water jars, saying nothing. Joseph quickly washed his face and hands before sitting down next to his father. The table was unusually silent, but Joseph expected that it was because the sons of Bilhah and Zilpah had received a tongue-lashing.

But it was not so.

His father stood up, and Joseph saw that he was holding a richly-woven robe, with colorful designs and the tiniest hint of gilt intertwined at the collar. He stared at it. He'd rarely seen anything so fine.

"Joseph, my son," Jacob said quietly. "Today you are seventeen years old. I gift you this, in honor of the day of your birth and in memory of your dear mother. May it serve you well, and remind you of the responsibility you have towards my house and this family."

Joseph stood slowly, in shock. Jacob's face was warm and smiling. If the others were not, he supposed he did not care—for the coat, shining in all its variant colors, was a gift from his father.

And it was so very beautiful.

3

He sat in his father's tent the next morning, still perhaps a little besotted by Jacob's gift and words from the night prior. Wearing the fine robe against the chill that had returned, Joseph watched the thick drapes of wool that formed the walls of the tent drift slightly with the outside breeze. The brazier flickered, casting warm light on the rippling walls.

His father peered over his shoulder, critically eyeing the neat cuneiform lines Joseph had stamped into the soft clay tablet he was holding.

"Only twenty jars?" Jacob repeated.

"Only twenty," Joseph returned, casting his glance down at the tablet once again. "Though," he said thoughtfully, rubbing his temple with the reed stylus, "old Mizzah may yet be in the city. He's likely to know who has more. Or we can wait until the olives ripen."

Jacob snorted. "I'll not be beholden to Mizzah any more than we already are this season. He already convinced Levi to trade perfectly good honey for those blasted obsidian knives."

Privately, Joseph thought the knives quite spectacular, but did not say anything. "So we wait, Father? We'll be here several more weeks if we are to make the oil before we move north."

"It would seem so." Jacob looked at him expectantly.

Joseph shifted slightly, wondering what his father was about. "Father?"

He chuckled. "My dear son, I am waiting for you to tell me what we must do next."

Mind racing, Joseph shook his head. "I—what do you mean?"

"If we are to stay here several more weeks, what must be done?"

"Well, the flocks will not last, I think. We ought—to move them north?" The ending came out like a question. Joseph hoped this was what he was getting at.

Jacob laughed a little and rubbed his knees. He looked warmly at Joseph. "Well done. I shall send your brothers north in the next week or so with the flocks. We will follow a few weeks after."

Nodding a bit, Joseph smiled slightly at his father's pleasure. Jacob had been teaching him all the ways of their livelihood for the past several months, but never had he so directly relied on Joseph to state the next course of action.

"Your mother would be very proud of you."

Joseph looked up, a little stunned. This was the second time in the span of a day that his father had spoken of Rachel. He felt an unexpected prickle of grief, but his father only continued. "You will lead this family well, one day."

The world careened to a stop; for a brief moment, the dancing fire in the brazier ceased to crackle, and even the sound of the wind disappeared. Then Joseph's head cleared, and all was as it should be. Or at least, most of it. He stared at Jacob, convinced he had misheard.

"Father?" he ventured with effort, for his throat seemed to want to close. "What do you mean?"

Jacob came and put a gentle hand on his shoulder. "Only that of all my sons, you are the one most deserving."

Mind spinning once again, Joseph dared not say anything else, for his father did not. He watched him go to the other end of the tent to pull on his outer cloak. Jacob would go to walk the camp now, as he did often in the afternoons.

Is he speaking of—the birthright? Reuben's birthright?

There was nothing he could do to learn more. He stood, bowed, and exited his father's tent in a daze.

He lay awake that night, staring up at the wooden poles that supported the tent, their farthest ends barely lighted by the glow of the dimming braziers.

Someone snorted in their sleep—*Asher, most likely*—and Joseph grimaced. Since the incident in the fields yesterday, not a single one of his older brothers had spoken peaceably to him. Sharing a tent with the sons of Bilhah and Zilpah, as he always had, had never been more miserable.

Asher snorted again, and someone smacked him. The sound ceased, and slow breathing again reigned throughout the tent.

Left again in relative silence, Joseph's thoughts turned once more towards the injustice of it all. He scowled. For them to be so irresponsible, and then not even Judah to defend him when he told Father? What had they expected him to do? It was ridiculous.

He was willing to admit that perhaps he ought to have respected Reuben's place and gone to him first, but he quickly forced the thought down. *Reuben would have gone to Father regardless, and the result would have been the same.* And, all duty towards his father or eldest brother aside, it served his brothers right to have a boy put them in their place if they aimed to be so foolish themselves.

He thought back to only two nights ago, when he had firmly believed that one day his brothers would change, would become more levelheaded. He sighed. At the moment, that appeared to be quite an unreachable prospect.

And in heaven's name, what had his father meant when he said, *Lead this family well?*

His head spun, no answers to be found.

Joseph sighed deeply, and his thoughts drifted to Dinah.

In his mind's eye, he saw her in the women's tent, lying there surrounded by the Canaanite women who had never once ceased to blame her for the massacre at Shechem. He scowled again fiercely, and his stomach knotted. To be *raped*, for there was no other word for what had happened, by the prince of that city, and then to have Simeon and Levi murder *every single man* in Shechem in her name? His heart ached for her.

A change, nearly any change, might serve her well. But it certainly could not be *marriage*. He shuddered. The sight of her hollow eyes after she returned from Shechem had never left him.

What change?

He rolled over and sighed again, feeling singularly helpless.

He had no idea.

Judah grinned at him, and Joseph laughed in turn. He glanced over the vast field, shot through with canals, taking it in and calculating its yield.

It would be enough.

He looked again to his brothers. All eleven of the men reached for the last piles of grain and began to bind them. Joseph did the same.

Once they finished, they laid the sheaves on the earth, ready to bring them to the storehouses.

But Joseph's sheaf would not lie. It rose and stood upright. His brothers looked on in astonishment. A few called out.

Joseph saw his brothers' sheaves beginning to bend and wave. They also arose and, forming a circle, bowed themselves towards his own sheaf, which stood tall in the center.

In the far distance, the wide river flowed.

He awoke with a start to the deep darkness of the early morning. The braziers had gone out. Sweat dripped off his brow, and he sat upright in confusion.

Only a dream.

But it did not seem like one, somehow. He tried to shake off the crawling feeling that skittered up and down his spine, as if someone had been watching him in his sleep. Yet his brothers slept on, and not a single one stirred.

He laid back down and let out a long breath. Still his skim crawled.

All their sheaves of wheat bowed down to mine.

What had it meant?

Outdoors, a single gust of wind set a chime hung nearby into motion. He nearly bolted upright again, but then the strange feeling ceased altogether, as if someone had snuffed out a lamp.

Joseph lay there, unnerved and utterly still, until he threw off his sheepskin blanket. He was suddenly far too hot to remain under it. But the moment the cooler air reached him, sleep inexorably grasped at his mind. He struggled against it, trying to focus on the strange dream.

It was no use.

No other dreams found him that night.

The next morning dawned cold and clear, and when he awoke the sons of Bilhah and Zilpah were, blessedly, already gone. He rubbed his eyes and squinted in the bright light. The events of the middle of the night seemed immaterial, almost as though he had imagined it all.

Almost.

He knew he had not. Joseph combed out the knots in his hair and put on his new robe, brows knitted in perplexity, before stepping out of the tent. The morning meal would be soon.

He caught the eye of Mehetabel as he did so. She was a little way away, leading Benjamin along, her two sons following. Benjamin squealed when he saw Joseph, stretching out his free hand.

Joseph smiled in return and walked over, scooping the boy up. Mehetabel laughed quietly, Benjamin whooping in excitement. But once the little boy was at his eye level, Joseph frowned. Benjamin had seemed older in his dream, somehow.

"And how are you this morning, Joseph?" Mehetabel was asking.

Joseph had to shake himself a little. "I am well," he answered with a forced smile. To hopefully put her off any questions, he heaved Benjamin up a little farther on his hip and nodded smilingly at the boy. "And how is Benjamin?"

"He is blessed with boundless energy," she said with a wry quirk of her mouth. "He will make a strong man one day."

Somehow those words made the morning far more disquieting than it already was. He forced a laugh and searched for something to say in response. "Shall I bring him to the morning meal?" he looked at his brother and grinned. "Is he growing quickly? Is he old enough?"

Benjamin only looked at him, blue eyes round. Mehetabel laughed. "I suppose you might try. He may well be silent as a mouse, surrounded by all you big men."

"Ah, well, we shall try then." He hoisted Benjamin up onto his shoulders and turned towards the center of the camp and the canopy. Metal pans were clanging, and Joseph smiled at Mehetabel. "I will bring him back after the meal and let you know how it went."

He walked towards the canopy. Jacob was already there, and Benjamin clapped when he saw their father.

"Father!" Joseph called. Jacob turned. "I have brought a guest; may he stay for the meal?"

Jacob threw out his hands and came to them as they approached. Benjamin laughed, nearly leaping from Joseph's shoulders. "My sons!" Jacob exclaimed. "My littlest one," he said, putting a hand on Benjamin's head and then taking him up in his arms.

"Papa!" Benjamin exclaimed delightedly.

"Do you wish to stay for the meal, my son?" Jacob asked the boy with a smile. Benjamin was bashfully silent.

"He'll sit with me; I'll see to him," said Joseph.

Jacob nodded approvingly and handed Benjamin back to him.

The three of them walked towards the table and arrived at the same moment as Dinah and several of their brothers. Dinah touched Benjamin's head with a smile, but the others were sour-faced when they saw the boy. Joseph forced down a scowl, for his father's sake.

The meal went near-silently, and Joseph inwardly fumed. He knew it was because Benjamin was present. New thoughts drove the morning's unease from his mind. If they meant to make his brother their target as well—

He clasped the small boy, eating silently in his lap, a little more tightly. That, he vowed, would never happen.

He was still seething when he returned Benjamin to Mehetabel. She asked how it had gone, and Joseph responded noncommittally, but it was clear she noticed that he was not himself.

Then heading towards the donkeys, which he saw to every morning he was in camp, he stopped short when he saw that all ten of his older brothers were waiting for him.

A small part of him whispered that he should run, but he ignored it. Why should he? "What do you want?" he asked.

Reuben spoke for them. "Why did you bring the little one to the meal?"

"Why shouldn't I?"

"*Why?*" Simeon pushed forward. "We don't need another accursed son of Rachel trying to usurp us, that's why."

Joseph clenched his fists. "Benjamin is *three years old.*"

"So were you once, whelp, and perhaps we should have done away with you then!"

Roaring in rage, Joseph would have tackled Simeon had not Reuben, shouting, pulled Simeon back. Judah stepped between them and put a calming hand on Joseph's shoulder, flashing him a warning look.

Joseph ripped himself from Judah's grasp. "I've had it with the lot of you!" he shouted. "If I have Father's favor, *what of it?*" He glared at them and a terrible sort of mood overtook him. "Please hear this dream I had last night," he spat. "We were binding sheaves in the field. Mine rose and stood upright, and all of yours stood around it and bowed down to mine."

They all stared at him, dumbfounded.

"Now you tell me what that might mean." He looked at them grimly.

Too many of his brothers to count rushed him, but somehow Judah managed to roughly drag Joseph out of harm's way.

Simeon howled the loudest. "You think you will *reign over us?*" His other brothers cursed and thundered demands of explanation, surging forward.

Judah dragged Joseph back farther and finally placed himself between him and their near-manic brothers.

Male and female servants were appearing from all directions now, rushing towards the chaos.

"Stop defending him, Judah!" Levi bellowed, pushing forward.

"Enough! That's enough!" Reuben grabbed hold of Levi's collar and hauled him back. The others halted where they stood, glancing around in understanding. Reuben eyed the crowd worriedly. "That's enough for today," he repeated, voice stern.

He turned, and the others followed, casting dark glances over their shoulders as they went. Judah cuffed Joseph's ear and glared at him as he left. "You fool," he muttered.

And as quickly as that, they were gone. Joseph stood there, breathing heavily and grimacing at the pain in his ear, trying to ignore the whispers and glances. Setting his jaw, he dusted off his robe and moved purposefully toward the donkeys. The watching crowd, with nothing more to see, slowly dispersed.

A cold wind blew as Joseph lugged the sack of grain to the trough. His thoughts stormed through his mind unchecked.

They were impossible.

They were heartless.

Cruel.

Wicked.

They had threatened harm on Benjamin.

He grit his teeth and forced himself to breathe.

To be reasonable.

Simeon couldn't have *meant* it. Surely. None of the others had agreed. He forced another breath. They had all been angry. Judah was right. He'd been a fool, to mention his strange dream in anger. After all, it meant nothing.

Nothing.

Trough full, he set down the sack of grain and placed a gentle hand on the nearest donkey, rubbing its soft ears and nose. He took another breath.

"Joseph?"

He jumped and turned. It was Dinah, brows knitted in concern. "Joseph, what happened?"

Frustration returned. He picked up the sack before looking back at her again. "It was nothing." He walked past her and out of the pen to rest the sack next to the storage tent. The colorful ends of the tent's draped sides danced and snapped in the stiff breeze.

She followed him doggedly. "It did not sound like nothing. What did you say to them?"

"Me?" he wheeled on her. "You ought to ask what they said to me."

"Well, what did they say?"

Mouth half open, he forced down the words. It did not bear repeating. "Dinah, it was nothing."

His sister frowned at him. "As you like."

Joseph softened. "I'm sorry. It was only tempers flaring."

She was unconvinced, pursing her lips as she looked up at him, but nodded. "Very well." Standing on tiptoe, she kissed his cheek. "Do not let them bother you."

He smiled thinly in response and watched her go.

4

His father watched him with similar concern that afternoon as Joseph sat in Jacob's tent, running though projections of how much wool they might acquire during the spring shearing. He said nothing, and hoped his father would not broach the subject.

"Joseph," Jacob eventually said.

Inwardly, he winced. "Yes, Father?"

"I understand that you and your brothers came near to blows today."

Joseph determinedly stared at the tablet in his hands. "That is true."

"Why?"

Looking askance, he considered the events of the morning. They had all been to blame. And he was not about to bring his father reports of his brothers again, not with Benjamin suddenly thrust into the picture. Even if Simeon seemed only to have spoken in anger, it was not worth hearing such things said of his brother again.

"We were—angry. It was nothing."

He could feel Jacob's frown. "My son, you are better than that."

"I know it."

"Look at me." Joseph raised his head resignedly. "Your brothers have never learned that such actions will earn them little in life. You have time yet to learn it. Do so quickly and well."

"Yes, Father." In his mind, he blanched, and wished he could explain.

The flat roof of the house, whitewashed mud-brick, was cool under his

feet. Netted curtains, nearly as fine as spider silk, blew around him in the dim light. Scattered at his feet, he glimpsed piles of cushions.

In the far distance, the wide river flowed.

He looked up into the night sky. Thousands of stars lay there, flung out by the hand of God. And as he watched, eleven of the stars and even the moon came close to him, almost as though he could reach out and touch them.

Suddenly it was not night, but day, and the sun was there, with the moon and eleven stars. They came and rested in a circle around him, and bowed to him.

He awoke again to the dead of night, that strange crawling feeling skittering up his back. Joseph threw off his sheepskin blanket and gasped for air. He was burning hot and drenched in sweat.

Would this not cease? Two nights in a row was ridiculous. Had his father's words about his place in the family gone to his head?

Sleep tugged at his mind, as it had the first time, and Joseph did not try to fight it. But then, out of total silence, a single gust of wind set that same chime to ringing.

His eyes flew open. He lay very still.

It had to be a coincidence. It could be nothing more.

Then he thought of his father, who had wrestled with his God, and before that, had seen the angels of God traveling to and from the earth in a dream. Jacob had even heard the voice of God in that dream. He thought of his great-grandfather Abraham, who had made a still-stranger blood covenant with God. God had promised to prosper his descendants.

It cannot be.

He rolled over, but his mind spun, and sleep had left him.

It was a very different scene at the morning meal the next day. Joseph came late, just as the others were sitting, walking in a haze of sleeplessness. He must have looked horribly spent; he could feel the eyes of the others on him, even Bilhah and Zilpah and Leah.

"Are you well, my son?" Jacob asked quietly.

"Yes, Father," Joseph answered, trying to stifle a yawn as he sat.

"I think the dreamer has slept too much," he heard Levi mutter to Simeon.

Jacob glanced sharply at Levi and then turned to Joseph. "What is this Levi speaks of?"

Joseph stared down at the piece of bread he had just taken, and one of his brothers stifled a guffaw. He saw Dinah, from the corner of his eye, looking at him questioningly. Finally, Asher snickered. "Why don't you tell Father what you told us yesterday?"

"My son?" Jacob questioned again.

Resisting the urge to squirm in his seat, Joseph resignedly answered: "I had a dream."

"One dream?" his father asked.

He could not lie to his father. His brothers had set him up, without even knowing it.

"And another, last night," he finally added.

Asher and Levi hooted, and several of his brothers made sounds of disgust.

"Silence, for heaven's sake," Jacob said.

He relayed the events of the first dream without looking up. Then he rushed into the second dream, only wanting to get it over with. "I dreamt that the sun, the moon, and eleven stars came down from the heavens and bowed to me."

The table erupted in sounds of objection, and Simeon threw down his food and stalked off. Dinah was gaping at him, and Leah covered her mouth in shock.

"Enough!" said Jacob. The table grew silent. "I will hear no more of such things this morning."

Abashed, Joseph determinedly met no one's eyes for the rest of the meal. He stood to leave as soon as was permissible, hoping to see to the donkeys in relative peace.

33

But his father's firm hand on his shoulder stopped him short. "Joseph, I would speak with you."

His stomach sank.

He walked with his father, who guided him towards his tent. Joseph once ventured a glance backwards, but his father's eyes were distant, almost unseeing. They entered, and Joseph took a seat on a stool and waited for his father's reprimand.

It came forcefully. "What is this, Joseph? Shall I and your brothers and indeed your mother, may her memory be blessed, bow down to the earth before you?"

Joseph grimaced. The dreams, especially the second one, had not seemed *so* intensely egregious until his father spoke them out loud.

Then Jacob sighed, loudly. "My son, why did you speak of such a thing to your brothers?"

"I was angry."

"Look at me, Joseph."

He looked up. His father's gaze was unreadable. "Dreams such as these are not to be spoken of lightly."

Joseph stared at him. Jacob continued. "The meaning of any dream belongs to God. It is not for us to parade our own interpretations about. Especially interpretations of *such* dreams."

"Father," Joseph managed, bewildered. It was not quite the scolding he expected. "What do you mean? Do you mean to say that my dreams—"

Jacob held up a hand, and Joseph fell silent. "I will speak no more on this," his father said firmly. He held open the flap of the tent. Cowed, Joseph bowed and left in silence.

The dreams returned no more, and for that Joseph was grateful. A week passed, and if Dinah had ribbed him for a few days about the absurdity of it all, nothing else changed, except that his brothers became more quarrelsome by the day. That did not surprise him. He supposed they had expected the dreams to curb his father's favor.

The olives were rapidly ripening, but the sheep had less and less food as each day passed. Jacob announced his plan one day after the noon meal.

Simeon immediately objected. "Send us north to *Shechem*? We'll not be welcome there."

Reuben snorted. "Whose fault is that, I wonder?"

"There's no one left to be angry with us," muttered Gad.

"The grazing will be better there," Jacob said. "And it is not so far that we may not quickly join you as soon as the oil-making is complete."

"When do we leave?" asked Reuben, speaking for the brothers.

"The day after tomorrow," Jacob answered. "I will send all of you, save Joseph. Together you should be enough to watch the flocks, and watch them *well*." He eyed the sons of Bilhah and Zilpah pointedly.

Ten pairs of eyes immediately turned towards Joseph. "What then, he is not to come with us?" Levi protested. "Is he to make oil with the women?"

"My uses for my son are none of your concern," Jacob said sharply.

Grumbling, they turned and walked away.

Joseph thought his father might say more to him, to either explain what Joseph would be doing or offer a word of comfort against his brothers' actions. But he only turned to go, deep in thought. As he left, Joseph almost wished to ask if he could go with his brothers after all.

What am I thinking?

He shook himself. Why would he ask for what would amount to nothing more than weeks of misery, all to prove some point?

And what point? That he was *not* Jacob's favorite? No action in the land could make his brothers think that was not so.

Joseph walked off in the opposite direction, to the lone olive tree that sat on the northwest side of the camp. The other trees were farther to the west, ten minutes' walk. With a huffing breath, he sat down under it and drew up his knees, wrapping his colorful robe more tightly around his chest.

The grasses and scrub were totally brown now, waiting for the first rains of winter. He looked up at the sky and sniffed. There was no moisture in the air, just a dry, chilling cold that assaulted the nostrils and an endless, sharply blue sky. The insects of summer had gone silent, and the birds had fled south. The only sounds that remained were the rattle of the grasses and, faintly, the sound of sheep.

Looking down, he saw that one of the earliest olives had already fallen to the ground. Joseph picked up the deeply purple fruit, observing the hole some crawling thing had made in it, and looked upwards into the silvery branches. The dusty green leaves shook in the wind. The harvest would begin any day.

He glanced again at the little fruit in his hand, and then, on a whim, threw it as far as he could. It flew in a long arc before it bounced on the outcropping of a nearby stony hill and disappeared into a little valley below.

He sighed deeply and leaned back against the gnarled trunk of the olive tree.

There was little to mark the morning of his brothers' departure. The male servants came back from the fields, each driving a large portion of the sheep and working to cluster the animals into a manageable swath. His brothers spread out amongst them, long crooks in their hands, ready to drive them north. They had already said their farewells, Jacob promising to join them within the month. They said nothing to Joseph.

He stood with Dinah, watching them go. She looked up at him keenly. "Do you wish you went with them?"

Joseph glanced at her, then squinted at the shrinking forms of the flocks and his brothers as they moved away. "No."

She pursed her lips and nodded, before making her way to the weaving tent.

The oil-making went well, for a time. Joseph watched the male and female servants and the Canaanite women beating the fruits from the trees; the olives bounced down in large numbers and were carried to the cooking tent to be crushed and pressed. But after the second evening, Dinah and her mother came out shaking their heads. Leah left when she saw Joseph standing nearby, but Dinah came to him, mouth twisted to one side in displeasure.

"What is it?" Joseph asked.

She shook her head again. "We think it has been too hot, with too little rain. Many of the olives are small and have little pulp."

Joseph thought back to the oil production tallies his father had requested he make daily, and mentally envisioned scratching out the projections he had done on the side.

"How many?" he asked. "What portion of a basket?"

Dinah twisted her mouth again. "A third, perhaps."

He winced. "It will not be enough oil then. Father will have to trade for some before we leave."

"Can we not do so after we go north?"

Joseph considered. "I've no idea where Father plans to winter or which families may be there. He may decide to wait until then, but I do not know if it would be wise. We may not find anyone with any to trade."

"But does anyone in Hebron have any? If all the trees are like this, it may not be so."

"There may be some from last year. Or someone may need something else more."

Dinah sighed. "I suppose you had better go and tell him."

When he did, Jacob was not pleased. He frowned and stroked his beard, turning to face the wall in thought. Joseph stood near the door of his father's tent, pouring over the wet clay tablet on which he had recorded the tallies earlier that day.

He thirded the amount he had projected and subtracted that. The results were not promising: twelve jars, perhaps.

Maybe they could stretch the old jars and the new—thirty-two jars in total—through to the next autumn, but he did not believe his father would think it the wisest course. He waited for Jacob to speak.

It was some time before his father did so. "Tell me what you are thinking, Joseph."

Joseph looked at his father in surprise. There it was again—his father's deliberate testing of Joseph's decision-making abilities. He rocked a little on his feet and thought of Reuben, and of Simeon's anger, and of Benjamin.

Still, he must answer. He shook his head a little. "We will have a little more than thirty jars if all goes as it does now. It will likely not be enough." He looked up at his father. "We ought to see if we can acquire more before we go north."

Jacob nodded slowly. "Why would we not trade for oil later in the year, after we move northward?"

Joseph repeated what he had already considered with Dinah. "I suppose we could, but it would not be a certain thing. If we attempt to get some now and succeed, it will be one less thing to worry about. And with the sheep already gone northward, we can spare the time."

His father smiled a little but did not say anything in agreement. Then he shooed Joseph out. "Away for now, my son. I must think."

5

At the evening meal, Jacob announced his plan to send Joseph and a male servant into Hebron the next day to see if there was any oil to be had. Joseph left early the next morning, with a Canaanite boy in tow. Ezer was a year or two Joseph's junior, one of the oldest children who had survived Shechem. Joseph had always found him rather sullen, but then, he supposed, Ezer had good reason to be.

The frosty air nipped at their ankles, and the chill dew on the grass bit at their sandaled feet, but the view of the dawn over the hills was pleasing to see. They walked in silence, Ezer clearly not wanting to talk and Joseph unable to find anything of interest to say.

The bright hues of the sunrise had melted to pale blue by the time the pair approached the city gates. They had just opened for the day, and a few other small groups trickled in with them. The city square was sorrowfully empty in the cold morning air, nothing like the bustling and colorful market of summertime. Without the draped canopies set about to mark the different stands of the traders and merchants, the mud-brick walls of homes loomed sternly over the square. Joseph glanced over the emptiness and bit his lip. Then his heart leapt.

There! At the farthest end of the square, under his ancient canopy that once upon a time had probably been green, sat Mizzah.

Joseph approached with a smile, Ezer following like a surly shadow.

"Ah! Young master Joseph!" Mizzah stood up, a hand on his back as he attempted to straighten. "I thought your family would be gone by now. How is your father?"

"Well, thank you," Joseph answered. There was a line of sorts to be walked with Mizzah. He could be shrewd—Jacob would say *too shrewd*. Joseph continued carefully, for there was no way for him to have the upper hand in any sort of bargain that might be struck. "We are only looking to trade for a few jars of oil before we move northward."

Mizzah regarded him for a moment, knowingly. "Ah. As many are, I'm afraid." He shook his head. "A foul business, this past autumn."

Joseph cocked his head in return. "So, not everyone is looking for oil?"

The old man gave a guffaw and a little smile. "No, not everyone, but many."

Shrugging a little, Joseph glanced over the man's wares, spread on the ground across a thin blanket. He nodded towards the two large jars at the back of the array of items. "Those cannot be oil, I imagine."

Mizzah laughed. "No indeed, young master. Empty, those are."

"Hmm, not much use then."

The trader continued laughing. "You are a sly one, son of Jacob. Tell me what you are getting at, and we will make this more quick, I think."

Smiling, Joseph answered: "Suppose you find me some oil, and in return I start by taking those jars off your hands. They'll be a hindrance on your journey for the winter, empty as they are. We also have plenty of wool blankets to trade. Those, I think, will be much more worth your while in this weather."

The old man stroked his beard. "I'm not sure I know who wants to trade their oil."

"It seems as though you know who isn't in need of any. Perhaps you can start there?"

With another laugh and clap of his hands, Mizzah slapped him on the shoulder. "Well said, young master! But what are you offering *them*, now? It had best be something special."

"I have three jars of desert honey from south of Beersheba. With the rains so little this past autumn, I doubt there will be any like it again for some time."

"Hmm," Mizzah's face was impassive, but his eyes were twinkling. "I am leaving for Joppa in less than a week, but I'll see what I can do."

Joseph smiled. "Excellent."

"Now, how many blankets have you to trade?"

"Plenty, as I said."

Mizzah snorted and grinned. "I don't think I ought to name my price until I hear yours."

"I already named my three jars of honey. I think it's only fair you give your price now."

The trader eyed him again before finally smiling broadly. "For the entertainment you've brought me this morning, young master, I'll concede. Fifteen blankets."

Pausing thoughtfully, Joseph ran a hand through his hair before saying: "Nine."

"Thirteen."

Joseph had been hoping for ten, but he knew now that number would not do. "Eleven."

"Done." Mizzah slapped him on the shoulder again. "Now, then—is there anything else I can interest you in? How does your brother get on with those knives?"

Laughing, Joseph shook his head. "Well enough, but I have no need of one."

"Ah, but I saw your face, lad, when he bought them."

Shaking his head again with a smile, Joseph raised his hand and took his leave.

"Come back in two days, young master," Mizzah called after him. "And bring your wares."

Jacob was pleased with the results, though Joseph had been a little concerned about the two large jars that were, for the time being, rather useless. His father paid them no mind.

"Take some balm," his father advised the night before Joseph was to return to Hebron. "In case someone requires a little more persuasion."

The oil-making had continued and Joseph's re-worked projections seemed, so far, to be correct. Jacob looked them over and frowned. "Try to get five jars, at least," he said to Joseph. "And if that is not possible, then anything you can acquire must be enough."

Joseph set off again the next morning with Ezer following, leading two of the camels. It was likely they would only need one for the oil, but it never hurt to show one's expectations, Joseph decided. The first one came loaded with blankets, well-woven. Joseph had placed one of Dinah's making on top, with a clever design that mimicked braiding around the edges. He had hidden the little clay jar of balm among them. The second camel carried the honey.

Mizzah raised a hand in greeting when he arrived. "Welcome, young Joseph!" The old man looked him up and down. "That is quite a coat."

Joseph nodded in thanks. He hadn't worn his father's gift the other day, purposefully. It wouldn't have done to let Mizzah know Jacob had seen a profitable year, for then he might have asked for more.

"Your father must be doing well."

"Well enough," Joseph acknowledged with a smile. "And what have you found for us?"

"Two jars is the best I can do, for your three jars of honey."

"That's it?" Joseph cocked his head.

The trader nodded.

Shifting on his feet, Joseph finally answered: "I suppose it could be done. But my family may have more luck than that ourselves, if we wait to trade until after we move northward."

"That may be," Mizzah agreed. "But then, you may not."

Thinking again, Joseph struck on an idea. "Mizzah, how much for your knowledge?"

"My *knowledge*?"

"Yes—of which family has oil to spare now—" his eyes flicked up to glance at the old man "—which ones had oil to spare last week, which ones will decide they have more to spare before you leave for Joppa, and which ones will finally have some to spare after the harvest is complete in a few weeks' time."

Mizzah laughed outright. "Ah, I see. No, no, young sir. You'll not cut me out of this. My knowledge, if I have any, will come with two jars of oil."

Joseph nodded. "Very well. Then what is your price for oil and knowledge?"

Mizzah glanced at the camels behind Joseph. Stepping towards the blankets, he fingered them thoughtfully. "These are well-made. They will do for my payment as go-between. For the knowledge—" he looked towards the second camel. "A fourth jar of honey, for my own keeping."

Such a brazen offer was not unlike the old man, so Joseph laughed in turn, and Mizzah grinned knowingly. "I'm not prepared to trade so much for information that may prove less than useful," said Joseph.

"And are you willing to go north without oil?"

"Perhaps."

"Hmm," Mizzah replied, still amused. "Well, son of Jacob, how do you propose we solve this?"

Reluctantly, for it seemed there was not much more bargaining that could be done, Joseph reached into the pile of rugs and pulled out the little jar. "This, for the information."

The trader plucked it from his hands, opening the jar and sniffing the aromatic resin. "It is good," he acknowledged. "Very good. But, for such a trade, I cannot promise I will not act on some of that information before I leave."

"That is fair, I think."

The old man smiled. "Very well, then."

He hoped that his father would not think his idea a harebrained waste, so Joseph explained it as quickly as he could while standing in the doorway of his father's tent. Then he looked up apprehensively.

Jacob looked thoughtful. "You suggest we speak to each of the families on our own now?"

"Yes. I thought that perhaps in a few weeks' time or even sooner some may decide that they have enough oil for trading."

His father's thoughtful expression did not change. "It will keep us here longer, if we have to wait for the other families to finish their harvests."

"Yes, I did think of that, but only after the fact. I am sorry, Father."

"No, no," Jacob stood up with a grunt and waved his hand in the air before coming forward to rest it on Joseph's shoulder. He looked at him fondly. "It was well done, Joseph."

The days stretched out into weeks. Still no rain came, though clouds now scudded across the sky, and a hard wind blew in the nights.

Jacob had visited all the families Mizzah had suggested. Most were herding families like themselves, but one or two lived in Hebron. Of them all, only two families showed interest in trading oil, and only after they had finished their harvests.

"It seems Mizzah was quite honest with you, about only having two jars to trade," Jacob admitted to his son one day after the evening meal. The others had dispersed, leaving only the two of them at the table, eating some dates. "We will be leaving Hebron at least three weeks late, since the other families are not so far along in the harvest as we." He paused, and his eyes narrowed in thought for a long moment before he continued. "Joseph, I think I shall have to send you to your brothers in Shechem tomorrow. Let them know we will be later than we intended and bring word of how things are proceeding back to me."

Joseph's heart dropped a little. His father had asked this sort of thing of him once before, the previous spring, and while a small journey on one's own was pleasant, this particular end destination was certainly not. But he could not say such things. "Of course, Father."

He found Dinah a while later, with several of the other women who were scrubbing out pots with sand down at the little rivulet that had once been a sizable stream. She stood up as he approached and wiped her hands on her shawl. "What were you and Father talking about for so long?"

The wind was picking up as the sun set, and Joseph pulled his robe a little more tightly around himself. He glanced westward at the last rays of the sun gleaming on the horizon. "We'll be here later than we expected, so we can trade for oil. I'm to go to Shechem tomorrow to see how our brothers are faring."

Dinah blew out a little puff of air. "No doubt you will not enjoy the task."

"No doubt."

She looked at him, eyes direct. "Joseph, can you not—*try* to get along with some of them, at least?"

"Dinah! They give me no peace. None of them."

His sister looked down and sighed. "I know it." She twisted her mouth in displeasure before looking back up at him. "But for heaven's sake, telling them that you have dreams where they will one day bow before you cannot help matters."

"I only did that because I was angry." He paused, thought, and then threw caution to the wind. Dinah would understand. "Simeon *threatened* Benjamin." It was good to finally say the words out loud.

She paused, face unreadable. "Simeon is a brute and an idiot," she said finally. "His words mean nothing. Reuben and Judah would never let him talk that way if he meant anything by it."

"That is what I told myself."

Dinah shook her head. "You must learn to ignore him. All of them, until the time comes when things may change."

Joseph laughed a little. "I think that time may never come."

"For you? I think it will. It must. Men who are brutes eventually

45

become dull drunkards, and then they no longer care what you do, as long as you provide them with wine."

He winced a little at her biting words. She never used to speak in such a way. Joseph put his hands gently on her shoulders. "And for you?" he asked. "Shall not change come for you as well?"

She looked up at him a little sadly and shook her head a second time. "I am not a favored son. The only change in my future is marriage."

Joseph looked at her solemnly in turn. "Then if my change comes, as you say it will, and it is in my power—if you find yourself mistreated, I will come for you."

His sister looked away and bit her lip. Her eyes squeezed shut and a single tear dropped down her face. Quietly, she pulled him close.

6

The sun was stretching its first rays over the eastern horizon when Joseph said farewell to Benjamin the next morning. Still sleepy-eyed, the boy was rubbing his eyes with one plump hand, which then traveled up to tug at his tousled curls.

Joseph picked him up with a smile and spun him around. "I will be back in a few days." He set the small boy down and pulled him into an embrace. Benjamin clutched at his arms and then gazed at him owlishly when Joseph let go. "A few days," Joseph repeated. "I'm going on a small journey, that's all." Hand in his mouth now, Benjamin finally nodded.

Giving him a quick kiss, Joseph turned to go. Mehetabel led the boy off to the side with a smile. A camel was waiting for Joseph, loaded with a blanket and food for himself and his brothers. "Safe journey, my son," Jacob said. "May God, who has walked before my fathers, Abraham and Isaac, and who has walked before me, go before you as well."

Joseph bowed his head in acknowledgement of the blessing and turned to go, giving Dinah a quick embrace before he mounted the camel. He waved from atop his perch as the camel got to its feet. "Farewell, I will see you soon!"

And then he was off, jouncing along with the rolling motion of the camel's movements. The air was brisk, but not quite as cold as it had been, and the sky promised no rain. If he continued without interruption, he would be there by evening.

The morning passed uneventfully, the numbing jostle of the

47

camel the only real nuisance. He watched the hill country go by. He had seen it lush and green in the past, but all the grasses and brush had browned to a dull color, almost that of smoke. Only the trees on the higher slopes still held their rich green hue.

He passed a few traveling trains of families, all headed northward for the winter. Some processions stretched almost a league in length, scattered throughout with animals and great folded tent walls.

The day passed on. The wind picked up and blew strongly out of the north, whistling down the long valleys and carrying dust that smarted in his eyes. He pulled his robe more tightly around himself and put his sheepskin blanket over that. Vigorously rubbing his hands over his face, he managed to bring a bit of life back into his nearly-numb cheeks and nose.

Evening was approaching by the time he marked the high valley of Shechem, sitting between the mountains Gerizim and Ebal. Once familiar, it had been over three years since he had seen it. He urged the camel forward.

The valley was near empty, and the city, off in the distance, showed no signs of habitation. Above all, there was no sign of Jacob's flocks, though the swaths of green that painted the ground proved that the grazing was still good, and the mountains shielded the valley from some of the wind.

Joseph wandered for some time, urging the camel over and around small rises in the surrounding hills, looking for where the flocks could be hidden. On a larger hill, just as the sun was setting, he looked out over the valley again. Three campfires could be seen, winking in the low light, but none were surrounded by sheep.

Frowning, he decided to try the next valley over and was halfway there before he came across a man. "What are you seeking?" the man called out.

The man had just dismounted his donkey, which was laden with baggage. He looked to be about to set up camp for the night.

"I am seeking my brothers," Joseph answered. He preferred not to give his father's name in this region, but there was no way around it. "The sons of Jacob. Please, do you know where they are feeding their flocks?"

A quick flicker of distaste crossed the man's face. "Another son of Jacob? They are no longer here, boy. I heard them say they were to travel on to Dothan."

Confounded, Joseph couldn't help the sound of frustration that escaped him. "I see," he said finally. "Thank you, sir."

The man watched him go without offering to share a fire.

He could not travel on to Dothan tonight. It was not a long journey, but as all journeys it was better taken in daylight. Joseph traveled away from the man, to the northern edge of the valley, and dismounted the camel near a stand of olive trees.

Irritably, he tied the camel to one of the trees. It immediately took to foraging through the branches and leaves. Unloading his supplies for the night, he set up a small camp and struck a fire. Finally sitting and leaning his back up against a tree, he closed his eyes and sighed in frustration.

Why had they gone on to Dothan? Those had not been their instructions, and there was plenty for the sheep to eat here. He guessed it had been some untenable idea of pride. He ran a hand through his hair in frustration. The day's ride in the wind had tangled it hopelessly, and his fingers caught in the strands.

Still indignant, Joseph forced himself to eat some almonds and part of a loaf before rolling over to sleep.

The next morning dawned cold and clear. The blue of the sky seemed almost brittle, and the valley was covered in a thin sheet of frost. Stamping his feet and blowing on his hands, Joseph kicked some of the sandy soil over the smoldering remains of his fire and loaded the camel for the ride to Dothan.

The camel was ornery in the morning chill, taking three promptings before it knelt for Joseph to mount. At length, it rose to its feet, Joseph astride, and he continued northward for the second day in a row. It was less than a third of the distance he had traveled yesterday, and for that, at least, he was grateful.

Before midday, he saw the walls of the small city in the far distance. And from the rise on which his camel stood, he could see, spread out to the west, large flocks of sheep.

Shaking his head, he urged the camel forward. It was not long before he could make out the ten forms of his brothers. He noted with some ire that they were not spread out amongst the sheep, as they should be, but were instead gathered around what looked like an old well.

They walked to meet him as he approached. Joseph had expected some form of jeering upon his arrival, but instead they were oddly silent.

He was just about to dismount, the camel halfway kneeling, when Simeon and Levi leapt forward and grabbed him.

Joseph yelled in surprise. The camel bellowed and staggered as he slipped from his seat. He hit the ground, his brothers still tightly gripping his arms. "What are you doing?" Joseph shouted, trying to wrench himself from their grasp. "Stop!"

Outrage and shock quickly turned to fear as the others converged on him like a storm.

Still yelling, Joseph kicked, arms held fast, against the grappling hands of his brothers. Someone forced his hands behind him. Someone else caught a leg. Still his brothers remained eerily silent.

Panic rose up in him. The world blurred. He looked around wildly.

"Reuben!" he screamed, catching a glimpse of his oldest brother. He stood a little away from the scene, grim-faced. Naphtali wrenched Joseph's arm roughly in response. Lightning pain shot down from his shoulder. Joseph cried out.

Then, in his haze of growing fear, Joseph caught sight of Judah. He was standing near Reuben, face pale.

"Judah!" Someone attempted to put a hand over his mouth. Joseph bit down, and there was a yell. The hand vanished. *Help me!*

Simeon grunted in triumph. Joseph's robe ripped from his back, its seams splitting.

Eight pairs of hands hoisted him into the air. And he screamed, one final, meaningless time.

He was thrown. Down, down, into the well.

His head smacked on the rock bottom of the dry pit.

And the world went perfectly, mercilessly, black.

Joseph's first waking thought was that his brothers had really tried to kill him.

His second thought was that they had not succeeded, and now he would starve to death at the bottom of this well.

Joseph tried to force himself upright, but the world spun violently. Every muscle protested. His stomach heaved, and grey spots danced across his vision. Breathing heavily, fingers grasping at the dust and rock under his hands, it was a long moment before he made it onto his knees.

Sharp pain lanced through his hands, and he looked down at them. They were raw and bloody. Then he looked up at the small blue circle of sky, many cubits above him. It seemed to shrink as he stared at it, the distance becoming wholly irrelevant. It was high above him, and that was all that mattered. Joseph stumbled to his feet, ignoring the wave of dizziness, and rushed to the sides of the well, screaming and clawing at the rough stone. He found no purchase and beat the walls with his fists, leaving smears of blood behind.

Then he heard voices.

They are still there.

Howling in rage, he stumbled backward towards the center of the pit, shouting their names at the circle of blue, until nausea found him again. He tripped over bloodied feet and retched.

He gulped for air. "Judah!" he screamed between gasps, trying the most likely brothers once again. "Reuben! For the love of God, please, get me out!"

51

There was no response.

Desperation grew.

"Please! Am I not your brother? What have I done to deserve this?"

No one responded.

Terror. His mind was a wild haze of despair.

"Have mercy! I will do anything you ask!"

"Please! In the name of God I beg you!"

An hour passed.

His throat was raw from screams that drew no response. He licked his lips, parched and tasting of blood. The noise of talking grew silent. Horror spiked through him as he strained to hear a sound, to let him know that they were still there.

That there was still hope.

Silence.

Had they left? Blind panic rose up in him.

And then, miraculously, a rope slid down.

Crying out in shock and relief, Joseph stumbled over to it, gasping repeated thanks, ready to kiss the feet of whoever it might be. He gripped it with all his remaining strength, wincing as his bloody hands slipped on the rough fibers of the rope.

It jerked and twisted as he was hoisted upward, but still he clenched at it, grimacing. As he neared the top, he looked up, expecting to see Judah at the other end, alone and come back for him. Or even Reuben.

It was not so. All his brothers were there, save Reuben. Many hands pulled him up. Behind his brothers stood another group of men with a caravan of four camels.

Traders, Joseph thought in confusion. He stood unsteadily on the rim of the pit, his brothers' hands still holding him fast. He looked around in bewilderment.

And then his brothers were binding him with the rope.

In a flash, he understood the terrible thing that was about to occur. A frenzy overcame him. He shrieked and struggled, but Gad and Asher held him down. Soon his hands were bound, and

Simeon was dragging him towards the traders. Joseph buried his feet in the gravel and pulled against him with all his might.

"No," he screamed with everything he had left. "Please, no. Have mercy!" He caught sight of Judah standing to the side, even as the others came from behind and forced him forward. "Judah. Please!"

Dan laughed in his ear. "You've Judah to thank for this plan, boy."

He felt the blood drain from his face, and he locked eyes with Judah.

His brother stared at him, stricken.

And then, setting his mouth in a tight line, Judah turned away.

Joseph screamed wildly as Dan shoved him towards the camels.

He pulled and kicked, but it was no use. They reached the caravan. The traders looked on dispassionately. One took the long rope from Simeon and bound it to the saddle of the last camel. And then, inexorably, the caravan began to move.

The final camel grunted and bellowed as Joseph fought against the rope, still pleading in desperation. Muttering, one of the traders approached and roughly forced him forward before landing his whip squarely across Joseph's shoulders.

Crying out, he had no choice but to move, shoulders searing with pain.

His brothers had already turned away.

7

The day passed in a nightmarish, pain-filled haze. Joseph attempted to resist once more and only received a blow to the ear and a second lashing for his effort. They stopped once, but the traders gave him nothing to eat nor drink. His already injured feet, bloody from the fall, chafed on the grit in his sandals, trapped there from his earlier struggle. He could see bruises blossoming on his arms, and his shoulders burned with pain.

They moved slowly southward, but not on any roads that Joseph knew, and passed no one. The cold wind picked up once again and cut through his tunic, and he was shivering by the time they stopped for the evening. He crumpled to the ground in exhaustion.

He didn't know how long he sat there in near-stupor before he heard one of the traders calling out: "Get him some food and fire, Kedar. He'll be no use to us if he dies on the journey." Their dialect was similar enough to be understood—through the fog of his thoughts he recognized their speech to be that of Ishmaelites.

Someone roughly pulled him to his feet and placed him before the fire. His hands remained tied. Water was poured into his mouth and some dried meat of unknown origin shoved into his grasp.

The stop in constant movement brought ringing to his ears, and his head began to throb. The meat swam before his eyes, and after a moment of agony, he vomited. He heard the traders laughing, from very far away, and then he knew no more.

Joseph awoke an indeterminable amount of time later to a rocking sensation. He blinked and squinted. It was daylight, and they were moving. He had been thrown facedown over the back of one of the camels and tied there. His mouth felt as though it had been scrubbed out with foul wool.

There was a trader walking nearby, and when Joseph raised his head, groaning, the man glanced towards him. "Oho!" he exclaimed to the others. "He's awake."

He wanted to ask for water but thought that might put him at risk of another lashing. Instead, he managed a thick: "Where are you taking me?"

The trader laughed. "It's almost winter, boy. Where does one go to escape the cold and bring back wares so enticing that no one can resist?" He looked at Joseph expectantly, but he had no response. "Egypt, halfwit," he spat.

The world, which had still been spinning indistinctly up until that moment, instantly came into sharp focus. Joseph felt his blood turn cold.

His brothers, his own brothers, had actually done this. He was not going to Joppa, or Tyre, or to some trading port in Canaan from whence he might make his way home. He was going to Egypt.

Some unholy mixture of fury and terror rose up in him. Heaving ragged breaths, he gasped out: "Please. My father will pay you double, *triple* to bring me back to him unharmed."

The trader only laughed again. "Boy, you do not know our business well. Or your brothers, which surprises me." He glanced at Joseph. "Oh yes, the sons of Jacob are well-known. We will not cross them. And Egypt will give us enough for you regardless."

Joseph knew the sound that came out of him was like that of a caged dog, but he did not care. All fear of a lashing vanished. He struggled against the ropes and spat in the man's face.

"Coward! Wretch!"

The man seized Joseph's hair in response and shoved his face deep into the camel's saddle and baggage, so that he could hardly breathe. A heavy blow from the man's walking stick landed across his back. Joseph cried out. Finally, the trader dragged his head up again, and he gulped for air. "That's enough from you," the trader snarled. "Or there is plenty more of that."

Exhaling with a groan, Joseph lay splayed out across the camel's back, barely able to move. The trader released him roughly and walked on with a mutter and wave of his hand. The world spun and rocked and throbbed, and a single thought slowly coalesced in his mind.

Oh Dinah, take care of Benjamin.

No one else would.

Then realization settled in his stomach like so many rocks.

They will do the same to him.

Waves of horror swam through his mind, his thoughts subsumed by primal fear.

They will do the same to Benjamin, and I am powerless to stop them.

Finally, in despair, he did something he had never presumed to do before.

"God of my father, Jacob," he whispered. "God of my fathers before him, Abraham and Isaac. If you are listening to me, have mercy on Benjamin. Have mercy on me."

He was too starved and thirsty to struggle when the traders let him down from the camel that evening. He sat dully by the fire, eating and drinking the small portions greedily.

"Aye, a bit of want takes the fire out of them." The leader, whom Joseph had learned was called Hadad, laughed.

The wind blew in the brush around them, and Joseph said nothing. The fire and the food were too important.

The days blurred together, one much like the other. He walked now, tied by the long rope to the last camel, as they made their way down from the hill country and towards the plains. One day he saw the sea from afar, a thin blue line that could be glimpsed from the top of a ridge. He could not admire the sight, though he had seen it only once before in his life. And still the wind blew, sharp and insistent, but as the days passed to weeks, the chill of it lessened, and the trees shrank in size until they vanished. The traders kept off the main roads for many days, and gagged him once they joined a great southward road.

Groups of other traders and travelers passed occasionally, accents no longer those of Canaan. He heard the voices of Midianites and speech he did not recognize.

Brush turned to desert until great jagged hills of rock and sand were all there was to see. His daily gag was removed. The sea appeared again to their right, a brief glimpse of vivid turquoise against the brown of the land. Then they turned farther southward, and immense dunes of sand grew before them. Joseph stared. Not even in the desert south of Beersheba had he seen such expanses.

After many days among the endlessly crawling dunes, they stopped at a small pool that bubbled up out of the ground and then vanished. Joseph was too tired to wonder about miraculous water in such a vast desert, even as he sat amongst reedy plants that squeaked in the wind and the tallest, thinnest palm trees he had ever seen.

Kedar, the man he had talked to on his first day in the caravan, fed him near twice as much as usual that night. Though Joseph did not say anything for fear of losing the food, Kedar noticed his surprise and laughed. "We've got to get you ready to sell. No one buys scrawny slaves."

"Quiet, Kedar!" Hadad yelled from the other side of camp. "Don't provoke the boy."

Mind dull from lack of food and exhaustion, Joseph felt he ought to say something, but stupidly found he had nothing to say.

Kedar laughed again and knocked Joseph's head as he left.

Joseph's legs swung excitedly as he sat on his father's shoulders. His

mother stood next to them, the fresh, sweet scent of her styrax-perfume wafting towards them in the morning air. On her other side stood her father, Laban.

The group stared out over the grassy fields of Padan-Aram in awe.

A man and a woman, black braids flying as they shouted to one another in a strange language, each sat astride a running creature so magnificent that Joseph's heart ached. Many more pranced in a herd around the two and their mounts. The animals' long dark tails flowed in the wind.

"They are beautiful," Rachel breathed. Her blue eyes were wide with pleasure.

"They are more costly than they are worth," Joseph's grandfather Laban grunted. "Ummah traded half his wheat crop for just three of them."

His mother shook her head. "Surely they took advantage of him. That is ridiculous."

Jacob shrugged a little, shifting Joseph on his shoulders as he did so. "The horses come from the steppes on the far side of the Tigris and Euphrates. Beyond Ur. That is a long way to bring such beasts."

Eyes momentarily drawn away, Joseph looked southwards to see a camel train rounding a nearby hill. He watched them for a moment before a terrible scream from one of the horses made him whip his head around to stare at the herd.

The horses flew, rearing, running, dashing away down the field.

The man and the woman called out and forced their mounts to calm before urging them to run after the others.

"Useless creatures," Laban said with a grunt. "Spooked by a camel."

The small group turned away to head back into their own fields, but Joseph craned his neck to watch the horses until they were out of sight.

Joseph awoke and sat up, taking a moment to gather his wits. He half-expected to be in his bed, but instantly realized that it was not so. Hands numb from the rope and body protesting each movement, he lay back down on the sandy ground with a groan.

Then the dream came back to him.

Not a dream, quite. A memory.

He rolled onto his side. His heart wrenched, and he grimaced against threatening tears.

It had taken place before his family had left Padan-Aram for Canaan, many years ago. Why had it come to mind now?

He pushed the thoughts aside angrily. His mother was gone. Now his father was taken from him as well.

Joseph lay there, motionless. At length, however, he was struck by the distinct feeling of warmth. The food from the night prior spurred his brain to sharpness. Wasn't it nearing winter?

Sitting up again, he looked around in confusion. The sky was a brilliant blue, and the air was cool under the odd palms, but a warm wind was blowing out of the south. One of the traders who had taken the last watch was chewing on a thin strip from one of the reeds, apparently unperturbed. A strange white bird with a black head, wading at the far side of the pool, was the only other creature moving.

The numbness was leaving his hands now that he sat upright, setting them needling. He moved his fingers distractedly. For the first time in weeks, he had the presence of mind to truly appraise himself. His bruises and cuts from the fall had all healed, though his feet were caked in dried earth and his hair was knotted and grimy. His shoulders still ached from the lashes, and the cuts caught oddly under his filthy tunic. The rope had rubbed his wrists raw. He grimaced.

Then Hadad was awake and ordering the camp to rise and make ready. Joseph was, to his surprise, again given food and water.

"Haste," Hadad said, "and we may arrive the day after tomorrow."

Dread settled in Joseph's stomach.

They fed him three times that day. With each meal his mind grew clearer, and his panic rose.

The caravan passed others on the road who jabbered in a language he had never heard—blunt-sounding, its words seeming to hang fitfully with no conclusion. They wore white, and their eyes were smeared with black paint.

Still the camel dragged him along.

His mind raced as he stumbled behind the animal, thoughts finally able to progress sensibly. He would be sold—as a, as a—slave, never to see Benjamin nor his father nor Dinah nor anyone he had ever known again.

And what did they think had become of him?

Was he dead?

He must be.

It could not remain so. He must return to them. His heart wrenched, and his terror rose to a breaking point. He cried out, resisting and burying his feet in the sand as he had in Canaan. They would not lay a hand on him this close to his sale. The camel grunted.

"Not this again," Hadad growled. He came toward Joseph and pushed him roughly forward. "Move, boy."

"No. Please!" Joseph implored, gasping. "I will do anything."

"You will *walk*," Hadad said, forcing him forward again.

Joseph dug his feet in and screamed. "I will not."

"Very well." Hadad waved and the men came forward and seized him. They bound his feet, gagged him, and once again tied him over the top of the camel. He roared through the gag even as the futility of his actions grew clearer by the moment, for the caravan only continued.

Still they fed him, but the rest of the time he was kept tied and gagged. Then, with no explanation, they retied him in the late afternoon the following day, so that he was no longer lying over the top of the camel's saddle, but sitting forcibly upright.

Soon after, the road gained the crest of a monstrous line of dunes, and Joseph understood.

In the broad, flat lands below flowed a wide river, its delta flung out northwards, painting the desert in swaths of shining green and blue. Towns and lush farmlands, too expansive to fully take in, dotted the green landscape. He looked south, and the river continued to the very horizon, its borders still edged with growth and life. At the center of it all, where the river transformed into the magnificent delta, lay two of the largest cities Joseph had ever laid eyes on.

His mouth would have been left gaping if not for the gag, for the cities were walled in their entirety, filled to bursting with neat houses and the tallest buildings he could imagine, gleaming white on the river's edge. And between the cities, on the far side of the river, sat six shining white structures with sides of triangles, reaching farther into the sky than anything around them.

Kedar must have seen his face, for he laughed. "Those are Memphis and Heliopolis. We are headed south to Itjtawy, the capital."

To be informed that neither vast metropolis below him was the center of power in the land drained the remaining life from Joseph's limbs.

He could not live here. He could not be a slave here. So much power, so remote. He would be here the rest of his life, with no hope of escape. He shut his eyes.

The camels lurched forward. Their road joined with others. Soon the jabbering language surrounded them as the caravan and hordes of travelers in white made their way towards the cities. But they entered neither, passing Heliopolis and instead following a road that led south along the green banks of the river. He stared across it at the glimmering white structures, their triangular sides reflecting the sunlight like bronze. Memphis, larger than Heliopolis and with shining white walls, loomed to the south of them.

A gaggle of the strange white birds with black heads leapt from the reeds at the water's edge and flew overhead. The air was barely cool. This was an entirely new world, nothing like Canaan.

And I will never see Canaan again. Oh Father, forgive me. I tried.

8

At noon two days following, Itjtawy sprang into view as the road rounded a bend in the river, shaded by palms. They had passed many more of the shining triangular structures and villages, flung out along the river's path like beads on a string.

The city itself sat on the opposing side of the river, bright white against a wide fan of green land and fields that expanded westward. It rose from the riverbank, all stone and grandeur. Boats busily crossed the river before Joseph, full of cargo and passengers. His mouth grew dry under the gag.

God of my fathers, have mercy.

The caravan reached a scattering of square buildings near the riverbank, pale and built of mud-brick. They passed by them with a small crowd of other travelers. Wide stone steps led down to the river's edge where sat wooden docks. Boats were tied and waiting.

Voices swirled around him and he understood nothing. Hadad pulled aside a man who looked to be in charge and spoke to him in the jawing language. The black-rimmed eyes of passers-by regarded Joseph, sitting tied, gagged, and perched atop the camel, but no one seemed troubled by it. Then the entire group was moving down the dock toward a massive boat.

Joseph had never been on a boat in his life, though he had seen the fisherman on Kinneret bring in their catch, and the traders arrive in Joppa. This boat rivaled the sea-boats at the harbor in Joppa, and as the crowd and the traders and the camels boarded it, the wooden deck rocked and creaked. His stomach lurched.

They crossed the great river slowly, making for a similar dock on the north end of the city. Other boats, both smaller and larger, could be seen north and south of them, sailing unconcernedly up and down the shining waters as though it were the most natural thing in the world.

Itjtawy grew before them, fully walled except towards the water, and a league of docks spread out to meet the newcomers. White-washed buildings seemed to stretch farther westward into eternity. To the south, grand gleaming buildings were seated on a bluff high above the river, with great stairs leading down toward the banks.

Once at the dock, the boat again groaned worrisomely. Joseph's hands, tied to the saddle of the camel, found purchase there and gripped it so tightly that his knuckles turned white. Although the boat continued to protest and rock, everyone stepped off and reached the shoreline without so much as a glance of concern at the wooden beams that supported them.

Hadad took the reins of the first camel, and the other three, tied in a line, followed.

They entered the city. A dizzying array of sights and sounds and language assaulted Joseph. Traders and merchants filled the square, hawking myrrh and balm, feathers and strange animal skins, pottery and silver, and scores of wares Joseph had never before seen. Men and women walked among them, dressed in white, eyes painted. The women were bareheaded, glossy black hair adorned with beads. The men wore no beards, many with heads shaven or hair cropped shockingly short. A few wore white, draped headdresses. Joseph thought there were a handful of men who wore their hair shoulder-length, as he did. He stared, then, when one man removed his hair completely before placing it back on his head.

Utterly overpowered, he did not notice that the caravan had stopped moving. Hadad had found an empty space in the square. His wares were few, but as he spread out his spices and other goods, prospective buyers arrived. He seemed to be well-known.

It had been a mere fifteen minutes before a large man walked toward them wearing a fine belt and a white tunic. After greeting Hadad, he looked up at Joseph, still gagged and tied on the back of the camel. He laughed outright.

Hadad held his hands up somewhat defensively and appeared to be explaining something in Egyptian. He gestured towards Joseph, and the man's expression became calculating.

Joseph froze, feeling as though he might never breathe again.

God of my fathers, have mercy on me.

He looked around wildly. There was nothing he could do.

Kedar came and untied him from the camel. The other men dragged him down and held him fast. The Egyptian walked over and grabbed his chin, peering at his teeth around the gag and making a pleased sound. But then he looked Joseph up and down and frowned, grabbing one of his shoulders.

Joseph winced in pain.

The man roughly tugged the collar of Joseph's tunic down below the long wounds across his shoulders and Joseph cried out as the cloth caught on the angry flesh. The man held up an exasperated hand and turned towards Hadad. The trader again held up his hands defensively.

They spoke for several minutes, back and forth.

God of my fathers, have mercy on me.

He fought against the grasping hands of the traders, fear rising once again. The men held him in place.

God of my fathers, have mercy on me!

Unexpectedly, the Egyptian nodded and turned to go. He studied Joseph as he left but said no more.

Exhaling, Joseph watched him leave in relief.

Hadad glanced at him and then went back to his sales. The men put him back on the camel.

Evening drew near, and the square grew quiet. The sellers dispersed, and the traders began to pack up their wares and the items they had acquired—feathers, silver, and delicate, colorful pottery.

Joseph guessed they would camp outside the city gates, but instead they turned to travel deeper into the city. They passed rows of houses and shops, sitting along a maze of dusty streets. From his perch atop the camel, he looked over courtyard walls and saw high lit windows in the buildings beyond.

It was only a matter of time before he noticed that the houses they were passing were growing larger and larger. The courtyard walls grew so that he could no longer see over them, and still the houses grew grander. The tops of palms and young sycamores reached above the walls, rustling quietly in the evening light. Voices and occasional laugher could be heard. Then the men stopped walking.

The gate of a courtyard on their right opened, and Joseph saw the man from earlier that day. He stiffened.

The man walked toward him, followed by several others dressed only in white skirts. The traders pulled him down from the camel.

God of my fathers, have mercy on me!

Screaming through the gag was pointless. Indeed, resisting at all was pointless.

But he did.

He roared and flailed his bound arms, and yet he was still inexorably dragged into the courtyard.

The gate shut behind them.

He was forced to the ground. His hands were untied but he could not move—one of the men sat on him, and another pinned his left arm. His right hand was roughly grabbed, and a painful scraping began. Joseph yelled through the gag again and tried to pull away, but many hands held him fast.

He tried to buck off the men, to keep them from whatever aberration they were attempting, but it was futile. Finally, after what seemed like hours, they hauled him to his feet.

The tall man from the market shook him roughly and then held up Joseph's right hand for him to see. A line of strange symbols had been scratched in black ink into his skin. The man motioned to the gate and then to Joseph's hand. He shook his head. The message was clear.

You cannot leave. You belong to this house.

Joseph awoke with a groan. He looked around, bewildered, until the events of the previous night came rushing back to him. He was in a dimly lit room, only a few faint slivers of light shining through high windows. He rolled over on the rough mat he had been given. Six other men lay asleep, spread across the small room.

Sitting up stiffly, muscles cramping from days of being bound, he caught a glimpse of the scrawl on his right hand. The skin was reddened around the marks, and it burned as though he had caught it in a cookfire. He shoved it bitterly into the folds of his tunic and put his head in his other hand. Fighting despair, his face crumpled against threatening tears.

God of my fathers, have mercy on me, he had repeated. Where was that God who had led his father and grandfather and great-grand-father away from every sort of trouble and had prospered them, even in the face of adversity?

And what of his brothers who had done this? Was there no justice? His heart pounded in his ears.

How could they have done this? How could they have *dared?* His thoughts turned towards home, and he imagined the moment his brothers spoke to his father. A lie, no doubt. *Your son Joseph is dead.* He saw his father's face, ashen, clothes rent.

He saw Benjamin, faultless except for the name of his mother. His blood boiled, and he almost screamed at the silent room in helpless rage.

Then the door burst open. Joseph nearly jumped out of his skin, breathing labored. The tall man walked in, and the six sleeping men, jolting awake, quickly stood and rolled up their mats. They adjusted their white skirts and ran hands through close-cropped hair. It seemed to be some sort of routine. The tall man spoke rapidly, gesticulating, and one by one the men bowed and left. Each reached into a small pot by the door as they did so and smeared black paint on their eyes. Soon only the tall man and one old man remained. They turned towards Joseph.

The tall man, obviously the one in charge, waved his hand disgustedly when he noticed Joseph still seated. He stepped over and hauled him to his feet. Gesturing towards Joseph and the other man, back and forth, he spoke rapidly. The old man snorted a little in response and shook his head. There was amusement in his face, but the way he set his eyes on Joseph made him think there was also a bit of pity.

He was pushed out the door and through a bewildering set of corridors and turns before exiting into the courtyard. The morning light was dim, and the air had only a faint chill.

They brought him to a small overhang of reedy slats around the corner of the main house. There were large jars of water there, and Joseph realized with some small bit of gratification that they meant for him to bathe. He did so, glad to scrub the grime away. He gently felt his shoulders, doing so for the first time in weeks. Two long lines, tender and raised, traveled across them. He winced.

When he was done, they had a white skirt waiting for him. Nothing else. No tunic nor sandals. He balked, but his own tunic was filthy and his sandals ruined. He put the skirt on, feeling naked and wishing for something more.

The old man guided him to a wooden bench and bade him sit. Before Joseph had any idea what had happened, the man smudged his eyes with the black paint. Recoiling, he felt the tall man's hands grasp his arms, holding him in place. The old man looked at him, and Joseph again thought something like a flash of pity crossed the man's face. He then held up a little jar of something that smelled like salve and applied it to his shoulders. It stung for a long moment, then tingled away into something vaguely cooling.

Joseph thought they were done, but it was not so. The tall man held him down even more tightly and the other man produced a razor. He snatched up Joseph's hair in his hand.

It was idiotic to resist at this point. What would be the point? Pride? He had little left to be proud of. He grit his teeth. "No," he whispered. The tall man held him down. "No!" It was a yell.

It was futile. The thing was done.

Joseph stood, tattooed, skirted, painted, and shaved, in a line with the six other men he had shared a room with the previous night. A group of unfamiliar men stood opposing them, and behind each line were two rows of women, dressed in simple white frocks. The tall man stood at the head of both lines, and a few men and a woman stood with him.

Everyone was silent, waiting in the courtyard. Palms and a sycamore grew taller than many of the walls and outer buildings, and a small pond, surrounded by fruit trees and flowers, bubbled quietly at the far end.

Out of the house stepped a man and a woman. They too were dressed in white, but it was the finest sort of fabric he had ever seen. The man's head was covered in a white headdress, and the woman's hair gleamed with gold beads. Around their necks and wrists more gold shone, mixed in patterns with colorful beads. Joseph stared. He had not thought so much wealth possible.

They walked towards the lines, the master stopping to speak to the tall man for a brief moment. Then they continued, the tall man following.

The master stopped when he came to Joseph. He looked at him curiously before turning to the tall man and asking a brief question. The man answered, and the master nodded before moving on. The lady's eyes never left her bracelets and skirts, which she played with continuously.

Turning when he reached the end of the lines, the master addressed the group. Joseph bit his lip against rising frustration as he listened to the babble. There was not a single word in all of the Egyptian jabber that was familiar.

The master and his lady left, and the servants began dispersing across the courtyard. Joseph stood, uncertain, a vague dread growing in him at the thought of simply continuing to stand there. It could not end well. He cast a glance about furtively.

A hand tapped on his arm. He turned to see the old man from his room. Motioning Joseph forward, he led him towards a group of men gathering by the gate. The tall man let them out as they passed the gatehouse, and another man was waiting for them outside. He shooed them forward.

They jogged down the dusty street past white courtyard walls with trees overhanging them, their overseer occasionally shouting in hoarse tones. Joseph assumed he meant to hurry them along.

It was some time before they reached a break in the walls, and the river came into view on their left. They were herded down a slope toward it before continuing southward, parallel to the shore, running down a dusty path cut through the tall grass and reeds. On their right, they passed the tallest building yet, painted white with flashes of gold, high walls encircling courtyard upon courtyard. Great steps led up to it from many sides, and colorful patterns marked the rooflines. Many pillars could be seen amongst the maze of walls. It was surrounded by a large complex of tall white buildings.

Joseph watched it pass in disbelief. He thought of the lord's house in Shechem, with its grey walls and all of ten rooms. In other circumstances, he might have laughed.

Still they ran on. The buildings gave way to fields, spread out among the fan of green that grew westward out of the river. Joseph saw that it was shot through with canals. In its far distance, a lake was shining. Down they ran, off a rise and into mud.

They ran westward, the mud sucking at their feet. Gradually, it decreased to a mere dampness. Jogging past large fields, Joseph saw workers, dressed like himself, planting.

Comprehension dawned, and resignation settled in his bones.

They followed a canal, brown water running through it in a long course from the river's edge. It reached an expansive grouping of fields and split into many branches. Here they stopped their run.

The work began.

The day was long, with few rests. They were planting wheat. They pulled unwanted growth from the field, bent completely over until Joseph's back shrieked with pain. The moisture in the ground brought the warm air of midday to near-sweltering. The next day they began making long furrows and on the third day they laid the seed. Indignation and fury rose in Joseph, relegated to such work. They seethed in him, greater each day. Then, all at once, they surrendered to sheer exhaustion and crumbled into vague, bitter despair.

The work shifted to a more distant field—barley.

Days settled into a week, then two, in unrelenting routine.

Sleep was followed by a half dazed-meal, followed by a day of toil in the fields, then another meal spent in stupefaction, before Joseph fell onto his mat for a few blessed hours of oblivion. His skin burned and peeled until he was nearly as dark as the Egyptians, and every muscle and bone screamed in protest until, one day, they became resignedly silent.

God of my fathers. His mind spoke bitingly to the ceiling one night in a rare moment of wakefulness. *Have You not seen me? Did You not hear my cries for mercy?*

There was only silence.

9

It was his sixth week. The planting ended, and there was a day of comparative rest, ordered by the master himself, Lord Potiphar.

On this day, his mind a little more clear from the extra hour of sleep they had been allowed, Joseph realized he understood Egyptian. Or rather, parts of it. It was not at all as if someone had unexpectedly uncovered a lamp, casting light onto mystery in a moment of triumph. It was more that words he had begun to recognize separately began to connect to the words that preceded or followed them, larger meaning growing as they did.

He sat with the old man from his room, Menkare. Joseph did not know if he did it from some thought of kindness, or if he had been ordered to, but the man had seen to it that Joseph was never completely without understanding of what he was supposed to do.

They had been set to scrubbing out clay pots, for a purpose not yet revealed. It would, Joseph thought resentfully, be unlikely that he would ever be told the purpose. He looked out across the courtyard, where the lady of the house, Tetisheri, as well as several friends, sat under the fruit trees. They were laughing in amusement at the fish that had just been stocked in the pool.

His thoughts flew to Benjamin. He would have loved to see the fish.

Anger bubbled up again, and he grit his teeth, scrubbing the pot he was holding vigorously. It was no use to think of Canaan. It never was.

Menkare glanced over at him curiously. "You are angry again today, my young friend."

Joseph understood the sentence, but did not have the words to answer. He looked at Menkare and grunted before returning his attention to the pot.

He felt the man's eyes on him for a moment longer before Menkare turned back to his work. They scrubbed in silence for a time.

"He who spits into the sky will have it fall on him," Menkare said at length. It sounded like a maxim.

"What?" Joseph asked.

The old man looked up from his scrubbing and gestured towards Joseph's hand. "You are not here of your own choosing, that much I can see." It was then that Joseph noticed Menkare's hands, free of any tattoo. "You did not hire yourself to this house. You cannot pay off a debt and then go on your way. You are far from home and now a part of this household. It seems as though you have a right to be angry. But I would ask, after your weeks here, if it is truly useful to be so, or if you are spitting into the sky?"

Joseph's brothers would have called anger useful in a heartbeat, but the true impotence of it all did strike him. What use was it? What could he actually gain from privately seething until the day he died? He scrubbed on.

But staring up at the ceiling that night, he scowled. It was easy to advise that someone end their anger, especially when one did not know what had been done to the other person. His mind whirled, thoughts of his father and Benjamin and Dinah flooding through his mind.

He ground his teeth and rolled to the side, one hand gripping and twisting his mat fiercely.

It was the day after when Joseph found that Menkare had been right.

For he broke.

A fierce cloud of wind and dust had assaulted the city in the morning hours, but by the afternoon it had cleared, and he was sent to the stables as though nothing had happened. The overseer who took them to the fields, Apepi, had learned that he was experienced with camels.

When he arrived, he was immediately assigned the arduous task of checking their nails. The animals complained in the usual grunts as Joseph went over their feet.

Mind still dominated by Canaan and stomach clenching with anger, he went through the process livid. And when the third camel spat at him, barely missing his face, he stopped only a handbreadth short of striking it.

He looked around, frozen in shock, before slowly lowering his hand. No one had seen.

Quaking where he stood, he backed away, wiping the brown liquid from his bare shoulder. He had never done such a thing. Camels were often peevish. It was to be expected. For that matter, it was to be tolerated. Camels did not forget poor treatment.

His eyes smarted against sudden, unexpected tears. His mind screamed at him that he must get back to work. And yet he could not force himself forward.

"You there! What are you doing?" Apepi turned from speaking with another slave and noticed him loitering.

"I'm—sorry," was all Joseph said. He took a breath and forced himself to return to the camel.

He finished as quickly as he could, going through the routine with brewing fear that he might lash out again. When it was done, he hoped somewhat irrationally that he might be given a moment of peace, but the overseer sent him to scrub the mud bricks surrounding the pond.

At least there was no one nearby, save the Lady Tetisheri's strange pet, a little grey-furred, worrisomely humanlike creature called a monkey. It clung to the edge of its cage, watching him scrub, and chattered each time he looked at it.

Face down, back to the ever-cloudless sky, he scrubbed, closing his eyes in shame. He recalled the time he had seen Dan strike a stubborn donkey over and over until its brays became fearful to hear. He had been ten, and his mother had led him away, her mouth a thin, tight line.

Was he any different? Anger had eaten them. He could not say when it had started; it seemed it had always been that way. Now it would eat him too.

The monkey chattered again and cocked its head when he looked up. Joseph scrubbed.

He sat on his mat that night, unwilling to sleep, fearful of what the next day would bring. His stomach knotted, and his head throbbed. Heartache tore at him and desperation settled in his bones.

After a time, he uncrossed his legs and moved to a kneeling position.

Mimicking his father, whom he had once seen pray so desperately for God's favor after the events of Shechem, he whispered into the dark: "Oh God of my father Abraham and God of my father Isaac—and God of my father Jacob. I am not worthy of the least of all the mercies and of all the truth You have shown Your servant—"

He stopped, for the words, once spoken by his father, rang hollow.

The thoughts of Joseph's heart, his ire at his father's God for ignoring him, came to his mind and settled there like so many rocks. His father's God must remember those thoughts as clearly as Joseph did. These grand words would mean nothing. Indeed, at this point, he would be patently false to speak to God in such a manner.

Still determined, for he had nothing else left to lose, he took a deep, shaken breath and ventured again. "Oh God of my fathers. If You will not deliver me from this house, then I beg You deliver me from myself."

The next morning he awoke before the tall steward of the house,

Pawura, burst in, as he did at the beginning of each day. Joseph frowned, marking the thinnest bit of light trickling in from the high windows. How one was ever to know the time without the outside light and sounds filtering through tent walls was a mystery.

He did not have to wait long. Pawura arrived moments later, and Joseph was sent after breakfast to chop lettuce in the wide garden behind the house.

"In the garden, it is the lettuces I have watered," he murmured to himself as he worked. The words tumbled out without a thought. His heart tore a little at the thought of Benjamin, but a small, fond smile tugged at his mouth. "Let the lord eat this lettuce!"

But then, in his mind's eye, he saw his brothers, and Benjamin, helpless before them. He took a deep breath and stood up straight. The long knife he was holding fell from nerveless fingers, its point driving deep into the earth. Shaking his head, he clenched his jaw.

He ran a hand through his cropped hair, casting his desperate gaze around the rear courtyard. Where was that miracle, the acts of God that always came upon his fathers? Anger rising again, he picked up the knife and went to chop the next head of lettuce.

His muscles tensed, and he clenched the knife. He could not bring himself to swing. The blow would have been so hard that the head would have gone flying.

Dropping the knife again, he swayed on his feet, irrevocably defeated.

"God of my fathers, deliver me from myself," he whispered, "and deliver Benjamin from my brothers, for I cannot."

No peace came to him and no miracle. But he found he could again grasp the knife without wanting to destroy something.

Swallowing once, he continued.

Joseph, along with seven other servants and slaves, was sent down to the fields after midday. They ran along the river called the Nile, Joseph dreading the afternoon ahead. Apepi shouted behind them as always.

But to Joseph's relief, they passed the grain fields and moved far-ther into the green region, which, together with the capital Itjtawy and its surrounding villages, the Egyptians called the Pa-yuum.

They had almost reached the shores of the far western lake when Apepi steered them north towards a grove of trees. Rows of sycamore figs were waiting for them, laden with the dusty-colored fruits. They were set to picking, first grasping at the low-hanging clusters and then sent up into the trees for the highest.

The fruit went into large sacks just as it had in Canaan, and Joseph was ordered to tie the full bags closed. He did so, and then paused. At home, he had always felt the bags and written an estimated number of the contents on each. It was simple, if one knew what a handful felt like, to cast one's hand in and around the bag and come out with a fairly accurate result. He looked about for something to mark the bags with before finding a firm bit of clay in the soil that would leave an orange streak behind.

He paused again. He hadn't the faintest idea how to number in Egyptian. Resignedly, he wrote on them anyway, in cuneiform. At least there would be some sort of record.

"What's this?" Apepi strode over.

"Numbers—" Joseph managed. He stood up, flustered. His mind raced, grasping for words. "In the bag."

Apepi stared at him. "You counted the figs in each bag?"

He hadn't counted, he had estimated. But he might as well be commanded to recite poetry in Egyptian at this point; to explain that was equally impossible. The number would be close, anyway. So he nodded.

The overseer cocked his head. He did not seem angry, but rather amused. "We have no need of that here." He turned away, calling everyone to pick up a bag so that they might return to the house. Joseph hoisted his, grunting under the weight, and furrowed his brow, perplexed. How could there be no need to count food? Even if there were plenty, it was irresponsible.

They reached the house near an hour later. Joseph's arms and shoulders protested from the weight, and they set the bags in one of the storerooms. He had not yet been in one, and as Apepi had said, baskets and sacks were strewn against the walls, all unlabeled. Joseph grimaced.

That night, as they filed into the small room to sleep, Joseph asked Menkare haltingly why no one bothered to keep records.

"They do," he answered. The old man had heard about the incident with the figs earlier that day and now looked at Joseph, bemused. "But no one needs to know how many figs are in a bag. There are what there are."

Joseph didn't have the words to explain all the situations in which knowing an exact or even estimated amount would be very useful. But he supposed a man as rich as Lord Potiphar would encounter none of them. He sighed, wiping the daily paint off his eyes at the pitcher by the door before falling down on his mat to sleep.

Winter, or a shadow of it, finally arrived many weeks later. No bitter wind blew, nor did frost paint the courtyard garden, but the air nipped at Joseph in the morning as he stood in the lines of servants and slaves, waiting to be addressed by the Lord Potiphar and his lady. It did not happen daily, but this morning they had been told to prepare the lines by dawn. The lord and lady eventually entered the courtyard, wrapped in long white robes to guard against the chill. He looked down at his own simple shendyt, as the white skirt was called, and tried to curb the bitterness that shot through him.

God of my fathers, he prayed silently in response, as had become his habit, *deliver me. Deliver Benjamin.*

What *deliver* meant anymore, in regard to himself at least, he was unsure. He only knew that without that prayer, he descended rapidly into anger-fed wretchedness. And that he could not endure in himself.

To his surprise, the Lord Potiphar announced that today was some sort of celebration. The slaves and servants reacted in jubilation, and Joseph was surprised when, en masse, they followed the lord and lady out of the courtyard and down the street.

He had been in the city very few times since his arrival, always either trapped behind courtyard walls or herded down to the river to work in the fields. Still, he had seen enough of it to decide it was a marvel. The streets were dusty but otherwise clean, refuse kept aside in ditches. Beggars were few.

They passed down the long street on which Lord Potiphar lived, the houses growing smaller as they descended the hill, until they reached the buzzing hub of the city, houses and places of business packed so close together that they shared walls. Then they turned westward, following the growing crowd, into a part of the city Joseph had never seen. The streets widened as the houses fell away, and they entered a vast square, surrounded by high buildings of stone. Painted in bright patterns of green, blue, and red, and covered with strange symbols, the buildings encircled the entire area. Giant stone figures stood between supporting pillars, the height of three men or more.

As they waited in the square, the stone and dusty earth turning even the winter sun to warmth, Joseph asked Menkare what sort of celebration they were there for.

"The Mysteries of Osiris," Menkare answered.

Who or what *Osiris* was remained to be seen. Joseph looked around. Lord Potiphar and Lady Tetisheri sat at the front of their household, housed under a fine canopy. A house-servant Joseph did not know stood near the couple, gently waving a fan. Other lords had arrived with their households, and the general populace was filing in as well on the opposite side of the square. It became obvious that there was not enough room for all and that the crowds would overflow into the streets beyond. Stunned, Joseph began a count to pass the time. To have so many people in one place was a little dizzying.

He had reached the astonishing number of 446, with the majority of the square left to count, when several men appeared at the top of the steps that led to the tallest building. The crowd erupted into cheers.

The men's green sashes, tied about their waists, flew in the wind, and they wore strange skins, golden with brown markings that flowered throughout the fur. They were shouting, but Joseph could not catch the words. The crowd cheered again in response.

Out from behind them came more men, holding aloft something Joseph could not quite make out. Behind them came several women, also with sashes of green, hands raised. Then, Joseph realized what the object was. It was a statue of a man, wrapped in burial cloth.

The crowd wailed in what could only be sounds of grief and mourning.

And then another man stepped forward. He wore a tall, elaborate mask with the face of a wolf. In response, the crowd cheered so loudly that Joseph thought the stone of the buildings might crack.

With a sickening wave of realization, it became obvious to Joseph that this ceremony must honor the gods of Egypt.

Yet another man, wearing a mask-head like that of a black jackal, came forward, and the crowd lashed out with venomous, hate-filled roars. Joseph's shoulders clenched. The slaves and servants of Potiphar's house, standing around him, raised their fists and spat obscenities.

Men rose from the crowd, gathering at the center of the square. They took up staves of wood that had been set at ready. Then some went to bow before the wolf-man and others went to bow before the jackal-man. All was still for a long moment until, to Joseph's shock, they turned on each other. Staves cracked on wood and bone, and blood began to fly. The crowd cheered wildly.

Looking on in growing horror, he struggled to watch. Not even the false Canaanite god Ba'al required this variety of depravity.

He turned his head and shut his eyes.

When Joseph heard that they were to attend the next part of the celebration the following day, his stomach turned. He could not do such a thing.

Mind racing that night as he lay wide awake on his mat, he tossed and turned as the hours passed, and his thoughts warred. "God of my fathers," he ventured finally, his voice the merest whisper. Unsure of what to say, he finally ended with: "if You will, lead me in a way that pleases You."

Sleep did not find him, and when Pawura entered the next morning to raise them all, he sat up resignedly. His stomach knotted with so much dread that he could barely eat the morning bread.

They stood again in their lines in the courtyard, and when Lord Potiphar and his lady came out of the house and made ready to leave, and the servants and slaves once again moved towards the gate, desperation took hold. Looking about wildly, Joseph took his chance.

Falling back in the crowd, he dashed behind a gathering of large pots that sat near the open gate and held his breath. He did not know what getting caught would cause and did not wish to find out, but anything was better than watching that loathsome play or anything like it ever again.

Heart pounding, he knelt, frozen in place, for what felt like an eternity. And then, miraculously, the gate shut.

Joseph strained his ears, listening for the telltale crunch of feet on sand that would prove that someone had remained behind. The sound never came. Slowly, disbelievingly, he got to his feet. The courtyard was empty.

His first thought was to run. He looked around the courtyard, towards the fruit trees that surrounded the pool. He could climb one, cross over the wall, and leave the city while the people celebrated their masochistic god.

But where would he go? Back to Canaan? He had no supplies and no protection. Then he looked down at the tattoo on his right hand and grimaced. He would not even get as far as the ferry-boat that would take him back over the Nile. He sighed in bitter resignation.

Quietly, in case someone remained inside, he stole towards the back courtyard, where the garden lay, and sat down against the wall of the house. He closed his eyes.

It was a beautiful thing to sit and be silent. The chirping of a group of swallows, dashing about in the morning air, filtered down to him.

Joy comes in the morning, his mother had often said.

Joseph was not so certain about *joy*, but it was the first somewhat pleasant moment of his life in months.

He sat there for some time before absently picking up a nearby stick. The sun had risen fully now, and far away he could hear the sounds of the celebration, alternatingly jubilant and despairing. To drown out the sound, he murmured to himself, scribbling the words into the sand:

What you are talking is nonsense.
The person who could come up with these ideas,
And accomplish them, doesn't exist!
These orders you are giving me and telling me to repeat back,
To recite over and over, I haven't the power to accomplish.
Come with me upstream of the city, on the city's edge,
And I'll show you a washery.
This big job you want accomplished—do it yourself!

He smiled slightly at the lines, remembering his father's animated reading of them, trying to keep the attention of his then-small son. Joseph supposed he felt a little more kinship with the washer now.

All at once the hairs on his neck prickled and he looked up.

A man was watching him.

Joseph scrambled to his feet in alarm, brushing dust off his shendyt and coming to the attentive stance that had become habit. Hands folded, head slightly down.

"What are you doing here?" the man asked. Joseph knew him

by sight, but not his name. He was the household scribe, and his skin was very dark brown.

"I—" every possible falsehood flashed through his mind, but all were idiotic. Finally, he answered, "I do not worship Osiris." It might have been folly, but he felt the sudden urge to look the man in the eye. So he did.

The scribe was regarding him inscrutably. Finally he spoke. "You did not ask to do this, I gather."

"No, sir."

The man gestured towards the cuneiform words in the sand. "You wrote this?"

"Yes, sir."

He pinned Joseph with his gaze. Uncertain of what to do, Joseph stared back for a moment before dropping his eyes uncomfortably. Finally, the man guffawed. "You are the one who numbered the figs, I take it?"

Finally having enough command of Egyptian to be able to explain, Joseph answered: "I estimated their numbers, but it is accurate enough. I have done such all my life. It is—" he searched for a word and, giving up, tried another approach. "I think it is important. If records are good, then one can make better trades. It may make all the difference, in a time of want."

The man's face was still inscrutable, despite his earlier bark of amusement. "I do not think Lord Potiphar has known want in all his life. But," he continued, "I see the sense of your words." He paused. "Where are you from?"

"Canaan, sir."

"You have not been a slave long, I take it."

"No, sir."

Eyes narrowed as he looked at Joseph, the scribe was silent for a long moment. "You read and write, I see. Do you know mathematics, above counting fruit?"

"Yes, sir." A vague, unexpected hope stirred in Joseph.

"What have you been doing since you came here?"

"Working—in the fields and in the courtyard."

The man snorted. "An excellent use of your abilities. What is your name?"

"Joseph, sir."

"Joseph. My name is Djaty. I am Nubian, and I do not care for the Mysteries of Osiris either. Such things are better left unperformed." Djaty shifted on his feet, ever so slightly. "Well, Joseph of Canaan, I have a proposal for you. I need an assistant, and I am willing to see how you perform. What say you?"

Mouth open, it took Joseph a moment to gather his wits. "But—I cannot read or write Egyptian."

"Then you will learn, and in the meantime you will do all my calculations for me, until the time comes when we may distribute the work differently. Unless you prefer the yard."

"I don't." Joseph had to work to keep the words from coming out in a squeak.

"Very well."

10

Djaty brought Joseph to Pawura that afternoon when the household returned from the celebration.

"Your assistant?" Pawura's brows knitted. They stood near the doorway of the house, and the tall steward glanced over the courtyard for a moment with a frown, attention drawn elsewhere by some happening. Finally, he looked back at them. "I heard about the figs, boy. You're most likely clever. You can read and write?"

"Yes, sir—in cuneiform."

The steward snorted, and Joseph thought he'd lost all chances with the man. "We've no need of that chicken-scratch here." But then he seemed to size him up. Pawura looked at Djaty. "You have until spring," he finally said. "If he's not serviceable for basic record-keeping by then, I'll send him back to the fields and yard. I won't waste my time nor Lord Potiphar's with an illiterate record-keeper."

Until spring? Joseph felt the blood drain from his face. He glanced at Djaty, whose face remained unreadable. "Of course," the scribe said. Then he added, "He will need to remain with me during the remaining days of the celebration. There is too much to be done."

Pawura snorted again, but then shrugged and nodded as he pushed past them. "Get to it."

They both stood in the empty doorway for a moment, Joseph watching Pawura walk away with growing dismay. "How," he breathed, "can anyone learn to read and write in three months? I can barely speak Egyptian!"

"You try," Djaty answered. "Or you will end up back as a yard-slave." He stepped inside, and Joseph followed. Instead of continuing straight on, towards the maze of servant and slave rooms, the scribe turned left into a part of the house Joseph had never seen. Trepidation growing, he trailed the scribe.

The corridor opened up into a grand pillared room, long, high windows letting in far more light than the slits in the walls provided the slaves and servants. Joseph cast his gaze around in wonder. Piles of cushions lay against walls painted in intricate designs, and low tables and chairs stood about the room, glimmering with inlays of gold. Thin curtains at the far end of the room danced in the breeze that came through the windows, hinting at more beyond. The very floor he walked on was inset with blue stones.

He would have stopped to gawk, but Djaty continued on through the room to another corridor. Joseph hurried behind him. After a few more turns they entered a small room. It was brighter than Joseph expected, for it had high windows on two sides. No decorations adorned the walls, but they were clean and whitewashed. Cushions and a soft mat lay in one corner, and in the other, an array of pots and boards and rolled scrolls. A few low stools added to the scene, along with several unlit lamps. "Sit," Djaty said.

Joseph sat.

"I do not know the cuneiform way, but Egyptian has two modes. You will need to know both to work under me. Hieratic, which is for record-keeping, flows from the hieroglyphs."

Joseph nodded in response. He would not go back to the yard.

"Then we will begin."

The evening passed in a blur. Egyptian writing, he learned, was a mad art. Symbols meant one thing at one time and a completely different thing at another. Sometimes they represented a sound, sometimes not. And hieroglyphs could be read any which way, seemingly depending on nothing more than the author's particular mood at the time of writing. Hieratic at least flowed in reasonable, consistent lines. Beyond that, Djaty threw mathematical calculation after calculation at him, apparently testing him. It was some time before the scribe nodded in approval.

Djaty put a reed pen in Joseph's hand and produced several large shards of pottery, presumably broken from old vessels.

"*Miw*," he said. Cat. He pointed at Joseph. "Write it."

Joseph bit his lip and furiously looked through the list of hieroglyph letters and determinatives Djaty had drawn out for him while he had been talking. It was long and apparently, also very incomplete.

Slowly, finding what he needed, he drew on the pottery shard. First the milk jug in a net, *m*, then the flowering reed, *i*, and last the quail chick, *w*. He thought he was complete, but then a realization struck him. He quickly drew the determinative cat image at the end of the word. For evidently, writing "cat" was not enough for the Egyptians.

Djaty actually laughed and then nodded. "Well done."

Supper was brought to them—a far cry from the bread and onions that had overrun Joseph's meals of late—garlic and a little fish, and lentils and melons. He tried to stop himself from gaping when he saw it. A prickle of shame ran through him. To be so beguiled by mere food was ridiculous.

He did not return to the small dark room in the servants' wing. Djtay kept him working late into the night until Joseph's head was nodding over the pottery shards, now covered in symbols and more often than not scribbled out with errors. The scribe finally provided him with some cushions, and he fell into a deep sleep near the door of the small room.

Joseph awoke with a start to daylight streaming through high windows. His immediate thought was that he had somehow slept through Pawura's customary morning bellowing. He sat bolt upright in alarm before looking about in confusion. Then he remembered.

He glanced around the small room. The pottery shards lay where he had stacked them, near the bed. The pen had somehow rolled in the night; perhaps he had knocked it with a wayward hand. He stood up to get it, immediately noticing how the cushions had favored him. He ached, as he often did, but not nearly as much. Picking up the pen, he stretched. The skin on his shoulders still caught a little, but he had resigned himself to the fact. The lashes from the whip had healed wrong, leaving two raised lines that traveled across his back.

It was only a moment longer before Djaty strode in. "Good," he said, seeing Joseph awake. "I was not about to let you laze about any longer."

Bewildered and wondering what time it was, which was nothing new, Joseph could only nod. Djaty handed him some bread and water and then had him scoop up some still-blank pottery shards into a basket. He led Joseph out into courtyard. It was silent, and Joseph realized with shock that the household had already gone. Apparently Djaty and his assistant were not beholden to attend the morning lines.

They continued towards the pool, and Djaty had them sit in the shade of one of the fruit trees. The little monkey was there, and it chattered insistently in its cage until it realized that they had not arrived to give it attention.

The scribe handed him a writing-board and unfurled one of the scrolls he had been carrying. Joseph noticed it was not animal skin, as he had thought. He looked at it curiously. It was almost cloth-like, but very coarse. Allowing no time for further study, Djaty immediately ordered Joseph to copy the first several lines of the scroll onto a shard. Uncertain as to the purpose, Joseph did so without protest. It was far better than the fields.

Djaty began work of his own, setting another board on his knees and setting his pen to a manuscript. Joseph looked back down at the scroll and pottery shard on his board.

The symbols running across the page were inked in black and

red, and many were unfamiliar. Still he saw many he remembered from yesterday—the flowering reed, *i*, and the desert hare, *wn*, and the determinative seated man. He could not read it, but he could make out some of the sounds.

When he showed his carefully copied work to Djaty, the scribe grunted in approval. "You have a neat hand," he said. "Though I can see your strokes are often in the wrong order. But you will not be etching temple walls. You will read this by the end of the week."

Joseph stared down at the pottery shard he had just written on and swallowed.

When the household returned that afternoon, Djtay pulled Joseph from their work in the courtyard garden and brought him to the fine room he had seen yesterday. Lord Potiphar and Lady Tetisheri sat within, house servants that Joseph did not know fanning them and standing nearby with plates of food and drink. Djaty bowed before taking a seat on a cushion. Flustered, Joseph quickly did the same.

Lord Potiphar was staring at him. He finally looked towards Djaty. "Is this not the Canaanite slave Pawura bought three months ago for the fields and yard?"

"He is, sir," Djaty answered. "But I discovered yesterday that he has been put to sore misuse. He is well-educated."

Now Lord Potiphar addressed Joseph, face intent. "Speak, boy. Where were you educated?"

Joseph swallowed. He had never been under the tutelage of a master, which he knew happened in such places as Tyre. He answered carefully, for he knew his accent was not good. "My father taught me, sir. My—grandfather's father was from Ur. My family has passed down the knowledge of that land."

"Hmm," was all Lord Potiphar said. He took a cup from a waiting servant and turned again towards his scribe. "We shall see, but if you think he is capable, I see no harm in it." The lady never looked up.

For a long moment, the master and his wife were both consumed with their cups of beer.

"Djaty," the lord said again after he had finished. "The Pharaoh maintains much interest in building a border fortification at the eastern edge of the Delta near Tjaru. In speaking with him, I suggested that some of the prisoners here in Itjtawy might serve as excellent labor—"

Joseph did not hear the rest of what Lord Potiphar said, for he was caught up in the startling realization that his master answered to the Pharaoh himself.

Broken out of his reverie a moment later, Joseph heard Djaty calling him to attention.

He was ordered to begin several calculations, about weights and stone and labor and things he knew little of. But the numbers, at least, were clear. Unable to do anything other than react, he scribbled furiously on the pottery shards. It was strange to draw out the cuneiform marks instead of pressing them into wet clay, but the results were the same. He read off the answers to Djaty, who wrote them onto his scroll as part of a letter Lord Potiphar was dictating, apparently meant for the nomarch—a type of governor, it seemed—who lived near the area in question.

They continued in this manner for some time before Lord Potiphar was satisfied with the letter. Djaty brought it forward, rolling it tightly together and wrapping it, and the master stamped it with his seal. "I'll see that it is sent," Djaty said. Lord Potiphar nodded. The scribe bowed and turned to go, and Joseph scrambled to his feet and did the same before moving to follow the scribe out of the room.

"You, boy," Lord Potiphar called.

Uncertain, Joseph turned. "Yes, my lord?" He tried to stamp the trepidation out of his voice.

"What is your name?"

"Joseph, sir."

"Joseph," the master repeated. "Well done."

As they crossed the courtyard, Djaty went to speak to the gate-keeper about the scroll. Standing several steps back, Joseph saw

Menkare across the yard, leaving the stables. Glancing around furtively, the old man quickly hurried over to Joseph.

"Where have you been?" he asked.

Joseph smiled a little. "I am working for the scribe."

Menkare glanced towards the well-dressed Nubian, still speaking with the gatekeeper. "Well, now," he said, eyes twinkling. "That is a stroke of luck. Here I thought I was going to have to tell you that I am leaving tomorrow, and wish you well. But perhaps I will have you wish wellness upon me."

"You've paid off your debt to Lord Potiphar?" Joseph asked.

"Yes."

Joseph smiled, broadly this time. He clasped the man's arm. "I wish you well. And thank you, Menkare, for everything. It was because of you that I stopped spitting into the sky."

The old man smiled.

Joseph lay awake that night on the cushions in the scribe's room, staring at the moonlight coming through the window that turned the small cracks in the mud-brick ceiling into deep canyons. Something was not right.

He bit his lip in concentration, trying to sort out the knot that had taken hold in his stomach. And slowly, almost as though he were drawing a pitcher from a well, realization came to him.

God of my fathers.

He sat bolt upright, the memory of two days prior flooding back to him.

God of my fathers, he had prayed. *Lead me in a way that pleases You.*

Joseph sat in the dark, shaken to his very core.

He had prayed for guidance. And he had received it.

So much so that he had ended up under the tutelage of the household scribe, sitting in the garden, writing and eating *fruit.*

God of my fathers, he had prayed, even before that. *Deliver me from myself. Deliver Benjamin.*

90

Had not that prayer calmed him, each time his anger and despair rose? Had it not steadied him and given him a reputation good enough so that he would be taken in by the scribe?

He had neither thanked his father's God nor even *recognized* any connection. He had even told Menkare that it had all been because of *him*. Had he thought it impossible that he would be answered by God?

In his mind's eye, he saw his father's face before him. *Our God is great, my son*, he had said once to Joseph. *And beyond understanding. His ways are great and even so His faithfulness to those who trust in Him.*

Sucking in a deep gulp of air, Joseph flung himself off the cushions and thrust himself facedown onto the floor. Djaty was asleep, but Joseph did not care if he woke the man.

"God of my fathers," he whispered. Taking another breath, he dared to speak the next words.

"*My* God."

Cringing on the floor, still in disbelief at his own ignorance, he continued, remembering the words of his father's prayer after Shechem.

Did God forgive? He did not know, but maybe He would at the least overlook. "Your servant is not worthy of the least of your mercies. Great is Your faithfulness, and great is my shame that I did not see it. May I never do so again."

11

Joseph awoke, and as he had every morning for the past three years, he immediately rolled off the soft mat.

"My God," he murmured, kneeling. "Thanks and all glory be to You, for what You have done for me, for Your servant is not worthy of the least of Your mercies.

"Comfort my father and Dinah. Give them peace in their lives. Deliver Benjamin from my brothers. And if it be Your will, deliver me from this place. And if it is not Your will, then give me the strength and peace to do that which is."

He looked up. Djaty was just rising. The scribe looked at Joseph askance, but said nothing. Joseph knew he had grown used to his assistant's strange habits.

"What is to be done today?" Djaty asked as Joseph stood up to scrub his face at the water pitcher. The other man had taken to letting Joseph remember the specifics of their duties regarding the border fortification project. Aside from that, after making a few suggestions throughout the beginnings of the process that had only seemed logical, somehow Djaty and Lord Potiphar had decided that Joseph was best suited to organize the prisoner transfers going up and down the river to Tjaru in the eastern Delta.

"I'll need a written agreement with Lord Potiphar's seal to bring to Nebit," Joseph said in reply. His tongue twisted a little, switching so quickly from his Canaanite prayer into Egyptian. He dried his face with a nearby cloth and quickly smudged his eyes over with the black kohl paint. It did wonders for keeping the glare of sun and sand out of the eyes. "He's not prepared to ship prisoners without some kind of guard and guarantee."

Prisoners had been leaving Itjtawy and all parts of the Pa-yuum for the past eighteen months to go northwards to work on the fortifications. But now the project was picking up speed, and prisoners from southward in Thebes and Abydos were being shipped there as well. There was so much movement, both in manpower and supplies, that the Pharaoh and his advisors had requested Lord Potiphar contract merchants to ship prisoners, as the royal and military fleets were overwhelmed.

Nebit was the first Joseph had approached, and he would need to find more. He reached over to the pile of papyrus scrolls in the corner and found the one that had come from the palace last week. He skimmed it over, refreshing himself on the number of prisoners it was requested they handle, then looked at Djaty, who was just getting to his feet. "I'll need to find three more merchants with sizable fleets. They'll likely ask for similar agreements."

The scribe nodded. "Very well, we shall get the agreement signed, and you will be on your way to Nebit. In the meantime, I will be working on Lord Potiphar's land acquisition documents."

They left the room a few minutes later. Lord Potiphar and Lady Tetisheri were just ending the breaking of their fast in the great room. Joseph and Djaty bowed as they entered.

"The morning finds my lord and lady well?" Djaty asked, stepping forward.

"All thanks to Sekhmet and Nefertem, yes," the master answered. "The prisoners and the land acquisition, I assume?"

"Yes, sir."

Lord Potiphar hmmed thoughtfully. "And we ought to discuss the prisoners first, I expect."

Joseph stepped forward. "Yes, sir." He quickly relayed Nebit's terms. "And I shall have to find three more merchants. I assume they will have similar demands."

"No doubt," Lord Potiphar said. He looked up at Joseph. "I know you will have looked into it, but for my own peace of mind—this Nebit is trustworthy?"

"Everyone speaks well of him. I have not heard of anyone who has been displeased with his services."

The mistress of the household laundry had entered and had been speaking with the Lady Tetisheri, but now she quickly exited. The lady turned. "Is he not the merchant who at times deals in ostrich feathers and Nubian ivory?" she asked Joseph.

"He is, my lady."

She smiled. "Joseph has chosen ably, my dear," she said to her husband. "My sister has bought from him; he treated her well."

Lord Potiphar nodded, and Joseph bowed slightly in acknowledgement of the lady's praise. "Write it out, then," his master said. "And I will sign it."

Bowing again, Joseph went to the cushions strewn in the corner to work as Djtay and the lord began discussing the details needed for the land acquisition. Setting up his ink and pen, Joseph rolled out a fresh sheet of papyrus and set it on his workboard.

I, Potiphar, Captain of the Royal Guard of the Pharaoh, who is the Lord of the Two Lands and High Priest of Every Temple, to the merchant Nebit, greeting.

Your request for guard and guarantee has been made known to me. Be it known that I will provide—

Joseph paused and thought, looking at the hieratic lines. As was his habit, he glanced over them, checking carefully for errors, for they were shockingly easy to make. He saw none and went back to his conundrum. How many guards?

Lord Potiphar easily had 100 at his disposal at any time who were not in any critical position and could be moved. He had heard his master say so once. If they hoped to have four merchants running prisoners at a time, Joseph hazarded a guess that five guards per ship would be the upper limit. He nodded to himself.

94

—five guards to travel with the prisoners and your men to see to it that all is well. I require that they be given rations in equal share with your crew.

I further pledge to guarantee any recompense deemed necessary by myself and the Chief of Police, should harm come to your property in so transporting these men.

Signed,

He left the bottom blank and looked over the second half. Finding a grammatical error, he grimaced and held his breath while he carefully painted around the hieratic, forming the word into the proper one—they were spelled similarly. Finishing, he blew worriedly on the scroll and held it up once the ink was dried. He squinted. The edit was not perfect, but it would do.

After letting it dry, he brought it forward and waited until Djaty and his master looked up. "Is it ready?" Lord Potiphar asked.

The Lady Tetisheri, who had moved to a chair toward the back curtains and had a servant girl seeing to her nails, looked on curiously.

Joseph nodded and bowed, handing it to him. Lord Potiphar looked it over, lined face further creased in thought. "Five guards—" he nodded approvingly. "Rations—and arbitration in the event of any damage." He looked up at Joseph. "Very well done." He stamped his seal into the bottom. Drawing a red cord out of his robe, he handed it to Joseph.

Bowing, Joseph quickly left the room. Stopping by the kitchens on his way through the courtyard, he took a piece of bread for his own breakfast. The women shooed him out good-naturedly, as they often did. Adjusting his shendyt and running a hand though his cropped hair, he made certain the red cord was tied to his wrist above the tattoo on his right hand before he walked towards the gates. Showing the cord to the gatekeeper, he was let out.

The cord lengthened the tether the tattoo had given him. With it, he could travel throughout Itjtawy and the surrounding area on his master's business. But he could not leave the Pa-yuum nor cross the river. He remembered the first time he had been able to read the hieratic scrawled across his hand. *Of Potiphar*, it said. Anyone could look at him and see to whom he belonged.

He walked towards the center of the city. The day would be hot. Living in Egypt, he had learned, was like living in a bread-oven for more than half of the year. He reached one of the main roads that flowed towards the market square. Glancing left, Joseph grimaced as he caught sight of the tall stone temples looming over the rest of the city. The gods of Egypt were complex, their ceremonies and myths dark and often ignoble.

Turning right, he was immediately pushed to the side by a sea of movement. "Make way!" a herald was shouting. A nobleman passed on his litter, flanked and carried by servants. The procession traveled up the street from which Joseph had just come, towards the palace. After a moment, the crowds continued on their original paths. He had almost reached the market when more movement disrupted the crowd. Five men ran past, carrying rope and spears. They were shouting—apparently a crocodile was on the river-bank near the ferry. The crowd called after them, invoking the protection of Sobek, the crocodile-god. Joseph pursed his lips and continued on.

The road opened up into the sea of color and sounds and smells that was the marketplace. Someone was selling roasted vegetables, the scent wafting over the crowd. A group of Nubian merchants had arrived with three monkeys like the Lady Tetisheri's, drawing a gaggle of delighted children.

Joseph caught sight of the place where Hadad had stopped the caravan of camels three years ago. His stomach lurched, and he quickly looked the other way.

My God, deliver Benjamin from my brothers.

For I cannot.

A moment later, he said to himself: *Benjamin is six*. It was an exercise he had done many times; somehow it helped him feel more connected to his family.

I am twenty.

Dinah is twenty-two.

My father—he stopped. *My father is 111.* He swallowed. His father was not young.

He pushed the thought away.

Joseph strode to the small building near the city gates, on the edge of the marketplace. Linen sheets hung out to dry fluttered off the upper roof, and the smell of cooking meat permeated the air. He entered the small courtyard and pushed open the door.

The room was cluttered, baskets and tall jars taking up most of the floor space. Nebit was inside, sitting at a low table and pouring over a papyrus. He looked up.

"Ah! You again. What does your master say?"

Joseph held out his papyrus. "I think you will find the terms agreeable." He made an effort to speak as clearly as he could. It did not matter so much at the house, but when representing the Lord Potiphar it was best not to give anyone a reason to think he could be taken advantage of.

Nebit took the document from him and stood up, perusing it. A slave girl came in from the back and placed a few strips of meat on the table. "You're doing well, I see," Joseph said, nodding towards the food. Meat was expensive.

The merchant glanced towards it and then nodded. "I've done quite a bit of work in Abydos; they always need supplies for the construction of the new temples there." He looked back down at the papyrus. "This is acceptable," he said after another moment. "But now we must talk price. To hire several boats and their crews is no small thing."

"It will be three deben of silver for one boat's journey to and from Tjaru," Joseph said firmly. "The Lord Potiphar and the Pharaoh do not bargain."

He had not expressly been told such a thing, but he knew what Lord Potiphar would wish, and four deben of silver was far too much. He kept his expression inscrutable and eyed the man.

Nebit puffed out a breath in defeat and then shrugged. "Who am I to argue?" He nodded towards Joseph. "Wait a moment." Finding a pottery shard, he quickly scribbled his acceptance on it and handed it to Joseph. "Take that back to your master. When will the first group of prisoners be ready?"

"Within the week."

Nodding, Nebit returned to his work without a second glance at him. Joseph worked hard to keep his expression neutral, but did not bow. Such things happened when one was a slave, he had discovered.

He was well aware that he *ought* to bow, but there were some things he could not bring himself to do.

He stepped outside. Three merchants more to find.

Joseph had been set to making copies of Lord Potiphar's land agreement, one for his master's own records, one for the seller, and one for the nomarch of that region, which was northward around Memphis on the southern end of the Delta. What his master planned to do with the land, Joseph could only guess, but after all it was not uncommon for Egyptian nobility to have more than one home.

In the middle of his second copy, a servant girl popped her dark head into the doorway of the scribe's room where he was working. "Joseph, the master wants you. He's in the stables."

Frowning, he set his work aside and strode out of the house and through the courtyard. A terrible screaming animal sound was coming from the stables. Slaves and servants alike had stopped their work to gawk worriedly. He hurried faster.

Entering the stables, he found Apepi and a few slaves struggling to maintain grip on a rope strung around the headstall of a rearing beast. The camels nearby bellowed in agitation. Lord Potiphar stood far to the side, looking grim. Skirting around the scene, Joseph approached the master.

"Joseph," Lord Potiphar said over the din. "This is a creature from your homeland, I think. Do you know how to calm it?"

A creature from Canaan? Joseph turned, mystified, and looked again. Sudden recognition dawned. It was a horse.

"Not from my homeland, sir. I saw a herd once in Padan-Aram, near the home of my grandfather. A nobleman had bought them. They are from beyond the Tigris and Euphrates, I think. I do not know why it is screaming."

They both turned, looking about the stables and back towards the horse, as if an answer might leap forward and show itself. But there was nothing. Finally Lord Potiphar called in exasperation: "All right then, take it back outside."

The men dragged it out into the courtyard where it pranced, mouth foaming, for another minute, sides heaving and eyes wild. Slowly, it calmed. Intrigued, Joseph stepped forward and held out a hand. It immediately shied away.

"*Don't* rile it up again," Apepi grunted, straining with the effort of keeping it in place.

A little cowed, Joseph stepped back and addressed Lord Potiphar. "I haven't any idea why it was screaming, sir. Perhaps it simply just doesn't like being in a stable?"

"It was in the stables of the Pharaoh when I purchased it."

At a loss, Joseph was about to admit defeat when a memory struck him like a lightning bolt.

"*Useless creatures,*" his grandfather Laban said with a grunt. Joseph stared out over the grassy field from his perch on his father's shoulders and watched the herd running wildly. "Spooked by a camel."

He whirled and stared at the stables, then back at the horse. "The camels," he said.

The other men looked at him in surprise. "What?" the lord asked.

"It is afraid of the camels."

The men stared at him, and one of the slaves snorted. "Afraid of camels?" Apepi asked in disbelief. He looked up at the creature. "Useless beast."

"You know this?" Lord Potiphar asked Joseph.

"I remember my grandfather saying as much."

His master nodded, satisfied. He turned to Apepi and the others. "Set the horse up under a canopy for the night. We'll see to finding better accommodations tomorrow."

They led the horse away to the other end of the courtyard, and Joseph was left with Lord Potiphar, waiting to be dismissed. Instead, his master turned towards him with a smile. "I have not yet known you to be without a solution. Well done."

Joseph's mind raced. How *had* he come to that answer? He could not have been more than four years of age when he had seen the horses. And to remember his grandfather's words?

As if in response to his thoughts, remembrance of the dream-memory he had once had of the event shot through him. He stared across the courtyard at the horse. A little stunned, he could only give credit where it must be due.

My God, thank You for Your continued favor.

He had to stop himself from simply bowing in response to Lord Potiphar's words, for his master next said: "I sometimes think Thoth himself has smiled on you."

Joseph balked. What could he say to it? They were his master's words. But the image of Menkare smiling came unbidden to Joseph's mind. He felt a prickle of guilt touch him. To not acknowledge his God again would be folly.

He shifted on his feet. "I do not know any Thoth, sir, but my God is faithful."

Lord Potiphar seemed taken aback. His lips thinned. "Perhaps Thoth is there, and you do not know it."

"My God would not allow it, sir. He is the only God." Joseph slowly realized that he was digging himself into a pit from which there was likely to be no return. He bit his lip.

The lord must have seen his discomfort, for he said, in a clipped fashion: "Perhaps it would have served you better to be silent on this subject."

Stomach churning, Joseph swallowed. "That may be, sir. But if my God is faithful, how can I be any different?"

His master stared at him before giving a quick bark of laughter. "Indeed. I suppose you cannot be faulted for that."

Lord Potiphar turned, and Joseph watched him go, breathing out a long sigh of relief. Unbidden, his mind cast back to the other two dreams, the ones that had so angered his brothers and confounded his father.

He had not thought of them much, if at all, in the past three years. Frowning a little, he pushed them from his mind. Even if this one dream had proven useful, the others had not been memories, and he doubted anyone would ever be bowing to a slave. It was clear his father had been mistaken in whatever it was he had thought of them.

In a way, they were the reason he was now trapped in Egypt.

He turned and made his way back to the house.

12

Joseph found three more merchants in a fairly short period of time, all well-spoken of. Lord Potiphar, he had discovered over the years, was a practical sort who rarely dealt in the sort of large-scale or rarity-based trade that these merchants took part in, except perhaps at the behest of his wife. But the good word of several stewards from other houses had been sufficient to help him choose them. Within the month, there were four respectable merchant fleets traveling downriver to Tjaru, filled with workers.

A papyrus had come just that morning from the prison stating that there were now only five prisoners free to be moved. It also gave detailed counts of expected arrivals and of those in the prison who would be shortly standing trial. Another round of transport ships would not be needed for several more weeks.

Taking the papyrus to Lord Potiphar, Joseph found him in the courtyard with Pawura, discussing plans to finalize accommodations for the horse. He waited until the master bade him come forward and then handed him the scroll.

Lord Potiphar read it thoughtfully, nodding. "No need to hire the merchant ships again for a little while, I see," he said. "Good." Then he pointed at the line about the men who would soon stand for their crimes. "There is one man in here who will need quite a guard when he is taken to trial." The lord looked up at Pawura. "I must go to the prison today."

The steward nodded, for he often accompanied Lord Potiphar on his visits there. But the master held up his hand. "I will not stop your work here. You have the horse to see to and the plans for Memphis. I will take Joseph."

Stunned, Joseph turned to look at Lord Potiphar, but could only bow. Pawura looked at Joseph for a long moment before bowing to the master as well.

Lord Potiphar turned toward the house, and Joseph followed, not daring to glance back. He could feel Pawura's eyes on him. They entered the house, and his master stopped in the great room. "Wait here a moment." He disappeared behind the thin curtains at the far end, which Joseph knew led to the family quarters.

Standing there with nothing better to do, he found his eyes drawn to the handfuls of beads that had been left on the table, near the alabaster Senet game-board. They had been left there, dregs from some project of the lady's. Made of something called *glass*, they were very bright in color. His mind was instantly on Dinah, who would have loved such a thing to weave into her designs. His heart clenched, and he bit his lip. Where was she? Had she married? Was she happy?

My God, give my father and Dinah peace in their lives. Deliver Benjamin from my brothers.

His master reappeared, wearing the rich collar and broad leather breastplate that marked him as the captain of the guard. They left the room and were soon out of the courtyard and walking up the street, houses growing grander as they climbed farther up the hill.

Joseph followed Lord Potiphar obediently, as he should, but he was acutely aware that technically he was now in the position of bodyguard. His master often walked to the prison with only one servant; it was not as if he were travelling to the marketplace. Still, it was, Joseph realized, a large responsibility on his own part. He hurried behind the lord. Even the group of girls walking on the other side of the street now appeared suspicious.

And why had he taken Joseph? The question rattled in his mind. Bought slaves were not often treated with the same trust as servants who had hired themselves out to a household. Especially after their conversation regarding the horse, where the Lord Potiphar had been obviously displeased, it was rather baffling.

Lord Potiphar turned and glanced at him with a bemused expression. "You seem disquieted."

"I—" Joseph hurried forward to fall in step with the man. "I am gratified you have taken me with you, sir."

"But?"

"But—" Joseph searched for a diplomatic way to phrase it. "I know that I am an unusual choice."

"Hmm," the lord said. "Let me be frank. You are an odd one, Joseph, with your one God, but what you have said about yourself is true. You are faithful and diligent. And if you believe that you are so because of your God, I will not dare to ask that you change your ways. It would be folly, I think."

They continued up the dusty road in silence for a moment, Joseph feeling rather relieved. The last great house had fallen away behind them, and the street was hot in the sun, with no trees reaching from behind garden walls to shade it. The road crested the hill and began to descend slightly, and in the distance, Joseph could see the palace, that marvelous building he had seen from the riverbank on his first day. Before it stood a complex of buildings, both administrative and military. In the midst of them was the prison.

"I have thought long on this." Lord Potiphar spoke again as they walked. A cluster of scribes hurried past in the other direction. "And yesterday I asked Djaty for his judgement as well. I have decided that you ought to begin to work directly under Pawura."

Joseph almost stopped short. "Sir?" he ventured.

His master glanced at him. "I will be sending Pawura to Memphis in the next month or two. There is much to oversee there, and I trust no one else with it. But while he is there, I will need someone to be my steward here."

Now Joseph did stop walking. Lord Potiphar turned around and looked at him. Knowing he should force words to come, Joseph still had none.

"Speak," Lord Potiphar said, laughing.

Joseph didn't much like Pawura; he was brusque and intense and, if Joseph were honest, reminded him a bit of his brothers. But the offer of stewardship, the amount of trust in him it spoke of—he had no words.

"Sir, I am—I'm honored."

Nodding approvingly, the lord waved him onwards. Joseph began walking again, but it was as though he were striding through a dream.

"There is much for you to learn," Lord Potiphar was saying. "But you will have the weeks under Pawura. Djaty is loathe to lose his assistant, but he agreed that you are well-suited."

"I shall try my best, sir," Joseph breathed.

They arrived shortly thereafter at the large complex of buildings that rose up before the grand palace walls. Lord Potiphar strode through the gates of the complex, and the six guardsmen held their spears up in salute. They moved through the streets, passing hordes of scribes and priests rushing about, as well as noblemen, who walked at a more leisurely pace. Many had servants following after them with fans.

The prison then loomed before them—a long, low building with thick walls and few windows. There was no courtyard in the front. They passed through the door and entered a small room.

"Intef!" Lord Potiphar called.

A man, perhaps the same age as Lord Potiphar and very broad, stepped through another doorway and bowed. "Captain."

His master nodded. "I'm here to discuss arrangements for Ranefer."

Intef snorted. "The man's mad, or brilliant at making play that he is. I've had to lock him away under guard."

Joseph listened to the exchange raptly. It was a far cry from mathematics and bargaining and copying documents.

"Show me."

Walking through the door from which Intef had come, they made their way down a long hall with rooms on either side. In the brief glimpses Joseph was able to take in the gloom, they looked

105

like storerooms and one poorly-lit record room with a low table. Then they went through a door at the end of the hall and were arrested by sunlight.

They were looking down on a vast courtyard, some six cubits below them. Several prisoners worked at brick-making in the center of it, and many soldiers stood at intervals around the perimeter.

Around the rim of the courtyard was a narrow walkway and, along the outer edges, a wall. Several doors punctuated it. As they began walking, Joseph realized that the wall, for the most part, was actually made from the backs of many of the other buildings in the complex.

They were led to a ladder and descended into the courtyard. Two guards immediately arrived to escort them as they approached one of many more doors sunken into the lower courtyard walls. A near-howling sound was heard.

"He's at it again," muttered Intef.

Joseph glanced about furtively. None of the prisoners seemed to be paying them any attention, but the ravings, growing louder as they came near, put him on edge.

A guard stood outside the door. The noise was coming from within, and Lord Potiphar looked though a small latticed window in the wood. "Ranefer!" he barked over the din.

The sound didn't stop.

"Ma'at have mercy," his master grunted. "How long has he been doing this?"

"He started yesterday morning. He's quiet for a bit, at times, but then he will start up again."

"He was perfectly sane before he arrived at the prison."

Intef raised his hands helplessly as they walked away from the noise back towards the ladder. "He stood near a wall and screamed the entire morning yesterday. We dragged him over to work on the bricks, but he hit another prisoner with one. We tried beating it out of him, but he seems bent on playing the madman. Or perhaps he's really cracked."

Joseph's stomach screwed itself up a little at *beating*, and he shifted his shoulders uneasily, but his master's next words drove all other thoughts from his mind. "A man on the brink of going mad is not sent to assassinate the Pharaoh."

Invisible as a slave often was, his expression must have been something to behold, for Intef caught sight of him and laughed outright. "Your man looks like he swallowed a frog."

Lord Potiphar glanced at him, and Joseph, a little flustered, quickly returned to the attentive stance he should have been holding. Hands folded, head slightly down. "My apologies, my lord," he nodded to his master and then to Intef. "Sir."

Intef cocked his head after hearing Joseph speak. "A foreigner? Sir, as warden—I must question his being here."

Astonished, Joseph felt the life drain from his limbs.

Not because Intef had called him a foreigner, but because he had not noticed that Joseph was one *until he spoke*.

Lord Potiphar only waved a hand dismissively. "It is well thought of, but Joseph is to be my steward while Pawura is away. You will see much of him, and I will vouch for him."

The prison-master seemed satisfied that he had done his duty and spoke no more of it as they continued talking, discussing the particulars of Ranefer's trial. Joseph knew they must have decided on how many men would guard the prisoner, and heaven knew what else, for they climbed the ladder and left soon after. He heard none of it. His ears buzzed and rang, and he felt ill.

His heart ached for Canaan, for his father, for Benjamin, for Dinah, as it had not in three years. He berated himself. Here he was, *pleased* that he would act as steward for an Egyptian master? Pleased that his master approved of him? His stomach wrenched. Three years had turned him into so much of an Egyptian slave that he not only looked and acted like one, but he had not even seen how—*changed* he had become.

They passed the gates of the large complex, and he trailed Lord Potiphar back toward the great houses, crossing the long corridor of sand which lay in between. To the west he could make out the tall wall that surrounded the city.

Still he fumed. What *right* had anyone here to make him their slave? He stared at Lord Potiphar's back as they walked. He, of such use to his father and beloved by him, firstborn of Jacob's favored wife.

He ought to have laughed in the face of every Egyptian since he had arrived.

The absurdity of the thought caught him, and Joseph bit his lip.

You are full of pride, son of Jacob, he told himself. *Firstborn of Rachel, beloved of your father and of such use to him.*

All of these thoughts were folly, he knew. He had a right to be free, but neither his name nor his mother's nor his father's had anything to do with the reality of his situation. Perhaps young Joseph, who had been dragged though the desert screaming like a wildcat, would have been horrified at it all. But the Joseph of now had nowhere else to go, and to throw away what little he had would be lunacy.

He clenched his jaw against sudden emotion and thought again of Benjamin, of Dinah, of his father. He felt lost, like a great wind had picked him up and torn him away from everything he had thought settled and familiar.

Joseph had believed, in some corner of his mind, that he had resigned himself to the fact that he would never see them again.

That was not true.

Oh my God.

Comfort them and comfort me. Give me peace. For I have little and need much.

Joseph set himself to finishing the copies of the newest land acquisition documents, no matter how long it took. Tomorrow he would begin work under Pawura, and he had decided that he desperately needed the distraction. Djaty was out of the small scribe's room, having a message dictated to him by the Lady Tetisheri, for her father in Heliopolis.

Working in the light of two small lamps, for the sun had just set, the sounds of the courtyard being swept and the stables being closed for the night filtered through the small windows. The household would soon be preparing for sleep.

Sitting on his knees, scribe's board in his lap, his pen flew across the papyrus; he was on the third copy, and by now he could have written the message out with his eyes closed. With a last scrawl, he finished the document. Blowing on the wet ink, he set it aside, spreading it out on the ground so it could dry.

He frowned, feeling lost. He might never copy a document again.

Joseph hated the feelings the day had stirred up in him. With every part of his being, he wished now that his master had never thought of making him steward in Pawura's absence. Even if it was an honor, there was a certain—familiarity to the work he had done under Djaty. In some ways it was the same sort of work he had done at home.

Home. He missed it terribly.

Sighing, Joseph tried shake himself out of his mood. Intef's words had rattled him far beyond anything he would have thought possible.

"My God," he murmured in Canaanite. He closed his eyes, and years of prayers flew through his mind. "Give me peace, for I have little and need much. And if it be Your will, deliver me from this place. And if it is not Your will, then give me the strength and peace to do that which is."

He opened his eyes, and Djaty was watching him from the doorway. His expression was amused. "I admit," he said in his dry way, "that I will miss my strange student."

Rubbing his face, Joseph had to laugh. "I am sorry to leave you. More than I can say."

"Ah," Djaty waved a hand as he stepped into the room. "You are better served elsewhere. There is more to you than letters and numbers. Me, that is all I know."

"I am grateful for what you did for me."

"So am I; you saved me from plenty of work. And now I shall once more have to do it all myself."

Joseph laughed again.

"We are not going to the opposite ends of the Nile, boy. If you like, I'll give you a list of calculations you can do for me every week."

Heart a bit lifted, Joseph made ready for bed. The lamps were blown out and the household was soon asleep.

But in the night, a woman screamed.

13

Joseph awoke, as he always did, vague hints of early-morning sounds filtering into his mind through the high window. He had learned to listen in his sleep. The merest hint of grey colored the sky and reaffirmed that it was time to rise.

As he had every morning for the past six years since he had become steward, he rolled off his soft mat.

"My God," he murmured, kneeling. His tongue stretched around the Canaanite words. "Thanks and all glory be to You, for what You have done for me, for Your servant is not worthy of the least of Your mercies.

"Comfort my father and Dinah. Give them peace in their lives. Deliver Benjamin from my brothers. And if it be Your will, deliver me from this place. And if it is not Your will, then give me the strength and peace to do that which is.

"Give me wisdom in this day, for I need much, and give me peace, for without You I have little."

Taking a deep breath, he got to his feet.

He washed and shaved, pulling on a fresh shendyt and tunic before securing it with a belt and brushing on his eyepaint. He frowned into the little silvered hand-mirror that always rested on his washstand. His hair would need to be clipped again. It was just growing long enough to curl, and that would be unseemly, by Egyptian standards.

Ready for the day, he stepped over to the door of his small room and swung it open.

A pottery shard had been placed up against his door and it tinkled on the stones of the floor when he opened it. He picked up the shard and chuckled. Djaty had left him another mathematical problem. The scribe did so every few weeks, and they had been getting more and more ridiculous over the past months. He took a moment to peruse it.

What is the height of a pyramid the side of whose base is 140 cubits, with a slope of 5 palms, 1 finger?

Joseph rolled his eyes. He had rarely done geometry before coming to Egypt, and Djaty knew it. He cocked his head and listened to the outside noises. There were no birds yet; he had a moment.

He flipped the shard over and snatched up a pen from his scribe's kit, which was resting on a stool in the corner. Pursing his lips, he thought on how to begin, and after a moment, began scribbling the work out in cuneiform. He knew it riled the scribe. Joseph could do mathematics in hieratic, but he disliked it. The Egyptian number system was near-unhinged, and it took quite a bit of effort to make his mind work that way. And if Djaty was going to give him geometry problems, then he would get cuneiform sent back.

Working for several minutes, he double-checked it all before writing the answer in hieratic at the bottom and circling it with a flourish. He set down the pen, put away his scribe's kit, and left his small room, shard in hand, walking down the long hall to set it against Djaty's door.

Then it was a quick walk through the great room and into the slaves' and servants' area on the other side of the house. Taking a breath, Joseph braced himself for the only part of his day he dreaded.

Sticking his head into the yard-workers' room, he bellowed the wake-up call. They shot awake and rolled their mats, and he gave them their duties for the morning. Planting was beginning today. He watched them go. Apepi met them in the hall, and

Joseph nodded to him before the overseer saw them off to a quick breakfast and then the fields.

He turned. The head handmaid and mistress of the laundry were waiting for him. He had found that they both had good heads on their shoulders, and they relayed to Joseph their plans for the day. He nodded. They were well-organized as usual.

Then they were off. One more room.

Putting his head in the house-workers' room, he yelled a second wake-up call. They did the same as the yard-workers, rolling their mats and waiting for instruction. There was much to do, for the lord and lady had just returned from a river-trip to Abydos, and were traveling again by river to their newly finished home in Memphis within the next week.

The house-workers filed out of the room, headed towards the kitchens and the great room.

Joseph took a deep breath. It was only a few minutes of each day, but he hated every moment of the morning instruction. It brought back too many memories of being a frightened boy who understood nothing of what was happening around him.

For another day, however, it was over.

He turned and walked back down the corridor and into the great room, stepping through the back curtains to ensure that the lord and lady's personal servants had themselves in order.

A handmaid, running down the hallway with a clean robe in her hands, nodded as she passed, bracelets jangling. The smell of perfumes wafted down the hall, and he heard Lord Potiphar and a manservant talking in the bathing room. Joseph took a second deep breath. All was well.

He stepped back into the great room. Soon, servants would be entering to lay food and drink on the table, but for the moment, it was quiet. Standing there, he thought over what still had to be done. The master's boat had only just been unpacked from the previous trip. Provisions for the lord and lady's next trip had been procured, but they still needed to be packed, as did clothes—which likely needed to be washed—and all manner of jewelry and perfumes. He considered. Perhaps some of the unperishable food could be packed in the later afternoon and even stored away on the boat, if the captain was ready and willing.

To add to this, Lord Potiphar was expecting a guest for the night, a priest from Heliopolis traveling upriver to Thebes. A special supper would be prepared, and then the man would walk with Lord Potiphar in a burial procession for a nobleman the following day, before continuing southward. Joseph had ensured that a cut of beef had been made ready, and he would send a few servant boys to the market to buy pomegranates and dates after the noon meal.

Certain, among all the things to be remembered, that he was forgetting something, Joseph frowned. Shaking his head a little, he forced his mind to move on. It would come to him, and such was the life of a steward, especially one with no formal training.

He had never studied under Pawura.

The night before Joseph was to begin, the former steward had assaulted the Lady Tetisheri.

She had gone late that evening into the great room, to gather up the beads Joseph had seen that very day. Pawura had found her there, and after a struggle, she had screamed.

The shock of it all sent turbulence rampaging though the household. No one had thought it of Pawura, least of all the Lord Potiphar.

As punishment, the steward had been killed.

Work in Memphis was put on hold, and Joseph was flung into the position of leading a house still stricken with unrest and abject horror. Lord Potiphar had somehow thought he could do it. *Blessed by Thoth*, was all had said, with a wan look. *Or your own God, maybe.* Djaty had helped Joseph as best he was able, but there was little the scribe knew about chores and trades and the daily challenge of having thirty people to organize. Joseph had drawn on every memory he possessed of how his father guided him in Canaan.

His prayers became desperate. *Give me wisdom in this day, for I need much, and give me peace, for without You I have none.* It had become the chorus of his day, chanting in his brain, until one day he realized that the house had not fallen down around him, and everything was running, if not smoothly, at least without outrageous incident.

The prayer itself had remained, a comforting reminder that his God had once again seen him through.

"Ah! Joseph!"

He turned and saw the Lady Tetisheri entering the great room through the curtains. He bowed as she swept forward. "I meant to ask you," she continued. "Are there any plums still to be had, for the supper tonight?" She came to stand by the table, one hand brushing through her black hair. The golden beads resting in it chimed.

"It is unlikely, my lady. They're a summer fruit. But I can have the servants look when they visit the market."

She smiled. "Of course. But it would make *such* an impression, to have them."

Privately, Joseph thought that any late-season fruit was predestined to be middling to bad, but since he could almost guarantee that there would be no plums, he let the matter lie. He bowed.

Servants began trickling in, carrying bread and fruit, and Lord Potiphar arrived a moment later. Their meal was soon underway, and once they were done, Joseph slipped off to have a bite of his own.

"The lady wants plums," he told the two servant boys as they stood by the front gate. They looked at him in disbelief, dark eyes perhaps slightly amused. "Look for them, but do not waste time if you do not see any. Dates and pomegranates will be enough."

Nodding, they dashed off down the road. They were, Joseph realized with a shock as he watched them go, Benjamin's age.

Benjamin is twelve.

I am twenty-six.

Dinah is twenty-eight.

He continued, though it rent his heart to do so. *My father is 117.*

115

As quickly as he had decided to perform the ritual, he pushed it aside.

Turning, he looked out across the courtyard. It had just been swept, and two servant girls were caring for the last bit of bush still flowering in the autumn. The little monkey watched them curiously as it hung from the roof of its cage. As it always did nowadays, it cast an occasional glance at the hoopoe-bird that lived in the cage on the other side of the pool, a more recent addition to the Lady Tetisheri's collection. She had added a cat as well, one that was supposed to stay in the house but regularly escaped outside to stare intently at the crowned, sandy-colored hoopoe.

He caught sight of the cat just then, smoke-grey and still as stone, once again sitting pertly near the pool and eying the bird. Rolling his eyes, he made his way over to the cat and picked it up. It protested—loudly—but did not scratch, even when the monkey called at it, teasing.

Carrying it inside, he set it in the great room, shooing it back towards the family quarters. Lady Tetisheri and two friends were in the back of the room, giggling over something. They looked up in surprise at his entrance and watched the cat run by before bursting into laughter again. Confused, but not overly perturbed, for that was their way, Joseph bowed slightly and turned to go.

"Oh, Joseph, don't mind us!" the lady called. "Come, come here for a moment."

A little puzzled as to what they could want from him, he stepped forward. The young handmaid who had been standing to the side, fanning them, flashed him a look he could not read.

"This, *this*, is the one who is trying to get me plums," Lady Tetisheri was saying to one of the other women. He did not recognize her as a friend he had seen before. The new friend looked at him with a smile.

It was almost as though none of them intended to say anything else, for only silence followed.

116

Bewildered, he bowed again, slightly. "Is there anything you need at present, my ladies?"

The women were growing red. One of them glanced at Lady Tetisheri, mouth twisting upward.

"No, Joseph, thank you," the lady answered. Her voice quivered ever so slightly. "That is all."

Bowing for a third time and thoroughly perplexed, he left the great room, only to stop in the hall when he heard the three ladies again burst into gales of laughter. It was only a moment before they began hushing each other.

He should not have gone back to listen, but the strangeness of it all compelled him. He crept back to the corner, where the hall met the great room.

"—didn't expect you to practically *introduce* me to a slave, Tetisheri!" one of them was saying in a fierce whisper.

"It didn't seem like you minded," came another voice, quiet and fighting against laughter. Someone snorted, and the conversation deteriorated into giggling.

Lady Tetisheri's voice finally broke through. "Indeed," she whispered back. "I think you were quite overpowered by him." Another round of giggles. "You stared at him as though Hathor herself had spoken in your ear."

"*Tetisheri!*" the first voice protested though gasps of suppressed laughter.

"I assure you," the lady continued. "It's perfectly understandable."

At that moment something was dropped in the courtyard.

Joseph jumped, the sound of shattering pottery bringing him to his senses. He hurried quietly out to see what it was.

Two menservants had collided in the hurry to prepare for the evening, and one had dropped a large water pitcher. A slave girl was already running to the scene to sweep up the shards. All looked well. Joseph nodded to them all; everything would soon be back in order.

He turned, pretending that he was observing those cooking in the kitchens, an area of grass-roof overhangs at the perimeter of the courtyard.

Inwardly, his mind raced, aghast. What was the lady thinking, talking in such a way to her friends? And about *him*? He felt sick. And to act the way they had to his face—did they think him an idiot? He would have put the pieces together, if not immediately, eventually. Then his heart nearly stopped.

Did they think he would not mind?

"Well. I know you well enough to see that your mind has left on a journey."

Joseph jumped for a second time. Djaty was standing nearby, looking at him bemusedly. "Where were you? Upper Egypt, at least. Maybe Nubia. How is my home?"

Attempting to brush it all away, or Djaty would become suspicious, Joseph shrugged a little and forced a laugh. "I simply have too much to do."

"Apparently so, your work this morning was not in hieratic."

He had to play along. He bowed a little. "My apologies, sir."

"Ah," Djaty said. He clapped him on the back and headed towards the gates, raising a hand. "You will do better next time!"

Joseph was again left with his whirling thoughts. *My God, have mercy on me.* How was he ever to stand in her presence again? To be silent and passive and know the sort of things that were going through her mind? He could not do it.

He forced himself to walk, to do something, anything. To stand there like carven stone would do no one any good, and further, would set curious eyes on him. Calling a manservant over, he sent him on his way to the docks. If the boat was ready, he could begin sending some cargo aboard. He looked around. A maidservant ran up to him, asking if the fruit was bought yet. About to shake his head, he saw the two boys running back through the gate. "No plums, sir," one of them said as they reached him. "But here are the pomegranates and dates." They were given to the maid.

Continuing in this manner for some time, he sent servants into the house to straighten and set the great room and table, much of which he would have normally seen to himself. The manservant returned; they could begin loading the boat tomorrow, but not today.

It was not many minutes more before Lord Potiphar arrived with his guest the priest. Joseph greeted them with a bow and led them inside to the great room, which was mercifully straightened and set to Joseph's satisfaction, as well as bereft of the lady of the house.

He waved some maidservants in, who approached with drink and fruit as the men sat and talked. Lord Potiphar's personal manservant, who played the lyre, struck up a gentle tune from his place near the curtains at the back of the room. Joseph stood near the entrance, waiting should he be needed.

Lady Tetisheri drifted in some time later, white skirts billowing and gems glinting, just before the meal was served. Joseph was caught between watching her worriedly and studiously ignoring her. She, for her part, did not seem to notice him at all. The beef was set out, and bread, pomegranates, dates, and date wine. Everything in good order.

Lord Potiphar and the priest discussed the temple buildings which were growing and springing up in Abydos, honoring Osiris. The priest shook his head. "I of course respect the people's growing adoration of Osiris. To be part of the living ones even after death is of utmost importance. But Atum-Ra is lord even of the underworld. Come visit Heliopolis when you are staying in Memphis, my friend. My fellow priests will show you how to balance them both within the Pesedjet, the Nine."

Joseph studiously observed the back curtains, blowing slightly in the evening breeze that came through the high windows. Of all the Egyptians' dizzying array of gods, Atum-Ra was often at the head, the sun personified, creator of the world and ancestor of the Pharaoh himself. He shifted on his feet. Atum-Ra had always galled him the most, and it had taken him years to understand why, but it was simply that he was a dim image of an all-powerful creator—his own God—yet he sulked and fretted like a child in the stories Joseph had heard.

Glancing back at the table, he noticed a manservant stepping forward at the lady's bidding to refill her glass of wine. Joseph frowned slightly. How many had she had?

He looked down at the blue stones patterning the floor and glanced at her again from the corner of his eye. She drank the wine swiftly and called for more.

The burial procession of the nobleman was a quiet affair, and Joseph walked slowly behind the lord and lady, a few other household servants completing their entourage. It was not the first procession he had attended with his master, and he chewed on his tongue to keep from focusing on everything that happened around him. They traveled along the west bank of the Nile, towards a field of low, flat-topped tombs.

Pulled along by several priests, the burial-curricle moved towards the nearest tomb, the mourners fanning out behind it. Many other priests in white robes walked before it, burning incense.

At the door to the tomb, the curricle was set before the dark opening and a High Priest stepped forward. The deceased, wrapped and head covered in a burial mask, was raised up for the mourners to see. The priest touched the leg of a calf to the lips of the painted face on the mask and began to chant.

"Your mouth is opened by Ptah,
Your mouth's bounds are loosed,
Thoth has come, ready with spells,
He looses the bonds of Set from your mouth.
Atum-Ra has given you your hands,
They are here, as guardians.

Your mouth is given you,

Your mouth is opened by Ptah,
With that chisel of metal
With which he opened the mouths of the gods.
Sekhmet speaks, who dwells in the west of heaven.
You stand amongst the souls at Heliopolis."

Joseph looked stolidly down, still biting his tongue. The Opening of the Mouth was part of a long ceremony meant to ensure that the nobleman would be comfortable in the afterlife. Sacrifices would be offered and the tomb laden with the tools and comforts that the nobleman would need in eternity.

The inside of the tomb itself would be painted with scenes both actual and fantastical. Inscriptions to Ma'at, the Egyptian goddess of truth and justice, would cover walls from top to bottom, the hieroglyphs listing the great and moral things the man had done. Interspersed within them, there would be some wrongdoings by the nobleman portrayed, written instead as spells of absolution. They would skew the scene, provide caveats, or even deny events entirely, so that he was shown to be innocent. And thus, the Egyptians believed, the man might be judged as worthy and without wrongdoing by the goddess and the god Osiris in the afterlife.

Joseph cast his eyes surreptitiously around him. The other mourners were rapt, listening to every word. For no Egyptian would be irreverent of death or the words they believed were needed to find life again afterwards. There was fear in their actions—those who could built tombs as soon as they reached adulthood, or sooner. To be without a proper burial was to be lost after death, without a future.

He went back to chewing his tongue. His God was not so easily fooled.

Silently, he counted the minutes until they left.

14

Two days later brought Lord Potiphar to him in the courtyard. It was afternoon, and Joseph was sending a third round of supplies down to the docks to be loaded. He had also just ordered more jars to be brought up from an old storeroom, for the lady had ordered that extra beer be taken along.

"Joseph, will you spare a moment?" his master asked.

"Of course." Joseph quickly turned—he hoped not too quickly. He tried to draw his mind away from the fear that spiked in him. There was no way the lord could know what his lady had said, and besides that, she had done nothing more since.

"I am afraid I will not be going to Memphis."

Joseph opened his mouth in sheer surprise, trying to formulate a response. Lord Potiphar held up a hand. "I know what you are thinking, but your time has not been so very wasted. Tetisheri will go, and some friends. You needn't change anything you are doing."

Bowing and wondering what in the world had happened, he ventured: "I trust all is well, sir?"

"Hmm," was all his master said for a moment. Then he continued. "Do you remember Ranefer? The prisoner I went to see, the first time you came to the prison with me?"

"The madman?"

"The same. What do you think has happened? There is another man now."

"Another madman?"

"Yes. His case is near the same as Ranefer's—another attempt on the life of the Pharaoh. He will be killed like the first, but before that, I have Intef recording everything the man says or does. This, I think, is not a coincidence. Nor do I think he is a madman. Two cases is too much. He is only play-acting, and I want a record of it."

"Do you have any records from Ranefer?"

"No. I wish I had. At any rate, I will ask you to accompany me to the prison today. I may have need of your brain."

"Of course."

Lord Potiphar put a hand on his shoulder before turning away. "Good man."

Joseph swallowed.

The lady was mercifully gone within the next day, with two friends and a gaggle of maids and menservants. She was not expected back for over two weeks. Lord Potiphar spent his days at the prison, or at the palace consulting with the Pharaoh, so the house was relatively quiet. Joseph set the household slaves and servants to scrubbing the entirety of the premises and washing all the curtains in the house, something that had been sorely needed.

He left one day to meet his master at the prison. The prisoner, Baufra, was not so violent as Ranefer had been, but twice as loud. Joseph unlooped the red cord from his belt and wrapped it around his right hand before stepping out the courtyard gates. His master had given it to him years ago.

The afternoon was hot for autumn, and the sun blazed unmercifully in the sky, its light melting the blue to near-white. He walked slowly in the heat, stepping to the side to let two litters carried by small armies of menservants go by. Their inhabitants were a mystery, shrouded by a layer of curtains. Joseph, bemused, watched them pass. He had always found them somehow comical. Lord Potiphar never used one, though the lady did on occasion.

At the entrance to the administrative complex that housed the prison, he waved his right hand vaguely in the direction of the guards. They let him through without even glancing at the cord. He was there often with his master.

Intef was in the front room when he entered. "Ah, Joseph!" he said.

He bowed slightly. "Is the Lord Potiphar here yet?"

The prison-master shook his head. "No, but have a look at this." He handed Joseph the long scroll that was being added to daily. It carried a list of everything Baufra had said or done since he arrived. Mostly it had been nonsense ravings, repeated words over and over that meant little. The only thing anyone had noticed so far was that the man called upon Osiris fairly often. Joseph glanced at the bottom, and his eyes widened.

Dedumose of Abydos will write it, it read.

Intef was looking at him, satisfaction in his features. "The man talked in his sleep last night. Dedumose is the High Priest of Osiris at Abydos."

Joseph looked up, eyebrows raised, considering all the doors this bit of information had flung open.

At that moment Lord Potiphar strode in, the manservant with him remaining just outside the door. Joseph handed him the scroll with a bow. "Ha!" Lord Potiphar said after reading it. "Well, that is interesting."

"It could be nothing," Intef said. "Though I hope it is not."

"If there is any chance a priest is indeed a part of this, you will have to use caution," Joseph murmured.

"Hmm," was all Lord Potiphar said. He glanced down at the scroll and then back up at Intef. "This is the first time he has talked in his sleep?"

"He is guarded at all times; it is the first time he was heard."

"Keep three guards at his door tonight. Tell them to listen as if their lives depended on it."

The prison-master bowed. Lord Potiphar turned his attention back to the scroll and frowned. Joseph watched him for several moments as he stood there, but then the lord turned to him. "What do you make of this?" He held out the scroll and pointed to a line a hand or so above the words from last night.

"Sand," Joseph read. "Sand … I have seen it." He shook his head a little at the ramblings and continued. "Ma'at! Sand! At the crocodile's mouth!"

"That is the sixth time he has mentioned Ma'at in the past two days," said Lord Potiphar. He unrolled the top of the scroll further to point them out. Intef came over to peer at it as well. "Prior to that it was only Osiris. Perhaps she is on his mind?"

Joseph nodded slightly. "I would not be surprised."

With a sudden flash of understanding, he looked back down at the words from last night.

Dedumose of Abydos will write it.

"Dedumose will absolve him," Joseph said.

Both men stared at him.

"Dedumose will write Baufra's spells of absolution from his crimes, before he is dead," Joseph said emphatically.

"By Thoth!" exclaimed Intef. He looked down once again at the papyrus, then looked at Joseph and grinned. "Captain, your man is quite something."

His master was looking down at the scroll, mouth twisted to one side in a smile. "That is why he is my steward."

They left soon afterward, Intef running down to the sunken courtyard to place a three-man guard on Baufra, Joseph and Lord Potiphar walking back through the complex. The manservant trailed a respectful distance behind, and they walked in silence until they were nearing the house.

"I shall write to the Chief of Police in Abydos directly," Lord Potiphar said at length. "Dedumose must be brought to Itjtawy for questioning. Will you find Djaty, when we return?"

"Of course."

His master spoke again after a moment, gruffly. "Joseph, I think I must tell you that the service you have provided myself and my house since coming to me has been nothing short of excellent. But you knew that," he said with a wry smile and a sideways glance. "Blessed by your God or Thoth, or whoever it may be, I have never known a house to run more smoothly."

"Thank you, sir," Joseph said quietly. His heart was gratified, but in the back of his mind, the shameless words of the lady leapt forward, and his stomach twisted.

"I have no sons nor daughters," Lord Potiphar continued. Joseph looked at him in sudden surprise at his frankness. "And, it seems now, I never shall. Or so that is what Tetisheri and I have been told." They had reached the gates to the house now, and his master shooed the manservant inside before turning again to face Joseph. He set a hand on his shoulder. "When I leave this life, I intend to free you, and give you all I own."

Stunned, Joseph could only stare in shock before finally bowing deeply. He tried to speak, but his throat caught.

Lord Potiphar smiled.

That night found Joseph kneeling in his small room, praying, as he often did, before sleep found him. His mind spun, but his heart sang in a way it had not in years.

Taking a deep breath, he thought carefully and flexed his tongue a little before beginning to speak the Canaanite words. "My God. Truly You are faithful. Great is Your faithfulness, and thanks and all glory be to You, for Your servant is not worthy of the least of Your mercies."

The taste, the *thought* of freedom, be it still far away, coursed through him like wine. He did not wish for Lord Potiphar to die, indeed, the man was kind. But freedom drew him in. "I know now You will deliver me from this place. Give me the wisdom and peace to do what is needed until that time. Protect Benjamin. Comfort him. Comfort my father and Dinah."

He paused and added, as he had been these last few days: "Have mercy on me, my God. Do not let the lady's words continue, or lead anyone to harm."

Joseph blew out the lamp and laid down on the mat, his mind too overwhelmed to allow him to do more than stare up into the darkness. He thought of his family, somewhere in Canaan. He would find them, somehow. He would see Benjamin, and Dinah, and his father. He would comfort them. He would appear before his brothers and his father and speak the thing they had done.

My father is 117.

The thought came unbidden to his mind.

He paused again.

What would it do to him? To know what his sons had done? He was old, and would be older still when the time came for Joseph to be free. Joseph's heart clenched, just a little.

It is no matter, he told himself firmly.

His God was seeing to it.

Lady Tetisheri returned fifteen days later, glowing and fawning over her long-absent husband. She brought with her a trunkful of new clothes and jewelry, and a second hoopoe-bird, desperately in need of a larger cage. Joseph immediately set two male slaves to building one near the first bird.

All was well, and she seemed to be ignoring Joseph completely, as she had just before she left. Perhaps she had realized that he had overheard her conversation, or at least that he was not a simpleton.

It did not last.

Joseph was preparing to retire the night of her arrival, and had only to straighten a final few cushions in the great room, when a hand brushed his shoulder. He turned in surprise, and there she was.

He recoiled.

She stared at him, black-rimmed eyes amused.

"Lady," he said finally. His heart pounded, and he took a step backward. "What can I fetch for you?"

"Oh," she said with a little smile. "I need nothing of that sort from you."

Joseph's breath caught in his throat. It was time to take a stand. "Lady, I will not hear this."

She cocked her head, a slight frown creasing her features, and she stepped forward. "You shall, for I am your mistress." Her voice dropped to a whisper. "Lie with me."

His jaw dropped, and he reeled back. Had she taken leave of her senses? "Lady Tetisheri," he gasped. "Your husband has committed this household to me with all his trust. He pays no attention to what I do to ensure its running and holds nothing and no one back from my command. I may do as I will with all of it—except you. It is wicked even to consider it. How could I betray him and so sin against God?"

Her face darkened. "You and your God," she spat. Joseph barely heard her. He was already moving swiftly down the corridor.

He reached his room and shut the door. Breathing heavily and leaning against it, he stood there in shock.

"My God, what can I do?"

The next day was a haze, and the next, and the day that followed. He worked. He stayed in the yard as much as possible. He ignored her.

She was not cowed. Her hand slyly slid across his arm when he served her and the master a plate of newly-picked sycamore figs. So subtly she played this game, no one could see it. Her eyes followed him across the courtyard from where she sat by the pool in the late afternoon. No one noticed.

Djaty left him another mathematical problem. He attempted it, and failed miserably, even in cuneiform. He put it aside. "Are you well, my friend?" the scribe asked. Joseph nodded and swallowed. Djaty gave him an uneasy look.

"Lie with me," the lady found a chance to say each day. No one saw, no one heard. Her hand dug into his arm—he pulled away.

Was this what had truly happened to Pawura? Fear clenched him.

His nights were filled with desperate prayer. "My God, You are faithful. Deliver me, for I know You are with me."

On the fourth day, he entered the great room to ensure that it had been properly cleaned and set. Lord Potiphar was to have another guest that night, and the Lady Tetisheri had gone out.

The room was empty. The cleaning had been rushed, it appeared at first, but as Joseph looked over the room he began to wonder if it had happened at all. Frowning, he turned to go and find the servants he had put in charge of the room.

But the back curtains unexpectedly parted, and he turned.

Lady Tetisheri stood there, face determined.

He whirled to go, but before he knew it, she was upon him. She clenched his tunic. "Lie with me," she hissed.

He tore away, and his tunic split, left in her hand. Down the corridor he ran, dressed in only a shendyt like a yard-slave. The lady shrieked, the sound following him through the house and grounds like her grasping hands. Joseph stumbled out of the door into the courtyard and turned in horror at the sound.

The scene in the courtyard seemed to stop in that moment, to freeze like the water he had once seen in a pot at his grandfather's home in Padan-Aram. The gazes of the workers, turning from curious to dismayed, were the only sign that time passed.

And then three house-servants burst from around the corner of the house. They caught hold of him, dragged him to his room, and roughly threw him down to the floor.

He tumbled across the floor as the door slammed shut.

On hands and knees, he gasped for breath, tasting blood.

"My God," he whispered, aghast.

He would be accused of rape.

That terrible crime that haunted his sister, that vile thing that had stolen her peace and left her with only bitter resentment towards so many in her life. The crime would brand him and follow him swiftly to the grave.

For he would be killed for it.

Disbelief coursed through him. It was farcical. It was ridiculous.

How could his God, who had seemingly watched over him despite what his brothers had done, allow *this*? To give him a promise of freedom, and then *this*?

Anger burned in his chest, and he rose to his knees and turned on the ceiling with a roar. *"My God! What have I done to deserve this?"* His breath came in gasps, the still air in the room pressing and palpable. "What have I done to deserve *any* of this?" he screamed again.

It was in that moment that he realized he was screaming to his God in Egyptian, not Canaanite.

His limbs went numb. Helplessness overtook him. He sat with his back to the wall and put his head in his hands.

Part Two
Faith

15

Joseph stepped out of the sucking mud with a groan. His legs burned with exertion. He bent over, gasping, wiped the sweat from his brow, and glanced around the prison-yard. Even in only the first glimpses of spring, Egypt was cursedly warm. The two other prisoners who had been kneading mud paused as well, stretching with grunts and groans and stumbling away from the muck for a blessed moment's rest.

He stared down at his feet, newly caked in the thick mixture, before looking back at the swath of mud with a grimace. There would be three days left of kneading before it could rest and then be made into bricks. There was another pit nearby that would be filled and kneaded while the first pit sat resting.

It was what the prisoners did while waiting to be transferred, either to the courts for trial or to Tjaru to work on the fortifications.

Joseph's mind wandered back to that time, when helping Djaty and organizing prisoner transportation were his domains. He wished now for any work like that, something to challenge his rotting brain.

Instead, he was destined, it seemed, to make bricks for eternity.

He had not been killed. He had seen Lord Potiphar only once after the incident four months ago, late in the evening. The lord had burst into Joseph's room, and Joseph had looked up from where he still sat on the floor. The man's eyes were like fire.

"The truth!" he snarled.

Joseph, numbed and dismayed, could only shake his head in stupefied silence.

Lord Potiphar stalked closer and threatened a kick. "The truth, now! I want to hear your words!"

He flinched, but somehow that action, so unlike his master, pushed him out of insensibility and past fear.

Feeling an unexpected wave of pity for the man, Joseph looked him in the eye, suddenly understanding that even in this state he held the power to shatter the man's world.

"My lord," he whispered finally. He had no other choice but to say the words. "I did nothing. I swear it."

The man whirled with a roar and left, slamming the door so violently that the wooden doorframe split.

That was the last Joseph had seen of him. Soon after, men he did not recognize burst into his room and dragged him down the hall and out into the courtyard. He had caught a glimpse of Djaty's stricken face before a bag was put over Joseph's head.

The Joseph who came to Egypt might have screamed his innocence so that every person in Lord Potiphar's household and the surrounding houses knew it. But the Joseph of now could not bear to do so. It would shame Lord Potiphar irreparably, and earn Joseph nothing at all.

He had thought he was being taken away to be impaled at the stake, but instead he found himself thrown down the ladder at the prison, into the sunken courtyard. And there he had stayed, no call to trial, no summons for a boat to Tjaru.

Intef, apparently, was equally concerned about Joseph's seemingly amorphous status. No one stayed in the prison for long—that was not the way in Egypt. But the prison-master had resignedly been forced to keep him working on the bricks with the other prisoners, who came and went.

Joseph stood upright and flung his hair, damp with sweat, out of his eyes. He squinted, eyeing the movements of the guards on the walkway that circled the lip of the sunken courtyard. If he was right about the time, they would bring down a jar of water soon.

Looking around at the dismal scene, he finally made his way to a low doorway, the entrance to one of the rooms built into the earthen sides of the courtyard. The wooden door hung open on loose hinges. He slumped down in the shade, and a skittering sound deep inside the dark room made him stiffen. There were rats, he had found, and plenty of them. He was learning to ignore them.

The prisoners would be allowed no more than a ten-minute rest, but none of the guards bellowed out the reminder. Intef, he guessed, had told them to let Joseph manage things.

The prison-master had not said as much, but his actions made it clear he thought Joseph innocent in the matter. Just as, Joseph guessed after so many months, Lord Potiphar did, for death had never come.

He grimaced. What would the man do now, married to an unfaithful wife? And one who had, it seemed, perhaps been unfaithful twice over. He grimaced again, thinking of Pawura.

And what could the Lord Potiphar do, with a rightly innocent slave, now accused of such a crime? If they wanted to avoid public scandal, then Lady Tetisheri had tied the lord's hands. Joseph must remain in forgotten oblivion.

So here Joseph was, back, for all intents and purposes, in the bottom of a pit. Only this time, there was no screaming nor begging. There was only a deep, impersonal numbness, as if he were watching it all from a distance.

He had thought he had seen his God guiding him, providing a way to reach freedom and home. He had been very wrong. The realization had been like someone stealing the floor from under his feet.

The noise of marching feet arrested his attention, and he looked up. Intef was coming towards the ladder, followed by two guards. He made his way down, looked around, and approached Joseph. The two guards remained standing by the ladder.

"How goes it?" the prison-master asked, by way of greeting.

Joseph shrugged. "As you see."

Intef leaned against the doorframe and looked at him. "You were right, you know."

Glancing up, Joseph eyed the man with a squint. "About what?"

"Dedumose. He was questioned at the palace. He had absolved Baufra. And Ranefer."

Joseph felt the wheels of his mind turning in response to the information, grinding and protesting after months of bricks and only bricks. Some small part of him that was not fully numb, the angry part, told him to shove it all away. Ignore. Why should he care about such things anymore?

But he was too curious. His brain finally formed the thought that had been rising to the surface. "Is he the one behind it all?"

The other man shook his head. "Likely not, from what I have heard."

Shifting thoughtfully where he sat, other questions came to Joseph's mind, faster now. What, if anything, had the man revealed about other conspirators? Who were his friends in Abydos and elsewhere? He bit back his tongue before he voiced them, finally wresting control from his curiosity. What was the point? He could do nothing from here.

Seeming to understand at least the general direction of Joseph's thoughts, Intef grunted. "Look. It's ridiculous to see you brooding like this. I'm going to give you something to do, and if you refuse so that you can spite your own self, I'll *order* you to do it."

Joseph couldn't help the small snort that escaped him. "What sort of thing would you have me do?"

"Organize prisoner transfers to Tjaru. I understand you were the original architect."

Surprised, Joseph looked up at the man. "Are you still using the same merchants? I can't hire any new boats from here."

"Sometimes the same, sometimes not. It depends on the time of year. I've been doing most of the logistics work, or one of my men.

To be frank, I'd rather someone else did it, and you need something better to do than make mud with these vagrants. I'll make sure you have the names and timetables you need."

Looking down, Joseph pushed his hair out of his eyes again. "I'll do it," he said finally. What else could he say?

"Good man." Intef rapped him on the shoulder and turned away, just as the guards called out and began to lower down the pitcher of water. Prisoners came running from all sides. Joseph observed them dispassionately, waiting for the crowd to disperse. There would still be water when they were finished.

He watched Intef climb back up the ladder and then make his way around the walkway towards the low building at the prison entrance.

"My God," Joseph said bitterly in Canannite. The prison-master disappeared into the building, and Joseph closed his eyes and grit his teeth. "Why are You doing this a second time?"

Save to pray for the well-being of Benjamin, Dinah, and his father, Joseph had not spoken to God in the past four months. He had not dared to stop praying for their protection, but it was pointless to pray about anything else. God had made it abundantly clear that He was not listening to Joseph's pleas.

Joseph had been so certain that God had heard him and was guiding him back to his family. For as soon as Joseph had prayed, all those years ago, for guidance in His ways, Djaty had found him. God had given Joseph his master's esteem and a promise of freedom as an answer to his faith.

Or so he had thought.

For then there was *this*.

And now, for whatever reason, the cycle, the same sort of chain of events that had given him so much hope previously, was starting again. A man had come and offered him work that would bring him up from the lowest parts of this place. Where that would take him, Joseph did not know, but there could be no promise of freedom for an enslaved prisoner accused of rape.

"My God," he said again. "Why not just leave me in the house

137

of Potiphar forever? It would have been better than this." The words, spoken without premeditation, tumbled out in Egyptian. He scowled at the realization and then cast it aside angrily. What did it matter? For there was silence in response to his words. There was only ever silence.

He scuffed his mud-caked heels in the sand.

Our God is great, my son. And beyond understanding. His ways are great and even so His faithfulness to those who trust in Him.

The words, his father's words that he had remembered when he first came to the house of Potiphar, came so clearly to Joseph's mind that he jumped where he sat. He looked around, perturbed and half-expecting someone to be standing nearby, speaking them aloud. But there were only the mud-brick walls and the men at the water pitcher. Frowning and a little uneasy, he looked up at the cloudless, blue-white sky.

"My father said that You are faithful," he said after a time, as if responding to the memory of Jacob's words. It was brazen to speak in such a way, maybe, and in Egyptian no less, but he was past caring. "I cannot see it. If all this is truly Your doing, You are capricious. You built me up in my father's house, then let me be sold as a slave. You built me up in Lord Potiphar's house, then let me be thrown in this prison. Now Intef wishes for me to do this thing. What of it?"

He scowled, and then sighed. He was talking to the air.

Then he tensed.

Even if he were talking to the air, the words, once out, provided a pathway to determining a clear series of tenets.

Either his God was false, or his God was true.

And if his God were false, then his father, who said that he had wrestled with God and seen God's angels ascending into heaven, and his great-grandfather, who said that he had sworn a blood-covenant with God—then they were false as well, for none of it could be true.

And if his God were true—then it was just that. He was true, and must be great, and beyond understanding, and faithful. Joseph's jaw opened a little as he considered this, every moment of his life boiling down to the stark choice he must make in naming the next tenet.

Either God was true, and therefore there was a purpose, somehow, in the chaos of his life. Or God was false, and therefore there was no purpose, and would never be.

He sat paralyzed by the thoughts running through his mind.

God must be true. He knew it with every fibre of his being. It was a conviction that came from his bones. The visions and stories and encounters and knowledge of his father, and of his grandfather, and of his great-grandfather—they were not tales woven to impress children around a nighttime fire. They were firm and real and experienced from generation to generation. He had never doubted it, not once in his life, even before he had ever dared to speak to his father's God. And once he had spoken to God—

Joseph recalled the Mysteries of Osiris play and how his refusal to attend and desperate prayer had led to his service under Djaty.

God is great.

God is beyond understanding.

They were truths, as surely as the sun rose and set.

God is faithful.

God is not capricious.

Joseph staggered to his feet and slumped against the doorframe. He felt as though he had just been gutted. "Oh my God," he whispered. "Then how could You have done this to me? How is this faithfulness? I have tried to serve You."

Another realization rocked him, and Joseph stood there, feeling as though a veil had just been lifted from his eyes.

To trust in God and serve Him must not be to ask for what seemed good and right and know that it would be granted.

To trust in God and serve Him must be to know that whatever happened, whatever it was and however terrible it seemed, would be used for His faithfulness—His purpose.

Defeated, Joseph clutched his head in his hands and pushed the thought away.

It can not be so.

It must not be so.

For he could take no more of this.

Joseph stared down at the sleeping man in distaste. He had been thrown into the courtyard some four hours ago, staggering and muttering and obviously drunk. A while later, when no one was looking, he had unceremoniously lurched into one of the dark rooms that edged the courtyard and become dead to the world. Unfortunately, the room he had chosen was the one Joseph had been using, along with another man.

A rare rain was falling in the wake of a dust storm, smacking the sand outside with wet pockmarks and rushing a blast of vividly cold evening air through the courtyard. Both of the other men were asleep now, and there was no space at the back of the room. Rolling his eyes, Joseph resignedly sat away from them, almost within the entry, and shivered in his shendyt. Trying to ignore his surroundings, he picked up the pottery shard and unrolled the papyrus he had been reviewing before the dust and rain began.

There were to be seven new arrivals at the prison that week, including the new man. Intef had begun having Joseph keep all such records in the past few weeks. It was easier that way for Joseph to organize transportation to Tjaru—four of the men arriving had already stood trial and would be added to the prisoners waiting to travel downriver.

One merchant ship was available next week, but could only take three prisoners with one guard. Joseph furrowed his brow, wondering if it wasn't better to wait for a different ship, arriving the following week—the passage on the ship available sooner was expensive even for four. He looked down the lists for the next available boats and their passenger loads and quickly scratched some cuneiform calculations into the sand.

He rolled his eyes a second time once he realized that it would be the same amount of money either way, and that the first merchant would be used the third week if he were not used in the first. These merchants, he decided, had become unexpectedly shrewd since he had first started hiring them six years ago. They had probably staggered their availability purposefully. He glanced at the prices a second time. They had gone up, as well.

Squinting back and forth between the prison-record papyrus and the pottery shard upon which shipping timetables were written, Joseph realized that the light was nearly gone. He sighed. There were no lamps for prisoners. Rolling up the papyrus, he set it and the pottery shard in a niche in the wall he'd been allowed to create. He ran a hand through his hair and beard and felt a sudden urge to go out and stand in the rain. Prisoners were allowed little by way of bathing. But he looked again and saw that the rain had nearly stopped.

Glancing again at the slumbering men, Joseph resigned himself to the fact that he would be sleeping in the doorway that night. He might have dragged the drunkard outside, if not for the sodden sand. He sighed again.

"My God," he murmured finally, preparing to sleep. He had begun praying again, morning and night, but had given up praying in Canaanite. At first, the thought of doing so almost frightened him, but eventually resignation had settled in his bones. His tongue, out of practice, staggered around the Canaanite words, and it made everything seem inaccessible, somehow. As if God had nothing to do with Egypt.

He still felt somehow that it was brazen of him to speak in Egyptian. But then, so also were many of his words. And God was the one who had sent him to Egypt to rot, after all. He did not know the consequences of speaking one's disillusionment directly to God, but he was past caring.

"Comfort and watch over Benjamin. Deliver him from my brothers. Give Dinah and my father peace in their lives." He paused, and grunted slightly. "If You have any, show me Your purpose here. Your faithfulness my father spoke of. Soon. *Why can You not allow me to return home?*"

He grit his teeth.

"For I do not understand You, *and I hate this.*"

16

J oseph!"

Turning quickly, Joseph saw Intef fairly flying around the rim of the courtyard towards the ladder. Glancing back at the two men he had been lecturing, Joseph gave them a black look before the guards led them off to opposite sides of the courtyard and locked them away in separate rooms.

They had arrived yesterday, both members of a criminal gang that had been hustling and pickpocketing its way through Heliopolis before coming to Itjtawy. Three merchants had been robbed before two of the members had been caught. The police were still searching for the other members, but in the meantime, these two seemed to blame both each other and the world at large for their misfortune. They could not stand to be near each other or anyone else without brawling, and Joseph had been forced to reorganize the sleeping arrangements and the brick-making rotations so that all-out chaos did not erupt. He was counting the days until their trial.

He looked now towards Intef, who had just reached the bottom of the ladder, and approached him. "What is it?" Joseph asked.

Intef pulled him aside and led him to an unoccupied corner. Two guards stood nearby, apparently not wanting anyone to come within earshot.

"I am sorry, but I am going to need you to reorganize the sleeping arrangements again." He looked quite apologetic, but Joseph couldn't help the look of frustration that crossed his face.

"Why?"

The prison-master's voice dropped to a whisper. "The Pharaoh ordered his chief cupbearer and chief baker to prison this morning."

Joseph's mouth dropped open, just a little. Such elite servants of the Pharaoh were deeply trusted, families often serving the throne for generations. Such a thing was near unheard-of.

"They'll need a room of their own," Intef continued. "They're not to speak with the other prisoners or make bricks. I'll need you to look after them." He glanced around before continuing. "They're accused of another assassination attempt."

"A third one?" It had been two years since the discovery of the priest's involvement, and Joseph had heard nothing more. He had been beginning to wonder if that had been the end of it.

"Yes. As we thought, Dedumose was not the sole architect." Then the man raised a finger and pointed at Joseph. "Now. You're not supposed to know any of this, so don't go attempting to unravel any mysteries while they're here."

"Of course."

"That said, if you hear anything of interest, let me know." Intef glanced over Joseph's shoulder. "How are our two friends?"

"Unmanageable this morning. They'll not be making bricks today; they don't seem capable of doing so without starting a fight."

Intef snorted. "Keep them in their cells on water and a quarter-loaf a day until they come to their senses."

"As you wish."

The cupbearer and baker arrived that evening. Evidently they were to be allowed many of the finer things, for Joseph was instructed to bring them razors, soap, and water, along with some fish and fruit. He studiously refused to look at the food as he brought it across the courtyard. He hadn't laid eyes on such things in two years.

The two men were sitting in the room Joseph had emptied for them. The occupants had been dispersed amongst the other rooms, making for some crowding and complaining that the guards had quickly shut down. The two belligerents Joseph had let be in their own rooms, and everyone knew it.

Nodding as he entered, Joseph set the items down near the door. The men eyed the spread and then him with distaste. "Is that all the bathing-water we are to receive?" one asked. "I am filthy with the sweat of the day."

Joseph glanced down at the two jars. One of them was more than he was allowed in three days. He didn't even think he had used that much daily when he had been steward in Lord Potiphar's house. He bowed a little. "It is, sir. I'm afraid it is actually quite exorbitant by prison standards."

"I can see that," the second man said, eyeing him.

Joseph bit his tongue. "Is there anything else you require?"

"No," the first said firmly.

Declining to bow, Joseph left.

The men were not talkative, at least in Joseph's presence, and did not succumb to flights of madness, false or otherwise, as had Ranefer and Baufra. There was little to report to Intef regarding them over the next week. On a different front, the belligerents grew hungry enough to consent to work, if not to lay eyes on each other without screaming. Joseph kept them on separate work rotations and hoped each might eventually be able to have a room-mate to remedy the overcrowding.

He was looking over the latest prisoner lists for Tjaru. A boat would be ready at the end of the week for nine prisoners and three guards, which would have cleared rooms, except that he knew four prisoners were expected today and five more the next.

Joseph sighed and rubbed his beard. Intef allowed him a few moments with a razor every several months, and he gratefully sawed off most of his hair and beard, but it always quickly came back with a vengeance. He finally understood why Egyptians shaved and bathed like madmen. The heat made anything else near-intolerable.

Unexpectedly, the cupbearer and baker begin speaking in raised tones. Joseph looked up from his seat against one of the walls of the courtyard. They were in their room, as they always were, and he guessed they were going off about the rats again. The rodents were a constant nuisance, though not so bold as to be any real danger. Even so, the men were having none of it and often called him in to chase one out.

He walked over and peered into their room. The two men looked up from their seats on the ground, and Joseph was surprised not to see the usual anger or annoyance on their faces, but genuine dismay.

The three stared at each other for a long moment before Joseph ventured, for he felt he must say something to break the silence: "What happened? Why are you so distressed this morning?"

Looking at each other uneasily, the two men did not speak for some time. Finally, the baker, whom Joseph had learned was the less ill-tempered of the two, answered. "We have each had a strange dream, and there is no interpreter."

Joseph opened his mouth to answer and then stopped.

It was as if the world itself kept moving around him, and yet from far away, Joseph could hear, on the very edge of his understanding, a still, small voice. It spoke no words, only meaning. Uneasy, he tried to shake off the strange sensation, but found that it only grew. He felt that if he did not give words to it, the earth itself would cry out.

"The meaning of any dream belongs to God," he found himself saying and realized that he echoed his father's words from so long ago. He meant to continue his father's admonishment, to caution that interpreting such things was folly, but his tongue caught.

It was not what the voice meant for him to say.

"Tell them to me, please."

Astonished, the men gawked at him. Joseph stared back, thunderstruck by what he had just said. Yet somehow, he felt content, as though he had completed a task asked of him and completed it well.

Finally the cupbearer laughed. "Who is this God? You speak

well, foreigner, but I can tell you are not one of us. The gods of Egypt rule here, not your small deity."

"Hush," the baker snapped. "It is better than nothing. Tell him."

The cupbearer rolled his eyes. "I suppose participating in blasphemy is a small crime compared to the accusations leveled against us. Hear this then," he said. "My dream was vivid, like none I have ever before had. In it, there was a vine before me. On it were three branches, and they budded, flowered, and grew fruit. I admired the clusters of grapes, and the cup of the Pharaoh himself was in my hand. I took the grapes, pressed them into the Pharaoh's cup, and placed the cup in the Pharaoh's hand." The man looked up at Joseph, a challenge on his face. "So, man of God. What does it mean?"

Every part of Joseph screamed certainty that he should not know. How could he? And yet, like lightning, that still, small voice thrust meaning into his brain.

Stunned, a wild hope grew within him. Was this—God's doing?

Sudden guilt flashed through him. Why should he think such a thing? He knew the state of his prayers.

Trying to maintain a measured voice despite his whirling thoughts, he took a deep breath and slowly put to words the knowledge that had inexplicably entered his mind.

"This is the interpretation of it. The three branches are three days. Within three days the Pharaoh will restore you to his side, and you will place his cup in his hand, as you have always done." He looked at the man, and decided to seize the moment, even if it all came to naught. "When you see that this is so, please, remember me here. Mention me to the Pharaoh. You are right—I am a foreigner, from Canaan. I have done nothing here in Egypt to deserve to be in this place. I would only ask that the Pharaoh allow me to return home."

The baker whistled softly.

"Ha!" was all the cupbearer deigned to say for a long moment. Finally, he continued. "What a nice picture all that paints. Well, we shall soon see whether or not you are any good. Three days is not much time."

He made no mention of Joseph's request, and Joseph opened his mouth to reiterate, but the baker began to speak. "In my dream," he said eagerly, "there were three white baskets on my head. In the uppermost basket I carried all sorts of bread for the Pharaoh, but the birds came and stole it all away."

Like a thousand weights, the meaning fell on Joseph. He stared at the baker. Agape and struck with sudden cold fear at this gift that had appeared from the blue, his stomach turned.

"What is it?" the baker asked. He sat up straight, staring at Joseph. The cupbearer, roused, looked on.

Joseph swallowed. "This is the interpretation," he managed, voice hoarse. "The three baskets are again three days. But within those three days the Pharaoh will execute you at the stake, and the birds will eat your flesh."

The cupbearer scrambled to his feet, white. The baker roared wordlessly and lunged at Joseph, and Joseph, bewildered and horrified, hurried from the room. Guards rushed to the scene as the baker followed him out, shouting obscenities.

Joseph turned and watched, shaken, as the man was forced back inside.

Intef had actually ordered him to one of the rooms and bade him stay there. The door was not locked, indeed it hung open, but Joseph sat there in discomposure for some time. Leaning against the back wall, he listened to the scratching of a rat somewhere nearby, and the eternal sounds of brick-making continuing in the courtyard. His arms rested on his knees while his hands worried at a bit of cloth he had found on the ground. Heart pounding, in his mind there was nothing but turmoil.

Finally the prison-master stormed into view, blocking the light that streamed through the doorway. "What were you thinking?" he demanded. "Telling the baker he is going to be executed?"

There was no real way to explain it, the feeling that he could not have said anything else or the world itself might have screamed it

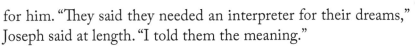

for him. "They said they needed an interpreter for their dreams," Joseph said at length. "I told them the meaning."

The other man stared at him, open-mouthed. "By Thoth," he said acerbically. "So you interpret dreams, too?"

Joseph shrugged uncomfortably, trying somehow to distance himself from the idea that he had predicted a man's death. "I did not like the interpretation any more that he did."

Leaning in the doorway, Intef shook his head. "*If* you are right, it would seem to me that an interpretation of that sort would best be kept to oneself."

"I could not lie."

Intef snorted. "Well, they will have me to serve them now, thank you very much. They don't want to lay eyes on you."

Joseph sighed and looked up. "I am sorry."

The other man snorted again and waved his hand before turning to leave. "What's done is done. We shall see if you are right."

Left to himself, Joseph leaned his head back against the wall and closed his eyes, utterly confounded.

"My God," he groaned. "I denied it at first, but this can only be Your doing. What is this You have done to me now?"

He prayed again, his mind in shambles that night. Intef had bidden him back to the room he shared with another prisoner. The man slept like the dead, and Joseph was left in the dark with his own thoughts. They spun uncontrollably in his mind, a mixture of dismay at what he had done and belief that, from God or not, it would all come to nothing.

Everything else had.

But there was also, he realized, for the first time in two years, a modicum of hope.

He whispered to the darkness. "My God, why did you put such words into my mind? Why did You force me to tell a man the day of his death?"

Joseph took a deep breath. His mind refused to steady. Trepidation crept into his voice. "Will it truly be that the cupbearer speaks to the Pharaoh, and I am freed? I am twenty-eight years old. Benjamin is fourteen. Dinah is thirty. My father is 119." His throat caught at the words.

"Is this Your will? Can I now return home? If it is so, then *why? Why did You force me to Egypt?*"

The days passed without incident. Joseph returned to his work, managing the prisoners and the transfers, and Intef saw to the cupbearer and the baker. On the third day, a new prisoner arrived, and desperate for space, Joseph placed him with one of the belligerents. Nothing happened. Inordinately pleased over the small victory, he missed the moment when the cupbearer and the baker were quietly removed from the prison.

That evening, as he sat gnawing on a piece of bread that was more stale than usual, Intef found him.

Joseph looked up.

The prison-master's face was white as the moon. He let out a long breath and stared at Joseph.

"The chief cupbearer has been reinstated," he said. "The chief baker is dead."

17

Joseph stared up at the mud brick ceiling in the dim morning light, every muscle and bone aching. Four years on the brick and sand of the prison floor had done that to him. Or maybe, he thought dryly, it was just age.

I am thirty years old.
Benjamin is sixteen.
Dinah is thirty-two.
My father is 121.

There was no mat to roll off, but he rolled over all the same, and onto his knees. His prayers had become more resigned over the years.

"My God," he murmured. "Comfort my father and Dinah. Give them peace in their lives. Deliver Benjamin from my brothers." He paused, and sighed. "What is Your purpose for me here? What is Your will? If there is none, why can I not return home? And if You have a will for me, *what is it?* I see nothing here. *Nothing.*"

He sighed again. Bits of his old prayers had returned over the years, and he had abashedly worked them in, hoping that God would take notice. Perhaps he had been angry, and he knew he was still bitter, but he was not disbelieving.

"If You have a will for me, then show it to me. Give me the strength to do it. Give me peace, for without You I have none." Taking a deep breath, he got to his feet.

It was the dead of summer, and lines of heat already crawled their way across the sunken courtyard, though the sun had barely risen. A ship to Tjaru had left yesterday, and the prison was near empty. Only three men were there besides himself, waiting for their trials. He would need to bellow for them to rise in a minute or two.

But for the moment, he took another breath and listened to the silence. No shouts of guards or prisoners, none of the relentless thudding and stamping and groaning of brick-making. He tried to force away the creeping wave of disquiet that always threatened at such times.

He had been here four years.

It had been two years since the strange incident of the cupbearer and baker's dreams. And the cupbearer, it appeared, had never mentioned his name to the Pharaoh—or had done so and it had not mattered.

I will never be free of this land.

He shook himself and grit his teeth.

Give me peace, for without You I have none.

The thumping steps of the guards echoed through the court-yard. Arriving from the low prison-building, they would relieve the guards who stayed at the top of the ladder overnight, and that would be Joseph's signal to awaken the prisoners for the day. But glancing upwards, Joseph frowned.

It was not only the guards, but Intef as well, and another man. Joseph cocked his head and watched. He never saw the prison-master at this time of morning. Intef caught his eye and began to hasten his pace. It was only a moment before he fairly slid down the ladder.

Concerned, Joseph strode towards him.

The man hurried forward and clenched Joseph's arms once he reached him. "You're to come with me."

Joseph took a step back, convinced he had heard the man's words incorrectly. "What?"

"Come, man!" Intef said. He stepped forward and fairly pushed Joseph towards the ladder.

"What?" Joseph said again, even as his feet began to move.

"Hurry!"

Completely bewildered and grasping for an explanation, Joseph began to wonder if somehow Intef were breaking him out of prison. The man urged him up the ladder, and as Joseph gained the top, he looked upward and nearly fell back down again.

The other man was Lord Potiphar.

Shaken, Joseph stopped short. Execution might be near.

"Up, man!" he heard Intef grunt from below.

Reluctantly, he crawled up onto the rim of the courtyard and stood to face his master.

"Lord Potiphar," he murmured, bowing.

The man looked him up and down, expression unreadable. "Joseph," he said finally.

Intef reached the top, and Lord Potiphar turned without another word. They followed him—Intef, several guards and the apprehensive Joseph—to the low front building of the prison. Entering one of the small, dark rooms, Intef shut the door behind them, leaving the guards in the corridor.

"It seems," said Lord Potiphar without preamble. "That two years ago you correctly interpreted the dreams of both the chief cupbearer and chief baker of the Pharaoh."

The prison-master gave Joseph a knowing look.

"I—" Joseph managed, stunned. He searched for words. "The interpretation came from God, sir. But I heard it."

"Regardless of the particulars, the Pharaoh is in need of your services."

Incredulous, Joseph stared at him.

"You will bathe and be taken before him within the hour." The man nodded to Intef. "I will be back shortly."

Lord Potiphar left the room. Joseph watched him go, wordlessly. The prison-master hurried Joseph across the corridor into the opposing room. Several jars of water lay ready, along with a razor, soap, mirror, eyepaint, and a change of clothes.

"Hurry!" Intef whispered. "Don't you want to be out of here for good? A direct service to the Pharaoh is always rewarded!" He slammed the door shut, leaving Joseph alone.

Joseph stood, immovable.

It was as though everything he had hoped and prayed for might actually come to pass, and he could not bring himself to believe it. He jumped when Intef banged on the door. *"Move, man!"*

Joseph moved. He bathed with a vengeance and shaved his beard to nothing and his hair down to less than a half-finger. The fresh shendyt and eyepaint somehow bolstered his brain to life.

Oh my God, are You truly going to accomplish this?

Guilt flashed through him.

What right had he to ask such things, now? After being so brazen in his prayers for four years?

He grimaced, resignedly continued, and stared at himself in the little silvered mirror before leaving the room. His face was thinner than he remembered, though all of him was rather lean from the prison, he realized. The white scars along his shoulders stood out starkly against his deep tan, and on his right hand, scrubbed clean, the slave's tattoo was again blatantly readable. Still, he must look more presentable than he had in years, and that was something.

Ushered by two guards to the front room, Joseph saw that both Intef and Lord Potiphar were waiting. Neither man said anything, though Intef's face betrayed some earnest anticipation. Lord Potiphar turned to go, and the guards urged Joseph forward. Intef slapped him lightly on the shoulder as he passed.

And with that, he walked out of the prison.

The world outside had not changed, though Joseph supposed he could not have expected it to. Whitewashed, mud-brick buildings still stood in dense rows; soldiers and lords, administrators and slaves milled about between them as they had always done. But then Lord Potiphar and the guards turned Joseph southwards down a road he had never traveled.

Instantly, Joseph was keenly aware of the full weight of his task.

The palace loomed before them, impossibly tall and shining white in the bright sunlight. Gold edged the many windows and doors, and over courtyard walls hung thick fruit trees. He looked up as they gained the top of a great stairway and passed onto a walk lined with colorful pillars the height of three men. The ceiling was densely painted with hieroglyphs and images, centuries of tales and myths.

The walkway led through a lush, sprawling courtyard where a brightly tiled pool dominated the center. Lords and ladies stood in low conversation, and servants and guards stood at ready. Many of the nobles looked up as they passed, several turning to whisper to those nearby.

Fighting down a spike of fear, Joseph hurried forward, for Lord Potiphar's pace had quickened. He heard the guards behind him do the same. Evidently the Pharaoh's request was known, for the crowd pushed forward behind them, towards the great doors they were now approaching.

Two guards, dressed in finery Joseph had not thought possible for mere soldiers, swung the doors open to allow them entrance. The crowd waited only a few moments before following them inside.

Within was a grand, many-pillared hall, with long, high windows, the largest he had ever seen. Hieroglyphs and murals covered the walls, and everywhere Joseph saw the flash of gold—in the bases and heads of the pillars, laid in between the blue stones that paved the floor, and on the great throne itself, standing on a high dais.

They walked towards the empty throne, and Joseph heard the crowd filtering into the room behind them, their whispers echoing off the high celling. The guards behind Joseph fell away into the crowd. Stopping several paces away from the high dais, Lord Potiphar knelt, and the entirety of the room did the same. Joseph quickly followed suit. The doors swung shut behind them, their carven wood allowing dappled sunlight to reach within the room, lighting the rich paintings and gilt like spots of fire.

The sound of footsteps echoed throughout the great room, and everyone bowed their heads. Joseph felt his heart begin to race.

My God, what is this? The prayer came unbidden to his mind, no longer able to remain suppressed by guilt.

A barrage of sudden realizations rocked him.

If God's purpose and will was for him to speak here, then Joseph had failed miserably before he had ever begun.

How could God be pleased with such brazen and capricious prayers as Joseph had offered up in the past four years? Further still, Joseph had lived all the time in Lord Potiphar's house convinced that God rewarded him for his faith and would do nothing else. As if his God were a dancing animal, pleased to perform for someone who gave it notice. He thought of Menkare, who had received Joseph's thanks instead of his God.

Shame filled him.

He could only hope, as he once had when he first arrived in Egypt, that his God might overlook.

My God. Please—I have already failed. Do not let me fail further.

The footsteps came nearer, and someone began to climb the stairs of the dais. Joseph's heart might as well have been in his mouth. The stones of the floor swam before his eyes.

He was about to speak for his God in a foreign land, to a man believed to be a descendant of Atum-Ra.

Please. My God—I see Your hand, even if I do not understand your purpose. If this is what You ask of me—do not let me fail You.

Do not let me fail You.

Ever again.

The room looked up. Joseph, breathless, quickly did the same.

A man whose aged face was like carven stone sat on the throne. A striped headdress of blue and gold covered his hair and a false beard sat on his chin. His white robes were ornamented with gold. Gems spread across his belt, collared necklace, and bracelets and rings. He looked down dispassionately at those before him.

On the steps to the dais stood a woman and two children—a wife, a daughter, and a son—all three in finery. They looked as aloof as the Pharaoh. Six servants stood near the scene, two waiting at attention and the others gently cooling the family with long gilded fans. Guards stood nearby.

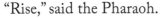

"Rise," said the Pharaoh.

Slowly, the room rose to its feet.

The Pharaoh's eyes fell on Joseph and then flicked to Lord Potiphar. "This is Joseph, the one of whom I have been told?"

"He is, your majesty."

"Bring him forward."

Lord Potiphar turned, and with a tilt of his head, bade Joseph follow. They moved toward the dais, almost to its first step, before Lord Potiphar knelt again, and rose. Joseph did the same, though his knees almost buckled. *My God, do not let me fail You!*

He stood on the left hand of his master and looked up at the Pharaoh. The man, whose face remained detached, spoke, and Joseph realized that though his face might be unreadable, tangible concern crept into his voice. "I have had a dream, and my magicians and priests cannot interpret it. I have heard it said by a man who has my ear, whom I trust, that you are one who can understand and interpret a dream. Is this so?"

Mouth as dry as sand, Joseph forced out an answer. "It is not in me to do so, but I have heard such interpretations from my God."

The Pharaoh's eyes darkened. "Cannot my priests do the same? I am the Living Horus. May I not hear the voice of my fathers, the gods of Egypt?"

Joseph swallowed. He knew instantly that his next answer would bring him swift justice. This was not God's way to freedom. It was only a test of faith after his time in prison and ridiculous misunderstanding of his God.

He would die not denying his God, at least. There would be purpose in it, somewhere. There must be. His life could not possibly be so useless as that.

"I do not know your gods, oh Pharaoh. I know One, the God of my fathers and my God. He is the only God, and He allows no others before Him."

His master stared at him. The room echoed with gasps and fierce whispers.

"You risk death with those words," said the Pharaoh darkly.

"I would do far worse not to say them, your majesty."

The man on the throne stared down at him, unmoving for a long moment. Then, unexpectedly, he put his chin in his hand. "I will tell you my dream. We will then see what power your God has."

Joseph and the entire room released an astonished breath as one.

Oh my God, Joseph prayed desperately. He felt as though a rock had fallen onto his chest. *Let me hear Your meaning as I did before.*

"In my dream," the Pharaoh said, "I stood on the bank of the Nile. Out of it came seven cattle, fine and well-fed. They grazed on the banks. Then, out of the river, came seven more cattle, yet these were poor and gaunt. I have never seen the like of their ugliness. They ate the seven fine cows, so that they were no more, but it did not aid them, for they were just as sickly and thin as before. I awoke, much troubled, and soon after fell into a second dream. Before me was a stalk of wheat, with seven good heads, ripe and full. But the east wind sprang up, and a stalk of seven more heads arose. These were thin, blighted and withered. They devoured the seven good heads, so that they were no more. And I awoke a second time."

The room was deathly silent before the Pharaoh continued. "Therefore, I told these things to the magicians and priests. But no one could interpret it for me."

Joseph feared that he would hear nothing—that the still, small voice had somehow never been from God and had only been the strangest bit of luck and coincidence. And, for a moment, there was nothing.

Then meaning slashed through his mind like a torch through the night.

He staggered ever so slightly, stunned at the revelation lying before him.

For it was nothing less than the doom of the world.

Hissed whispers flew back and forth amongst the nobles at his reaction.

"Your majesty," he managed, steadying himself with a deep breath.

"God has shown you what He is about to do. The dreams of Pharaoh are one and the same. Both the seven good cows and the seven good heads of wheat are seven years—good years, years of plenty. The seven ugly cows and the seven blighted heads of wheat are seven years of famine. Seven years of plenty will come, but after them will be seven years of famine, a famine so great and severe that the years of plenty will be forgotten, and the world will know nothing of plentiness. This thing is fully established by God, for Pharaoh has dreamed it twice. It will shortly come to pass."

Gasps and murmurs whipped about the room. Someone cried out in shock. Voices rose. The Pharaoh only looked at him, something in his eyes that Joseph did not understand.

His mind reeled. Why would God bring such a thing to pass? Why had his God revealed it to the Pharaoh of Egypt?

Joseph's brain unexpectedly settled, attempting to decipher it all but finding the purpose already laid out for him. Why it would happen, he still did not know, but the Pharaoh had been given warning so that Egypt might prepare. His thoughts raced.

"Oh Pharaoh," he said over the din. Slowly, as he spoke, the room quieted. "In light of this, it would seem wise to select someone with discernment to go out over the land of Egypt in preparation for this famine. Then they might collect one-fifth of each harvest grown in the seven plentiful years. Let it be stored under your authority in the cities. Then it may be opened in the years of famine and used as a reserve, so that your people will not perish."

The room was once again silent.

He looked around. Face upon face was staring at him, as if he had brought the sun down from the sky and claimed that it was something that could be held and measured.

Joseph looked back at the Pharaoh. The man regarded him a moment longer and then rose to his feet.

Every man and woman fell to the ground. Quickly, Joseph did the same. His breath came rapidly, and his heart pounded. The Pharaoh had not believed him.

The Pharaoh walked down the steps and stood by him. "Rise, Joseph, of Potiphar."

Slowly, Joseph gained his feet, looking around. The rest of the room remained on hands and knees. Bewildered, he looked to the Pharaoh, but he had turned to Lord Potiphar. "Of what crime was this man accused?"

Lord Potiphar looked up at them. "I have accused him of no crime, your majesty."

Silence continued to dominate the room.

"Is this why he was never sent to trial? Why then has he been in your prison, these past years? For it is two years at least since my cupbearer heard his dream interpreted."

Joseph pursed his lips and closed his eyes. The Pharaoh could not know what he asked. Finally, Lord Potiphar spoke. "My wife was—indelicate—in her behavior towards him."

The room broke into gasps and fierce whispering.

The Pharaoh's face was impassive. He turned to look at Joseph. Feeling that he should bow, but not certain he was supposed to after being told to rise, he could only assume the slave's posture. Hands folded, head slightly down. The Pharaoh held out a hand towards him. "He speaks the truth," he called out to the room. "I know it in my very soul. Where else may I find such a man, a man in whom is the Spirit of his God, who has shown me such things and given to him the interpretation?"

He turned and again looked at Joseph. "You say it is wisdom to set a discerning man over Egypt for this task. I say that your God, who will do this thing, has claimed you as that man. For as He speaks to you, there is no one as wise or discerning as you." He turned once again to the room. "I am Seshemtawy, He of the Two Ladies of Egypt, Sekhamaat, Hetepnetjeru, King of Upper and Lower Egypt, Khakheperre, Son of Atum-Ra, Senusret, second of that name.

"I name you free, Joseph, no more of Potiphar. I name you free and my vizier set over Egypt, and call you Zaphnath-Paaneah, *the God speaks and lives*."

18

The retinue behind the Pharaoh Senusret—his wife and children, the servants and guards, who had remained standing until this moment, dropped to their knees.

And Joseph stood, dumbfounded.

The Pharaoh continued to speak. "Without your consent no one may lift hand nor foot in all of Egypt. You shall be over my house, and the people shall be ruled according to your word. Only I shall be greater than you."

It was a dream.

It could only be a dream.

But it was not a dream when a horde of servants took him into an antechamber and dressed him in sandals and white linen robes finer than he had ever seen even Lord Potiphar wear. It was not a dream when a collar of gold and turquoise stones was placed around his neck or when the white khat headdress of the nobility was put on his head.

It was not a dream when the Pharaoh entered and placed his signet ring on Joseph's right hand. Or when he was walked back through the courtyard from whence he had first come, with guards and heralds shouting: "Bow the knee!" and all the men and women fell to their knees. It was not a dream when he was placed in a chariot behind two horses at once and driven through the streets of Itjtawy to the shouts of, "Bow the knee!"

And it was not a dream when he was taken to a house he did not recognize, was led through a lush courtyard, through a bewildering amount of rooms and corridors, and to a well-furnished bedroom.

The man who had led him inside bowed and shut the door.

Shocked, Joseph could only stand in place. He heard Intef's voice: *"Move, man!"*

Had that only been this morning?

But there was nowhere *to* move. Or rather, there was nowhere he was required to be.

How bizarre.

Reeling, he slowly sank down to the floor and pulled off his khat headdress. He leaned his head against the wall and blankly stared at nothing, openmouthed.

"My God," he finally managed. But no other words would come.

Joseph sat on the floor for a good hour, rooted to the spot with his thoughts unable to do anything more than be suspended in silent disbelief.

"My God," he eventually tried again, but there were no words to express the depths of his incredulity.

At length, he realized that despite being placed in a bedroom, it was not night—though evening was nearing—and also that he was hungry. Not that *hungry* had meant much in the past four years; it had become simply a vague, dull ache that arose at times and little more.

He managed to get himself to his feet and sidle to the door, replacing his khat. For some reason he found he had to screw up his courage to open it. Still, he did, and almost slammed it shut again when he saw the same man standing outside.

The man looked at him with an expression Joseph fancied was slightly bemused. He bowed. He was young and wore a dark wig. "Good evening, sir. My name is Anhotep—I am your steward."

Joseph fought the urge to bow in return. He wasn't supposed to do that.

What did one *do* when one was not meant to bow?

He finally nodded. "Of course, thank you, Anhotep." His mind finally put together the fact that the steward must have been stand-ing there the entire time, waiting for—whatever Joseph would do. Joseph put himself in Anhotep's position. To wait on a lord who had no idea how to be one?

Good heavens!

And where had this house come from? Even if it had not sat empty for long—he remembered the glimpses he had caught as he walked in—it had been nothing less than affluent perfection. He had seen servants moving about in orderly work and had smelled the aromas of clean air, and perfumes, and roasting meat. He looked at the man with sudden respect. "You have done very well today, I think," said Joseph. "It cannot have been easy."

He didn't know what he expected the man to do, but when he only bowed again and said: "Thank you, sir," Joseph found himself a little disappointed.

There was silence again for a moment.

Then Anhotep spoke. "If you'll follow me, sir, the evening meal is almost ready."

So he was ushered down several corridors until he entered the great room. He nearly stopped short. Twice the size of Lord Potiphar's and three times as grand, he sat at the large table and glanced around at the room furtively while meats and beers and plums and melons were fairly thrown at him. Stones in patterns of blue and green sparkled on the floor, and the walls and pillars glowed with images in white and gold and red. Everywhere the furniture shone with gold, and netted curtains, nearly as fine as spider silk, danced throughout the room in a breeze that came through the high windows.

He did not eat much, or rather, found that he could not. Whether that was because he was accustomed to the lack of food in the prison or because he found it highly disconcerting to have people standing about watching him eat, he was unsure. Eventually, he rose, not knowing what else to do, and returned to the bedroom.

Joseph shut the door and sat down heavily on the bed. Hands in his lap, he stared at the golden signet ring, the Pharaoh's cartouche in the center, and at the slave's tattoo, right below it. "My God," he breathed, some semblance of his thoughts finally trickling into words. "What is this You have done?"

He had, in so many words, told God that he did not believe there was any purpose for his time in prison, then challenged God to show him one.

And how could God's purpose have been anything like *this*? How could it have been? Since Joseph had arrived in Egypt, he had struggled. First, he had been angry. Then he had misunderstood his God. Then he had been bitter, unbelieving in his prayers. And further, he had been blatantly selfish in his unwillingness to acknowledge that God might have any plan better than Joseph's own wishes. How could God *reward* any of that with *this*?

"My God," he whispered. "I do not deserve this."

His mind flashed back thirteen years, to the dreams, near-forgotten until two years ago, that his father had thought so strange.

I saw eleven sheaves of wheat; I saw the sun and moon and eleven stars. All bowed down to me.

His eyes widened in shock, and he slowly pulled the khat from his head.

Had this been God's plan? God's purpose? Had he been shown it from the very beginning?

There could be no other explanation. No other meaning. For the country of Egypt had bowed to him that afternoon.

God had chosen him to do this thing, long ago.

Joseph slowly closed his eyes, the weight of it staggering, and repeated his prayer from that morning. "My God. Let me not ever fail You again."

Joseph awoke, and it was light. Decidedly so. He sat bolt upright. He had missed it—Pawura's bellowing, or Djaty's harrumphing, or the small sounds of morning filtering through a high window or a prison doorway. One of them. He had missed it, and now he was late and negligent.

Looking around and completely baffled by his surroundings, the events of the previous day finally trickled back into his mind. He fell back down on the bed in a daze.

He had not slept on a bed since he was seventeen.

Up. He must get up. He had no notion of the time, but he expected a vizier had far more to do than a head-prisoner or a house-steward.

Rolling off the bed, he took a deep breath, and knelt.

"My God," he whispered. He paused.

Did God forgive? The question that had come to him when he first arrived at Lord Potiphar's house again haunted his mind. He did not know. Clenching his eyes shut and grimacing, he spoke the prayer he had neglected in the prison. "Thanks and all glory be to You, for what You have done for me, for your servant—" his throat caught. "Your servant is not worthy of the least of Your mercies." He took a deep breath.

"Comfort my father and Dinah. Give them peace in their lives. Deliver Benjamin from my brothers."

He paused. To pray for his own deliverance was no longer right, for he was free. He was free and, it seemed, the second most powerful person in all of Egypt. His mind still reeled with the knowledge. "If it be Your will, God, let me see them once again, Benjamin and my father and Dinah." He paused for a second time.

It felt almost wrong to ask for such a thing with the knowledge he now had. Shameless, in light of his bitterness.

It would take a second miraculous act, for he could not leave this place with such responsibility as he now had.

But how could he not ask? He sighed.

"I am astonished and bewildered and *grateful* for what You have done by Your hand. I do not understand it. But my heart begs You to let me see them. *Please*, my God." He paused again, and finished. "In this task You have given me, give me wisdom in this day, for I need much, far more than I ever have before. And give me peace. Without You I have none."

Joseph slowly got to his feet and looked about the room. A small doorway led to a bathing-room with an antechamber of sunken stone footbaths and an inner room with tall pots of water and a corner paved in stone. He gladly used it before dressing in clothes and what he guessed was an appropriate amount of jewelry, which he found in the several trunks in the bedroom. He found a hand-mirror on a small table and a palette of eyepaint and, once done, sat down on the bed again and breathed.

My God, give me wisdom in this day.

I have none.

He stood and walked out the door.

Anhotep was standing there, and another manservant who was holding bottles of what looked like bathing oils. They both stared at Joseph in surprise before the man whisked the bottles behind his back. Anhotep quickly nodded, and the man scurried away. "Good morning, sir," his steward said, without missing a beat. He bowed.

Watching the other man disappearing down the corridor, Joseph's perplexity turned to understanding. He ought to have known; Lord Potiphar's manservant had helped him ready each morning. He frowned a little and then decided he did not care if he had made an error. Who needed help bathing, really?

"Good morning," Joseph answered, turning back towards the young man.

His steward was urging him down the corridor within the next moment. "The morning meal is ready, and there is a message from the palace. Shall I have it read it to you?"

"No, I will see to it myself, thank you."

Out of the corner of his eye, he saw the young man nod the tiniest bit, as if he had made a mental note of something. Perhaps he had been unsure if Joseph could read. Joseph grimaced internally, not envying Anhotep's position. It would have been easier for them both if they sat down and had a frank discussion about how things should be. But that would likely have been unseemly and an insult to Anhotep if Joseph asked to do so. As if Joseph thought the steward could only do his job with prompting and hints.

He managed some bread and melons for the morning meal and hid the waiting eyes of Anhotep and three other servants behind the scroll from the palace.

Joseph was to report after the noon meal. The time seemed excessive; he expected that would not normally be the case and that this was a leniency for his first day. He still had no real idea of the time but hazarded a guess that the morning was half-gone from the light streaming through the windows.

With the meal out of the way, Anhotep offered to show him the house and gardens. Having nothing else to do, Joseph accepted, and spent an hour being completely overwhelmed by the scope of what was apparently his. The garden was full of tall, thin palms and stout plum trees, surrounding a pool with yellow and green stones gleaming at the bottom. Lotus flowers floated serenely on the surface. Stables lined the courtyard, waiting for animals to fill them, and the house itself held no less than twenty rooms.

Stairs led up to the rooftop, boasting a serene view of the Nile, which could be accessed by a short path and stairway at the back of the courtyard. The servants' quarters were not even attached to the house, but sat in the back of the compound. There were many profitable fields associated with the house as well, Joseph learned, out toward the lake Mer-Wer in the Pa-yuum wetland. There were no slaves yet in the house, and for that Joseph was grateful. He could not have stomached it.

By the end of the tour, Joseph had to resist the urge to sit down and stare dumbly at it all. But, looking at the position of the sun, it would soon be midday.

"Shall you walk to the palace or shall I call the litter, sir?" Anhotep asked.

Joseph almost burst out laughing at the thought of himself in a litter. "I will walk, thank you, Anhotep," he managed. He turned a little when the steward called for some menservants and tried to straighten his face.

The four servants followed him out the gate, and Joseph was keenly aware that he would have no idea which way to turn. To his surprise, however, he found that it was not true. He had passed this house many times with Lord Potiphar, on his way to the administrative buildings and prison. Turning left down the street, he found that the four servants quickly enveloped him, two in front and two behind. He fought the urge to grimace.

This home was far closer to the palace than Lord Potiphar's, and within minutes they reached the gate of the administrative buildings. The guards bowed deeply when he passed. Not knowing what else to do, Joseph simply nodded.

They passed through the streets of the complex, and Joseph found, to his shock, that the crowds fell away before him. Many bowed and whispers flew back and forth. Perturbed, he tried to catch their words, but could not. Entering the gates of the palace, they continued up the grand stairway and into the main courtyard.

The nobles milling about near the pool stopped and bowed; he looked around, but no one would meet his eyes. A group of young women who had been standing on the pillared walkway before them quickly scattered to either side to allow him passage. Uneasy, Joseph found none of them would meet his eyes, either. He was about to look forward again, for it was all too disconcerting, when he saw that one of the young women, the farthest away from him, had raised her head and was staring straight at him.

Their eyes met, and Joseph realized that she must have thought him no longer looking in that direction. Her expression went from one of slight worry to sheer terror before she wrenched her gaze away. Stunned, Joseph quickly looked forward, deciding to force his gaze on no one else.

Am I—am I somehow now an object of fear?

His mind raced as they approached the great doors of the throne room. The guards again bowed deeply and ushered him away from the doors and through a smaller entry that opened to a long hall. His servants bowed and waited outside, and Joseph was left standing in the empty corridor. He glanced up and down the hall. It bordered the courtyard, wrapping around it with several entry points both from the inner palace and the outdoors. Its high ceilings were painted with gilt.

Joseph had waited for several minutes, wondering if there was something he ought to do that he was unaware of, when he heard footsteps. They were coming around a nearby corner, and he turned to see if it was the Pharaoh—but it was not.

It was Lord Potiphar.

He did not see Joseph at first; he was looking down at a scroll that he was reading. Joseph stood rooted to the spot, unable to think of anything to do or say, before the man finally looked up and stopped short, not three cubits from him.

His former master stared at him for a long moment before slowly bowing. Joseph gaped. When the man raised his head, Joseph was surprised to see resignation verging on despair written across his face. "Tell me what it is you will have done to me," Potiphar murmured.

Stunned, Joseph could only shake his head. He supposed he could have any number of things done to anyone, now. The thought was dizzying. He looked back at Potiphar. Had he been living in fear since that moment in the throne room yesterday?

The thought that he could do anything at all to Potiphar had never crossed his thoroughly bewildered mind, much less the idea that is was practically expected. He shook his head again. "I—do not wish to harm you," he managed.

The other man stared at him in obvious disbelief.

"I—" Joseph tried to think of a way to express his whirling thoughts. "How could you be expected to choose a slave's honor over your wife's?"

Potiphar grimaced and hung his head. "All the same," he

answered. "I have wronged you. And I have ruined my case further by not saying so to you before you became vizier."

Unsure of what else to say, Joseph stepped forward. He very slowly clasped the other man's shoulders. Potiphar did not move. "I wish no further ill on you," Joseph finally said quietly. "I think you have already suffered much."

Silent, Potiphar lightly clasped his shoulders in turn but did not meet his eyes. Then he stepped back, bowed deeply, and slowly walked past Joseph down the corridor. Stricken, Joseph watched the man depart.

A door opened near him, and he started. A man, standing in the ingress, bowed. "My lord Zaphnath-Paaneah, the Pharaoh is waiting to receive you."

Nodding, Joseph hoped he looked serene, but the weight of what he was about to do now fell squarely upon him.

My God. He recalled one of the first prayers he had ever spoken. *Lead me in a way that pleases You.*

He entered.

170

19

T hree men within bowed deeply when he entered, and Joseph, once again only able to guess at what he was meant to do, nodded. The Pharaoh stood near the back of the room, and Joseph approached him before bowing in turn. The other three men fairly crumpled to the floor in response, and Joseph wondered if he were not supposed to bow so deeply, for the others' sake.

Still, Pharaoh Senusret seemed pleased and the men unperturbed when they and Joseph rose.

"My new vizier," the Pharaoh said. He motioned towards the three other men. "Here is my son, Sonbe, the Lord General, and Khnumhotep, the Treasurer over Egypt, and Seneb, Overseer of the Granaries." All three again bowed, and Joseph wondered that the Prince Sonbe had not been in the great hall yesterday. There had only been the young boy and his older sister.

Pharaoh Senusret turned to face the wall of the antechamber and stood there thoughtfully. It was a long moment before he turned back to face them all. He looked at Joseph. "Seneb tells me that the granaries do not have the capacity to store such amounts of grain as you spoke of yesterday."

Joseph bowed a little and then turned to Seneb. "I am not surprised. For the present, however—have we granaries in each large city? Or at the very least, each nome?"

Seneb nodded. "We have least one in each nome, my lord, though it may be small. However, many are put aside for temple use only."

Mind working, Joseph turned to Pharaoh Senusret. "If it pleases

171

your majesty, it would seem best to first purchase or rent many places in each nome, to be used for storage, before the next harvest. It may be necessary to build more as well, even within the first year, but if there are some buildings already in place, the process will be simpler."

The Pharaoh nodded. "It is well thought of." He nodded to Seneb and Khnumhotep. "See to it that the vizier has full access to the treasury and granary records so that he knows how best to proceed." The two men bowed in acknowledgement, and the Pharaoh dismissed them with a wave of his hand. They quickly left the room the way Joseph had come, and he was left with only the Pharaoh and his son.

"I have spoken this morning with Potiphar," Pharaoh Senusret said to Joseph. "What is it you will have done to my captain of the guard?"

Joseph told himself that by now, he ought to be used to feeling completely blindsided by others' questions or actions. However, he was not. He shook his head and bowed a little. "Yes, your majesty —I saw him just a moment ago, in the corridor. I—" he paused. "As I told him, I wish him no ill. He has suffered enough by what has transpired."

The prince openly gaped at him, but the Pharaoh's face remained impassive. "It is the duty of the vizier to uphold the laws of Ma'at— her justice, honor, and truth. Do you deem this justice?"

Joseph considered. His father's words from long ago came to his mind. *There are three things God requires of those who follow Him—to act justly, to love mercy, and to walk humbly in the path God has given them.*

"Perhaps not, your majesty," he answered slowly. "Perhaps it is mercy. And that, together with justice, I think must be the duty of every man to uphold."

Sonbe's eyes flicked back and forth between them. Joseph tried to read the Pharaoh's face, but it remained like stone. He had no idea if his words were too bold.

172

Finally, the Pharaoh gave a rumble of approval. "You speak honestly," he said. "And that is the first principle of Ma'at. If you think thus, I will allow it."

Relieved, Joseph bowed again.

"I will let you see to the records now," Pharaoh Senusret continued. He swept away without another word and clapped his hands twice. A second door, though which Joseph had not come, was opened by a guard who had been standing outside. The prince bowed to Joseph before following his father. Then the first door opened, and another guard showed Joseph out.

He was quickly led down the corridor by two waiting menservants. They passed several doors and eventually entered a large room filled to the brim with scrolls. The treasurer and overseer of the granaries were within, as well as several scribes. With many bows, Joseph was shown to a selection of scrolls laid out on a table. He looked through them briefly.

When he came to the previous years' granary records, he frowned. Many residents had paid their taxes in grain, but many had not. He looked at the numbers. "Is it anywhere recorded the fraction of those who paid in grain, as opposed to those who paid by other means?"

Seneb shook his head. "No, sir."

Joseph frowned more deeply and looked farther down the papyrus. He could perhaps extrapolate the fraction in each nome, if the tax records were good enough. And from there he could calculate the average field yield from last year, within each province. The average from two or three prior years would be useful as well. It would take much time.

He considered the next steps. "Who can I send to speak to the merchants here in Itjtawy? Some of them may have storehouses they are willing to rent, or sell."

Khnumhotep bowed slightly. "I can send a man out, my lord."

"Very good." Joseph nodded, paused, and on an impulse, began to tightly re-wrap the scrolls he had opened before picking them up and turning to the two men. He wasn't certain if this would be allowed, but there was no point in refusing to test it. "I will be taking these for further study."

The men in the room simply bowed.

Joseph had to force down the bit of heady rush that stole through him. "Please send your man to me once he has completed his enquiries."

Another bow from the man, and Joseph left the room, clutching the scrolls. He walked down the corridor, blowing out a breath in bewilderment as he went. It would be easy to become petty with such treatment. When he reentered the large courtyard, the four menservants surrounded him again, but not before offering to take the scrolls. Joseph declined. The least he could do was carry scrolls.

They passed again through the courtyard, and once again men and women bowed, and no one would meet his eyes. It was the same as they walked through the streets outside the palace. He glanced furtively in the direction of the prison as they passed. Had he truly woken there just yesterday morning?

Reaching the house, they entered the courtyard, greeted by Anhotep. Joseph felt a small kind of relief. His steward, for whatever reason, was one of the few people in the city who would look him full in the face.

What sort of talk was happening about him?

When Joseph indicated that he planned to pour over the scrolls for some time, his steward nodded and carefully questioned him about the midday meal.

Midday meal? Joseph hadn't even thought of it; he was not in the least bit hungry.

He thought he could have knocked Anhotep over with a feather when he asked how much food had been prepared and if the great room had been made ready for a meal yet?

Standing up a little straighter, Anhotep answered, "None of that bears any considering, sir."

Joseph cocked his head a little. It was a pretty answer, and certainly the correct one to give, but it could not be *true*. He wondered if Anhotep knew anything of his past. Finally, he nodded. "Very well. I am happy to sit for the meal if all is ready. But *if* the great room has not been prepared, I will take a small plate in the study." He had seen the small room on the tour that morning. With high windows on two sides, it reminded him of the scribe's room in Potiphar's house.

If Anhotep felt any emotion, he did not show it. He led Joseph though the apparently unready great room and several corridors before bowing at the entrance to the study. Joseph entered and let out a long breath, setting the scrolls down on the large table that sat within. It was not tall, but cushions and a stool were spread around it. The walls of the room were bright white, and a pattern in yellow, blue, and green flowed where they touched the ceiling.

He sat down to work.

The next morning found him awake some time earlier. There was a swallow's nest somewhere near one of the high windows in the bedroom, and their small trilling sounds called him to wakefulness. The morning went far more smoothly, though he outstripped Anhotep and was sitting there in the great room perusing a scroll when the steward walked in. His steward started but otherwise said nothing.

Retreating to the study after the meal, Joseph poured over the tax records from each nome. He'd accrued a large pile of pottery shards and was scratching cuneiform calculations on them, one after another. He knew by now that he could have an army of scribes arrive instantly to do it all for him, but then he would never learn the details and circumstances of each nome. The provinces were all very different from one another.

Anhotep appeared at the door. "Sir, you have a visitor."

Joseph looked up, surprised. Who in heaven's name would be visiting him? "Send him in." He waved a hand and prepared to meet a stranger.

175

Except it was no stranger.

It was Djaty.

He stood up in delight, but to his shock, Djaty bowed. Joseph quickly tore off his khat and stepped forward, clasping the man's shoulders. "No, don't do that," he fumbled. He pulled the man into an embrace. Djaty chuckled, and the scribe pounded him several times on the back.

"It is good to see you, boy."

Joseph stepped back with a grin. "What brings you here?"

"Ah, well," Djaty said with a strained look. "The Lord Potiphar and the lady are off to Memphis for an extended visit. They will have little need of my services there, so I am here, with his blessing, to assist you however you may need in the meantime."

Surprised, Joseph shook his head slightly. "Well, I don't have a scribe here as of yet, but Djaty—I don't want you *working* for me."

The scribe pursed his lips and raised an eyebrow. "Joseph," he said dryly. "I will tell you something. I am working for you, no matter where I stand. The entire country is."

Rubbing the back of his neck, Joseph had to laugh a little. He supposed it was true. "Well," he conceded, "if it is what you wish."

Djaty nodded and smiled. Then he happened to glance down at the work spread over the low table. His eyes fell on the pottery shards. He raised his hands and groaned. "This nonsense, again from my student?" he exclaimed, waving at the cuneiform. "On *official business?*"

Joseph smiled. "Not on official business, yet. I'll record the necessaries in hieratic when I've finished."

"Or I can do it for you. In hieratic, the first time."

Grinning now and shaking his head, Joseph again took a seat at the table and motioned for Djaty to do the same. "I'd appreciate that, but I'm trying to learn about each nome by doing the calculations."

"Hmm," Djaty sat back. "Well, I am at your disposal."

It was a strange thing to hear. Joseph sat in silence for a moment.

"Djaty," he said finally. "Are Lord Potiphar and the lady gone to Memphis because of everything that has happened here?"

"Of course they are. The row they had the night you were made vizier was a thing to hear. They were both near-panic. What they expected you to do, I cannot say. But they certainly did not expect *nothing*. Now they simply want to escape prying eyes."

Joseph pressed his temples. "You know that I never harmed the lady." It was almost a question.

The scribe snorted. "Of course I do. The entire charade was ridiculous. Anyone who wasn't convinced became so once you were not killed. But it was quite hushed up outside the house. That is why they left; now everyone has eyes on them. Public scandal is a vicious thing."

Nodding slowly, Joseph sighed.

Djaty leaned forward. "You look tired."

Did he? He felt more rested than he had in years. He waved a hand and looked up. "I am all right. It is good to see a friend. Most people seem to hold me in some kind of dread."

The scribe regarded him seriously. "You have done something rather frightening. To speak for your God, who is going to send the world into famine? To seemingly be the sole person who can save us all? That is quite a thing."

Joseph drew his mouth into a thin line and sighed.

Khnumhotep's man arrived late the next afternoon. He bowed and handed Joseph a small roll of papyrus. On it were the names of several merchants who were willing to rent or sell storehouses, the locations of each written next to them. Most were on the northern edges of the city, along the Nile. "Thank you," Joseph said presently, handing it to Djaty for his perusal. "Tell your master I will visit the storehouses over the next few days." The man nodded and bowed, but he was only gone for a moment before Anhotep appeared.

"A message from the palace, sir. You're needed at once."

Nodding, Joseph stood and left Djaty to his work calculating how much could be spent yearly on such matters. He was soon on his way to the palace, the customary four men surrounding him. Once they arrived, he was ushered down the long corridor to a room he had not yet entered and shown inside.

Pharaoh Senusret stood there, as did three others—an older man and woman, and a young woman whose eyes remained downcast. The family, as it seemed, bowed as he entered.

"I have before me Potiphera, the High Priest of Atum-Ra in Heliopolis," said the Pharaoh. The man bowed deeply again. "His daughter, Asenath, will be your wife."

20

Joseph nearly choked. This time the young woman bowed. He looked at the family, then back at Pharaoh Senusret. There was nothing he could say, nothing that could be done, for this was very clearly the doing of the Pharaoh, who stood quietly, gauging his reaction. He swallowed hard.

"Pharaoh is gracious."

Before he knew what was happening, Pharaoh Senusret placed a marriage contract on the table. Potiphera signed, for himself and for his wife, as Joseph expected. Then Asenath stepped forward and signed for herself. He watched the penstrokes she made, firm and quick. She was literate. Many women were not.

She held the pen out to him, still not raising her eyes until the very moment he took it. Her gaze flicked up to meet his, and he recognized her. She was the young woman from the courtyard, the one who had looked at him.

Even now, there was terror in her face.

Clenching his jaw in sudden distaste, he glanced over the document. The Pharaoh seemed to have worked out all the particulars; evidently he would be given thirty deben of silver and four camels for the marriage, and in exchange Joseph would provide twenty deben of silver. Resignedly, he signed "Zaphnath-Paaneah" at the bottom. He set the pen down, and it was done.

The Pharaoh put her hand in his, and Joseph found it was shaking. His mind flashed to Dinah, returning from Shechem, the moment now seventeen years past. He saw her face—hollow, empty, joy stolen by a man who had taken it from her. He almost dropped the woman's hand as if it burned.

"May Hathor bless your union," the Pharaoh said. "In two days' time, you shall be celebrated."

Joseph bowed, and Asenath did the same, but not before he quickly dropped her hand. They were now obviously meant to leave. Joseph did so, wondering what the woman would do. He found she walked silently by his side.

He stole a glance at her as they moved down the corridor. She was very beautiful, he admitted to himself, with eyes painted in black and green, and gold woven throughout her hair, but her face was strained beyond what he thought possible.

Stepping out into the heat of the courtyard, Joseph almost stopped short, for out of nowhere a litter had appeared. They were urged into it by Joseph's four menservants and several others he did not recognize. Finally mastering his wits, he managed to offer her his hand as they entered. She touched it, but only for a moment.

He stepped in and closed only the thin inner curtains. The heat was intense, though the purple light of sunset had already arrived.

The gaggle of servants lifted the litter, and they were off. The platform tilted oddly and rocked like the deck of a boat. Joseph resisted the urge to grimace—he'd ended up in a litter after all.

Inside was all smothering heat and even more smothering silence. Joseph glanced again at Asenath, who still kept her eyes downcast. He tried to think of something to say, but the only thing he could come up with was to introduce himself, and she already knew full well who he was.

Who he was. The thought lambasted him like a stampede of cattle. Aside from everything Djaty had said, he was a foreigner, a former slave, a former prisoner, and formerly accused of rape.

Good heavens, no wonder she is petrified.

He was surprised she'd taken his hand at all a moment ago.

So he let her be. When they arrived at the house, a crowd of servant girls who he assumed to be hers greeted her and led her away.

Joseph stood watching the scene in something like bewilderment for a long moment. Trunks had arrived in the courtyard and servants were hurrying back and forth. He watched one maidservant rush by holding a black cat he did not recognize. Then he caught sight of Djaty, who was standing under the colonnade at the front of the house, openmouthed and with one hand on his head.

Joseph wanted to pull off his khat and fan his face with it to clear his mind, but he knew that would have been unseemly.

"Sir?"

He started and turned to see Anhotep standing nearby. His face was calm, but the expression of his eyes was ever so slightly flustered.

"My lord, are you well?"

Clearing his throat, Joseph managed: "Yes—yes, I am, thank you." Suddenly he found he wanted to capitalize on the moment, tell the young man that he was doing an excellent job of things despite the chaos. Treat him as a friend. But that too, would have been unseemly.

Wouldn't it?

Then he decided that he didn't care. If he began to worry all the time about seemliness, he would stop getting anything else done. And right now he needed a distraction.

"I expect you are as surprised as I am," he finally said, and quirked a strained smile at Anhotep.

His steward actually gaped a little at how freely he spoke. "No—yes—sir," he finally answered, as if agreement were the only thing he could express.

Joseph had to resist the urge to purse his lips a little, but then decided that he ought to expect little else, at least right now. "I'll let you see to it," he said. "You have done well."

Anhotep bowed and turned away, leaving Joseph standing in the courtyard.

His thoughts, freed from the conversation, instantly spun into a whirl. What was he to do? He cast about for a solution and seized on the idea of quietly returning to the study.

181

But it was not to be.

One of the new maidservants approached him with a bow. "My lord, the Lady Asenath is ready for you."

If the ground had opened up and swallowed him right then and there he would have thanked it.

My God—how is this Your will?

He nodded to her distractedly. He wanted nothing more than to run, but it was better to somehow show Asenath that he meant her no harm, and further, that he had absolutely zero intention of touching her. His stomach knotted, and he made his way hesitantly to his bedroom and pushed open the door.

Asenath was sitting on the bed, arms crossed around herself. The outer panels of her white dress spread out around her like ibis' wings. She was beautiful.

She was also terrified.

Joseph almost turned heel and fled, but he stopped himself. What good would it do? It would only extend her misery.

My God, help me!

Slowly, he shut the door behind him and slid down to sit on the floor in front of it.

He sat, for he did not know how long. But at length, he glanced up, and saw Asenath staring openly at him from her seat on the bed. Her eyes darted quickly away. Fear had not left her gaze, but he saw that there was now something more in it—perhaps perplexity.

He seized the chance. "Lady, I will not harm you."

She did not answer, dark eyes wide as they stared at the floor.

"Lady, if you say the word, I will leave this room at once. I will not harm you."

Her mouth opened just a little, then snapped shut.

Silence filled the room.

Joseph sat for a moment longer, and making the decision, rose to leave.

There was a gasp, and a smacking sound as if something had hit the stones of the floor. He turned and started in dismay. The woman had flung herself off the bed and fallen to her hands and knees. Her mouth began to work and she looked as though she might burst into tears. Far different from her silent terror, it was infinitely more disturbing.

"Forgive your maidservant," she gasped, "for failing to please my lord, and treat her kindly, though she has been remiss."

Joseph gaped at her. He knew what she had expected of him, but had not thought she would blame herself for his actions. He slumped back down to the floor. "Lady," he said helplessly. "You are very beautiful. But I will not force you." A part of him shuddered. "I have seen a woman to whom it has been done. I will not see another."

She did not move.

My God, help me.

He stared at her, not knowing what else he could say. But then Asenath spoke. Her words were breathless, but clear enough.

"They say you can see into the souls of men and tell them the day of their death. They say your God has given you power to bring about the end of nations."

Skin crawling, the words filtered into his mind. *This* was the reason for all of the fear that followed him? He leaned weakly against the wall and shook his head. "It is not so," he answered. "I am not a god; I am only a man, and the only power it seems I have is to hear my God speak if He chooses it."

She was silent again for a long moment. Then she shifted, sitting slowly back on her knees but with eyes still locked on the smooth white stones of the floor. "Then why has your God chosen to punish the world with famine?"

Taking a deep breath, Joseph shook his head again. "I do not know. But Egypt will remain safe. God has seen to it."

They sat in silence for some time. Finally, Joseph shifted a little, trying to think of something, anything to say. He glanced again at Asenath, and though she still looked toward the floor, he thought he noticed a sort of dissatisfaction in her face. He cocked his head slightly and took the opportunity. "Have you more questions for me, Lady?"

Her eyes flicked towards him for a single moment. "None, my lord."

"I think it is written on your face."

Asenath bit her lip and looked away. "Did you rape my lord Potiphar's wife?"

"No."

She looked back at him. Met his eyes. She seemed—not unconvinced, but still dissatisfied.

"Has not he said as much?" Joseph asked. "And is being put in prison the usual punishment for slaves who rape their master's wives?"

She looked away again, but not before he saw her eyes glance towards the tattoo on his right hand. "No," she said finally. "And why then did you not punish him?"

Again the idea that he ought to exact revenge on Potiphar. He sighed a little. "He and his wife have been disgraced. I do not wish to do more to either of them. What would be the point of it? I would take no pleasure in it."

The woman stared at him, blatantly. Almost disbelieving. "Where are you from?" she asked.

"Canaan."

Her face was inscrutable. "Your ways are not like ours."

He nodded, just a little. "They are the ways of my God."

"The one who will punish the world?"

"The one who sent the Pharaoh dreams so that Egypt might be saved."

Asenath looked to the side, considering.

Joseph glanced upwards towards the high windows. The light had gone and only a few lamps lit the room, casting high shadows upon the walls. "The evening meal will be ready," he said quietly. "Will you come?"

She was still for a long moment. Then, almost resignedly, she got to her feet.

He escaped to the study after the awkward meal. Djaty had evidently fled after Joseph's return, and he rather dreaded what the scribe might say when he next saw him. Pouring over Djaty's calculations regarding what the treasury might spare for purchasing or renting storehouses in Itjtawy, he did some preliminary projections for materials and labor if, in years to come, they might need to be built.

Then he returned to working out the average crop yields by nome, and had almost finished averaging one with the greatest yields yet when he felt his head nod. He almost dropped his pen.

Shaking his head a little, he set the pen down and rubbed his face. Asenath had, apparently, gone to bed some time ago. He cringed at the thought of returning to that room. Blowing out a quick breath and picking up the pen, he was halfway through the next calculation when he realized he'd done it all wrong. His eyes blurred.

Resignedly, he stood up and found he could not force himself to move from the room.

Then he made a decision. It would be the talk of the house if someone saw him in the morning, but what did it matter? He pulled off his khat and jewelry and set them on the low table, and then stretched out on the cushions.

He was quickly asleep.

21

He awoke before dawn, disoriented, before the events of the previous day came rushing back. Groaning a little, he took a moment to gather his wits.

Then he rolled off the cushions and onto his knees, taking a deep breath.

"My God, thanks and all glory be to You, for what You have done for me, for Your servant is not worthy of the least of Your mercies.

"Comfort my father and Dinah and give them peace in their lives. Deliver Benjamin from my brothers.

"My God—give me wisdom this day, and strength, and peace—for what am I to do about this woman? Please show me. What is Your purpose in this?"

His stomach twisted a little at his words. Maybe the purpose of this was to firstly let him flounder a bit after what he had done in prison.

Sighing, he stood and gathered his things, realizing that if he hastened quietly, none of the servants would be the wiser regarding what had occurred. Anhotep had quickly realized that Joseph preferred to take care of the morning and evening routines himself, and had stopped sending menservants to the family rooms before the morning or after the evening meals.

Although— He paused. *Maidservants might be expected to come around now. Hopefully not at this time.*

Holding a small lamp, he stole down a corridor to a washroom connected to rooms that currently had no use. Joseph had noticed that pots of water and jars of soaps and oils had begun appearing and refilling consistently in the washroom he used, and he hoped this one would be similar.

He fumbled around in the dim light of the unfamiliar washroom and discovered that there was water, but nothing else. He grimaced, but it was better than nothing at all.

The sun was beginning to rise when he finished. Joseph hurried back down the corridor to the bedroom—and hesitated.

He had to; there was no choice. As vizier, he could not wear the same clothes two days in a row. Looking down at the ones he had put back on, he grimaced. Especially not clothes he had slept in. Gritting his teeth, he quietly tapped on the door.

For a moment nothing happened, and he thought he would have to rap more loudly. But then the door opened the tiniest bit. Asenath looked up at him, eyes wide, before pulling open the door for him.

"I'm sorry to wake you," Joseph murmured as he stepped in. He moved quickly to one of the trunks. "I only need some clothes."

"No, I—" she paused, looking rather taken aback, and watched him. "I was awake."

She continued gawking as Joseph found clothes and jewelry for the day and snatched up the palette of eyepaint and hand mirror.

"Where did my lord sleep?" she finally ventured.

"The study." He glanced at her and found that she was shaking her head, ever so slightly. "I'm off today to view some storehouse locations; you'll have the house to yourself. Please, do whatever you wish."

Openmouthed, she watched him go.

"This will be the place," Anhotep was saying. The young man shaded his eyes against the sun and glanced from the storehouse down to the river, which flowed on the other side of several fields, cutting a line of deep blue through the land. Joseph had requested that

Anhotep come; an extra pair of observant eyes was always useful. Three other servants stood nearby. Evidently four was to be the number of his permanent entourage.

Joseph looked at the old, mud-brick building critically. It was smaller than he had hoped. "Perhaps it can be expanded if we choose to use it," Joseph said. Anhotep nodded and scribbled on the papyrus he was holding.

Turning to look in the direction they had come, Joseph sized up the distance between the storehouse and Itjtawy. It was not too far; fifteen minutes' leisurely walk. He looked out at the slaves working in the fields. *Or five minutes' run.* It was not far enough to discourage thievery, certainly. There would have to be a permanent guard.

He glanced again towards the Nile. The owner had evidently once used the location to store goods headed up or downriver, for there was a dusty path leading towards the water, and a small dock at the end of it. "Remind me which merchant this belongs to?" he asked.

Anhotep looked down at the papyrus again. "His name is Nebit."

Joseph frowned. Hadn't he hired a Nebit, years ago?

Then, Joseph noticed a man coming up the road from Itjtawy, if not in a flat run, then something close to it. A servant puffed along behind.

"My lord!" the man called as he approached. He stumbled forward the last few cubits before bowing deeply and stuttering out his next words. "My apologies, I did not know you meant to be here today."

Joseph shook his head slightly. "Don't trouble yourself. I am only looking at possible storehouse locations."

Nebit bobbed his head up and down, but like the others, would not meet his eyes. "Of course, of course. Would my lord like to look inside?"

Joseph studied the man. He *did* know him. He was the first merchant Joseph had ever hired, ten years ago, for the prisoner transportations to Tjaru. He was inclined to raise an eyebrow in resigned amusement at how desperate to please the man was. It was a far cry from their first meeting. Joseph doubted the other man remembered him. "Certainly."

The man quickly moved towards the door and stuck a large key into the lock. The hinges creaked as the door swung open. Joseph and Anhotep stepped forward, and the other men followed them inside. Joseph looked around the space. It was not large, but it could do for a start.

At that moment, a group of rats charged out from around a large pile of broken pottery that sat in the center of the room. Nebit and his servant yelled. Joseph's servants followed suit and even Anhotep danced around the horde of rodents. Only Joseph remained still, watching the rats dispassionately. After the rats had vanished into the dark corners of the room, he realized all his companions were staring at him. They quickly averted their eyes.

Clearing his throat slightly, Joseph asked: "Merchant Nebit, how much would you sell this place for? Unfortunately, I think the rats may necessitate a lowering of price." It was too good of an opportunity now. The rats would make it sell cheaply enough to cover much of the expansion costs.

Nebit cast a quick glance around him and then rubbed his chin with a sigh. "Fifteen deben perhaps, my lord—in silver."

Joseph had to bite his tongue back from the immediate instinct to name a lower price. Twelve would be sufficient and reasonable, but there was no way for him to engage in such bargaining now. Nebit would likely sell it if he asked for two deben. Or one. He thought carefully. Perhaps there was another way to maintain fairness. "I shall see what the other merchants in the area will sell theirs for. I will send word to you if I am interested."

"My lord," Nebit said quickly, with a deep bow. "Perhaps ten deben?"

"Suppose we agree on twelve. And I'll see you receive your payment today."

He thought Nebit seemed a little bewildered at the reverse

haggling that had occurred, but the man again bowed deeply and expressed his gratitude before leading them back out into the heat and sun. He soon departed.

Joseph turned to Anhotep. "We'll need to do something about the rats, aside from enlarging the building."

To his surprise, his steward smiled slightly. "Certainly, sir."

Joseph returned very late that evening after seeing two more storehouse locations that were not satisfactory. Asenath had already eaten and was sitting on the cushions, quietly talking with a maidservant, when he entered the great room. A lyre rested in her lap, and the black cat he had seen yesterday sat curled at her feet. Its steady green eyes turned to watch him enter. The maid stood and bowed, and Asenath nodded slowly.

Joseph wanted nothing more than to escape to the study, but Anhotep had obviously instructed the servants to serve a second full meal, since several quickly burst from a passageway to lay the table with food. He sighed inwardly and sat down. Knowing he ought to say something, he cast about for a topic that was innocuous enough to discuss in front of the servants.

"Your day went well, I hope?" he finally said to Asenath.

She nodded slightly. "It was well enough, thank you. And yours?"

"Also well enough. Thank you."

There must be more that could be said. Something, anything at all. He finally thought of the lyre. "Do you play?" he asked.

She quickly looked down at it. "Yes—would my lord like to hear it?"

Inwardly he berated himself. Of course that would be the response, and there was now little way to mitigate it. "Only if it pleases you," he finally replied.

She immediately prepared to play, and Joseph knew there would be no way to tell if it pleased her or not. Still, when she struck the first sweet notes, and her face softened a bit in appreciation,

Joseph knew at least that she was a lover of the art. Asenath played for some time, weaving between one song and the next, until his meal had finished.

He wondered, as she ended the last strains of her final song, if she had continued playing on purpose, for no other conversation had been required.

"Thank you, you play very well," Joseph said to her as the meal was being cleared away. She lowered her head a little in acknowledgement but said nothing.

Joseph could feel the eyes of the servants darting back and forth between them. He quickly excused himself and retreated to the study.

It was some time later when he was roused from his work by the sound of a throat clearing. He had papyrus and pottery shards spread all over the table, and four lamps had been lit, their light playing on the white walls. The sounds of the house had quieted, and he knew everyone was retiring for the night.

So he looked up in surprise at the sound. It was Asenath, standing in the doorway and holding the cat tightly in her arms, almost like some sort of shield. Surprised, he stood quickly and motioned for her to enter. He wondered if he ought to replace his khat, which he had thrown haphazardly onto the table when he entered but then decided that would look rather absurd. "What can I do for you?" he asked, and, not knowing what else to say, continued, "Will you sit?"

She looked around silently before taking a seat on a cushion opposite from where Joseph had been sitting. He sat in turn and waited for her to speak. It took some time, for she opened her mouth, closed it again, and stroked the cat silently for a long while before beginning. "My lord, forgive me if I am too forward, but I am at a loss to understand you."

Joseph paused. "How so?" he ventured after a moment.

Her lips became an even tighter line than they already were, and she looked him straight in the eye. "It has been my understanding

191

that marriages not made from love can be difficult, but I have never heard of one beginning in this manner."

He actually found that he laughed a little. Running a hand through his hair, he nodded. "Neither have I."

She must have expected more of an explanation, for she remained silent and eyed him dubiously. Finally he shifted uncomfortably. "Would you prefer that I had acted differently on some point?"

"What would you prefer?"

Joseph gave a helpless bark of laughter. "I am beginning to think I would prefer my opinion not to be the pinnacle of everyone's concern."

Asenath actually gaped at him.

Looking back at her keenly, Joseph asked: "Why is that so difficult to believe?"

"Because," she answered. "Because—no one talks that way, my lord."

"And am I the only one who thinks that way?"

A measured look. "Perhaps."

Joseph gave her a measured look in return. He thought he had hit upon something. "Do you believe me?"

She hesitated.

"I would beg you answer honestly."

Looking away for a long moment, she glanced towards the dark windows. "As I said, my lord," she murmured finally. "I do not know what to make of anything you have done. Or said."

"Perhaps," Joseph said slowly, "in time, we can come to understand one another."

Asenath sat, stroking the cat for some time. "It is not lost on me that I might have been treated very differently upon coming here," she said finally. "If I may—who was the lady? The one who was—mistreated?"

"My sister," Joseph tightened his jaw and looked away. "She was fifteen."

Her lips pursed, and she looked down. "Where is she now?"

Taken aback, Joseph shook his head a little. "I—I do not know. I have not seen her in thirteen years."

192

To speak those words aloud was unexpectedly difficult.

The next question hung the air, but Asenath appeared unwilling to ask it. Joseph shifted again. "My father has twelve sons," he began slowly. "I am the youngest but one. He favored me, and when I was seventeen, my brothers—" He actually had to pause. Throat tightening, he swallowed. "My brothers, I suppose, decided they were done with me. They sold me to some merchants. That is how I came here."

It was a moment before Joseph realized that she was the first person to whom he had ever told that story. He looked up at her and saw that her brow was knitted in consternation.

"What an abominable thing," she breathed at length. "If this is true, then your God has smiled on you. No other man has risen from slavery to become vizier."

A wave of guilt slashed through Joseph. For it seemed indeed that God had smiled on him, and he still could not understand why. "Perhaps," he said.

"The sight of me gave no pleasure to my own father," Asenath murmured after a moment. "I am his only daughter; there were no sons. He wished for a priest to serve after him in the temple of Atum-Ra. I was of little use." Her face tightened again, and she unexpectedly rose to her feet. Still clutching the cat, she looked down at him. "I came here to tell my lord that he ought not to sleep on the floor."

Joseph attempted to keep himself from gaping at her. "If you wish it," he answered slowly. "But will you call me by my name?"

"Yes, Zaphnath-Paaneah."

He realized with a bit of surprise that she had no reason to know his true name. "No—that is not my real name. Joseph."

She paused, then attempted the strange name. "Joseph." Then she surprised him once again. "What does it mean?"

"May God Add."

Again pursing her lips a little, she nodded. "If you are Joseph to me, then I must be Asenath to you."

"Of course, Asenath."

22

Djaty did not appear the next morning, and for that Joseph was grateful. He did not think he could manage any questions about the delicate situation that was his marriage, well-meaning though the scribe would certainly be. But the celebration was to be that evening, and perhaps Joseph would have to answer questions anyway. Or perhaps no one would say a word to him or even look him in the eye.

It had been strange the previous night, each of them on the very opposite edges of the bed, Joseph hardly daring to move so as not to startle her. Asenath was rigid. When he had rolled off the bed in the morning to whisper his prayer, she watched him in openmouthed astonishment. "Where is your God?" she asked, looking around the room.

Explaining that there was no carven image of his God had taken some doing.

He worked alone for some time in the study, but was roused by Anhotep, who leaned his head around the doorframe. "Sir? Your four camels have arrived."

Once in the courtyard, he watched them coming through the gates, coaxed along by a group of servants. One of the animals spat.

Joseph caught sight of Asenath, watching from under a nearby fruit tree, when her cat, perturbed by the scene, leapt from her arms. "Aya!" she exclaimed.

The cat dashed by him, and he scooped her up. She yowled a little in protest, and Asenath hurried over. "I am sorry," she said breathlessly.

"Don't trouble yourself," he said as she took the cat from him. He nodded towards the camels. "What do you think?"

"They are four of my father's best. Three females and a male."

"I'm sure they will be excellent." He scrambled for something further to say. "The Pharaoh has several horses. Have you seen one?"

Something like excitement flashed across Asenath's face but was quickly quashed. Joseph found, a little disconcertingly, that he would not mind seeing it there again. "Yes," she answered. "They are beautiful."

"Perhaps," Joseph said on a sudden whim, "we shall have to acquire one ourselves."

The gamble paid off, for her face lit. "In truth?"

"I think it would be a worthwhile endeavor."

To his surprise, when he glanced at her again, he saw that her face was buried in her cat's fur. But the corner of her mouth was just visible, and she was smiling.

They were evidently to be taken to the palace for the celebration, again in a litter. Anhotep had informed him, with eyes to the floor but in no uncertain terms, that this was the way it must be. Joseph had almost laughed; it had been somehow refreshing to be told what to do, even if it had been done squeamishly. So Joseph stood, waiting in the courtyard under the shadow of the colonnade, watching the litter be made ready.

Asenath had been preparing with her maidservants since the mid-afternoon. He had no idea what could take so long as to necessitate three hours of preparation—he had done it in twenty minutes. He looked down at himself, checking over the robes and jewelry. Had he forgotten anything? All seemed in order.

Then Anhotep emerged from the house with Asenath and three maidservants behind him, and Joseph thought he knew what had taken three hours. Her hair was braided and caught by beads of gold and woven through with gilt wire, eyes rimmed in black and green and lips and nails colored in red. She wore a necklace in green and gold over her long white dress and on her wrists and ankles hung purple beads. He approached, and she smelled of sweet perfume. He had to fight the sudden urge to stare.

She was—beyond compare.

Joseph couldn't quite suppress a smile as he offered her his hand. She took it, lightly, and hers was not shaking.

The litter ride was long, for the carriers walked slowly, with a long retinue of maids and menservants behind, waving blue sashes. Revelers who would join them at the celebration met them along the road, cheering and falling in step with the procession as they made their way towards the palace. Asenath smiled and nodded serenely at the crowd that had gathered to watch, as if she had done this sort of thing her entire life. And, Joseph realized, she probably had. Following her lead, he did the same.

They were carried into the wide courtyard before the doors to the great hall of the palace. It had been done up with white curtains and lamps, and bowls of flowers and fruits rested on low tables that surrounded the pool and lay under the pillared walkways. Music was playing, lyres and flutes and drums. Soon guided to a table near the head of the courtyard, Joseph sat and watched others file in, listening to snatches of their conversations and feeling rather lost.

Asenath stood nearby, talking to several other women who greeted her. Dancers and acrobats soon arrived. Pharaoh Senus-ret entered after some time, and the courtyard bowed as one. He walked with the queen and the two children, the older girl and the boy, whom Joseph had seen the day he interpreted the Pharaoh's dreams. He frowned a little, again puzzled, and looked around the courtyard until he caught sight of Sonbe, the king's son and lord general. He was seated at a table some distance from the head of the courtyard, where the Pharaoh sat with his family. Joseph glanced back and forth between them.

It struck him that Asenath might have an explanation, so after a moment of deliberation, he ventured to ask her as she returned to sit. He leaned towards her. "Why does the Lord General Prince Sonbe not sit with his father?" he murmured.

She looked at him in open astonishment. "You do not know? He is not the son of the King's Great Royal Wife. He will not be king." Asenath nodded towards the boy at the table with the Pharaoh Senusret. "It will be the young Senusret, third of that name. He and his sister, Sithathoriunet, are her only children."

Joseph frowned slightly and glanced again at Sonbe before looking back at the young Prince Senusret, wondering if there was not a story there he knew well.

Slaves came around now, with platters of beef and bread, plums, figs, and melons, and cups of date wine. A tattooed hand set a cup before him, and Joseph found he locked eyes with the boy to whom it belonged, before fear shot through the young man's eyes, and he scurried away.

Wrestlers emerged, battling near the pool to the delighted cries of the revelers, who shouted out encouragement as they ate. When one fell in, the crowd laughed uproariously, and the wrestlers bowed to their audience before beginning again.

After the meal, the wrestlers departed, and the music continued as gifts were brought forward. Silver cups in the shape of lotus blossoms, golden bowls, necklaces, and jeweled collars. Rings of silver and bracelets of sparkling glass. A flowering plant in a painted urn and a hoopoe-bird in a gilt cage. Camels and cattle and donkeys, left outside the gates. And a giant urn, richly decorated, too large to be of any real use and far too wildly garish to be left out on display as a piece to admire.

Joseph had to look down slightly so as not to be seen laughing at it. He glanced at Asenath, who looked serene, but happened to glance his way. When she saw his face, her eyes widened and her mouth worked. "If you want us to use it to water the camels, I have no objection," Joseph whispered.

She quickly looked away and covered her mouth.

More gifts came forward, painted urns less large and more

handsome, chains of gold, alabaster jars of perfume and spices and oil. Asenath's parents came last, bowing before them and leaving a carved trunk full of fine linen and golden beads. Joseph glanced at her and saw her face, impassive.

The sight of me gave no pleasure to my father, she had said. He felt a stab of pity for her, alone with a father's distaste and no siblings for playmates or confidantes.

The celebration ended soon after. It was late in the night, and the full moon had risen. A breeze, warm but cooler than the hanging air, came blowing off the Nile as the litter carried them home. Joseph thought that Asenath would retire once they arrived, but she rounded the corner of the house and went up the narrow staircase that led to the roof.

Anhotep approached as Joseph watched her go. "Have you need of anything, sir?"

"No, thank you," Joseph answered quickly. He glanced at the steward. Emboldened, perhaps, by his success in making Asenath laugh, he found himself determined to make another attempt at some sort of friendship with the man. "Get some sleep, Anhotep. I know the morning after the master returns late from a celebration is never easy." Anhotep looked taken aback. "Yes," Joseph continued. "For you are bone-tired, and the servants don't want to waken either, so you have to bellow twice as loud as usual, and only the mistress of the laundry and her workers look like the living, since they retired before anyone else was able. And then the train of party-gifts starts to arrive, and there is nowhere to put any of them."

His steward gaped at him. "How do you know that—sir?"

Joseph laughed a little. He hoped he was making headway. "Did no one tell you that I was a steward, once upon a time?"

Anhotep stared at him for a long moment, and then Joseph saw understanding dawn on his face. "You were Lord Potiphar's steward."

"Yes."

The man was nodding, almost to himself. Joseph cocked his head. "What is it?"

He quickly stopped the motion. "I—" he paused, a little flustered, perhaps, that he had been caught. "I was only thinking, sir, that it makes several things make much more sense."

Amused, Joseph asked: "Such as?" He hoped the man would answer and not close up.

"Such as—" Anhotep's mouth clamped shut, and Joseph began to think he had only succeeded in making him feel uncomfortable. But then the steward began to fumble through the next sentence. "The things you know, sir, and—"

"—the things I don't know?" Joseph finished for him.

Nervously, the man laughed a little. "Yes."

Joseph found himself chuckling again. "As I said the other day, you have done very well, especially considering whose house is in your charge."

"Thank you, sir."

"You have done far better than I would have. You must have had good training."

"My family has served nomarchs for generations."

"Ah. *Far* better training than me. Well done."

His steward bowed slightly, and smiled.

He was washing off his eyepaint at the washstand in the bedroom when Asenath entered. She nodded a little before sitting on the bed and slowly beginning to work the braids and gold from her hair. "Was the rooftop pleasant?" Joseph asked.

"You can see the Nile from there," she answered. "I never could in Heliopolis. It is tranquil." He thought she would not say more, but she did. "And did you enjoy the celebration?"

Joseph paused. Had he enjoyed it? He didn't know that he felt one way or another about it. He had not exactly known anyone present. "It was—" he didn't have a word.

She was looking at him quizzically. "Have you been to one before?"

He smiled, finding himself a little diffident. "No."

199

Her hands, which had been working through her hair, stilled. She set the bead she was holding on the growing pile in her lap. "I ought to have thought of that," she murmured.

Waving a hand unconcernedly, he sat down in a nearby chair. "It is no matter."

Asenath looked at him curiously as she went back to her hair. "If I may—what is it like? To have your life so much in tatters and then to be suddenly given such power?"

Joseph thought for a moment. "It is strange. Very strange. I have already told you that it is disconcerting to have no one speak contrary to you." He frowned and shook his head. "But really, I am working, Asenath. It is what I have always done. In that way, at least, it is not so different."

At length, she asked quietly: "How do you do it?"

"Do what?"

"Speak without bitterness. You have had a much worse lot in life than I, but no one would know it."

Pursing his lips and rocking back in the chair, he thought for another long moment before answering. "When I was a boy, I did not know my God. Not truly. Even now, I do not think that I do. But my father told me that there are three things that God wishes of me. Of everyone. To act justly, to love mercy, and to walk humbly in the path God has given me.

"When I came to Egypt, I was angry, and bitter. It overwhelmed me. It drove my father's words from my mind. But I had seen anger and bitterness eat away at my brothers, and I knew they would do the same to me. For the first time, I looked to my God. More than anything in the world, I did not want to become like them.

"When I was sent to prison unjustly, I was bitter once again. How could my God allow such a thing to happen after I had served Him? But my father had taught me that God has a purpose in the paths He chooses for those who follow Him. I could not see it, but if I were to believe in my God, a part of me, at least, knew that I had to accept it."

He looked to the side, realizing that he was about to voice the very doubts that had been crawling through his mind since he had become vizier. He ought to have balked, he told himself, at revealing such thoughts—but to have someone with which to share them was unexpectedly relieving. "I cannot say I did this well. I did not lose faith in my God, but I do not think I ever truly admitted that God could have any sort of purpose for my time in prison, until the morning when I stood before the Pharaoh.

"I have made poor decisions and raged at my God. I have told Him I could not see any purpose in what He was doing. I wonder then why I am here, in this position." Joseph looked at her evenly. "But I know that God has placed me here, so I will do the task He has given me. I will be grateful, act justly, love mercy, and walk humbly. And I will not doubt Him ever again."

Asenath had once again stopped working her hair and was looking at him, expression mystified. "You say you do not know why you are here? You believe your God has rewarded you with wealth and power and a task of grand importance, and you do not know why?" She shook her head in disbelief.

"My father is not a kind man," she said. "And my mother often felt the effects of his anger. My faith in Atum-Ra and all the nine divine gods of the Pesedjet, whom my father serves, *never* grew stronger in this adversity. You are here and rewarded because of your faith in your God. Even if one questions or rages or acts in error, it is still faith if one does not abandon what one believes."

Joseph stared at her. He found he had nothing to say.

"I know of no one else who has withstood such trials, and whose belief has only grown stronger as a result, who then questions whether or not they have served well. I have never heard of such a thing."

He finally found his voice. "It is wrong to question and rage and act in error."

"I suppose. But it does not seem to me that you have continued to do those things."

Deliver me from myself. Give me wisdom, he had so often prayed. *Give me peace.*

From the first moment he had asked, as an angry, frightened yard slave, he had been delivered from himself, been given wisdom, been given peace. Even when he had so wrongly understood his God.

And because of it, he had always found his way back, a little closer, to acting justly, and loving mercy, and walking humbly.

It does not seem to me that you have continued to do these things.

It was true.

But he *had* done those things, regardless. In Potiphar's house. In the prison.

His guilt remained.

Why then had he been given *the Vizierate of Egypt?*

His thoughts cast about in emptiness for a long moment, looking for an answer. There was none.

But then, instead of an answer, the question returned, quietly insistent.

Did God forgive what had been done?

God was all-seeing, all-knowing—how could He forgive such things as what humanity did? One could only live as best as one could, and pray it was enough to please Him.

Couldn't one?

More questions shot through Joseph's mind.

Why then did he know that his forgiveness of Potiphar was what must please his God?

Did God forgive?

How could God ask those who followed Him to love mercy—if He Himself did not?

Why had he prayed for wisdom and peace, and received those things, when he had made such grave errors in misunderstanding and anger and doubt?

You must love mercy.

God must forgive.

It was the only explanation.

202

Yet Joseph had never once asked for forgiveness.

Perhaps his God had known he would.

"Oh, my God." He had not known he was about to speak the words out loud.

"Forgive me."

Joseph lay in the near-darkness, staring up at the strands of moon-light that crept through the high windows and washed the walls and ceiling with ghostly hints of color. Asenath was asleep, breath-ing softly. He glanced at her and could just make out her face, peaceful and unmoving.

She is not frightened.

The thought was gratifying.

Then he frowned a little, considering her. She had said little else following their conversation, instead absorbed in her own thoughts. He wondered what truly went on in her mind.

And how had she been able to see so clearly what he had not? It was bewildering to realize that he had come to such a critically altered understanding of his God because of this Egyptian woman.

Perhaps this had been God's purpose.

Or perhaps—there was more.

He looked at her again and, unexpectedly, had to stop his hand from reaching out to brush her hair. Joseph smiled a little, in resignation.

"Bless you, Asenath," he finally murmured.

23

Pharaoh Senusret looked thoughtfully at the long list of grain averages from each nome, and the further projections Joseph had made for the next seven years. They stood in the great hall that day, at the foot of the tall dais where sat the Pharaoh's throne. The treasurer over Egypt and the overseer of the granaries, as well as several men who were apparently local officials, stood nearby. Many scribes sat in the room as well, putting to record everything that occurred.

"There are some storehouses in the area that I am purchasing or renting from merchants, to use for the first harvest," Joseph said. He thought of the three he had seen that morning with Anhotep, all good. "It is my hope that around Pharaoh's other cities, similar places may be found. But construction of such sites will have to begin immediately for the smaller nomes, and likely within two years for the larger nomes, which have storehouses already available for use.

"There is enough in Pharaoh's treasury to fund such projects without halting work on the fortifications at Tjaru, if local resources are used well and not wastefully. With Pharaoh's permission, I will see to it that all this is done."

The Pharaoh nodded. His son, the Lord General Sonbe, stood behind him, face impassive. "It shall be done as you say," the Pharaoh said. He turned to Seneb, the overseer of the granaries. "Prepare that word be sent to each nomarch. Zaphnath-Paaneah will tell you what is to be said." He turned. "Come, my son."

Pharaoh Senusret left, followed by the Prince Sonbe. The man bowed to Joseph before leaving, but in the expression of his eyes Joseph saw something he did not like, something shrewd.

Joseph regarded him as he left. Then, brushing it aside for later, he turned to Seneb. "This is what must be said."

Seneb nodded to the scribes, who each produced a new roll of papyrus.

Thinking for a moment, Joseph began slowly.

"I, Zaphnath-Paaneah, Vizier of the Pharaoh, who is Lord of the Two Lands and High Priest of Every Temple, to each nomarch in his nome of Egypt, greetings.

In keeping with the Pharaoh's wish to prepare Egypt for the coming famine, I require that word be sent to me if such places of storage as can hold grain, well-kept or easily made so, sit ready in your lands.

A list of each, if such exists—its size and location and the price of its use—is required with haste. I also require that a list of possible sites for future storehouses, and the manpower and supplies available, be sent.

Bring your men to the ready, for building, for sowing, for harvesting. Await my further instructions.

Zaphnath-Paaneah, in the name of the Pharaoh"

He touched the signet ring on his hand, which he would use to approve each document, and then quickly crossed his arms. There was no point in bringing extra attention to the tattoo which sat next to the ring; he knew it drew eyes, even if his gaze seemed to repel them. "When will we expect to have word from each of the nomes?"

"A month, my lord, for the farthest nomes, but far sooner for those nomarchs in the larger cities on the Nile," said Seneb.

Joseph nodded. "It is well; the largest cities will be the ones most likely to have storehouses available. Let us look ahead then. We must begin designs for storehouses to construct in the farther nomes, so that we are prepared when their responses arrive. Have your architects ready to meet tomorrow."

Seneb bowed.

Joseph left soon after, adding the meeting to the ever-growing list of duties that was running through his mind. That, and the forty-two transcriptions of his letter which would be delivered in the morning, ready for his seal and then couriered to the nomarchs.

Notices and orders and requested approvals had begun appearing in his study, brought in by scribes and messengers from the courts and palace. The results of a land dispute between two merchants. A complaint against the Chief of Police. A request for approval to open a new quarry near Tjaru. Dozens more.

His head throbbed thinking about it all. That morning, he had requested that Anhotep look into getting a few runners for Joseph's own use. He knew it would soon drive the steward to distraction if he continued having his staff pulled away at all hours to courier responses and approvals back to the palace or elsewhere. Joseph knew he needed some scribes, as well. Or an assistant. Or ten.

The entourage of four men followed him through the streets. He'd managed in the past week to make them agree to walking closely behind him, rather than enclosing him like the four corners of a room. However, Joseph found he was then unexpectedly free to observe the reactions of those he passed. He quickly noticed something which he had not when ensconced by menservants.

Everyone gawked at him when they thought he was not looking.

He supposed that there was nothing to be done about it, but it was disconcerting all the same.

The road through the administrative complex was almost behind him when, from the corner of his eye, he saw a face in the crowd that neither gawked nor quickly looked away. Joseph only caught a glimpse of the man before he disappeared from view, for the crowd was shuffling to make room for the vizier.

But it had been Intef, and he had been grinning broadly.

Joseph arrived home a little while later, bolstered somehow by the fact that there was another man in Itjtawy who would look him in the face. He walked through the gates and saw to his left Asenath and several menservants, standing near the pool.

She was pointing upwards at the wicker construction that was being built, a large cage for the hoopoe-bird that was a wedding-present. Asenath had immediately felt sorry for it in its small cage, and had let it have the run of several baskets taken to bits and roped together as its new cage was being built.

He hadn't seen what she had done with the monstrous urn. Approaching, he thought perhaps he might ask her, but he had only just reached the pond when he heard the gates to the courtyard opening once again.

Joseph turned and saw Djaty stride through. It had been two weeks since the wedding, and this was the first Joseph had seen of the scribe.

Djaty's eyes lit on Joseph and he smiled widely.

As Joseph forced himself to smile in response, he saw Asenath turn curiously to observe the newcomer.

"My friend!" Djaty said as he approached. He bowed a little, and before Joseph could protest that action, quickly clasped his shoulders. "Congratulations are in order, I think."

Hoping that Asenath would somehow know that nothing the talkative scribe was about to say was meant to be offensive, Joseph nodded. "Thank you." He turned. "Asenath, may I present Djaty, scribe in the house of Potiphar and my good friend."

The scribe bowed deeply. "A pleasure, Lady."

She smiled, and Joseph thought it looked genuine. "I am glad to meet you," she answered.

Djaty smiled in turn. "I had been thinking, just two weeks ago, as I watched the piles of work in his study begin to grow, that a wife might be just the thing for him. A fortunate event, indeed."

"Indeed," Asenath murmured.

"But may I say, my lady, that I have known your husband since he was a boy who could barely stammer out a sentence in Egyptian. You could do no better."

Joseph resisted the urge to drag Djaty away from the scene. It was obvious that the scribe had deduced even more than Joseph had expected and knew exactly what he was doing.

"Indeed," she answered again. Perhaps her tone was slightly cooler.

"Djaty," Joseph cut in. "Perhaps we ought to begin our work. I will have forty-two dispatches to seal in the morning."

"Of course," the scribe bowed once more to Asenath and turned with Joseph to move away from the scene.

He had to bite his tongue from instantly reproaching the other man. His new position, he realized, would make it difficult to rail anyone. How could one chide a person—gently—if they knew that one could have them thrown in prison—or *killed*? Not that Djaty would think that, of course.

"Djaty—" was all he managed after considering carefully how to begin, for the scribe actually interrupted him.

"I know," he answered. "I'm not to interfere. Noted, and my apologies."

"Thank you."

They entered the study a moment later. "Woosh!" Djaty said, looking about at the stacks of papyrus and shards of pottery. "There is more here than I expected."

"And near-none of it is related to the granary project," Joseph answered, a little grimly. "I've done all I can regarding that until the morning."

"You need an assistant, boy. Most high officials have one, you know, along with some scribes. It is respectable to want to examine everything, but it is not so respectable to kill yourself."

Joseph pulled off his khat and ran a hand through his hair. "I have been thinking that myself." But to *find* people who both worked well and were not going to jump every time he breathed? It sounded like a nightmare. "In the meantime I have you, and I thank you for it."

"You are most welcome. But I have to tell you, Lord Potiphar will be returning within the week, it seems."

Sighing a little, Joseph took a seat, already feeling defeated. "Well, we shall do what we can in that time."

The evening meal was coming to a close, and Joseph wished he could think of more to say to Asenath. But she could be so very reserved, and it seemed that she and she alone determined when she was willing to converse. He admired her mind, though, or what he had seen of it.

However, that evening Asenath made no attempt to escape the great room after the meal was finished, something she often did. Not that Joseph could blame her for it; he knew he did the same.

Instead, she nodded a little to him and moved to a pile of cushions where her lyre rested. A maidservant sat nearby, and Asenath began to play, softly.

The servants had begun to clear away the meal when Joseph's eyes lighted on Anhotep, standing quietly near the front of the room as he always did during meals.

It was then that an idea struck him.

Perhaps it was ludicrous. But if he was to have an assistant, for it was becoming abundantly clear that he must, why not choose someone whose organizational abilities he had confidence in? Not to mention who had the ability to maintain composure in Joseph's presence.

He turned and reached behind him, to a scribe's kit and several pottery shards he had left on a small side table upon entering for the meal. "Anhotep, will you come here for a moment?"

When the steward arrived, Joseph motioned for him to take a seat, and he set the kit and shards down on the table. Anhotep looked thoroughly mystified, but sat. "Perhaps I am being untoward," Joseph began. The young man looked even more puzzled. "But I have a question for you."

Quickly scrawling one of the Egyptian proverbs he knew on a shard, he handed it to the other man. "What does it say?"

Anhotep frowned but quickly looked down at the hieratic lines. *"If you do good to a hundred men and one of them acknowledges it, no part of it is lost."*

"Good." Joseph handed him a second pen. "Now, can you transcribe it into hieroglyphs?"

The steward looked as though he had been asked to bring Joseph the moon.

"Only to the best of your ability. I am simply curious."

Sizing up the sentence, it was a long moment before Anhotep began. Joseph watched him. It would be a true testament to his schooling if he could muddle through something even close to correct. Outside of the scribes, not many could. If he could do that, and a few mathematics problems besides, he was as well-educated as most nomarchs. The sounds of the music slowed, and Joseph glanced at Asenath. She was watching them curiously.

Anhotep pushed the shard back towards him, and Joseph turned to look at it. He picked it up and eyed it critically. It was fairly well done—not perfect, by any means, but legible. "You were well-schooled," said Joseph.

"Thank you, sir." His steward paused. "May I ask what this is about?"

"Yes, in just a moment." Joseph finished scribbling on a second shard and pushed it across the table. Anhotep took it. His steward seemed to mentally throw his hands into the air before beginning the three calculations Joseph had given him.

He worked fast, faster than Joseph could in the hieratic system. It was only a minute before he handed the shard back to him. Joseph nodded slowly. "Well, Anhotep, I will now answer your question. If we were to find someone to take on the more mundane aspects of your work, I am wondering if you would like to assist me in mine."

His steward gaped at him. "Me? Sir, that is not really my place."

Joseph set his elbow on the table and held up his slave's tattoo. "Nor is this mine, apparently, yet here we are."

210

Anhotep looked rather at a loss for words. Joseph shifted in his seat. "Let me say, that if you do not *want* to do it, that is an entirely different thing. I can find someone else. But you have a good mind, and that is worth quite a bit."

"No sir—I—I'll do it, certainly. I would be honored." Anhotep actually had a small smile playing on his face.

"Excellent."

"Thank you, sir."

Nodding, Joseph paused. "One more thing," he said after a moment, quietly, so that Asenath would not overhear. He hoped that he had developed enough rapport with the man for him to be willing to answer. "Since my becoming vizier, it seems that much of Itjtawy has held me in some kind of dread. Why not you?"

The other man paused for a long moment. "Well, sir," he said finally, and Joseph thought there was the smallest hint of dryness to his tone. "It did not seem to me that the man who arrived at this house, so completely out of sorts, was one prepared to call death down upon a nation."

Joseph laughed outright. "I am grateful for your perceptiveness."

He lay in bed again that night, staring up into the darkness. Asenath was still and quiet, and he thought her asleep. So when she spoke, he nearly jumped out of his skin.

"Joseph?"

"Yes?"

"I want to tell you something."

This was unlike her. He turned his head but could barely make out her profile. "Of course."

She was quiet for a long moment, and Joseph wondered if perhaps she was reconsidering. But then she spoke, rapidly. "When I was sixteen, my father promised me to one of the Pharaoh's most honored generals. He was sent to war in Nubia soon after the betrothal, and we had no news of him for a year. When we finally did, it was to learn that he had died." Asenath paused. "My father waited for a long while, I suppose, for another match he deemed advantageous."

"I am sorry," Joseph answered. It was trite, but it was all he could think to say.

He heard her hair brush the bedding as she shook her head. "There is no reason for you to be."

"It must have been difficult for you. Was there not ever—someone you preferred?"

"No." He was surprised at her vehemence. "You know what I have told you of my father. He has served Atum-Ra and all the nine divine gods of the Pesedjet all the days of his life, but they never curbed his temper, nor protected my mother." He heard her take a deep breath.

"But you, Joseph, are—*kind.*" Her voice cracked, but she quickly continued. "You treat others with kindness, with no thought to who you are or how far they are below you. You have forgiven one who has greatly wronged you. You say your God has required this of you, that you have followed Him, and He has helped you. Then I say to you, *I want to serve this God to the end of my days and beyond.* And I say—" her voice hitched again, and Joseph listened in growing astonishment. He was stunned to feel her hand brush his, tentatively. His fingers closed around hers. "I say," she repeated, "I suppose I have wished for someone whom I could trust. And I—trust you."

24

Joseph held the papyrus scroll up to the light that was shining through the high windows of the great room. He frowned. It was a dispatch from one of the small nomes in the Delta and had arrived that morning, apparently through the rain. Aya, the black cat, watched him unblinkingly from her seat on a pile of cushions at the far end of the room.

Still frowning, Joseph picked up his pen from a nearby table and tried to outline the faint hieratic words back into existence. In the eighteen months since he had become vizier, rain had become more frequent. This was the first dispatch that had been ruined, however. He hoped it was not the first of many.

It was difficult going; the scroll waved haphazardly as the pen struck it, the lines sliding about under the tip of his pen. He furrowed his brow in concentration.

There was sudden laughter, and he looked up to see his wife standing in the doorway to the great room. "What are you doing?"

"Trying to decipher this message. It was ruined in the rain."

Asenath walked over and took the scroll; holding it up in the sunlight with two hands so that it was taut. "You have managed to get yourself an excellent assistant in Anhotep, not to mention five scribes, and I still do not think you know when to ask for help."

"Hmm." He grinned at her before beginning to write again. "But you are so very good at making sure I have help anyway."

She looked at him dryly. "If you need to learn a lesson, I don't have to be. I can drop this scroll, and you can go back to whatever it was you were doing a moment ago."

Joseph chuckled. "A fair point."

There was silence for several moments as he worked on bringing the symbols back to legibility.

"Can you make it out?" Asenath asked at length.

The writing was slowly coming back to life. Joseph squinted again and looked back at what he had managed so far. "It is from the nomarch at Sais. He writes with the nomarch in—somewhere—about a building project."

"Let me see." His wife turned in the light and looked at the papyrus. "Is it—Khasu?"

Joseph peered over her head. "I think you are right."

She turned again so that he could continue. Her face was teasing. "Now you see; this is why one asks for help."

"Hmm," he said again with a smile, pen scratching on the scroll. It was a minute or so before the rest became legible. "They will be in need of two storehouses each if the next harvest is to be like this one."

"Two each? For such small nomes?"

"The Lower nomes in the Delta seem to be producing quite a bit more than the Upper nomes. They've grown their average production by nearly half."

Asenath again looked at the scroll. "I know it is a good thing, but it seems as though keeping ahead of the crops will be quite a bit of work. We still have more than five years left until the famine."

"I'll need to travel to Memphis so I can meet with the Delta nomarchs. We will set up a plan for storehouses that everyone can accomplish without my being present." He grinned at her. "How is that for help?"

"A pretty start. But when you did so in Thebes last year, you and Anhotep stayed up for nearly a week straight working on logistics after you returned."

"I'll make a different plan this time. One that involves less of me and Anhotep."

214

At that moment the steward entered and, upon hearing his name, bowed and looked at them curiously.

"Anhotep," Asenath said. "My husband has volunteered less of yourselves for the work in Memphis than he did in Thebes. Hold him to it."

"Certainly, Lady." He looked at Joseph. "Are we going in Memphis?"

"It seems we must." He handed the scroll to his steward, and Anhotep perused it. Joseph turned to Asenath with a smile. "I have a proposal for you. Suppose you come with us, and ensure that we don't work ourselves to death?"

She looked at him warmly and lifted her face for a kiss. "I think that would be lovely."

He kissed her. "Well then, it is decided."

They sat on the roof that evening, listening to the sound of the wind blowing in the trees that grew in the garden. The sky was cloudless, with no sign of the recent rain. The stars shone brightly around the half-moon, throwing their silver light onto the Nile in the distance. Thin hanging curtains blew in the light breeze.

Asenath shifted slightly so that she was more securely under Joseph's arm and adjusted a cushion. Then she looked up at the sky. "Once, I would have told you that Nut and Khonsu show their true glory this night." She stared up at the stars and moon. "What are they, then?"

Joseph considered. She asked a question like this, every so often. "I do not know," he said. "But they and the sun move, as you see, in patterns. There must be a reason for it in God's mind."

"Perhaps it simply gives Him pleasure to know that it is beautiful."

He nodded. "It very well may."

The neighing of the horse in the stables echoed through the warm evening air. "She took a basket full of linen on her back today," said Asenath in response to it. "I led her around the courtyard and she was as docile as could be. I shall try it myself soon."

He had told her of the man and woman he had seen in Padan-Aram, the day they bought the horse. That had been six months ago, and the idea stayed with her. Eventually, she asked Anhotep to call in one of Pharaoh Senusret's horsemen to advise on how to train it. Evidently a few of them had managed to ride a horse as well. The man had been coming weekly.

"I will want to see it. But—take care."

She laughed. "Of course. When do we leave for Memphis? I should like to try it before then, but not if we leave too soon."

"Five days, perhaps?"

Asenath nodded. "The horseman is coming in two days. I will have him try it first, if he thinks the mare is ready. Then I shall try." His wife was silent for a moment and then laughed again.

"What is it?"

"I was only thinking that I could never imagine my father's household being one where I might try riding a horse."

Joseph debated before asking gently, "Will you want to go to Heliopolis and visit while we are nearby?"

"No."

Her voice was firm.

Pharaoh Senusret was old.

It was not as if Joseph had not noticed the fact before, only that now it seemed very obvious. The Pharaoh sat heavily in his chair in the meeting-room, two menservants waiting nearby to help him stand when he required it. His son, young Senusret, was a boy of barely twelve. But the Pharaoh had begun bringing him to such meetings. He stood always at his father's right hand, watching with dark eyes and very silent.

This day the Lord General Prince Sonbe had also arrived at the meeting, recently returned from patrols on the southern border. He too was silent as he stood near Master Seneb of the granaries.

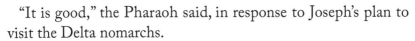

"It is good," the Pharaoh said, in response to Joseph's plan to visit the Delta nomarchs.

Joseph bowed.

"When you return, we will discuss what has been agreed upon. Do you expect it to be a plan that can be followed in the remaining five years with little alteration?"

"This is my hope, oh Pharaoh."

He nodded. "When will you leave?"

"In two days' time, if that pleases the Pharaoh."

"It is good," Pharaoh Senusret said again. He suddenly looked very tired. "I must retire."

The two menservants stepped forward to help the Pharaoh rise, and Joseph waited until he was on his feet before bowing.

As Joseph moved to leave, he caught Sonbe's eye. The man had been watching him. Joseph met his gaze, and the other man's eyes flicked away—but only to light on the Young Prince Senusret with a look that Joseph thought he knew very well.

His breath caught, apprehension dawning in his mind.

Turning amidst bows and forcing his face to remain impassive, he was silent until he exited into the great courtyard. Then he turned to one of the guards standing there. "Where is your captain?" he murmured.

"Here in the palace, last I knew, my lord. In the east wing."

Motioning for the four menservants who had been waiting for him to remain where they were, Joseph made his way across the courtyard. His thoughts flew. Sonbe was unhappy with his lot in life, that much had been obvious for some time.

But did he truly believe Sonbe capable of such treachery?

He wouldn't have believed his brothers capable of it.

Stomach cold despite the heat of the day, he quickened his pace. He had almost reached the eastern edge of the courtyard when, to his surprise, Intef stepped out from one of the many doors under the pillared colonnade. He looked up, saw Joseph, and grinned before bowing deeply. Joseph approached, smiling despite the situation. Unlike Djaty, he had only seen Intef a few times in the past eighteen months, and had never been able to convince him to stop bowing. "I'm sorry, Intef," Joseph said once he reached him. "But my matter is urgent. I must hurry and find Potiphar."

"He is just inside." Intef motioned behind him. His face was curious, but he did not inquire. "It is good to see you."

"You as well." He clasped the other man on the shoulder as he passed.

Intef turned and watched him go. "One of these days you must throw someone in my prison," he called. "Every nobleman does it at least once!"

Looking over his shoulder and waving a hand, Joseph soon found himself at the door from which Intef had come. He took a breath and entered.

Potiphar was within the small room, speaking quietly with two of his lieutenants. They started and stood to attention as soon as they saw Joseph. He nodded. "Captain, a word?"

The lieutenants scurried out an inner door and Joseph closed the one through which he had entered. Cocking his head silently, he eyed the inner door, and taking the hint, Potiphar quietly closed it. Glancing around the room and seeing only one small, high window in the white walls, Joseph moved as far away from it as he could. Potiphar followed suit.

Joseph opened his mouth to speak and stopped. Who was to say that Potiphar wouldn't side with Sonbe's claim, if he were to make one? He had not spoken to the man much in the last eighteen months.

A thought unexpectedly came to him. Would Potiphar oppose the young Senusret, simply for the chance that Sonbe might remove Joseph from office? The lord general obviously did not care for him. It struck Joseph how precarious his position might actually be.

My God—he ought to have prayed earlier. Much earlier. *My God, grant me wisdom, for I have little and need much!*

"What is it, my lord?"

218

It was very disconcerting to hear those words coming from Potiphar. He shook his head slightly, then came to a decision. He was leaving Itjtawy. There was no other choice. If he could not trust the captain of the royal guard, then his days were numbered regardless.

"Captain," he said quietly. "What are the chances that Prince Sonbe will make a claim for the throne?"

Potiphar shifted his stance, face impassive. "Perhaps it is likely. I have watched him for many years."

Joseph considered, for a thought had come into his mind. "Whatever became of the priest, Dedumose of Abydos?"

The other man stared at him. "He was killed. We could not discover who had hired him and the others. He would say nothing."

"And why exactly was the chief baker executed, near four years ago now?"

"Did no one ever tell you? He attempted to poison the Pharaoh." Potiphar shook his head. "You are not saying that the lord general has been behind this."

"How is it that it has *not* been discussed?"

"It has, once. Your predecessor, I am given to understand, broached the subject with the Pharaoh. He did not wish to hear it. That is why the vizierate was open to you."

Rubbing the space between his eyebrows, Joseph sighed. "I see."

"Why has this come to your attention, now?"

He searched for an explanation that did not sound fanciful. "In the past I have only observed that the lord general resents his position. But the Pharaoh has begun bringing the young prince to meetings of importance. I feel that Prince Sonbe's demeanor is now—different. Something is wrong."

Potiphar frowned. "I have never known you to act on mere *feeling*."

Joseph drew himself up. "Perhaps not," he admitted. He looked the other man in the eye. "I had my father's favor once. I became a slave in Egypt because my older brothers decided to rid themselves of me. So, if I am acting on feeling, I beg that you consider what I have just told you when I say again: *something is wrong*."

Silence reigned for several moments, then Potiphar shifted on his feet again and nodded, slowly. "What would you have me do?"

"I am to leave Itjtawy in two days. Can you have the lord general watched, without his knowing?"

"That, and more. I will have the kitchens watched as well. And, thanks be to Isis, the Pharaoh will not be leaving the palace in the coming weeks. There will be no need to protect him from crowds."

"Can you have the Prince Senusret watched as well?"

"You truly fear for him?"

"Yes."

"It will be done."

Joseph arrived home some time later, preoccupied, and, he realized, tired. Very tired. *Asenath is right; I do take on too much.* He knew there was a horde of papyrus in the study waiting for him to sort through. He had ordered everything possible brought to him before the trip, so it would not pile up while he was gone. Some of it Anhotep and the scribes could see to: general palace logistics, standard reports from border patrols. But other things, processes of the court and reports from nomarchs, he ought to at least look over himself. Some were notices of proceedings he needed to attend. What else could he delegate?

Perhaps once he finished in Memphis the reports from the Delta nomarchs would become more standardized. The reports from the Upper nomes had already calmed, to some extent, since his visit to Thebes the previous year.

"Joseph!" he heard his wife calling from across the courtyard. He turned to look and stopped short.

She was smiling at him from atop the horse.

He broke into a grin despite it all and made his way over to her. The horse-trainer was standing nearby, as well as several menservants. Two of Asenath's maidservants looked on from under the colonnade. "She is quite willing," his wife said as he approached.

She clicked her tongue and urged the horse onward a bit, to demonstrate.

Joseph grinned again and rubbed the horse's forehead as they came up alongside him. "You have done quite the thing."

"She is a kind one; she only took some getting used to the idea." She held out a hand, and Joseph helped her as she slid down. Asenath stroked the mare's neck. "Well done, my fine one."

They walked in step back towards the others, Asenath leading the horse. "You are tired," she said.

"That may be an understatement."

Glancing up at him, she put a hand on his arm. "Suppose you do no work on the river trip northwards."

"I think that is an excellent idea."

25

The river sparkled in the evening light, the bright lines of color that hung in the sky over the rocky western hills reflecting upon the water. From among the high papyrus reeds along the sides of the river came the clipped calls of an ibis. The water rushed pleasantly under the bow of the boat, dancing along the wooden sides and leaving white streaks behind them. Above the deck, the sail rustled in the breeze.

They would dock soon for the night at a small village on the eastern bank and reach Memphis the following afternoon. River travel was pleasant when one was being waited upon, Joseph had found with a bit of chagrin in the past year and a half. He shook his head a little and laughed to himself, remembering the first time he had been on a boat, tied to a camel, and all the times he had prepared Potiphar for such a trip at this, driven to distraction by the restrictions and changes in routine and supplies.

"What is it?" Asenath was looking at him curiously as they stood together at the bow.

"Oh, it is nothing. I was only thinking about how different my views on boats have become."

She cocked her head. "What do you mean?"

"Well, the first time I was on a boat, it was terrifying. And after that, it was always vexatious, to plan such trips as this."

"The first time?"

"Yes—" he stopped short. He hadn't thought of it, but it would seem terribly odd to an Egyptian to have never set foot on a boat until the age of seventeen. Joseph looked at her sheepishly. "I had never been on a boat before coming here."

It was as though he had told her that the skies were yellow where he came from. "There are *no boats* in Canaan?"

"Only on the coast. Or at the great northern lake. And shepherding is not a trade that makes any use of them."

She was glancing about with new eyes, peering at the water. Then she laughed. "I suppose it would be disconcerting." Then she paused and looked thoughtful. After a moment, she said, almost hesitatingly, "I have thought of something. I have never heard a word of Canaanite. My father had a Nubian scribe who would speak his language the moment you startled him. Nothing but Egyptian ever comes out of your mouth."

"I—" Joseph paused again, startled at the question. How long had it been since he had said a word in Canaanite? He had stopped using it to pray near the beginning of his time in the prison—had that really been six years ago? He was a little horrified at himself. "I suppose you are right. I hadn't thought of it."

His wife looked at him concernedly. "I think I have worried you."

He waved a hand. "No, it's all right. I was only surprised to think of it. I stopped when I was in the prison. It was becoming too much of a chore to speak in it." Joseph frowned. "Which is odd, really."

Asenath touched his hand. "Perhaps it is difficult for the mind to continue easily speaking something that it never hears. One surely cannot forget such a thing."

Had he? He looked around him, attempting to dredge up Canaanite words.

Boat.

River.

Sky.

Mountains.

He thought further.

I am going to Memphis.

I am thirty-two years old.

223

It is not so very hot today.

The words came to his mind with some small effort, as though they had been dragged up a ramp that led from the dock to the deck of a boat. But they came.

"No," he said after a moment. "I don't think I have."

"Good," Asenath smiled, relieved. "I was afraid for a moment it would be my fault that you discovered something awful." Then she looked at him, a smile still playing on her features. "Will you say something? I want to hear it."

"What do you want me to say?"

"Oh, anything that comes to mind." An arch look grew on her face. Turning to face him and leaning against the bow, she said, "Perhaps that I am the cleverest woman in Egypt?"

Joseph chuckled, and came to put an arm around her while thinking through the Canaanite sentence. "Asenath is the cleverest woman in Egypt—and the most beautiful."

She laughed and leaned against him. "It's lovely. It flows like the water."

"Say *shalom*."

His wife frowned and attempted it. "*Shalom.*" She looked up at him. "What does it mean?"

"It is a greeting; it means *peace*."

"Like *em hotep*?" She rolled her eyes and made a wry face. "*Shalom* sounds far better."

Joseph laughed again.

The high white walls for which Memphis was known loomed before them, standing long and tall on the western bank of the Nile. The boat continued a small distance upriver, past the bustling port, heading towards the sprawling residences that sat to the north of the city. In the distance, both north and south, Joseph could make out tall pyramids, fairly glowing in the sunlight, strung along the western bank south towards Itjtawy and northwards on the plain towards Heliopolis.

They arrived at a private dock, and a man was there to meet them. "My lord," he bowed deeply. "My lady. Welcome to Memphis. My name is Huy. I will be pleased to serve you while you are here."

Following the man, they made their way down a wide street toward the gates of a residence situated on a rise above the Nile. Anhotep and a handful of servants followed behind, the rest remaining to unload the boat.

There were several such houses in cities throughout Egypt for the vizier's use. Joseph had been to the ones in Thebes and Abydos the previous year. This one, however, was easily the largest of them all. Asenath smiled when they reached the courtyard, admiring the tall palms and sycamore figs. The garden was well-established, and the pond stocked with fish.

"I am sure you will wish to rest this evening," Huy was saying. "I am told that the nomarchs of Lower Egypt have begun to arrive this day. Tomorrow Nomarch Harwa will be pleased to host the gathering in his offices here in the city."

Joseph nodded. "Excellent."

Huy turned to Asenath. "Perhaps, Lady, you will wish to visit the Temples of Ptah while you are here, and ask blessings upon this project on your husband's behalf?"

Asenath's face became impassive, that expression Joseph had seen so much of when they were first married. But knowing her now, he could see the quick flash of disquiet that passed through her eyes. She took a measured breath. "Thank you, no."

Joseph watched Anhotep's eyes dart back and forth between the two. It was a massive breach in protocol.

His wife continued, voice even. "Be assured that I shall certainly ask blessings, but not of Ptah."

If Huy was surprised, he managed not to show it. "Very well," he bowed. "Please, if you will wait for only a moment, there will be a meal very soon." Anhotep followed the man into the house.

As Joseph and Asenath walked towards the pool, she sighed a little. Joseph thought that she would speak about what had just passed, but she did not, so he did not press her. "Look at these trees!" she said. "They have been here for ages. The day the Pharaohs moved the capital away from Memphis was a sad one indeed."

"Why did they move it?" Joseph asked as he looked up at the regal sycamore under which they stood. He had never heard the reason.

"Why does any ruler do anything? Ease, I suppose. And power. The Pa-yuum is fertile, after all, and well-placed in the center of the country, between Upper and Lower Egypt." She looked thoughtfully into the depths of the pool for a long moment. "Do you know, this is the first time I have had to refuse a temple visit?"

He observed her steadily.

"Everything is quite comfortable in Itjtawy. Anhotep knows our ways—the entire city does. No one asks such things of us." She looked up then, for Anhotep was approaching.

"I'm told the meal is ready," he said.

Joseph took Asenath's hand. "You did well," he murmured as they walked.

She bit her lip and squeezed his hand in return.

"Impossible!" the nomarch from Imu waved his hand. "My lord, my nome does not have the manpower to accomplish this!"

Anhotep, Joseph was amused to find, looked indignant to hear Joseph being spoken to in such a way. For his own part, he found it refreshing to not be placed on a pedestal. Over the past several days, it had become obvious that these Delta nomarchs put a little less stock in the Pharaoh Senusret's decisions regarding both Joseph and the interpretation of the Pharaoh's dreams.

Joseph had to remind himself not to lean back against the wall nearby. He would have done so had he been haggling in the marketplace, a quiet way of showing that one was unperturbed. But he was not in the marketplace; he was in a grand pillared hall, surrounded by nomarchs. In such cases, the vizier must stand and make himself an untouchable object, especially if those around were not going to do it for him.

"What are your numbers?" Joseph asked coolly.

"My—numbers? My lord?"

"Yes, the exact number of the men in your nome who may work on the storehouses. I am not prepared to send men from Itjtawy or anywhere else to assist anyone without the necessary information."

The nomarch turned to the scribes behind him, and they shuffled through several rolls of papyrus. Several of the other nomarchs did the same.

Anhotep leaned toward him and fought a smile. "If they can source both the supplies and manpower locally, that will be *much* less work for us."

"I expect they can. These are not the Upper nomes. They are all much nearer to one another, and have more resources."

"My lord," The nomarch from Imu called. "I have 600 men at a time who can be spared."

Joseph nodded. "You may have a dilemma, but perhaps not an *impossible* one." He turned to the nomarch from Sais. "How many men do you have?"

"Near 2,000, my lord."

"It seems," Joseph said to the room, "that perhaps you may be able share men amongst yourselves. Let us have a number from each nome."

They went from nomarch to nomarch, each relaying their numbers. Anhotep scribbled them down until all twenty had been recorded. Perusing the papyrus after it was complete, Joseph again addressed the room. "The nomes in Upper Egypt have found it possible to fully construct a sizable storehouse during the growing season so that it is ready for harvest. This takes near five hundred men. If each nome is to construct two, we can see that the nomarch from Imu has a point. However, the nomarch from Sais will have extra men. He shall send them, for one season, to Imu."

A murmuring grew about the room, and many nomarchs shifted where they stood.

"It will not be easy," Joseph said, "but it is necessary. I cannot remove men from the fortification project at Tjaru or from assisting the Upper nomes if you have enough men here. And it seems you may. Let us continue with the numbers."

They went, one by one, through the nomes. Memphis could share men, as could Sais, and several others. Timetables were drawn up; agreements were sealed. The nomarchs looked sour but did not protest.

It was nearing evening when Joseph left, Anhotep falling in step next to him and four menservants trailing behind. Memphis was sprawling, many times the size of Itjtawy. They walked through square upon square of grand buildings, and over all stood the tall walls of the great temple of Ptah. Joseph gave it little notice, though Anhotep glanced at it as they passed. It stood with high stone walls, vast carvings etched upon it, and proud statues, larger than three men, guarding the entrance. Before it stood a wide courtyard milling with priests and worshippers.

Joseph saw his steward shake his head a little, but he said nothing. "What are your further plans here, sir?" Anhotep asked presently.

"I do not wish to leave tomorrow, in case one or more of the nomarchs decides that there is a further issue. Perhaps the day after, or in two days. I shall see what Asenath wishes."

They arrived at the house after some time, and Joseph saw that Asenath had just returned as well. He offered her his hand as she stepped from the litter. "Smell this," she said, holding out a small alabaster jar with a painted blue rim. He sniffed and quirked his brow. It was sweet and fresh, and oddly familiar.

"Do you like it?" she asked with a smile.

"Yes, but what is it?"

Her eyes twinkled. "Is it familiar?"

"Yes," he laughed. "But what in heaven's name is it?"

"The merchant called it a balm of styrax."

Recognition dawned and he smelled it again. "My mother wore this in Padan-Aram."

She smiled again. "I hoped you would know it," she said. "The man said it was from just north of Canaan. I thought it a pleasant smell before I even knew what it was. I shall wear it, I think, if you do not mind."

"Of course I do not. I am glad you found it."

They turned and walked slowly through the courtyard towards the house. The evening meal would be soon.

"I think my business here shall be ended after tomorrow," he said after a moment.

"Really? After I forced you to retire early last night?"

"I promised you I would see to it that there was less work."

His wife laughed. "Forgive me; I doubted you."

Joseph shook his head and smiled. "I suppose you had reason to. When would you like to leave? Have you seen everyone here you wished to?"

She had been making her rounds, visiting old friends from Heliopolis who were in the city. "Yes," she said. They entered the great room, and she took a seat heavily on the long row of cushions that lined one wall. "I feel I am done explaining that no, I would not like to visit the temples of Ptah. Or Sekhmet. Or Nefertem." She put a hand to her eyes. "No one says as much to me, but I believe we are commonly spoken of in Memphis as heretics."

Joseph leaned back on the cushions as well. "They shall see in five years, I suppose."

Asenath shook her head a little. "Joseph, they shall only see that the God of your family is *a* god. A powerful one, perhaps. But to convince an Egyptian that there is only *one* God—" she sat back upright and looked at him earnestly. "That is quite another thing."

"You are convinced."

"There are not very many so sick of the gods as I was. It will take something far greater than this famine to prove God's sovereignty to Egypt, I think."

229

"What could be worse than seven years of famine?"

She shook her head. "God knows. Perhaps He plans. But it will not be this."

26

The slight rocking of the boat was soothing, and the sun was sending delicate fingers of light over the eastern hills when Joseph awoke. He stood to glance out the high windows and saw that they would be landed at Itjtawy within the hour. Already the white pyramids to the west were dropping behind them. "Asenath," he murmured. He reached over and gently shook her awake. "We will arrive soon."

"Mmm," she mumbled, taking a moment to master herself. "All right." She slid off the bed, and they both knelt.

"You today," Joseph murmured.

"My God," Asenath said. "Thanks and all glory be to You, for what You have done for us. Your servants are not worthy of the least of Your mercies. Show us Your purpose for our lives and grant us wisdom and peace." She paused, and added: "And if it be Your will, show us how we might serve You in a land that does not."

"Comfort my father and Dinah," Joseph added. "Give them peace in their lives. Deliver Benjamin from my brothers."

"Search our hearts," Asenath said. "And show us what is in them that does not please You."

It had been her idea to add the supplication, saying that it had always troubled her to be told that Osiris and Ma'at would weigh the heart after death, but knowing that much of what was done in life could be excused or glossed over with the help of a priest or scribe.

They stood, and Joseph added in his mind, as he often did:

231

I am thirty-two years old.
Benjamin is eighteen.
Dinah is thirty-four.
My father is 123.
He sighed.

They made ready for the day, and Asenath's maidservant had almost finished helping her with her hair when they docked in Itjtawy. Then, unexpectedly, Anhotep appeared in the doorway, face pale. "Sir," he whispered. "I don't know what, but something has happened. We have been stopped at the main docks, and there is a military contingent waiting for you."

Asenath went white and shooed out the maidservant. "What?" she hissed. She looked at Joseph. "Do you know what this is about?"

Joseph sat down heavily on the bed. Blood rushed in his ears as he stared blankly at the wooden decking that made up the floor. "Perhaps," he murmured at length. He glanced up at them both. "It may be the Lord General Prince Sonbe."

His wife's eyes went wide. "What about him?" She stared at him for a long moment. "Do you mean that he has *taken the throne?*"

"I don't know." Joseph turned to Anhotep. "If I must leave with them, will you ensure that Asenath is taken safely home?"

"Of course, sir. I'll call for the litter and have everyone accompany her."

She was looking between them wildly. "You don't mean to go to the palace."

"There may be nothing else I can do," Joseph said. He stepped towards her and clasped her hands. She gripped his in return, knuckles white, but face now measured.

"With God's favor, all will be well," he said, kissing her quickly. "Do not come out until they leave or I leave with them," he whispered as he turned to go. "It may be better that way."

He stepped from the room and walked slowly across the deck, followed closely by Anhotep. The servants and the boat's crew stood looking on in stunned silence. At the top of the ramp, Joseph drew himself up and looked down at the contingent. They stood at attention, almost like a guard of honor, but there was a tense air about them. "What is the meaning of this?" he called out.

"My lord Zaphnath-Paaneah," said the lieutenant carefully. He would not meet Joseph's eyes. "The Lord General Prince Sonbe demands your presence."

Joseph shifted ever so slightly. This was not Memphis, and there were no cynical nomarchs here. If there were ever a time to test the limits of his power, it was here and now. "Who is he to halt me here and demand my presence?" His heart pounded in his chest.

"My—lord—" the lieutenant gasped. "I am merely sent to deliver a message."

"It is offensive."

The lieutenant collapsed to his knees, and his contingent did the same. Joseph allowed his eyes to glance over the docks for the briefest moment. It was still early, yet activity had already begun. Several merchants and their servants, and a few tradesmen and women, watched from the outskirts of the scene, gawking. *Good.* They saw him as in control, not the lieutenant and his men.

"I will send a message in return. Tell the Lord General Prince Sonbe that he will await me at the noon hour in the great hall of his royal father."

"Yes, my lord," the lieutenant gasped. He scurried away with his contingent.

Joseph only watched them go for a moment before he turned. He stared across the Nile and blew out a long breath. "Sonbe will not be pleased," he murmured to Anhotep.

"Yes, sir, but least he knows you do not mean to so easily give way to him."

He shook his head. "I serve the throne. If the Pharaoh and the young Prince Senusret are dead, then I am at his disposal and have made a very poor showing here."

Anhotep gaped. "Surely he would not do such a thing without your backing. It could start a civil war."

Joseph only shook his head again. "As lord general, he may be willing to take that risk."

He arrived, ten minutes past the noon hour—for he intended to make Sonbe wait—to a silent palace. Guards stood at their posts, but no noblemen or women roamed the large courtyard as they so often did. The strains of music were silent. Joseph approached the doors to the great hall and set his jaw.

My God, help me!

The guards swung the doors open, and quickly shut them once he entered. The long room was empty save for a few guards standing in the far corners, and two men—the Prince Sonbe and Potiphar, standing in front of the raised dais on which sat the throne.

Joseph nearly stopped short upon seeing Potiphar. The man shot him a stricken look.

Sonbe turned. "Ah," he said coolly. "My lord Zaphnath-Paaneah. I had hoped to see you this morning."

"I was sorry to be forced to decline your invitation."

The prince shifted. "I will be blunt. My father is dead. I intend that the throne be mine."

Breath catching, Joseph turned to Potiphar and hoped his face remained impassive. "How did the Pharaoh die, Captain?"

"He fell ill, my lord, three days ago. The doctors have said his lungs became full. He passed in the night."

It was a strange kind of relief, to know that Sonbe had not done it, for there was no poison that could do such a thing. "I did not kill my own father," the prince spat, as if he had guessed Joseph's thoughts.

"Not for lack of trying, I think," Joseph answered.

Sonbe stared.

"I am given to understand your father trusted you," Joseph continued. "I am also given to understand that my predecessor did not. Nor do I." He crossed his arms. "I will not back the claim of a man who was neither the chosen of his father nor a worthy son."

234

The prince drew himself up. "I thought as much."

Joseph's heart thundered in his chest. "Where is the young Prince Senusret?"

"He and his sister still live, if that is your question."

"Let me see them."

Sonbe pursed his lips. "Very well." He motioned, and two guards at the far end of the hall opened a door. Through it were marched the Prince Senusret and the Princess Sithathoriunet. The boy was rigid and white, the young woman studiedly expressionless. As they were forced to a stop, they both looked at Joseph. The boy's eyes were pleading.

It was incongruous, but Joseph was somehow reminded of Benjamin and Dinah. His heart wrenched.

He tore his eyes from them. "The Prince Senusret, third of that name, will succeed his father," Joseph said. "I have spoken."

"I have heard your words." Sonbe cocked his head. "Potiphar, Captain of the Royal Guard," he said after a long moment. "You do not fear this one and his divination as so many do. Nor do I." He glanced at Joseph. "Arrest him, and the boy, and the girl, and I will erase the shame he has brought you from the record-books."

Joseph again caught his breath.

"It shall never again be spoken of. Your name shall be read with honor. But *this one*—" he raised a hand and pointed his finger at Joseph— "shall not be killed. He shall be sent to Tjaru, with nothing but a shendyt and the tattoo on his hand. *As is fitting.*"

Potiphar stared at Sonbe. The princess, shocked out of impassivity, slowly put a hand to her mouth.

Silence filled the room. Joseph raised his eyes to look at Potiphar, but the other man would not meet them. *This is why one takes revenge,* Joseph thought to himself, desperation rising. *If you do not, you leave yourself vulnerable.*

Oh my God! Let it not be so. I have tried to serve You. Forgive me where I have not. But do not let an act of forgiveness meant to honor You be the destruction of all I hold dear!

235

"Guards!" Potiphar's roar ripped through the silence. The young Prince Senusret started and shook where he stood.

Potiphar leveled a finger at Sonbe.

"Arrest this man."

The funeral procession of the Pharaoh Senusret spanned near a league. It moved along the west bank of the Nile, mourner after mourner following the curricle of the Pharaoh with slow steps. The pyramid ahead glimmered in the raucous sun, the morning already hot.

Drawn by two cattle, the curricle continued onward. Before it, many priests in white burned incense, letting the sweet smoke spread as they walked. The queen and her two children walked slowly beside it, followed by many members of their household. Behind them walked Joseph, and on his arm, Asenath.

The sound of weeping came from the long lines behind, and in front of him, Joseph had glimpsed the princess's and queen's faces, crumpled and tear-stained. But it was the young prince's face which tore at him the most—jaw set, but with eyes so wide and despairing that no one could mistake his anguish.

They continued on.

Reaching the pyramid, the dark opening in the side was revealed, and the curricle came to a halt before it. The High Priest approached the curricle and performed the Opening of the Mouth. Joseph looked away.

Gifts were brought forward, family by family, mourner by mourner, until the ground sparkled with gold and silver and jewels. And then, without a word, the curricle was brought inside the tomb.

The people turned, for the slow walk back to Itjtawy.

Joseph and Asenath stood, watching them go. Anhotep and a few servants stood silently behind them. His wife squeezed his hand, gently.

Then Joseph noticed the young prince. He stood staring at the tomb and those bringing the funerary gifts inside, as if he could do nothing else. Surrounded by servants, he still looked very alone. Frowning slightly and pressing his wife's hand in return, Joseph left her and moved towards the boy.

"Your Highness?" Joseph asked quietly as he approached. The boy turned, and Joseph saw tears hanging in his eyes.

He stared at Joseph. "What am I to do?"

"You are to be Pharaoh," Joseph answered as gently as he could. "But you are to surround yourself with those of your own choosing, whom you trust, so that you are not alone."

"Will you serve me as you have served my father? Will you save us from the doom of which my father was warned?"

"If it is your wish, I will serve my God while in your service, and do this thing."

With a shuddering breath, the boy nodded. "It is my wish." He looked up at Joseph, and with a sudden grit to his teeth and fire in his eye, said, "I will not be the Pharaoh under whom Egypt crumbles."

"Your father has given you a strong foundation."

The young Senusret drew himself up and squared his small shoulders, though his face was still disconsolate, and turned away. The servants followed. Joseph moved to go, but stopped short when he saw Potiphar standing nearby, watching him. Just moving out of sight over a rise in the road, he caught a glimpse of the Lady Tetisheri. She looked at him and moved quickly away.

He and Potiphar had not talked since the day in the great hall. There had been little time, with the preparations for the Pharaoh's funeral and the young prince's approaching ascension to the throne.

Joseph bowed his head a little and offered a small smile. Potiphar came forward.

"Thank you," Joseph said as he approached. "You held my life and much more in your hands. Many men might have chosen other than what you did."

Potiphar shook his head. "It should not have been something

the prince thought would tempt me." He took a deep breath. "I have wronged you, and greatly. You showed me mercy. How could I do anything else?"

"All the same, I am grateful to you."

"And I to you." Unexpectedly, Potiphar clasped his shoulders. "Blessed by Thoth," he said quietly. "Or One far greater. I am glad to have known you, Joseph."

It was a hot walk back to the city, and the sunlight shone dizzyingly off the golden sand and red hills, but Joseph found that he was content as he walked back with his wife. Glancing out over the wide river, he saw an ibis rise from the tall reeds and palms, its black head and white wings stark against the whitewashed blue of the sky.

They finally came to a field, shot through with canals. Heads of wheat drifted back and forth in the wind. Joseph nodded to himself, scanning it and thinking of the hundreds of fields and canals, both old and new, that grew under the blessing of God. They stretched throughout the Pa-yuum and beyond. It would be enough.

He looked down at Asenath.

Do not let an act of forgiveness meant to honor You be the destruction of all I hold dear, he had prayed in that moment of dread.

All that I hold dear—

He looked around himself, at the river, the land, the city, and lastly, at the wife God had given him.

I am happy here.

My God.

Thank You.

27

The walk home was desperately hot. It always was these days, though spring had barely arrived.

Joseph made his way through the marketplace with two men in front and four behind and Anhotep walking next to him. It had to be so these days, every time he went to and from the city gates. The marketplace was far too busy, with foreigners coming to buy grain. He would never get through unscathed without the seven of them; the crowds would mob him with requests for favors and blessings and supplications for first spots in the grain lines.

The streets cleared as they made their way out of the marketplace, and the two men in front dropped behind with the other four. Anhotep frowned next to him, reviewing that day's trades and sales on a papyrus. "What shall we do if another group of Nubians attempts to trade in ostrich feathers?" his steward asked. He glanced again at the scroll. "The Pharaoh can only have so many, certainly?"

"I think we shall have to take it," Joseph said grimly. "They are desperate for food."

The years of famine had come two years ago, and one year ago the first group of foreigners had trickled in, saying that they had heard there was food to be had in Egypt. That trickle had become a steady stream and then a flood, of Nubians and men of the desert tribes to the west and traders from as far as Arabia and Assyria.

It had become so much that Joseph found he had to set aside time daily to travel to the storehouses that had been built near the riverfront to meet with them all. Translators had been found, and the hours he spent there were full of endless back-and-forth, languages mixing and services or strange goods being negotiated.

He sighed and looked up at the cloudless sky, hazed with dust and nearly white.

I am thirty-nine years old.

Benjamin is twenty-five.

Dinah is forty-one.

My father is 130.

His heart lurched. Were they surviving this?

Had his father even lived this long?

They reached the gates to the house and Joseph entered them gratefully.

"Papa!" His youngest shrieked from his spot under the rapidly-drying palms and then hurtled towards him, braided sidelock bouncing.

Joseph caught him in his arms and lifted him up. Ephraim screamed with delight. "Oho!" Joseph grunted. "You are getting heavy!" He set him down with a laugh.

"Papa, Papa!" the boy repeated, tugging at his robe. "Guess what?"

"What?"

"Come see!" Ephraim began dragging him in the direction of the sparse shade. Asenath rose from her seat there, wearing a sheepish expression. Behind her sat one of her maidservants, holding the makeshift collar of a skinny, tawny-colored dog. The hoopoe-bird sat in its cage nearby, looking on nervously.

His wife gave him a half-exasperated, half-amused look as he approached. "One of the kitchen maids found her at the gate and gave her a bit of food as a kindness. Now she has decided she will not leave. Ephraim has taken a fancy to her."

"Can I keep her, Papa?" Ephraim broke in.

Joseph looked at Asenath, who raised her hands helplessly. "I told him the decision was yours."

Just then the courtyard gates opened again and Joseph heard Manasseh enter with his tutor, who had taken him to the palace to hear a special lecture that day. "A dog!" he heard his eldest shout. The boy dashed over. "Where did you get it?"

"I found her," Ephraim answered. "I named her Mai."

Asenath covered her mouth with the back of her hand and cast an amused glance at Joseph.

"Mai?" Manasseh repeated. "*Lion?* Ephraim, you cannot name her that. She is a dog. A lion is a large cat." His older son's words were spoken kindly enough, but Joseph thought Manasseh fancied himself rather worldly-wise as he said it.

"She is the right color," Ephraim stated, as if that explained it all.

Joseph put a hand on Manasseh's shoulder to quiet him before he protested further. "Ephraim," he said. "Will you care for her? Will you make certain that she does not bother Aya or the hoopoe-bird? It is a large task."

"Oh, yes, Papa!"

Asenath laughed as the boys descended on the dog to play with and pet. Mai rose to meet them, panting and wiggling in delight.

His wife put her arm around him. Then she frowned. "Joseph," she said slowly. "Looking at the dog now—I think we may have to prepare for pups."

Asenath was right. Four pups were born, two males and two females. The first three were the same tawny color as their mother. Ephraim, upon seeing them, quickly named them Mai Two, Mai Three, and Mai Four. The last pup to be born was black as night. Apparently struck by the difference in color, Ephraim picked up the youngest pup and spoke softly to him for several moments. Then he set him down and promptly named him Mai Five.

"One would think we have a dynasty in our house and not a litter of pups," Asenath murmured dryly to Joseph.

Laughing, he gave her a quick kiss and made his way toward the storehouses outside the city gates. Anhotep followed him, as always, and six menservants.

When he arrived at the stand that had been set up for him, the crowds were the largest he had yet seen. They spilled off the pathway, all the way down to the riverbanks, and back towards the docks. As Joseph climbed the stand with Anhotep behind him, the crowds erupted in a cheer. Joseph nodded a little and sat down on one of the chairs under the canopy, and the nearby guards quickly urged the chaos into somewhat of a line.

The rolling sound of the Nubian language came to Joseph's ears. He looked up. There was a group of Nubian men near the front of the line, speaking quickly and carrying what looked like ivory.

Not ostrich feathers. Joseph nodded to himself.

And then, at the very front of the line, he saw a group of men in long, colorful robes, heavily bearded and looking very out of place. They were casting glances about themselves as if they could not quite believe what they saw. One spoke to another, and Joseph thought the sound of the language was the most beautiful thing he had ever heard.

Another of the group answered quickly, and a few others murmured in response. It was at that moment that something altered in Joseph's mind, and he realized that he could understand them.

They were speaking Canaanite.

Joseph nodded distractedly to the guard who approached to tell him that all was ready and turned his eyes back to the group of men. They were moving toward him. He cast his eyes over them again and felt his heart stop.

In a moment of sheer instinct, he stood up and whirled to face the other direction, hoping desperately that they had not seen his face.

He knew these men.

My brothers!

The world tilted disconcertingly before his eyes, and blood rushed in his ears. Blindly, his hand grasped the back of the chair. He tried to reason with himself. *It can't be them—what are the chances of it? I'm being ridiculous. Hearing the Canaanite has simply rattled my brain.*

242

And yet, deep inside himself, he knew what he would see if he turned.

No solutions flashed through his mind, no plan quickly formulated itself. There was only a deep sense of dread that seeped through him until his limbs felt heavy as bronze. His feet were rooted to the platform on which he stood.

And he could not keep them waiting any longer.

He set his jaw, and with great effort, forced himself to turn and look at them. His heart pounded. When they looked up—

They were bowed, faces to the ground. One by one, they raised their eyes to look at him.

It *was* them. As he expected.

For a long moment he stood there, waiting. Waiting for them to gasp and shout in recognition. But as he met the uncomprehending eyes of the group of men kneeling before him, he realized with a sort of relieved horror that they did not recognize him.

Rage boiled up in him.

He almost staggered at its onset. His mind reeled. He had not felt such white-hot anger since his first days in Egypt. He wanted to scream at them.

Snakes! Fools! How can you not recognize me? How can you not look on me and see a son of Jacob?

Seconds passed.

Joseph crossed his arms in front of him, barely breathing. Reason slowly filtered back into his mind.

He was no longer seventeen. Years in the desert sun had tanned him far darker than any of them, and he was clean-shaven, eyes painted, and wearing his khat. He was, to them, an Egyptian. And why should he not be? Even Intef had thought him an Egyptian, once.

Slowly, he lowered himself into his chair.

His heart still thundered in his chest. At any moment, something he might do could bring recognition to their eyes.

Then his breath caught.

Benjamin.

243

Mind racing, he searched the group, face by face, looking for a man—for he would be a man—whose face he could not identify. One by one he studied them, coming to grips with what twenty-two years had done to each of them. But there was no young man in the group with eyes the color of the sky.

He counted and found there to be ten of them.

Where is Benjamin?

Cold fear settled in his stomach, pushing aside the anger.

His brothers stirred uncomfortably, waiting for Joseph to speak.

He grit his teeth. And he spoke.

"Where have you come from?" he heard himself bark in Egyptian.

The group of brothers exchanged disquieted looks. Joseph knew they would not understand. Reuben raised himself up slightly, hands upheld. "Please, my lord—"

Joseph held up one hand and cut him off.

This would not do. He would not begin speaking Canaanite with them. Joseph did not know what he was about to do, but he would not break the ruse that had fallen so neatly into his lap. Not in front of all these people, if he could help it.

Turning to Anhotep, he murmured, "These men are from Canaan. Will you bring the translator?"

His steward looked at him questioningly, but nodded, and Joseph guessed what he would be thinking. Anhotep knew that Joseph spoke Canaanite. There was a flurry of activity, and then a translator rushed forward from the direction of the docks, the same one who had been translating for those who spoke Assyrian. He bowed quickly to Joseph.

"Ask these men from whence they come," Joseph said.

"From Canaan, to buy food," Reuben answered the translator quickly. The translator repeated his words, and both men looked expectantly up at Joseph.

Joseph looked again out over the men, still kneeling.

Before his mind's eye, there unexpectedly flashed the image of sheaves of wheat, bowing before his.

He stared, thunderstruck.

Opening his mouth to speak, for he knew he should, no words came.

"The meaning of any dream belongs to God," his father had said. *"It is not for us to parade our own interpretations about. Especially interpretations of such dreams."*

Such dreams.

They had been true—and not as he thought they had, telling him of God's plan to save Egypt. They had been fully true. Here were his brothers, bowing before him.

His brain did not give him even a moment to consider the knowledge in incredulity. Thoughts now flew by in rapid succession.

Father!

Is he alive?

Dinah!

And where is Benjamin?

Joseph stood abruptly. They must give him information.

"You are spies," he said sharply after a moment. He waved an imperious hand towards them and willed the goading to work. "You have come to see our land while it is weak."

The translator looked at him worriedly and quickly repeated the words.

"No, my lord!" Reuben gasped. The others cried aloud. "Your servants are honest men. We have only come to buy food! We are no band of spies—we are all the sons of one man!"

"You are spies," Joseph repeated grimly, determined to try again. The constant wait for the translator was agonizing.

"Sir," Reuben said. He held up his hands again, placating. "We speak the truth. Your servants were twelve brothers. We are all the sons of one man, who lives in Canaan. You see ten of us here. The youngest has remained with our father. One other is no more."

Benjamin is alive.

My father is alive.

—I am no more.

At this, he snapped.

They had stolen it from him. A chance to look after Dinah. There was not even a way to ask after her. Twenty-two years with Benjamin. With his father. And alive or not, God only knew how they had treated his brother in that time. He had not been there to watch over him.

I am no more.

His thoughts raced, frenetic. "You are spies!" he roared. A wave of grief and blind fury rose up in his body, and a haphazard plan sprang into his mind. "By the life of the Pharaoh, you will not leave this place until I lay eyes on this youngest brother. You will choose one man to bring him here to me. The rest of you will be kept in prison. If that man does not return with this youngest brother, then you are *not speaking the truth.*" He turned to the guards. "Take them away!"

The translator had gotten only halfway through his speech when his brothers jumped to their feet in terror. The scene flew into an uproar. Guards leapt from all sides, spears extended. They bullied the men away, down to the docks. Then they turned the corner towards the gates and the marketplace.

All fell deathly silent. The rest of the waiting crowds looked about them, wide-eyed, not speaking a word.

Joseph, feeling sick, quickly descended from the platform.

He had been alone in the antechamber of one of the storehouses, sitting slumped in a chair, khat in his lap and head in his hands, for less than a minute before he heard a determined knock at the door.

"Sir?" It was Anhotep.

He wearily lifted his head. His temples pounded, and every limb was heavy with exhaustion. "Come in."

His steward entered and shut the door firmly behind him. He took a deep breath and before Joseph could speak, said: "Sir, with all due respect, what is happening? Why have you put the Canaan-ites in prison?"

Joseph looked up. It was clear on Anhotep's face that he felt very out of his place.

"Sir, you are not yourself. This is not like you."

Standing up and leaving his khat on the chair, Joseph paced the room. Anhotep lowered his head in response, face distressed, and Joseph felt a prickle of guilt for putting the man in this position.

"Anhotep," he said quietly. He walked to the opposite side of the small room and settled heavily against the mud-brick wall. "These are the men who sold me into slavery."

The other man gaped at him.

"There is more."

"More?" his steward managed.

"They are also my brothers."

Anhotep stared at him for a full five seconds, something like horror on his face. "Your brothers?"

Joseph nodded.

"I–I do not know what to say."

Pursing his lips, Joseph walked back over to the chair. He picked up the khat, sat back down without putting it on, and looked at Anhotep tiredly. "Neither do I."

It had been a fey mood that had gripped him, but now it was leaving, pulling back like the waters of the Nile in famine and leaving nothing but hollowness behind. It struck him that he had not spoken to God once since he had first seen his brothers.

His stomach twisted in guilt.

Then, even so, his mind drew up against it, protesting that his anger, *this once*, was justified, throwing each wretched memory against the guilt. Raging in desperation. Every aim to force its retreat.

"What will you do now, sir?"

"I don't know."

His steward took a step forward. "You—do not want to make yourself known to them?"

Joseph looked away. "No. Not here, at least. And not now."

At length, Anhotep nodded slowly. "Very well, sir." He sounded ever so slightly resigned.

It was his tone which brought Joseph to his senses. Sudden shame rose in him. Anhotep disapproved of his behavior.

How much more did his God?

My God, forgive me.

Give me wisdom.

For I have none this day.

He drew his hand across his eyes. "You ought to tell me that, at the very least, they should not be left in that prison, and one sent back across the desert alone. For you would be right."

The other man looked taken aback. "Sir. I—many men would put them there, send them to Tjaru, and never speak to them again. Many men would count it as just. But it does not sound, to me, that such a thing would be right by the God you serve."

Joseph let out a long breath and closed his eyes. "Just so." After a moment, he heaved himself from the chair and slowly replaced his khat. "You asked me what I am going to do," he said. "I am going to finish my work, and then I am going to think."

28

He was home only moments before Asenath descended on him in the courtyard. "What happened today?" she whispered. "One of the maidservants came running up from the marketplace and said that you put a group of foreigners in prison."

Joseph gave her a meaningful look. They moved quickly inside to his study, and he shut the door firmly behind him. "I did," he replied quietly, hand still on the latch. He turned to face her.

"What did they do?"

Crossing his arms, Joseph looked at the floor. "Asenath, you must understand—" His throat caught, and he found that he could not finish the sentence. He looked up at her helplessly.

"Oh," she murmured, eyes wide, and rushed to him. She caught his hand. "What is it? What happened?"

Joseph shook his head and closed his eyes. He forced out the words. "They—are my brothers."

"*What?*"

He lifted his eyes, wordlessly.

"Did you quarrel?" she breathed.

"No."

"What did they say?"

"Asenath, *they didn't recognize me.* So I used an interpreter. I told them they were spies. And I put them in prison."

His wife stared at him, face moving from stunned to pained. She bit her lip and led him to the cushions that surrounded the table. He sat, and she knelt, still clasping his hands.

She took a deep breath. "Many men would have done the same." She gave him an earnest look. "Joseph, I grew to love you because of your kindness and the forgiveness you showed. Even if they are not innocent, their families will starve if you do not send them home with grain."

"I know it," said Joseph. He found his voice shook.

"Oh, Joseph," Asenath whispered. Tears hung in her eyes, and she embraced him. "I am sorry. I am so sorry. I wish to God that you never had this pain."

He returned her embrace tightly. "I must fix this," he murmured into her shoulder. She drew back to look at him. "I told them that one must return to Canaan to bring Benjamin here. But to travel alone these days is folly." Gritting his teeth, he continued. "If they do as I say, the brother who goes to retrieve Benjamin will die before he ever reaches Canaan. And their families will starve."

There was a determined expression on her face. "Let us fix it, then. I will help you."

After two days, it was the best plan they could devise. Joseph would send all but one brother back to Canaan, with enough food to last for some little time, and the vow that Benjamin would be brought on the next journey. "I must see him for myself," Joseph said to Asenath. The vehemence behind his words threatened to overtake his mind. "I do not trust them. I will not reveal myself to them. But I must know how they have treated him. If he is well."

Joseph sat at the small side-table in the bedroom, meaning to wash his face to prepare for sleep, but instead was lost in whirling thought. Shaking his head as he realized the level of his distraction, he pulled off his khat and scrubbed his hands though his lengthening hair. Curls were forming again; he hadn't had time to have it cut. He ran tired hands over his face. A headache was threatening.

Then, on an impulse, he picked up the hand mirror, stared at himself, and frowned.

He only had a moment, for Asenath walked in. Joseph started, almost dropping the mirror.

"Good heavens, are you all right?" she asked.

Pausing, Joseph thought. Was he? He had no idea. Then he sighed. "I was trying to see if I am so very unrecognizable." He looked up at his wife, a little abashed, before getting to his feet and walking over to sit heavily on the bed. "I have heard I look like an Egyptian."

She came to sit next to him. "Sometimes more than others," she said with a small smile, running a hand through his thick hair. "But I find you quite handsome whether you do or no."

Joseph found that a chuckle escaped him. The throbbing in his temples lessened slightly, and he gave her a kiss.

She put a hand on his shoulder, and her face grew serious. "You are thinking of your brothers?"

"Yes. I was prepared to have a confrontation, right then and there. When they did not know me—it was a relief, in a way. But it also made me more angry."

"You had a right to be," Asenath admitted. "But it might also be expected. In their minds, they know you as a seventeen-year-old boy. You are the vizier of Egypt, and a great deal more than seventeen."

"Oh, a great deal?" Joseph replied with a wry smile. He could not help it. She lifted his mood.

She gave him a dry look. "Yes, a *great* deal. But again, I find you quite handsome nonetheless."

"Well," Joseph said with a laugh, again scrubbing his hands tiredly across his face. "That, if nothing else, is a relief."

Joseph approached the prison with no small amount of trepidation. Next to him walked Anhotep, and behind him walked the usual four menservants, as well as the interpreter. With each step, apprehension grew in him that his brothers would recognize him, once they laid eyes on him a second time. More than anything, he did not want to give them any hold over him, not before he saw Benjamin.

Oh my God, help me. Give me wisdom. Lead me in a way that pleases You.

They entered the small front room of the prison, and as Joseph stood, eyes adjusting to the dim light, he was struck with the realization that the last time he had stood there, nine years ago, he had been a slave.

He only had a moment to contemplate it. There came the sound of hurrying feet, and Intef and two guards appeared in the doorway that led down the hallway. They bowed deeply, and Joseph took Anhotep and Intef aside, out of earshot of the others.

"How have they behaved?" Joseph murmured.

"They made a bit of trouble when they first arrived, bellowing at each other and us," answered Intef. "They're manageable now, though we don't understand a word any of them says. They have learned to make bricks quickly enough. They're waiting for you, as you requested."

"Thank you," Joseph said.

"Of course. You've certainly made good on my standing offer. Ten men at once! Are you making up for lost time?"

The prison-master meant well, but the jest rang hollow. Anhotep glanced at the man in annoyance. Joseph forced a small smile. "I would hope that this will not happen again. I will see them now."

Intef led him and the others down the narrow hallway, and they exited out onto the rim of the sunken courtyard. Joseph looked down into it with a sudden shot of morbid curiosity, but his attention was quickly arrested by the group of ten men. They stood on the widest part of the rim, surrounded by guards.

He had thought that he would be able to be measured and deliberate, but seeing them standing not five cubits away sent a shot of fear through him. His throat grew dry, and his heart raced.

They would recognize him, surely.

They dropped to their knees.

252

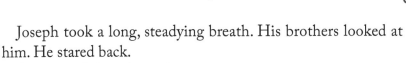

Joseph took a long, steadying breath. His brothers looked at him. He stared back.

And they did not know him.

They might never unless he allowed it. The thought bolstered him.

"I have decided," he said, once he mastered his voice. "Do this, and you will live and go free, for I fear your God. You say you have another brother, one who is younger. Is this truly so?"

The translator spoke, and his brothers murmured assent.

"And you say he is with your elderly father?"

"Yes, my lord," said Reuben.

"Then, if you are truly honest men, let one of your brothers remain here in the prison. The others may go, and take food for your families. When you next return, bring this youngest brother, so that your words will be proven and so that you will not be executed as spies."

Gasps rippled through the group as the translator reached the threat of execution. It was empty, but they could not know that. Levi made a desperate sound from the back of the group, his words hissing outward and meeting Joseph's ears.

"It is our guilt over our brother come back to find us."

Stunned, Joseph stood very still.

"We heard his cries for help and his fear, and we continued with the wretched plan," Levi said.

"It is as you say. This is our punishment," Judah murmured in response.

"Did I not tell you lot not to sin against the boy?" Reuben growled. "You would not listen. Now his blood is required of us."

In a daze, Joseph turned from the scene and stepped away. His breath left him.

After all these years, their first thought when facing trouble was—punishment—for what they did to him?

They felt—*guilt?*

He had never considered it. He had thought they would never have considered it again except with pleasure. If they considered it at all.

253

Had they instead lived twenty-two years with such horrific shame? His throat tightened, and he put a bracing hand on the low wall that overlooked the courtyard.

Oh God, what is this?

Tears unexpectedly hung from his eyes. He scrubbed them away, quickly. This would not do.

Help me!

He turned back to the scene, face as impassive as he could muster. His brothers still squabbled in hushed tones. "I have decided," Joseph said again. The men stilled. Joseph looked long at them, and then pointed a finger at Simeon. He would have enough reckless bravado to manage a prison sentence with no set end. "That one shall stay."

Two guards roughly pulled Simeon away, roping his hands together for the walk towards the ladder. The man shouted and struggled and cursed, but the brothers only watched in stricken silence.

"Simeon," Judah finally cried out. "We will return, I swear it!"

Joseph was not certain he could stand another moment of the scene. He whirled quickly. "Bring the rest," he shouted behind him. Back through the dark hall he walked, turning to Intef as they went. "Treat the man well. He will not be going to Tjaru."

The prison-master bowed in acknowledgement.

They all filed out into the street in front of the prison, and Joseph motioned to Anhotep. Blood rushed in his ears, and the world somehow seemed very far away.

His steward approached, eyes wide. "Yes, sir?"

Swallowing, it was a moment before Joseph could speak. The other man watched him worriedly. "Bring them to the storehouses and give them grain. But," Joseph glanced behind Anhotep at the troubled group of men. "Put whatever they pay you with back in their sacks. I will pay for it. And make sure they have enough to eat for their journey."

"Of course."

"I hope I have done—what is right," Joseph murmured.

Everything had become far more wildly complex than he had ever anticipated.

His steward could not know what his brothers had said, but Joseph saw he understood it had been important. "I think," Anhotep offered hesitantly, "that your God is pleased."

Joseph sighed. "I hope that you are right."

He watched his brothers leave, surrounded by guards and following Anhotep. Joseph felt, unexpectedly, as though a piece of himself were leaving with them.

Their admission of guilt had rattled him.

Had they—in defiance of everything, changed?

When they brought Benjamin, then he might know.

Spring had transformed into a raging summer that grew by the day. Joseph sat with Asenath and the two boys in the great room, one hand on Mai's soft ears. The evening meal would be soon. A brown haze was in the sky, and Joseph feared a dust storm might be on its way.

"I am not hungry," Manasseh said, sprawled facedown on the cool stones of the floor next to Mai and her pups. His game of Hounds and Jackals sat nearby, untouched. "I am too hot."

"It is hot," Joseph said. "But you have food, and many do not. You must eat."

The boy sighed, voice muffled. "I know."

Ephraim looked up from Mai Five, who yawned in his lap. "Mama, can we ride the horse?"

Manasseh groaned slightly. "Ephraim, it is too hot."

"It is hot, Ephraim," Asenath answered. "But perhaps it will be cooler in the morning."

Their youngest sighed.

Joseph might have laughed at the abundance of sounds the boys were making, but it *was* hot, and he felt like groaning and sighing himself.

Anhotep entered, his customary wig missing and head bare.

Ephraim sat bolt upright. "Anhotep! Where is your wig?"

The steward chuckled. "In safe keeping, young master. I found the weather too much for it."

"Will you make sure the servants have extra water, beer, food—anything they need?" Joseph asked quietly.

"Of course, sir." Anhotep held out a scroll. "I have word that several of the nomarchs from Upper Egypt are on their way to Itjtawy. They want to discuss having more grain shipped to them than what they already have."

"What?" Joseph frowned and took the scroll. He shook his head. "I find it difficult to believe they need it; we calculated what they would require." He squinted down at the list of numbers on the papyrus.

"Evidently the desert tribesmen have been trading for quite a bit of it."

Joseph perused the dispatch. "We ought to just have them come to Itjtawy to purchase or trade. They might be considered foreigners. But I'm sure the nomarchs enjoy the commerce it brings them." He glanced at Asenath. "We will need to host them for a meal of two, if not more."

She nodded. "Of course."

"I'll make preparations," said Anhotep.

Joseph had moved the hours in which he sold grain to foreigners to the early morning, closing all sales for the day before noon. The heat had become too much for anything else. He kissed Asenath's sleeping face as he left and stepped out with Anhotep and the servants into the pale light of dawn. Heat still pressed tightly around them, but it was bearable.

The nomarchs would come once again to his home near noon, and he would see to his second day's meeting with them. He was busy considering how best to approach their concerns, and so did not look out over the crowd when he arrived at the stand.

"Sir," Anhotep said quietly.

"Hmm?" Joseph said. He turned to glance at his steward as he took a seat under the canopy.

"Sir, look."

He looked, and there, in the crowd, was a young man whose eyes were the color of the sky.

29

It was as if every moving thing in the world careened to a stop, and all that mattered was that young man, standing there, surrounded by his brothers.

Benjamin.

He was tall, as tall as Joseph, and in his handsome face Joseph could see the likeness of their mother.

His heart wrenched.

"Anhotep," he breathed, still staring at his brother. "Please take them all to the house, and have Simeon brought up from the prison. Slaughter one of the calves to add to the meal. I will dine with them at noon."

The other man nodded and stepped off the platform, calling the group aside and leading them off. All of them cast glances back at Joseph, bewildered and a little uneasy. One of the granary officials stepped onto the platform to take Anhotep's place. Joseph pretended to read a scroll and tried to watch from the corner of his eye.

It was no use. His mind was a howling blank. He looked up and met Benjamin's eyes, just as his brother glanced backward over his shoulder.

Benjamin looked at him as Joseph remembered once gaping at Potiphar and all his seemingly impossible wealth. There was no recognition—*Why would there be*—only an awed stare of something like stupefaction.

His brother looked away, as though he thought he was being

impudent. Blood rushed in Joseph's ears. He wanted to scream and run after him.

Heart pounding, Joseph watched the group turn the corner onto the docks, and then they were gone.

As if waking from a dream, he again saw the crowds before him. He drew his hand over his eyes.

And he counted the hours.

If he could have run home at noon he would have, but the vizier could not sprint through the streets with six menservants and the translator puffing after him, driving the populace to dive out of his way. He grit his teeth and walked through the marketplace, through the lower streets, and up towards the grand houses. His heart was pounding and his stomach was so scrambled that he did not think he would be able to eat a thing.

The outline of his house was agonizingly far as he turned the street corner and began the long walk uphill. His pace quickened. *Blast decorum.*

It was only a moment before he burst through the gates and was relieved to see that the nomarchs had not yet arrived for their meeting. Asenath and the boys were out, as they had planned for the day his brothers returned. They likely had gone with several other families to the river. The courtyard was empty. He hastened inside and found his brothers there in the great room, seated on cushions, with a few servants waving fans nearby and another serving cool date wine.

The scene was so fantastically bizarre that he almost halted midstep.

His brothers started and jumped to their feet before bowing deeply. "My lord." Reuben hurried forward. He held an earthenware pot, painted white and run through with rings and lines of deep red. Levi and Judah stepped forward in turn, more pots in their hands.

The pots looked rustic against the rich paint of the walls, the sparkling stones on the floor, and the little alabaster jars and carved wooden boxes that sat on side-tables throughout the room. But they were, Joseph thought, quite possibly the most beautiful objects he had seen in twenty-two years.

"We have gifts for you, if it pleases my lord. Balm and honey and some spices. There is myrrh as well, and pistachios and almonds."

The translator relayed the message, and Joseph waited impatiently. The more he listened to the man, the more he decided that the translator's Canaanite was lacking.

"I thank you." Joseph was able at answer at length. He wondered what had possessed them to bring such things in a time of famine. It might be all they had left of each. He nodded, and two menservants stepped forward to receive the gifts.

Looking again over the group, his eyes lighted on Simeon. He did not look particularly worse for the wear. Intef, it seemed, had treated him especially well.

And in the center of them all stood Benjamin. Joseph met his eyes again for the briefest moment, but his brother quickly looked away.

"Is your family well in this difficult time?" Joseph forced out the words. His stomach knotted. "Your father, the old man of whom you spoke, he is still alive?"

"Yes, my lord," Reuben answered. Joseph's limbs went limp with relief. "Your servant our father is in good health." He bowed again, and the others followed suit.

Mouth dry, Joseph ventured, "Is this then your youngest brother?"

The translator spoke the words, and Benjamin's eyes widened slightly. He set his jaw and then stepped forward, casting his eyes to the floor. Judah set a hand on his shoulder. "Your servant's name is Benjamin, my lord," his brother murmured.

Joseph could not even touch him. He stood, paralyzed by his position of authority. Every part of his mind shrieked at him to take hold of the man and cling to him with all his strength.

"God be gracious to you." The words tumbled out of his mouth, hollow, as though he heard them from a great distance. The room

260

seemed to tilt and go grey. "Excuse me," he said to the unexpectedly blurred forms that stood before him. "I will return in a moment."

He moved quickly towards the doorway to the private rooms, and once he had turned the corner into the corridor, slumped against the wall. Joseph remained there for several interminable moments before heaving himself up and stumbling to the bedroom. Shutting the door firmly, he sat on the bed and put his head in his hands.

Joseph found his cheeks wet and scrubbed the tears away. "Oh my God," he whispered, voice ragged. "Give me strength. What am I supposed to do?"

"I will be back in a few days." His own words came, unbidden, to his mind. He saw Benjamin, three years of age and staring at him in the concerned way of a young child who does not quite understand.

"I'm going on a small journey," he had said to him. *"That's all."*

Words had never been more untrue.

Sudden rage boiled up again against the others. What they had done to him had also harmed Benjamin. To grow up with a dead brother, a dead mother—and, guilt-ridden or no, how could his older brothers have treated him kindly? It was clear Benjamin had remained behind during their first journey to Egypt because he was the favorite of Jacob.

He thought of Reuben and Bilhah. Of Simeon and Levi in Shechem. Of Dan, beating the donkey. He thought of himself. In Dothan. In the pit.

He knew his brothers.

They were not kind.

Grim determination took hold. He stood up. He would know for certain what kind of brothers they were to Benjamin. Walking to one of the carven chests that had been given him and Asenath at their wedding, Joseph opened it and searched inside the layers of delicate linen to take hold of one of the silver cups. Finely made, it was in the form of a tall lotus blossom.

Joseph stared at it, spinning thoughts coalescing into an idea.

He washed his face, and, taking a deep breath, set his jaw before returning to the great room.

Anhotep was waiting quietly to have the servants bring in the meal at Joseph's command. Joseph, entering slowly, set the cup down at his seat, making certain his brothers saw it. His steward stared at him curiously, and the translator stepped forward.

"You will be seated," Joseph said to his brothers.

The servants had prepared two long, low tables at the far ends of the room, one for his brothers and another for the nomarchs. Joseph motioned toward one. "Anhotep, please seat them in this order."

Taking up the cup and tipping it lazily on the tabletop, so that he appeared to swirl its contents, Joseph stared down into the imaginary depths for a long moment. At length, he looked up. Then he pointed to them one by one, in order of age.

Reuben.

Simeon.

Levi.

Judah.

Dan.

Naphtali.

Gad.

Asher.

Issachar.

Zebulun.

He paused at his place in their order and held them with his gaze. Their faces were dumbfounded.

"And Benjamin," Joseph finished after a long moment.

There was silence.

At that moment, the nomarchs bustled in, bowing to Joseph and then looking at his brothers with something like consternation. Anhotep led them to the second table.

The meal was soon served to Joseph, with many servants traveling back and forth to ensure that enough food was brought to his brothers and the nomarchs. His brothers gasped at the sight of the beef and even the bread, and though the onions and melons were, to Joseph's mind, a little poor, they dug into them as if they had never eaten in their lives. "Give the youngest extra food," Joseph murmured to Anhotep. He watched his brothers from the corner of his eye and then looked back up his steward. "Give him a ridiculous amount. Five times as much as he needs. I have an idea."

He found Anhotep in the courtyard that evening after the nomarchs had left, his steward ensuring that the kitchens and stables were in order before the household began to slowly turn towards bed. With a quick motion of his head, Joseph led the other man to the garden behind the house. It was fallow and empty. Quietly, he drew the silver cup from his robes and handed it to Anhotep. "When their sacks of grain are made ready, again put their payments at the top of each sack. But put this in the sack of the youngest as well. Send them away at dawn."

The man stared down at the cup he was holding and then back up at Joseph. "Sir—why are you doing all of this to the youngest?"

Joseph looked at him evenly. "I want to see if they will care for him as they ought. Or if they will rid themselves of him as they did to me."

His steward looked at him with feeling. "I will do it."

Clasping his shoulder, Joseph nodded. "Thank you."

Inside, the house was quiet. Oddly so, for Joseph had directed Anhotep to put all eleven of his brothers up in the guest quarters while he met with the nomarchs. Joseph could never remember them being so silent. He made his way to his bedroom. Asenath was there, sitting on the bed and slowly combing out wet hair. She looked up at him as he shut the door.

"Is it done?" she asked.

"Yes."

Joseph pulled off his khat with a sigh and fell face-up onto the bed. "I hope I am doing what is right."

Turning to face him, she drew up her feet and sat cross-legged next to his head. "Do you truly feel that you have to test them?"

He looked at her. "How else am I to know if Benjamin is safe? I cannot tell a thing from how they act in front of me. How else am I to know if—" He cut himself off and took a long, steadying breath. Despite the insistence of his reason that his brothers could never have treated Benjamin as they ought, their admission of guilt had awakened in him a distant, but captivating possibility. A tiny corner of his mind refused to abandon it.

Asenath frowned a little. "If what?"

"If I can—ever tell them who I am?"

She leaned over him, eyes compassionate. "My dear one. You could reveal yourself to them now."

"No." His mind shied at the idea, balking as he had once dug his feet into the sand to keep from being dragged to Egypt. "I must know if they have changed. I do not want to know them again if they have not. I do not want you to know them, or Manasseh or Ephraim. It would be foolish. It would be dangerous."

His wife set her comb in her lap. "Very well. And if they let Benjamin be blamed? What will you do?"

Joseph sighed again. "Then he will be better off than he was before, knowing. And then—I do not know, yet."

She frowned again. "It is not like you to have only part of a plan."

Looking at her resignedly, he quirked his mouth. "I know." He rubbed his face. "And I must resolve this, soon. I cannot remember a single thing I discussed with the nomarchs this afternoon. My God," he prayed aloud. "Give me wisdom."

Asenath put a hand on his chest and gave him a small, but fortifying, smile. "Take heart, Joseph. You have done all of this prayerfully. God is with you."

No sleep found him that night. Joseph turned, round and round, splayed on the bedding but found no spot that gave him rest. He finally gave up and simply stared up at the darkness for what seemed like hours upon end. When the merest light of dawn came through the high window, he rose. Pulling a light robe over his shendyt, he crept down the corridors to the entrance of the great room and listened.

Quiet voices came to his ears. Anhotep was sending his brothers away. With no translator to explain to them what was happening, their voices were strained, full of hushed confusion. He heard the doors to the courtyard open, and after several moments, they swung back shut.

He took a deep breath.

It is done.

The morning was a haze. Servants had been sent to postpone grain sales until the later afternoon. Half-cooked plans and eventualities so loudly buzzed in Joseph's mind that he almost left the bedroom for the morning meal without his khat and collar. Asenath looked up from her eyepaint and hand mirror just in time to warn him. Seated at breakfast, he did not know what he ate, or if he ate.

"Joseph?" Asenath's voice was quietly insistent. He felt a hand on his arm and shook himself a little, feeling as though he had just drawn up his head from a pool of water. She looked at him gently and then glanced towards Anhotep. Joseph turned to him.

"At your word, sir," Anhotep said.

Joseph nodded. It was near an hour past sunrise. It was time. "Yes, go," he said. "And when you find them, ask them why they have repaid my kindness with evil. Ask them why they have stolen my precious silver cup that I have used for divination."

His steward nodded, and he was gone.

Asenath put her hand in his.

30

Four hours later, his brothers entered the great room—dusty, breathless, and wild eyed—and fell to their knees in a tight huddle. Behind and around them marched Anhotep, the translator, and twelve guardsmen.

Joseph stood at the head of the room, heart pounding. He set his jaw and forced himself to begin.

He raked them all with a contemptuous glare. "What is this thing you have done?" he said. "Did you think a man such as I would not know who had done it? Did you not see me divine the order of your birth with that cup?"

There was a terrible silence as the translator finished speaking. Benjamin was white. Nearly retching at the unexpected sight, Joseph forced his eyes away from him.

"My lord."

He looked at Judah. The man's hands were raised in defeated supplication. "What can we say to these accusations?" His voice caught. "Indeed, there is nothing that can be said. How can we clear ourselves? God has seen the guilt of your servants. We are here, the one in whose sack the cup was found, and the others. We are your slaves."

Staring at the man in surprise, Joseph cocked his head. He tried another tactic. "Far be it from me to do such a thing. You have heard the words my steward was instructed to tell you." He gestured towards Benjamin. "Only the man in whose hand has been my silver cup shall be my slave. You and the rest of your brothers may return in peace to your father."

266

Wild glances flew between the brothers. Simeon shifted and tensed, almost as if he were about to lunge, but Reuben put a firm hand on his shoulder. Asher clutched Benjamin's arm.

Judah glanced behind to look at them all.

And then he stood.

The guards sprung forward, spears at the ready, as Judah raised desperate hands.

"Hold!" Joseph shouted.

The guards halted where they stood.

Joseph pinned Judah with a cold glare and took a step forward.

Perhaps Judah's initial actions were not surprising. But he would give in to Joseph's opposition now, for that was what Judah did. Joseph had seen him do it, more times than he could count. It was why he had ended up a slave.

Licking dry lips, his brother met his eyes and spoke.

"My lord—please let your servant speak, and do not let your anger rise against me, for truly your power is like that of the Pharaoh himself."

The translator finished the statement. No one breathed.

Stunned beyond words, Joseph looked at the other man, who seemingly would not relent. At length, he swallowed and tilted his head. "Speak."

Judah shrank with relief. Hands still uplifted, he spoke. "My lord knows that we have a father, an old man, and this one young brother, born in his old age. The young one's brother is dead, and he alone is left of his mother's children, and his father loves him dearly. And you said to your servants, 'Bring him down to Egypt, so that I may see him and know that you are honest men.'

"So it was, when our food began to run out once again in Canaan, that we went up to your servant our father, and told him of your words. He said, 'Go back and buy us some food.' But we said, 'It is as the man said. We cannot go down without our youngest brother.'

"And your servant our father replied, 'You know that my wife bore me two sons. One went away on a journey, and I said, "Surely he is torn to pieces," and I have not seen him since that day. But if you take this one from me also, and some harm befalls him and he should die, then you will bring down my grey head in sorrow to the grave.'

"Therefore, my lord, when I now come to our father, and the youngest is not with us—since their lives are so bound together, when he sees us without him, it will kill him.

"Your servant promised his father, saying: 'If I do not bring him back to you, then I shall bear the blame before you forever.'"

Judah took a deep breath. Joseph could only stare at him in abject disbelief. "Now, therefore," Judah continued, voice becoming clear and determined. "I beg that my lord allows your servant to remain as your slave instead of the youngest, and lets Benjamin return with his brothers. For how can I return if he is not with me, and so bring yet more evil upon my father?"

Quiet, pressing and palpable, lay over the room in the wake of Judah's speech. No one moved. Joseph could only continue to stare at the man.

Judah.

Judah, whose idea it had been, when all the adversity had become too much, to sell him.

"Please, my lord," Reuben spoke now, hands raised as he knelt. "Take any of us, but let the youngest return to his father in peace."

All of his brothers cried assent.

Joseph found he had taken a step back.

Their words rang in his ears.

Take any of us, but let the youngest return to his father in peace.

It could not be.

The words, impossible though he had believed them, had been spoken. They stormed through his brain and broke down every last shred of restraint that held him together.

A sob, unexpected, burst from his lips. He whirled away from his brothers to face the wall and struggled to think. "*Out!*" he finally roared. "*Everyone leave us!*"

All the guards and the translator scrambled from the room. Only Anhotep remained, glimpsed in the very corner of Joseph's vision, to cast him one worried glance before he, too, disappeared. The doors fell solidly shut.

Another sob wracked his body and he leaned, helplessly, against the wall. Disbelief coursed through him.

Was he truly going to do this?

Take any of us, but let the youngest return to his father in peace.

The words churned in his mind, beating down the last walls of denial.

Oh my God, what is this miracle You have done?

He could stand it no longer.

He tore off his khat and turned again to face his brothers. "*I am Joseph!*" he howled in Canaanite.

The words hung in the air. Eleven men stared at him, dumbfounded, for what seemed like an eternity.

And then recognition dawned in Judah's eyes. Making a strangled sound, he fell to his hands and knees.

Nine other men followed suit, falling prostrate in what looked to Joseph to be pure despair. Only Benjamin remained standing, shock and bewilderment on his face, before he, too, slowly began to kneel, looking in stunned confusion at the others.

"Please—don't," Joseph said with effort, stepping forward. But they would not look up from the floor. Only Benjamin flicked his eyes towards him.

"Please," Joseph said to his brothers again, voice cracking. The room seemed to be suspended in frozen silence. One of his brothers made a choked sound. "Please, stand up."

He saw Naphtali look up first, slowly. Then Reuben and Dan. But still no one stood.

"Please," Joseph begged again. "Do not—do not be afraid! I will not harm you." His tongue felt unexpectedly thick, and his mind struggled against the sudden demand to produce Canaanite words. He forced down the spike of panic that shook him.

269

Taking another desperate step forward, Joseph bent down and clasped Benjamin's hands, pulling him up. They stared at each other, eye to eye, Joseph slowly shaking his head, tongue cloven to the roof of his mouth.

Benjamin grasped at him as though he might disappear before collapsing on him with a gasp. "What miracle is this?"

One by one, the eyes of their brothers, stricken, moved upward to look at the two of them. No one stood.

Benjamin turned and looked at them all in consternation. "What is this on your faces?" he demanded. "Do you not see that this is my brother? My eyes remember him, young as I was. What are you doing?"

Not one brother moved. Then Judah locked eyes with them both, first Benjamin and then Joseph. "What fate have you prepared for us?" he asked quietly.

Joseph felt his heart wrench. He raised a hand, keeping the other on Benjamin's shoulder, and looked at their faces. Wretched. Despairing. "I will forgive it—I *have* forgiven it. I swear it!"

He could see in their faces that it was not enough. Not a soul believed his words. "Brothers, please!"

"Do not be afraid?" Simeon's tone rose, wild. "Do you not remember what we did?"

"Of what are you all speaking?" Benjamin's voice, low and with an undercurrent of threatening, broke in.

All eyes turned to stare at him.

"Benjamin." It was Judah who broke the silence. "Our crimes against your brother, and indeed against you, have been very great. Joseph—was Father's favorite. And in a vile fit of anger and jealousy, many years ago, we sold him as a slave into Egypt. He was not dead, and we knew it."

Casting his gaze over them all, Benjamin's face was pale. Then he rushed at Judah. "You *snakes!*" he roared. "You sons of—"

"Benjamin!" Joseph nearly shouted. He stepped between Judah and the livid Benjamin and grasped his brother's flailing arms.

"Do not start this anger and—jealousy again!" Benjamin stared at him and gaped wordlessly. "Benjamin," Joseph repeated, quietly. Then a realization rocked him. "Do you not see that through this, God has saved us?"

With a cry, his brother tore away before staggering several steps backward. Joseph came to stand near him. He did not dare to turn around and see his ten other brothers' faces.

"I thought you dead! For twenty-two years I was allowed to think you dead!" Benjamin spat. He looked up and glared at their other brothers. "Our father still thinks him dead!"

"There is truth in your words," Judah said. "It is a crime that cannot be forgiven."

The others murmured hoarse assent.

Benjamin's only response was a strangled snort.

Joseph turned to them in desperation. "Can you all not see? You—intended it for evil, but God has sent me here!" He watched their faces change from sheer fear to something like incredulity. "For the saving of lives. Many lives. This famine—it will last for five more years. Our God has sent me ahead of you to protect you and your families. You must go and tell Father and all our family to come here to Egypt and I will—provide for you." He left Benjamin's side and ventured among them, trying desperately to coax them to their feet. "Please, look at me! Stand up! *I will not harm you!*"

Slowly, one by one, they stood. Eyes darted back and forth. None looked toward him.

It was Reuben who came to him first. Standing just out of reach, he finally set his eyes on Joseph and seemed to take him in, mouth working. He shook his head, wordlessly.

Joseph, not knowing what else he could do to make them see, went to him and clasped him in his arms.

Reuben, rigid, gave a sudden sob. "I did not protect you from them as I ought. Forgive me."

"It is forgiven, I swear it." He felt Reuben shaking.

One by one, he went to his brothers, for the others would not come to him. Simeon would not once meet his eyes. Heart wrenching, Joseph came last to Judah, who could only clasp his hands and shrink down to his knees. "The wretched idea was mine," he whispered.

Slowly kneeling so that he could look him in the face, Joseph answered: "Yes, but the result—it is our God's," His voice cracked. "Judah, in the end, God has used it for great good. You must see this."

Tears poured from Judah's eyes. "My influence was so great, I might have saved you."

Joseph had no answer. "It is forgiven," he finally managed. It was all he could say.

Judah stared at him before finally pulling him into a tight embrace.

He found the others feebly crowding around, nervously laying hands on him. When they finally parted, Joseph found Benjamin watching them all, stricken.

Going to him, Joseph put his hands on his shoulders. "Think on it, Benjamin," he murmured. "They did not—they did not intend for the crime to be against you." His brother remained motionless, and Joseph slowly dropped his hands.

He looked at the ten other men who watched them. There was a heavy silence. It was Levi who spoke first. "Joseph," his voice shook. "Please, how did you come to be here?"

The question rocked him.

It was not a question he was prepared to answer. Not only was the story difficult in its points, but the more Joseph spoke in Canaanite, the more fatigued he felt his mind becoming. His words were stilted, and he knew it. The worrisome question of whether or not he could even tell a story in Canaanite shot through his mind.

At the very least, he decided, he should not try right now. Not when he could hardly think straight.

"I will tell it," he answered reluctantly. Perhaps, if he could manage it, it would make his brothers see what God had done. "But the—tale is long. Will you join me for the noon meal? I will tell you then."

The brothers nodded and murmured acceptance as one, and

Joseph thought the response rather hasty. Uncomfortably, it struck him that they would likely treat any request of his as a direct order, for the time being at least. "Very good," he said quickly, trying to feign ignorance.

Benjamin's eyes flicked up to look up at him again. "Joseph," he said quietly. "Did you single me out so as to test them?"

Joseph gave Benjamin a measured look. "Yes. As you see, they are—they are willing to give their lives for you, and for the sake of our father. That, I think, is something rather worth considering."

His brother would no longer meet his eyes.

"I will have you all again shown to—guest quarters," Joseph said. "The meal will be soon and this room must be made ready. If you will wait just a moment?"

He walked quickly towards the main doors of the great room, putting on his khat on as he went. Pulling the doors open, he strode through and almost ran into Asenath.

She made a surprised sound and stepped back as Joseph reached out to steady her. He saw Anhotep standing nearby. His wife grasped his arms in breathless questioning. Anhotep's face was worried.

"All is well," Joseph said in Egyptian. His tongue felt a kind of relief.

31

Asenath almost collapsed in his arms at the affirmation, and Anhotep took a deep breath. His steward came forward. "See to it that they are again given quarters," Joseph murmured to him. "Give the youngest his own room and keep a manservant with them at all times. I told them everything. The youngest is quite angry; if there is fighting, send word to me. They are all invited to the noon meal."

Anhotep nodded and called for servants. Several rushed down the corridor almost immediately. They came so swiftly that it was obvious they had been gathered nearby. Joseph pursed his lips as he watched them pass, but found he was more inclined to be amused than anything else. It must have sounded like quite a scene, even if no one listening had understood what was being said.

His wife put her arms around him and let out a deep breath. Joseph held her and rested his cheek in her hair. His heart, he realized, was pounding.

"I am sorry," she whispered. "You must not think I was listening at the door. I was only worried after I heard you had sent everyone out. I," she laughed a little, "I suppose I was planning to rush in, dragging Anhotep with me, if things went ill."

Joseph chuckled. "Don't worry. I am gratified."

She pulled back, looked him up and down, and led him down the corridor towards the doors to the courtyard. "You need to sit."

He followed, unprotesting, until they came to one of the benches near the pool. They sat, and the morning sunlight played on what little water there was, throwing flashes of light on the surrounding stones.

"So, Benjamin is angry," Asenath said after a moment.

"Yes. I had not thought of it." Joseph sighed and put his hands to his temples. "I do not think he will easily forgive them."

Asenath looked pensive. "One cannot blame him."

"It may be that he relents in time," Joseph said. Then he frowned. "But, Asenath—there is something else. They are afraid of me. Mortally so at first. I said over and over that all was forgiven, but even now, if I raised my voice, I think they would all go faint."

Staring at him, resignation came over her face. "I suppose it would be so." She gazed down into the water, and it was a long moment before she spoke again. "Joseph," she murmured. "You did not expect any of this, and it is complicated, but—are you happy?"

He looked at her in surprise. "I—" He could not quite describe how he was feeling. "I will be, I think," he said slowly. "Eventually. And once I realize that, this time, it is not a dream."

She quirked him a fond smile.

The noon hour approached more quickly than Joseph thought it had any right to, and Asenath retired to the bedroom to make ready. She was sitting on the bed, holding up a hand mirror and carefully repainting her eyes.

Joseph was ready. Now he was pacing the floor in growing agitation.

He saw his wife looking at him in the reflection of her mirror before she turned her head. Her brow creased. "Are you all right?"

Stopping short, he pressed a hand to his temples again. "Asenath." He swallowed. "I told my brothers I would tell them of how I came to be here. I have been trying to work out what I will say. But it is as I feared. I have *forgotten* so much Canaanite."

A worried look flashed across Asenath's face, but she stifled it almost instantly. "You spoke to them earlier," she said. She carefully put down the eyepaint and mirror and came to stand with him. "It cannot be as bad as you think."

"That was a conversation," Joseph said desperately, trying to explain. "And that was hard enough. But when one tells a story, one uses words that are less often heard. These are the words I cannot seem to remember—a Ishmaelite caravan, for instance. I cannot remember how to say this in Canaanite."

She looked away, expression concerned, and Joseph saw her mind working. "You must find a way," she said, turning back to him. "Use other words. Can you not say *traders* or *slavers*? It may be less correct, but at least you may complete your story."

Something inside of Joseph squirmed at the idea. His brothers would notice, if they had not already. Then it struck him that, more than it would shame him, it would shame *them*.

He could not. They were wretched already.

But there was no other choice.

"Very well," he nodded and took a deep breath, and began in Canaanite: "The—traders passed through the desert and—" he grunted and shook his head. He had leapt into the sentence without thinking and had used an Egyptian convention in the ordering of his words. Joseph tried again, carefully, and completed the sentence.

Asenath linked their arms and squeezed his hand. "It will come, Joseph. If not tonight, then later. It is the language of your family. If God is willing, and I believe He is, you will hear it often from now on." She stood on tiptoe and kissed his face. "It is time, I think."

Nodding despite himself, he murmured "Of course," and they walked out the door, through the corridors, and into the great room.

His brothers were just being shown in from the direction of the guest quarters. He looked at them all; none of them looked any worse for the wear, and Benjamin seemed complacent enough.

His wife squeezed his hand again, and he looked down to see her smile encouragingly. There was a light in her eyes, and that strengthened him. "May I introduce my wife, Asenath," Joseph said with careful Canaanite as they approached.

"*Shalom,*" Asenath said, surprising him. Joseph smiled.

His brothers showed equal surprise and murmured the greeting in response, with respectful bows. "Please tell them they are most welcome here," she said quickly to Joseph, in Egyptian.

"My wife wishes you to know that you are most welcome guests," he translated. The eleven men nodded and bowed again in response.

"Please, sit," Joseph said quickly, gesturing towards the long, low table that still sat near the entrance of the room. As the brothers found their places, he turned and saw that his and Asenath's own table was still set apart. He considered it for a moment before coming to a decision. "I will sit with my brothers," he said quietly. "You need not."

Asenath brushed it off. "We will sit with them, together." With a quick gesture, she called the servants over, and they made room at the large table. Joseph's brothers, unaware of the breach in custom that was being committed, only looked on curiously. The servants, Joseph could tell, were more than a little bewildered.

Once they were all seated, the food was served, and his brothers murmured in appreciation. But the conversation threatened to turn to silence as they ate. After a moment, Joseph took a steadying breath and then addressed his brothers. "You all, no doubt, still want to hear my story. I will tell it, if you wish."

"We will hear it," Ruben answered for them all. The rest nodded.

So Joseph, resignedly, began.

Despite all the things he had ever done, or been forced to do, in his life, the retelling of that story proved to be one of the most difficult. It caused unexpected depth of feeling in him, which must be hidden for the sake of his audience. He must also phrase it properly, for the same reason.

And yet, no matter how hard he tried at these things, Joseph knew that the sound of his derelict Canaanite heaped guilt on their heads regardless.

He felt Asenath's hand on his knee several times, under the table, in silent support.

When it was finally over, he met the eyes of his brothers for the first time since he had begun speaking. On their faces he saw a strange mixture of horror and bewilderment.

"God has done this," Joseph said, in closing. "There can—be no other explanation. Thanks are owed to Him. He has worked many evils for good."

"Thanks be to Him," his brothers murmured in response as they cast unreadable glances at once another. Joseph thought it sounded rather halfhearted.

The room descended into silence once again. It continued on for several vexatious moments before Asenath ventured: "May I know of your families?" Her request was in Egyptian, and all his brothers looked to Joseph for a translation.

"My wife wishes to hear of your families," Joseph interpreted quickly. He touched her leg in silent gratitude.

His brothers began talking, quietly at first, then more readily. Joseph translated the fairly simple phrases for Asenath, and it was far easier, he found, than speaking in Canaanite himself. They all had children, save Benjamin. Dinah was mercifully well, happy, with children of her own. His heart lifted in relief.

Bilhah and Zilpah were still living, though Leah was not. Joseph's stomach knotted as he thought of his father. But then Reuben asked after his family, and Joseph told of Manasseh and Ephraim.

An hour passed quickly, though Joseph did not know quite how, and the servants came to clear the remainders of the meal. He felt the danger of silence returning, but Asenath rose to her feet. His brothers, not seeming to know what else to do, rose as well.

She held up her hands and thanked them for joining the meal, which Joseph relayed. She told them that they were welcome to remain in the great room, or to go to the courtyard or rooftop, or return to their rooms. When Joseph had finished translating, she nodded smilingly, they nodded back, and Joseph nodded as well.

"I will see you this evening," Joseph said. "I must soon go to the granary." He paused. "I hope your afternoon is pleasant," he finished lamely. There seemed little else to say.

The brothers responded in kind, and the party dispersed. "Bless you," Joseph said quietly to Asenath as they left the great room. His wife squeezed his hand.

Joseph was distracted again for the entirety of his time at the stand, but Anhotep took notice and spoke for him as often as possible. It seemed an eternity before they closed for the night and turned towards home, the light coming long and orange through the near-evening sky.

His mind finally settled as he walked. Why was he so desiring to reach home? The vexation of the midday meal was not lost on him. What would he speak to his brothers about when he returned? Or would they only stare silently at each other? They could only speak about their families for so long.

He had turned the corner from the marketplace, nodding reflexively to those who stepped out of his way or bowed before him, when he saw Djaty puffing down a side street towards him. Slowing, Joseph smiled in welcome.

The scribe grasped his shoulder concernedly before falling into step with him. Anhotep fell a bit behind with the six menservants. "What has happened?" Djaty asked Joseph.

Frowning now, Joseph looked at the other man. "What do you mean?"

"I heard there was a row at your house this morning. With some men from Canaan."

Understanding dawned in Joseph. He remembered the servants darting into view as though they had been standing just around corners. "Where did you hear it?" he asked with a resigned look.

Djaty looked sheepish. "You will be pleased to know that I heard it from Lord Potiphar, who heard it from the Pharaoh and

Princess Sithathoriunet, who heard it from the chief cupbearer. I am afraid I do not know where he heard it."

Joseph drew a hand over his eyes.

"The rumor is you were rather out of sorts." Djaty gave him a measured look. "Joseph of Canaan, do you know these men?"

Nodding, Joseph took a deep breath before answering. "They are my brothers."

The scribe stopped short for a long moment before hurrying to catch up. "What fortune!" he gasped. "For you to see them again!" Then he frowned. "But, the story is that you had put at least one of them in prison."

"I did."

Djaty waited for him to continue.

"I have spoken of it to few," Joseph said at length, lowering his voice so as not to be overheard by the menservants walking behind. "I became a slave in Egypt because they sold me to traders, in order to rid themselves of me."

"*What!?*" the scribe exclaimed with a hiss, wide-eyed. "I had assumed—never mind what I assumed. What are you going to do to them?"

"Nothing."

The other man slowly closed his eyes. "Of course. I forget to whom I speak. You *do* understand that no one would fault you for it?"

Joseph looked at the other man with a small smile. "Yes."

"Very well, then."

"Djaty, they have changed. Greatly. I have found that out."

"It does not change what they did."

"No, I suppose not."

They reached the gates of his house and Djaty turned to face him. He jerked his head toward the courtyard walls. "Are they within?"

"Yes."

The scribe shook his head. "I wish you well in this. And happiness, I suppose. If it is possible in such a situation."

"I hope it is."

Djaty clasped his shoulders and left as the gate opened. Joseph turned inside.

Immediately he was near-tackled by Manasseh and Ephraim. Mai followed them, bouncing at their heels. "Papa! Papa!" They shouted. He drew them into an embrace.

"We have met your brothers!" Manasseh exclaimed. "Mama has told us their names, but we cannot understand anything they say."

Ephraim looked up at him owlishly. "Will you teach us how?"

Joseph supposed he would have to. "Of course," he said with a smile, trying not to show any sign of concern. His youngest immediately took him by the hand and began dragging him towards the pool. There sat his four oldest brothers, who had been watching them surreptitiously.

"I want to tell them that my dog's name is Mai," Ephraim said with glee. Mai, hearing her name, came up behind, panting with excitement. Joseph approached the group with some trepidation but forced a smile.

"You have met my sons, I hear," he said in Canaanite, by way of greeting.

Quickly getting to their feet, his brothers nodded and smiled in turn, and it seemed genuine. Judah put a hand on Ephraim's head. "Ephraim, I think?" he asked. Then he looked at the elder. "And Manasseh."

Manasseh bowed a little upon hearing his name and smiled broadly.

"Papa, may I introduce Mai?" Ephraim broke in.

Joseph had to laugh at his son's determination. "Very well." He knelt down and put his hands on the boy's shoulders. "Listen carefully." He switched to Canaanite. "My dog's name is Mai."

Puffing himself up to his full height, the boy proclaimed: "My dog's—" he broke off and frowned at Joseph.

"Name is Mai."

"My dog's name is Mai!"

281

His brothers laughed. "Well spoken," said Reuben.

Ephraim looked at Joseph expectantly. "Reuben says that you did well," Joseph said. The boy beamed.

Manasseh produced a ball from the folds of his shendyt and the two ran off to the still-shady ground below the fruit trees. Mai followed enthusiastically.

The five men watched the boys go, and Joseph sat down on the low edge of the pool, for there was no more room on the benches. He waved a hand when his brothers tried to offer him a seat.

The evening air, though warm, was less hot than it had been, and the palms in the courtyard rustled pleasantly in an unexpected northern breeze.

"They are fine boys," Levi said as the other four sat.

"Thank you. Ephraim is a bit—tenacious."

Judah snorted a little, but then instantly appeared self-conscious. Joseph looked at him curiously, and would have asked that he speak whatever had so amused him, except that he looked so uncomfortable that Joseph decided to let it be. So they descended into silence.

At length, Joseph decided to speak the question that had begun to gnaw at him since earlier that afternoon. At any rate, it could not make the silence any worse than it was. "How is our father, truly? Is he well?"

His brothers looked to Reuben, who rubbed his hands over his knees before answering. "He is. He is very well, especially for his age." He paused and looked Joseph in the eye. "You will see him. I swear it to you."

Joseph looked down and swallowed. "I am grateful."

Silence reigned again, except for the sound of the two boys playing, which drifted over from the trees. Joseph glanced towards them.

"God has truly blessed you here," Judah murmured after a long moment.

With a small smile, Joseph nodded. "He has."

Their conversation was arrested by the sound of someone exiting the house. It was Benjamin. He stopped and looked at them for a long moment before turning the corner to climb the stairs to the rooftop.

"How is Benjamin?" Joseph asked.

His brothers turned to regard him. "Not well," said Reuben.

"Who can blame him?" muttered Simeon.

Rubbing a hand over his face, Joseph sighed. "Perhaps I ought to—speak with him."

"You do not have to advocate for us," Levi broke in.

He returned Levi's gaze levelly. "Suppose I want to?"

The others were silent.

"I do not want divisions to begin again. You watched over Benjamin for twenty-two years. I do not want to destroy that."

"It would not be your doing," Judah said. "It would be ours."

Joseph gave him a strained look. "All the same, I do not want to see Benjamin lose you."

"He will not lose us," said Reuben. "Though we may indeed find that we have lost him."

They were roused by the call to the evening meal. Manasseh and Ephraim went racing by. The five men stood and turned to go inside, and Joseph was gratified to feel Judah clasp him lightly on the shoulder as they went.

32

That night, Joseph shifted about for more than an hour before coming to the realization that he was unlikely to get any sleep for the second night in a row. His thoughts spun, dwelling on the rift that his revelation had opened between Benjamin and his brothers.

He threw his arm over his eyes in frustration, and the idea of the rooftop in the moonlight unexpectedly beckoned to him. Carefully, so as not to disturb Asenath, he slipped out of bed, quietly taking a light robe from a trunk.

Leaving the room, he made his way to the rooftop, Aya watching him impassively from her seat on a cushion in the great room as he walked past. Once outdoors and on the roof, he sighed in relief as the breeze touched his face. The air held a hint of cool for the first time in months, and the moon and stars were bright, glinting off the Nile.

He moved to the edge of the roof, through a line of hanging curtains, and started in surprise as another person jumped to their feet a few cubits away.

It was Benjamin.

Neither man moved for a moment. Then Joseph took several steps towards his brother. Benjamin silently covered the rest of the distance until they were standing side by side at the edge of the roof.

His brother peered at him. "Now I see you," he said, almost to himself. He quickly clarified. "I mean, you look rather more like the person I remember."

Joseph laughed quietly and ran a hand through his hair. He had clipped it very short less than a week ago, but he was not wearing his khat, and his eyepaint was gone. "I am surprised you—have a memory to build from," he answered, with some curiosity. "You were only three years old."

Benjamin shook his head. "I remember." His voice turned a little grim. "I remember the last time I saw you. You picked me up and spun me around and said you would be back in a few days."

The scene once again came vividly to Joseph's mind. He no longer saw the Nile before him, with houses and palms running down to the river. He saw tents, and scrub brush, and heard the chatter of Jacob's household. He saw the curly-headed boy, with wide blue eyes, and picked him up, spun him around. *"I will be back in a few days."*

The boy put his hand in his mouth and finally nodded.

Joseph turned to look at the man next to him. "I am so very sorry, Benjamin," he whispered, gripping his shoulder. "I wish to God I could have somehow remained a part of your life."

Benjamin took a shuddering breath. Joseph could hear the anger that laced it. "You also say that our God has saved us through this."

"Can you deny it?"

"There ought to have been another way!" Benjamin spat.

Thoughtful for a long moment, Joseph tried to put into words the understanding of their God that had slowly grown in him over the years. "It may be that there was," he agreed slowly. "But God has bent what has passed to His will, regardless.

"And truly, how are we to—decide such things? For He is beyond understanding. Has not Father said as much to you?" He glanced at Benjamin, and saw a flash of recognition pass across his face. "And He is faithful. Benjamin, there are many parts of this path that I would not trade for anything in the world."

"Your family," his brother responded in a sort of resigned acknowledgment.

"That is a large part. And I know I would not trust God in such a way as this without—having been here these twenty-two years. I would have had no reason to do so."

Turning from the view of the river, Benjamin leaned against the low wall of the roof and eyed him. "Speaking Canaanite is difficult for you," he said abruptly. It was not a question.

Shifting on his feet, Joseph did not answer for a moment. His brother's tone was accusatory, but not towards him. "That is true."

Leaping forward, Benjamin grasped him by the shoulders, and actually shook him, once. "Joseph!"

Joseph could only look at him stunned silence.

"How can it be that you are not angry with them?"

His mind raced to find the words needed to explain something so difficult to express. "I was angry," Joseph said finally. "For quite a time. I was angry even this morning. But if I had spent the last twenty-two years being *only* angry, I would still be a slave in—the lowest level of Potiphar's house." A firmness grew in his voice. "I would have thought—and ruminated, and—seethed, until I thought of nothing else, did nothing else, except what came from that. That is no way to live.

"I chose to look to our God. I have been angry many times, and not only from our brothers' actions. But God has shown me how to walk in a way the pleases Him. Has not Father spoken to you—with such words as these? That we must act justly, and love mercy, and walk humbly in the path God has given us?"

His brother stared at him. Then his head dropped, and his hands slipped from Joseph's shoulders. He slumped down to sit on the wall and rested his head in his hands. Joseph heard him sob. Stomach wrenching, he put a hand on Benjamin's shoulder.

"I have heard Father say it. But I am not like you," Benjamin whispered.

Joseph shook his head and searched for more of the right words, trying to help his brother understand the truth that the past twenty-two years had taught him. "It is God, Benjamin. You must ask Him to lead you."

Benjamin, Joseph guessed, had never asked something so personal nor so direct of their God before. He might never have spoken to God at all. Joseph likely never would have himself, had he remained in Jacob's household. The world was familiar there, and anger and revenge were happenstances so common that one hardly thought of them. It was simply life, and one would move forward, eventually. But an anger like Benjamin's could have no easy revenge, and it cut too deep to be forgotten.

So Joseph sat down next to Benjamin, put an arm over his shoulders, and prayed, in Canaanite, for the first time in thirteen years.

"My God—thanks and all glory be to You, for what You have done for us. For truly—You hold great mercies for us, and Your servants are not—not worthy of the least of them. Show us Your purpose for our lives, and grant us wisdom and peace, even when we have no reason to have it.

"Comfort our father as his sons are in a strange land. And I thank You, my God, for keeping Benjamin safe through all these years and for giving Dinah a life in which she finds joy. Give Benjamin peace, and show him that in You—he may find that which he needs to continue onward in a way that pleases You."

Silence followed, and the yapping of a fox came in on the wind that rustled through the palms. Neither man spoke, but Benjamin reached over to put an arm over Joseph's shoulders in turn.

After a time, he reached forward and fingered the edge of Joseph's robe. "Did you know old Mizzah? *Now, boy, you are looking here at the best cloth in this part of Canaan. What will you pay for it?*" Joseph laughed; his brother's impression was flawless. Benjamin looked up at Joseph and quirked a smile, which he saw was thin, but genuine. "What is this stuff? It's splendid."

"It's linen," Joseph answered, trying to think of a Canaanite equivalent. He did not think there was one. "It comes from flax—a plant, not an animal."

"A plant," Benjamin murmured. "They are doing that in Assyria, I think."

The thought stuck Joseph that he was now extraordinarily far removed from his family's way of life. His heart rent, a little. "Benjamin, how is our family? Is everyone well, truly? Where do all of you—camp at present? Are your neighbors peaceful?"

His brother looked down. "We have moved ten times since the famine came. Right now, we are camped near Bethel. There is another encampment nearby; they and those in the city are hungry, just like us. But everyone is well, and Father is well, hale for his age. But I wonder what he—"

Joseph looked at his brother keenly. "You wonder how he will take news of me?"

"Yes."

Sighing, Joseph folded his arms.

"I should allow you to sleep," Benjamin said finally. Seeing Joseph's quick glance, the other man shook his head. "I will be fine. I will try, for your sake. If it will give you pleasure. But I will need time."

They both stood up, and Joseph nodded. He led the way down the steps from the roof and inside. They stopped for a moment at the doors to the great room before parting ways. "Goodnight, brother," said Joseph, clasping Benjamin's arm. Benjamin did the same before pulling him into a tight embrace. Joseph held him and closed his eyes.

"Goodnight, brother."

Joseph looked out over the crowd. The heat had again grown to near-unbearable levels after the one day's respite, and the sun was now directly overhead as the noon hour approached. He turned to Anhotep and wiped his brow.

"Have the storehouses closed for the day. We will none of us benefit if we faint from the heat."

His steward nodded and turned away, and Joseph watched the guards slowly herd the crowd back towards the docks. He sighed, and then stifled an unexpected yawn. Two near-sleepless nights had caught up with him.

Heaving himself from his chair, he slowly made his way down from the stand and toward the docks. Anhotep fell in step beside him, and the six menservants followed. He had been summoned by the young Pharaoh Senusret and was not about to walk to the palace or force anyone to follow him. Perhaps it was outrageous to order a boat to take him from one end of Itjtawy to the other, but there it was. At least no one would collapse while doing it.

A hot wind brushed around them, sand spitting up from the ground to catch in his sandals. His eyes, even with the protective paint, smarted. Anhotep furrowed his brow. "This may be the worst day yet," his steward murmured.

"I think you are right," Joseph answered as they walked up the ramp to the deck of the small boat. They took a seat under a canopy, and the sail was slowly raised by the shipmen. The dock fell behind them as the boat began to move, but no cooling breeze blew on the water as it had so often in the past. The wind remained hot.

They watched the city go by to the west. Street upon street of houses, and soaring above them, the massive stone buildings of the temples, sat baking under the sun. The tall, thin palms growing throughout the city were dusted and browning.

"It is only the second year," Anhotep said, voicing Joseph's thoughts.

"I know it." He looked at the man and smiled thinly. "But we have enough. More than enough."

The other man looked pensive. "Sir," he ventured after some time. "Do you know why your God is doing this?"

Joseph looked again out over the buildings to the west. The city was falling away, the last large houses slipping by. He watched his own house pass, and then before them loomed the administrative complex and the palace. Beyond spread the wide fields of the Pa-yuum, empty, the color of soot.

"No," he answered.

"I find it strange," Anhotep continued hesitantly, "that the

God who has done this is the same one whom you say has pleasure in your overlooking the offences of Lord Potiphar and your brothers."

"Perhaps it is strange," Joseph answered with some thought. "But has He not also provided for us?"

Anhotep looked out over the city. "We might have fared very differently, if not for you," he acknowledged. "Do you think He sent you here?"

"I do," said Joseph, slowly. "Though I do not know why He chose me." He paused. "Perhaps then, it is not so strange that both things you have mentioned were done by God. My time in Egypt before I knew you was—often unpleasant." Anhotep looked at him steadily. "But, looking back, we may comprehend the purpose of it. I think it must be the same for this famine.

"I have learned not to trust what I see before me. My vision is limited. What I must do is continue forward, with faith that, in time, God will reveal His purpose. He has always had one. And in the meantime, we are provided for."

The boat came to a slow halt at the private docks of the palace. Several shipmen leapt out to tie it fast. "I hope you are right, sir," Anhotep said as they rose.

Joseph favored him with a faint smile. "At this point, I have had too many strange happenstances in my life to be capable of believing anything other than what I have just told you."

His steward gave him an acknowledging nod as they disembarked, the six menservants following. Again they walked through the waves of heat, the shade from the rows of distressed palms and fruit trees helping little. The gardens of the inner courtyards were near-empty in the heat, and Joseph saw men with large pitchers, pouring water over the trunks of the remaining fruit trees. As they reached the tall doors to the great hall, his companions stepped aside, and Joseph entered.

The Pharaoh stood there, speaking quietly to Potiphar. The captain of the guard bowed as Joseph approached, then quickly made his exit. The young Pharaoh favored Joseph with a smile. "If I understand it aright, you are deserving of felicitations."

Joseph bowed to the tall youth. "Thank you, Pharaoh. It is as you have heard; my brothers have come from Canaan."

"How do they fare?"

"Not well, I am afraid, your majesty. They came to buy grain. It is my intention to offer them sanctuary in Egypt."

The young Pharaoh Senusret nodded. "It would be well done. Tell them to bring back with them all of your family and their households. Tell them that you will give them some of the best of the Delta land, and send them back with carts, and donkeys, so that they may travel easily." He paused, and looked at Joseph. "Tell them as well not to worry about their goods, for Egypt will provide for them. It is only right that Egypt do such a thing for one who has done so much for Egypt."

Struck, Joseph bowed deeply.

It was early in the morning several days later when Joseph sent his brothers on their way, carts and rows of donkeys at the ready, loaded with food and other provisions. He handed out changes of garments for each man for the journey, and at the end of the long line, came to Benjamin. "I wish I could come with you," Joseph murmured.

The young man looked at him wryly. "I am going on a small journey," he answered. "A *truly* small one. I will be back, soon."

Smiling, Joseph pulled him into a tight embrace.

"Here," Joseph said when they parted. He handed him a sack full of neatly-folded garments. Many deben of silver sat on top. Benjamin looked down at it and then looked up, astonished. "I would give you the cup, but it was a wedding present."

Benjamin snorted and pulled him into another embrace.

His brothers left soon after. "Do not argue along the way!" Joseph called after them. His words were met with several conscious glances backwards and raised hands of acknowledgement. Judah turned and, with a little trepidation, flashed him a smile.

"You have my word."

Joseph found that he believed him.

33

Winter came, without attracting any notice at first, for the weather did not change. Cloudless day followed cloudless day, and waves of heat crawled along the ground. But the shadows grew longer with time, and one day at noon Joseph walked home from the granary and realized that it was not sweltering.

Asenath greeted him with a smile as he entered the courtyard. She was walking the horse, and the courtyard around her bustled far more than it had in previous months, servants hurrying to accomplish tasks that had been put off in the heat. He saw several men on the roof, inspecting the whitewash, and another, sweeping near the pool. "Good afternoon," his wife said, kissing him. "It is a beautiful day."

He laughed and walked with her as they continued the circuit of the courtyard, past the gatehouse and toward the kitchens. The mare nudged at his robe and khat, looking for treats. "I'm afraid I haven't anything with me," he said with a laugh, but rubbed the horse's forehead. She shook her head primly.

"I have been practicing the greeting again," Asenath said. "I think I have it. Will you hear me?"

"Of course."

She had come to him a week ago, concerned that she would not be able to greet his father properly. Joseph had tried to tell her that it would not matter in the least, for how could anyone expect her to speak Canaanite? Jacob would simply be glad to meet the wife of his son. But she had been adamant and had asked to be taught a few phrases.

Asenath had struggled with the sounds of Canaanite, at first. The abrupt syllables of Egyptian, that Joseph had first noticed all those years ago and that had slowly become his normalcy, leapt before his ears again in full force when applied to Canaanite.

"Peace be with you, my daughter," Joseph said, in Canaanite.

"And peace be with you, and all health, and the blessings of our God. I pray that on this family, God grants prosperity in this land of Egypt," she returned carefully.

Joseph smiled broadly. Her determination had paid off—the Canaanite was rather good. He put his arm around her. "That was well said," he replied, switching back to Egyptian. "You will do excellently."

She smiled in turn. "Ephraim asked me again this morning when your family will arrive."

"Of course he did," Joseph laughed.

Despite his laughter, he felt a little distant from the prospect, as though it was something talked of but that could never truly come to pass.

They walked the horse the rest of the circumference of the courtyard before Asenath stopped at the door to the stables. A manservant strode over to assist her. "I'll see to her," she said to Joseph. "Go and refresh yourself for the meal."

He was halfway across the courtyard when there was a small commotion at the gates. Frowning slightly, he turned to see what it was. A man was coming through, dusty, heavily robed, and heavily bearded. The guard was leading him in with a smile.

"Judah!" Joseph couldn't help the astonished shout that escaped him. Before he quite knew what he was doing, he found that he had raced across the courtyard and embraced his brother, hard.

Judah actually laughed and thumped his back.

"Are you all here?" the Canaanite, put to unpremeditated use, poured out of his mouth in such a shamble that he would have been surprised if Judah understood him.

Somehow he did. "I came ahead; they are nearing the Delta, and will wait there for directions."

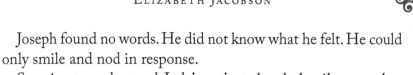

Joseph found no words. He did not know what he felt. He could only smile and nod in response.

Seeming to understand, Judah spoke to break the silence as they began the walk across the courtyard towards the house. "Phew! It's hot."

"Hot?" Joseph asked. "It is cooler than it—has been in months."

Judah looked at him askance. "I remember how hot it was last time. It is certainly less hot, but it is still hot."

Chuckling, Joseph acknowledged to himself that, more likely than not, he was only used to the Egyptian weather. Or, it could be that Judah was wearing layer upon layer of wool. "Come," he said. "I have just the thing." They walked into the cooler shadows of the house, and he heard his brother give an audible sigh of relief.

He led him through the great room and into the family rooms, finally opening the door to the antechamber of a bathing room. Judah shook his head a little, then immediately rolled up his sleeves and dunked his head and arms deep into one of the tall pots that sat near a footbath, sunken into the stone floor.

Joseph turned and grabbed a few of the oils off a shelf and readied one of the footbaths with scented water. "I'll leave you be," he said smilingly when Judah's head resurfaced.

"Ah, stay," Judah grunted as he sat down on a stone bench, kicked off his sandals, and put his feet in the water. "I haven't seen you in months."

Gratified, Joseph grinned and sat down on the opposing bench, pulling off his khat.

"I think, Joseph, you may be the second richest man in the world," said Judah after a long moment as he flung back his wet hair. "However," his brother continued after another moment, "this land of yours is still an oven."

Laughing again, Joseph shook his head. "I think the King of Assyria might take issue with your first statement. I admit that your second statement, however, is completely accurate."

There was a silence, but Joseph was surprised to find it companionable. At length, however, he found he needed to ask the question that had begun to hum insistently in the back of his mind, understanding that it might drive a wedge between them but needing to know all the same. "How is our Father?"

Judah's eyes immediately clouded. "He is well," he said. His voice was very quiet. "He is anxious to see you."

"And I him," Joseph murmured. He did not press further.

Silence followed, a little more strained. But after a time, to Joseph's surprise, Judah spoke. "How are *you*?"

He must have looked a little vacant, but Judah's question shook him back into the present. "What?" he managed in Canaanite, biting back the Egyptian equivalent that had almost leapt forward in his surprise.

"How are you?" Judah repeated. He motioned vaguely to the world at large. "You seem to be having to manage rather a lot. You are saving half the known world, at least."

Joseph couldn't help the small smile, thin though it was. "I am well," he said. "You will all live, Egypt will live, and, God willing, half the known world will live. I could—hardly ask for more."

Judah breathed a small laugh and shook his head. "I suppose not." He shifted a little in his seat and sighed. Joseph saw his eyes land on the tattoo on his hand and then quickly flick away. "It will be good to see you and Father reunited," Judah said quietly.

Finding the sentiment behind the words almost too much to imagine one of his brothers saying, Joseph managed another smile. Judah met his eyes, but his gaze was now a little haunted.

The next day was a whirl of activity. Joseph made arrangements for Master Seneb of the granaries to oversee the trading of grain for the next two weeks, and a boat was prepared at the docks, loaded with provisions and trunks of goods and clothes. Judah put himself to work wherever he could, counting provisions or ensuring items were accounted for, though Asenath and Anhotep were horrified, and Joseph protested.

Manasseh attached himself to Judah like an awed shadow, using the Canaanite words Joseph had taught him in the last few months and learning more by the day. Ephraim, too young to be anything more than beside himself with excitement, ran circuits around the courtyard unless stopped, followed by Mai and a string of now-large pups.

Two days later, Joseph left his home with his wife, his sons, and his brother, and boarded the boat that would take him to his father. Ephraim, his hand firmly in Asenath's, tried to run aboard with a shout of glee. Asenath pulled him back and spoke to him quietly.

Judah shook his head a little and turned to Joseph with a smile. "If you wish to know what Benjamin was like growing up, look to Manasseh. He is just like your brother, curious and practical. But Ephraim—he is you."

Joseph laughed in surprise, having difficulty remembering ever being so full of energy.

"Papa!" Ephraim called. He was standing now at the railing with one of the maidservants. Anhotep had gone to talk to the captain, and Manasseh had followed. Asenath came and linked her arm in Joseph's.

"Ephraim!" Joseph called back with a smile.

His son giggled. "Look!" he pointed upriver. A flock of ibises came flying overhead, black heads outstretched and white wings shining. The group watched them travel by, Judah murmuring appreciatively.

"Very beautiful," Joseph said. Ephraim, still struck, continued to watch them until they were out of sight.

They left soon after, Itjtawy dropping away behind them and the pyramids on the western bank growing and shrinking one by one as they passed. Judah watched them in fascination for some time from his seat under the canopy before finally venturing to the railing. After a moment, Joseph followed him.

His brother stood at the railing, knuckles tightly grasping the wood in what Joseph realized was discomfort. Though Judah would have, by now, been ferried across the Nile multiple times, Joseph knew that did not immediately translate to ease on a boat. Still, he said nothing, for Judah did not. He focused instead of the pyramids, shining white in the morning sun.

"They are tombs, you say?" Judah asked after some time.

"Yes."

"That seems rather a lot of work to only be buried in."

Joseph nodded. "It is. The young Pharaoh is already building his, near Memphis. We will pass by." His face fell a little. "The Egyptians—place rather a heavy emphasis on preparing for the afterlife. And unfortunately they go about it all wrong."

"Asenath and your sons follow our God. That must be due to you. Even your steward spoke to us of God."

Surprised, Joseph looked at Judah. "Anhotep did?"

"Yes, when we arrived with Benjamin and told your steward that our silver had been returned, the first time. He told us it was a gift from God. I was surprised he knew the name."

Joseph shook his head a little and smiled. That sounded like Anhotep.

"I do not know if I would have been as strong as you," Judah said at length. His voice was strained.

Perturbed, Joseph peered at him, but his brother still stared out at the pyramids. "What do you mean?"

"I am sure it must have been near impossible to avoid hearing of their gods, every day. It is only a small step to then become caught up in them. And as a slave—" Judah's voice faltered, and he cleared his throat. "I think I would have given up on our God and given in."

"And now?" Joseph asked evenly.

"Now?"

"After you know what He has done. Would you still?"

"No."

"That is all that matters, then."

Judah finally looked at him, expression unconvinced. Joseph leaned down, elbows on the railing. "God forgives, Judah. Did you know that?"

"God—what?"

"I have made far too many mistakes myself to believe anything else. I would not still see Him in my life if He did not. He would have given up on *me*."

His brother was gaping at him. "*You?* Make mistakes?" He shook his head, almost wildly, and then put his hands to his temples. "How can you say that of yourself and still deign to look me in the eye? If you have made mistakes than I am truly lost. I—all ten of us—we are not worthy of forgiveness, least of all yours."

So that was it then. Frowning a little, Joseph stood upright and tried to sort his thoughts into Canaanite before answering. "Judah—I gave you my forgiveness, I swear it. You—all of you—insist on tormenting yourselves. You offered yourselves up for Benjamin, for his sake and for our father's. You have changed."

"Joseph!" Judah threw up his hands violently. Any cowed restraint he had been hanging on to vanished. "You are fooling yourself. What can you expect? We—*I*—am not like you. No one on this earth is *like* you! And just because you take it into your head to show us mercy does not mean that it is the *right* thing to do!"

Joseph was taken aback. To finally get such raw truth out of his brother was far more than he had hoped. However, he instantly realized that he had made an error in showing it.

Judah looked at him, then looked around. His brother's eyes widened a little and he quickly put his hands down. "I am sorry," he murmured.

All eyes were on them, the servants and boatmen gaping. Joseph supposed it was because someone had raised their voice to him. Only his wife and sons were unconcerned; he saw that Asenath had wisely taken them to the stern. He looked back at Judah and quirked a grin. "Don't be. I haven't been yelled at in years. It is very refreshing."

Judah sighed and seemed to shrink. He leaned, defeated, on the railing and looked down into the swirling green depths of the river.

"Judah, if God has shown me mercy for the things I have done—and used the thing you did against me for such great good, how can I not show you mercy when you ask for it?"

"I did not ask for it. Reuben did," Judah said with some bitterness. "He was the only one not complicit in my plan."

Joseph had not known such a thing, but he did not say as much. "Do you *want* it?"

"Do I—what?" Judah glanced at him, bewildered.

"If you seek forgiveness and mercy, I have given it. I think now you must also seek it of God and of yourself. And to do that, you must be willing to be forgiven."

The string of pyramids that spread out north from Itjtawy had fallen behind them, and now only swaths of reedy papyrus and thick palms, still vibrantly green so close to the river, lined the banks. Joseph saw a crocodile slowly slide into the water.

At length, Judah answered. "Joseph, you must understand that what you are saying is difficult to hear. We have caused not only you but so many others great pain. Our father—we might have killed him. His grief has been great. Both these twenty-two years and now."

Joseph could only put a hand on Judah's shoulder. "Perhaps, in time, your sorrow will not feel quite so fresh. And perhaps kinder memories will begin to take its place. Know then that you already have my forgiveness, and that God will give His as well. Has Father not told you that there are three things which God wishes of you? To act justly, to love mercy, and to walk humbly in the path God gives you? How can God ask something of you that He Himself will not grant?"

The Canaanite, he realized all at once, had come out rather well. Perhaps the practice was starting to take hold.

Judah was silent. But, very slowly, he in turn placed his hand on Joseph's shoulder.

Joseph awoke at dawn the next morning. The small cabin the boat provided rocked back and forth with the flow of the river. Thin streams of light trickled through the curtain that hung in the doorway.

Today. Today they would land in Heliopolis. Today Joseph would see his father.

His heart lurched into his throat, and he sat upright, head in his hands.

It was as if the full weight of that knowledge had finally settled on him.

I am thirty-nine years old.

Benjamin is twenty-five.

Dinah is forty-one.

My father is 130.

I am thirty-nine years old.

I have lived longer in Egypt than I ever did with my family.

The final thought fell on him like so many rocks. Cold fear spread through his stomach.

Who, exactly, did his father expect to meet?

It was strange; he had spent so long consoling Asenath that she need not worry about meeting Jacob. Now, he found that he was feeling something close to terror. His father would likely not even recognize him. His brothers had not.

Asenath stirred and saw him sitting there, unmoving. She rose and put a hand on his back. "Joseph?" she whispered. "What is wrong?"

He shook his head a little. "It is nothing," he managed finally, voice low, for the walls were thin.

"It is not nothing." She peered at him.

Joseph sighed. "I only hope—my father is pleased with me."

She gaped at him. "Joseph. What nonsense is this? How could he not be pleased with you? You have served God well, not to mention you have saved them all."

He knew it, for it was logical. But for some reason, in this moment, logic did not seem like enough. "I could pass him in the street, and he likely would not know me. I will not be what he expects."

"Perhaps. But that does not mean that he will not be pleased."

Running his hands roughly through his clipped hair, he lay back down. Asenath followed suit and looked at him. "He is your father, and he loves you. He will be overjoyed to see you."

Joseph looked at her and put a hand on her face. "Asenath is a beautiful gift from God, the cleverest woman in Egypt."

His wife laughed quietly. "Say it in Canaanite."

34

They passed the high white walls of Memphis that morning, and not long after Heliopolis rose up before them on the east banks of the river. Here the Nile began to branch into many forks, and it was northward of Heliopolis, on the easternmost branches, where Joseph had set aside land for his family. It was well-watered and would still feed sheep even in these hard years. There was one small town nearby, Per-Sopdu. They could trade if they wished or isolate themselves if they wished. It was perfect.

Once at Heliopolis, Asenath cast a measured look at the city as they disembarked. They would not go in, and Joseph knew she was grateful.

Heat rose to greet them as they stepped onto the land. The wet Delta soil filled the air with a heaviness, making it seem almost thick. Joseph glanced down at Manasseh and Ephraim, whom they and the maidservant had worked to ensure looked perfect, and at Asenath, who somehow managed to look even more so.

Three chariots sat waiting, one sleek horse attached to each. Judah looked at them appreciatively. "I was told our family will be camped just north of the city," he said.

Joseph nodded. They stepped into the chariots, drivers holding the horses steady, Joseph and Asenath in the first, Judah in another, and Anhotep and the boys in the third. It was only a moment before the drivers sped them away, along the eastern city walls.

Riding in a chariot was never smooth, but it had never bothered Joseph before. Now he found that he clamped onto the side of the

303

chariot until his knuckles were white. Asenath put a hand on his arm. He felt his stomach knot.

The city passed by in a rush, and soon Judah pointed to a grove of palms and papyrus reeds on its northern edge. Placed near it were many long, large tents.

The color assaulted Joseph first.

There was no white linen here. Blue cloth, and red and yellow and green, splashed in wide patterns on the sides of the tents.

Then the sound of sheep, spread northward on the still-grassy Delta soil.

Last, the smell of roast lamb.

It was as though a floodgate opened in his mind.

His father, smiling over him and checking his figures. Dinah, balancing a water pitcher on her head and walking as proudly as a queen. Benjamin, on his shoulders.

He stepped off the chariot in a daze and pulled off his khat, letting it fall.

Judah leapt from his chariot and bellowed at the top of his lungs. People began to appear amongst the tents, walking towards them.

Joseph desperately searched the growing sea of faces, young men and women and children that he did not know. Then, among them, he saw Levi and Asher. The crowd parted, and he saw Benjamin.

And on his arm, an old man.

Joseph took a step forward, mouth slowly moving but no sound coming forth.

The old man's eyes fell on him.

Taking another step, and another, Joseph made his way forward until the old man stood before him. The man's hands were outstretched, shaking.

"Father," Joseph finally whispered.

With a cry, Jacob flung himself on him. He sobbed, and shook, and Joseph grasped at the old man as though he might vanish. His cheeks were wet, and he buried his face in his father's shoulder. "Father."

Jacob clung to him, hands finding his head, his hair, his arms, as if to prove that he was actually standing there. "My son," he finally whispered. "My own son. Thanks be to God." Gently, he pushed back Joseph's head to look at him and seemed to drink him in. "Now I can die, for I have seen that you live."

He clenched his father's arms. "Do not say such things!" he gasped through tears.

The old man actually laughed and pulled him into a fierce embrace. It was a long moment before he looked into Joseph's face again. Jacob put his hands on Joseph's head and smiled.

"I do not know why your brothers did not know you."

Joseph laughed, a lightness he did not know existed coursing through him. He pulled his father to him again.

After a time, he heard footsteps behind him. They turned. Jacob, one hand still on Joseph's arm, stepped forward, gaping. Asenath had come, Manasseh and Ephraim on each hand. Asenath offered his father a tentative smile as she and the two boys bowed. "Father," said Joseph. "This is my wife, Asenath, and my sons, Manasseh and Ephraim."

In wonderment, Jacob placed a hand on each of the boys' heads and kissed them one by one. Then he turned to Asenath and offered her his hands. She clasped them and bowed again. "Peace be with you, my daughter," he said, voice shaking.

She took a deep breath. "And peace be with you, and all health, and the blessings of our God. I pray that on this family, God grants prosperity in this land of Egypt," she murmured. Her eyes flicked to Joseph, and he smiled.

His father looked back at him as well, surprised and delighted, before turning back to Asenath. "I thank you."

Smiling again, she bowed.

A hand grasped Joseph's shoulder, and he turned in surprise. A woman stood there, smiling tentatively, eyes brimming with tears.

"Dinah!" Joseph shouted after a moment's staring. She laughed and wrapped her arms around him, and he picked her up and spun her around.

"Oh Joseph!" she said through tears as he set her down. "Oh Joseph, *look at you!*"

He laughed in turn as two young girls and an older boy came running up behind her. "Look at you," he returned with a smile.

His sister looked down fondly at the three. "My husband is with the sheep. You will meet him soon. But this is Sarai, and Adah." Joseph put his hands on the girls' heads, and they smiled. Dinah motioned her son forward. "And this one—is Joseph."

Joseph looked at her in surprise. The boy smiled in turn, the image of his mother, and bowed. He was a year or two older than Manasseh. Joseph bent down, to his height. "It seems we share a name. I am glad to do so."

"I am glad too, sir. That is," the boy paused. "I am glad that you are alive to share it."

Laughing again, Joseph turned and motioned his two boys forward. Dinah looked at them, eyes wet but face beaming. "These are my sons, Manasseh and Ephraim." He set his eyes again on the boy. "I am sure they would enjoy some playmates, but they will not be able to understand you, at least not for some time. Will you help them?"

His namesake nodded eagerly. "Of course, sir! Come," he took Ephraim by the hand and motioned to Manasseh. His older son grinned, Ephraim waved, and they were off running. He saw other children trickling out from the crowd to join them.

Jacob came forward, Asenath's arm in his. Dinah clasped Asenath's hands. His brothers came up from the crowd, Benjamin giving him a tight embrace and a resounding clap on the back. The others came one by one to greet him, reservedly but warmly. Jacob put a hand on his shoulders. Asenath smiled up at him, and Joseph pulled her close.

My God. Joseph looked up to the sky. *Thank you.*

The sounds filtered into his mind slowly—the clang of cooking-pots, steps on sand, the snort of a donkey. The rustle of fabric in the wind. For a moment he was seventeen, ready for a day with the flocks or for going over plans with his father.

Then he opened his eyes, and he was thirty-nine, with his wife next to him and his two sons asleep on bedrolls at the other end of the tent.

He took a moment to gather himself. There had been celebration late into the night, with roast lamb and date wine and music and dancing. His father sat him at his right hand, and Dinah took Asenath under her wing. Manasseh and Ephraim ran and played ball with their cousins.

It ought to have been a dream, but it was not.

Asenath stirred next to him, and they all four made ready for the day. Asenath had just finished braiding Ephraim's sidelock as they moved to stand in a circle by the opening of the tent.

"Our God," Joseph spoke. "Thanks and all glory be to You, for what You have done for us. Your servants are not worthy of the least of Your mercies, and that which You have given us in these recent days has been very great. Show us Your purpose for our lives and grant us wisdom and peace. Show us, oh God, how we might serve You in a land that does not.

"We thank You, for the peace You have given to us, and pray it upon those in this family who have not found it."

"Search our hearts," Asenath said quietly. "And show us what is in them that does not please You."

Joseph looked around at his family.

I am thirty-nine.

God is great.

Beyond understanding.

His ways are great and even so His faithfulness to those who trust in Him.

Anhotep arrived that afternoon, with six chariots, ready to take a group back to the river and onwards to Itjtawy. Joseph's brothers had balked, eyes wide, at the mention of going up to the Pharaoh with Joseph and their father, but such a ceremony like this would have to be.

Joseph thought he saw relief in the faces of the brothers whom he did not choose to accompany him. Benjamin would come, and the four eldest. Reuben and Judah looked grim, and Simeon and Levi seemed rather ill. Only Benjamin appeared relatively unaffected, if quiet.

"Follow this branch of the river northwards for twenty leagues," Joseph told his brothers who would remain with the camp, "and you will be in the twentieth nome and the land I have set aside for you. Per-Sopdu is its only town, and it will be nearby. We will return in a few days' time.

"In the meantime, we will go up to the Pharaoh and tell him that you have arrived. I will tell him that you are shepherds and herders and that you have brought all your animals with you." He turned to his five brothers who would come with him. "The Pharaoh will ask you your occupation, and you will tell him that you and your fathers have cared for livestock all your lives." They nodded. "He will then formally give you the land."

They nodded again. Farewells were given. Dinah came to him last and held him tightly.

"I will be back in a few days," Joseph said to her with a small smile. "I mean it, this time."

She laughed and hit his arm before wiping away a tear.

"It gives me joy to know that you have found peace and happiness with your family," Joseph said. "I prayed to God to give you that, every night."

His sister looked at him. "My dear brother. You must have had other things to worry about."

"I did. But that does not mean I would forget you."

Dinah pressed his hand. "Thank you."

Jacob endured the journey by boat with much stoicism, though Joseph could tell that he did not like it. His father often stood nearby him, one hand on his arm or shoulder, though he did not always speak. He watched Manasseh and Ephraim play on the deck with moist eyes, and taught them the Canaanite words for *boat* and *river* and *water*.

When they arrived at Itjtawy the next day, every man dressed in his best, he saw his father look on the city and the palace complex looming in the distance and swallow, once.

Asenath kissed Joseph, and she and the boys took their leave as Anhotep and several menservants stood ready to escort Joseph and his father and brothers to the palace. Joseph offered his father his arm as they disembarked. "God has truly blessed you here, my son," Jacob said, voice small, as he looked out at those already bowing on the palace docks.

They walked down the ramp to the dock, the others following behind, and Joseph smiled a little. "He has, but I am grateful that through it I may help my family."

Walking through the courtyards and gardens, courtiers and nobles skirting out of the way and bowing in their turn, Jacob watched the scenes for some time in silent astonishment. "I remember your dreams," his father said at length. "Do you?"

"I do."

Jacob squeezed his arm. "My dear son. I am so very *proud* of you."

Joseph looked at his father, gratified.

Reaching the carven doors to the great hall, Joseph turned to his father and brothers, who looked a little ashen. "I will enter first," he said. "Wait a moment." He nodded to the guards, and the doors swung open.

The young Pharaoh Senusret sat on his throne, a small smile playing on his face. Four servants stood nearby with large fans, and Joseph saw Potiphar with several guards a few steps behind them. They bowed. "Zaphnath-Paaneah," said the Pharaoh. "You have returned."

Bowing, Joseph returned his smile. "I have, your majesty. My father and all my family have come with their flocks and livestock. I have sent them into the twentieth nome near Per-Sopdu, and there I have given them land. I have here with me my honored father, and five of my brothers."

"I would greet them."

He bowed again and turned. The guards opened the doors, and Joseph motioned his brothers inside. They walked with some apprehension, clearly overwhelmed and glancing furtively around them, trying in vain to take everything in. They bowed deeply before the Pharaoh.

"What is your occupation?" the young Pharaoh asked.

They looked to Joseph, and he suddenly realized that he would have to translate. He clenched his jaw a little and then began.

"Your servants are shepherds, both we and our fathers. We have herded livestock all our lives. There are no pastures left in Canaan for our flocks. We beg the honor of being allowed to dwell near Per-Sopdu."

The Pharaoh nodded. "I am Netjerkheperu, He of the Two Ladies of Egypt, Netjermesut, Kheper, King of Upper and Lower Egypt, Khakaure, Son of Atum-Ra, Senusret, third of that name. I name it so." He turned to Joseph. "The best of Egypt is before you and your father and brothers who have come to you. Let them dwell there, and indeed, if there are any among them whom you deem able, put the royal flocks under their care."

"Pharaoh is gracious," Joseph responded after giving his brothers the translation. They bowed a second time. He turned again to the doors, and they opened, and Joseph went to his father and brought him in on his arm. Jacob inclined his head to the young ruler and did nothing more. Struck and rather proud of his father, Joseph let no emotion cross his face.

The Pharaoh looked only a little awed. "Jacob, father of Zaphnath-Paaneah, you are welcome in this land."

Quietly, Joseph translated.

"What are your years?" the young Pharaoh Senusret asked.

His father looked rather amused. "My years have been one hundred and thirty; they have been few and often evil. I have not attained the age of my fathers in their pilgrimage on this earth."

"Your years bring you honor, few though they may be in light of your fathers," the Pharaoh answered. "Will you bless me in the name of your God, the God of Zaphnath-Paaneah, who spoke to my father?"

Stunned, it was a moment before Joseph could gather his wits to translate. But Jacob only nodded with a small smile when he heard the request. "Blessed be the Pharaoh Senusret, whose land God has chosen to prosper in adversity. And Blessed be God Most High, Possessor of Heaven and Earth, who has done these things."

Joseph could have laughed, knowing the heresy his father spoke and the willingness with which the Pharaoh heard it.

Our God is great, and beyond understanding.

So he turned, and spoke the words of his father to the Pharaoh of Egypt, the so-named son of Atum-Ra. And the Pharaoh inclined his head ever so slightly, in gratitude.

Four days later, they stood looking down on the encampment near an offshoot of the Nile, deep in the Delta. In the distance sat the town of Per-Sopdu, and near the camp, sheep and cattle grazed on swaths of still-green land. The Delta lay before them, shining paths of water glinting in the sunlight. Joseph turned, and saw on his left Benjamin, and Judah, and Reuben, and Simeon, and Levi. Benjamin and Judah grinned at him, and even his other brothers smiled. He turned to his right and saw his father, looking out over the land and moved by the sight.

Jacob turned to him and smiled.

"Look, Father," Joseph said quietly. "See what our God has done for us."

Author's Note

I never set out to write historical fiction, but somewhere along my writing journey, the idea for this book jumped out of the bushes—or the Bible, I guess is more accurate—and grabbed me. It never let go until I had finished. In the several years that it took to complete, I learned more than I had ever expected about Ancient Egypt during the Middle Kingdom, when the Pharaohs Senusret II and Senusret III reigned.

Did you know that, if you're writing a story set in Ancient Egypt, you can't just pick some nice colors at random and say that they're painted on a wall? Nope. You most certainly cannot. Because every color had symbolic meaning in that culture.

This is the sort of thing that this middle-school math teacher was faced with while writing this book! There is more on my blog. Lots more. #yikes

And if you are an expert in Ancient Egypt—I know, and I'm sorry. I know that having horses, even as a curiosity owned by the mega-rich, in Egypt circa 1,800 BC might be stretching it somewhat. I know that Joseph's boat, as described, might be too big. I know we don't have actual documentation of wedding celebrations—which I still find patently bizarre. And I know that there's probably other things I missed entirely.

Math is so much easier. 1 + 1 = 2. Always.

That said, I hope the remarkable story of a man growing in his faith despite extreme adversity, the heart and purpose of the Joseph narrative in Genesis, remains firm and even perhaps enhanced by the *stretches* I allowed to take place within the setting. My humble prayer is that the indelible truths of God's providence are well-translated in this retelling of the Genesis account. And may we, like Joseph, learn a little more each day how to "walk by faith, not by sight."

I thoroughly enjoyed writing this book. If you enjoyed the story would you consider doing two things?

First—and this is a big request—would you consider leaving a review wherever you bought this book, or on your favorite social media platform? Word-of-mouth is the best way to introduce this story to other readers, and your voice can help do that. Leave a review and tell a friend!

Second—I love connecting with my readers. I invite you to stop by my website or my social media pages and say hi!

Elizabeth Jacobson

www.headdeskliz.com
https://www.facebook.com/headdeskliz
https://www.instagram.com/headdeskliz

Acknowledgements

First, I want to thank my Lord and Savior, Jesus Christ. *Soli Deo gloria.*

Next, to Mom, Dad, and James, who let me sit in the corner and write for years and years growing up, knowing that if they managed to come within eyeshot of the screen somehow (I was *purposefully* in the corner, after all), I would instantly minimize my document. It was a long time before I was willing to share my writing with much of anyone, but your respect for my passion despite me not letting you see a jot of it meant the world to me. Thank you.

Also, Abi, Alley, and Claire—my amazing beta readers. Thank you for believing in this book enough to read an early draft. Thank you for your honest critiques and your encouragement. I could not have done it without you.

To my grandmother, who read an entire printout of a draft and notated edits by hand—I am so thankful for your support and wisdom.

To all my family and friends who gave encouragement, or read drafts—thank you!

And last, but certainly not least, to Mike Parker and WordCrafts Press—thank you for believing in my book and for your patience and guidance.

About the Author

Elizabeth Jacobson is a middle-school math teacher in sunny California who loves the Bible, fantasy, and science fiction. She got bit by the writing bug at age thirteen and has been frantically putting words on pages ever since. Her goal in writing is to share with the world the most important message anyone can express: the Love of God and His Son, Jesus Christ.

Not by Sight: A novel of the Patriarchs is her first novel.

Connect with Elizabeth online at:

www.headdeskliz.com